# FOLK-SPELLED

## AN IMMORTAL HOLMES NOVEL

FORTHRIGHT

FORTHWRITES.COM

Immortal Holmes, No.1
**Folk-Spelled**

Copyright © 2025 by FORTHRIGHT
ISBN: 978-1-63123-095-0

Illustrations by Mart Lett | www.mart-lett.com
Jacket Design by BumbleBess | BumbleBess.com

TWINKLE PRESS

*because you might be standing*
*on the Brink of Wilds*

# Table of Contents

V

FIFTH OF FOREST

"Fifth of forest, gathering wolfberry, thornapple, and comfrey."

# FOLK-SPELLED

# 1

## The Green Man

Still not fully awake, Varti finished stretching in the back stairwell of The Green Man. Sunrise was at least two knells off, so nobody else in the three-story tenement was stirring. The building itself seemed to sigh in sleep, its abundance of carved planks and fancywork panels tensing against the turning season.

Thumbing the side door latch, Varti pushed and stilled, suddenly alert. And not because of the sudden wash of chill air.

Something was wrong.

Something had changed.

For as long as he could remember, this door had opened with a faint squeak. Releasing the clockwork latchkey—one of The Green Man's few nods to revolutionization—he triggered it again. The mechanism spun silently. He bent, but he couldn't see much in the dim, and his duty lamp was on its hook upstairs. But yes, there was the faintest whiff of oil.

How oddsome.

Who would have bothered?

I

Mr. Whilom liked to boast about his building's unique ambiance and historical significance, but he wasn't the type to tinker. Most repairs were unobtrusively handled by Varti himself, small tasks that Mr. Whilom accepted as his due, as if tenants should serve their lessor as they would some landed lord from bygone days.

Could Phil be responsible?

Varti supposed it was *possible*, but he doubted his quartermate had noticed the squeak, let alone silenced it.

He gazed up the stairwell, then along the little-used back hall. No other signs of tampering presented themselves. Nodding—even though he wanted to shake his head—Varti straightened, employed the latch, and stepped into an alley so narrow, the door's edge brushed through damp leaves on the vine-draped brick of the neighboring building. Cold mist hung thick in the air, softly dripping from foliage just beginning to turn copper and red.

For several moments, he stood there, listening.

A scuffle and retreating skitter. Probably a rat.

The faint hiss of escaping steam. In this part of the city, patching pipes wasn't a high priority.

Farther off, the bright double-ding of a trolley leaving Rowan station, regular as clockwork.

Nothing else out of the ordinary, yet Varti couldn't bring himself to dismiss the oiled lock.

With quiet deliberation, he closed the door, pulled a few coins from his pocket, and chose the most tarnished bobbin. He crouched to lean it against the door's rusty kickplate, where it was barely visible. And feeling increasingly foolish, he chose a smooth stone and set it a handsbreadth farther along the seam.

Just to see. Because as far as Varti knew, nobody but he and Phil ever used this door, which was only convenient if you wanted to avoid busybody lessors and chatty neighbors. Or in Phil's case, for smuggling in overnight guests.

Promising himself to take a closer look in better light, Varti moved to the alley's end, bounced a few times on the balls of his feet, and took off at an easy jog.

Only now, during the last knell of echoing time, were the streets so empty.

Only now, before his tocking in the bowels of the Bastion, could he pretend.

That his stamina served any purpose.

That this patrol held any meaning.

That he should continue, despite everything.

Yet he was keeping a promise to his fourteen-year-old self to learn every part of Newcomb. Varti no longer remembered *why* he'd settled on this particular challenge, why he'd decided that in order to protect Newcomb, he needed to know it.

Here he was, fourteen years later, still keeping his vow. Varti guessed he knew the city about as well as anyone could. Every hex and high street and ginnel and bridge.

So though fog obscured the scenery, Varti ran confidently toward the double row of fountains that gave the next-along district its name, crossing Foundry Road into Fullnis Park beyond. He lengthened his stride and swerved onto one of the footpaths that wove between the trees. Here was a caged and tamed fragment of forest. Werifesteria trees towered as high as the city walls, their blue-green leaves and starry tree balls creating a sanctuary—living and lush and possibly sacred. It was certainly more to Varti's taste than the many chambers of

3

the Composite Cathedral.

He sometimes crossed paths with other joggers here. Athletes. Soldiers. Badges like him. So he wasn't surprised when he heard footfalls coming up behind him. Except their cadence was off. Glancing over his shoulder, he yelped, dodging sideways and increasing his speed.

A ... dog?

It was just a dog.

Varti slowed to a more comfortable pace, and the animal matched it. All very companionable, but this was the second oddsome thing in less than a knell. Indeed, it couldn't have been more than ten knicks since he'd left the Drears.

Dogs weren't exactly common.

Oh, there were the purebred and pampered royal dogs, of course. And Varti occasionally saw pets in the Terraces, where houses boasted yards. But those were small breeds. Lap dogs. Big hounds like this were better suited to downslope farmsteads. He'd also heard of hunting dogs being used by gentry in the Lake District. But inside Newcomb? No. A dog like this didn't belong in the city.

Varti gruffly remarked, "You're common as cobbles and just as underfoot."

It felt strange to speak. He rarely did away from home.

Head tilting to one side, the animal looked at him as if questioning his words. Well it might.

"Fine weather, wouldn't you say?" Another lie. Only ever lies. Because dogs didn't speak and the day would break in a dismal mood.

The hound wuffed, its tongue lolling as if in laughter.

Varti slowed to a stop.

4

So did the dog.

"You look ready to tear my throat out."

The animal was extraordinarily large, with smoky gray fur that frizzed every which way. Its eyes were as silver as the surrounding mists. With a decidedly clownish air, it sank back on its haunches and waved its front paws. Utterly harmless.

Clearly male. No sign of a lead. No owner in view. The beast was breaking laws simply by being here, but at least he wasn't aggressive. Varti stepped closer, slowly reaching. He should look for a collar.

Shortish, flopping ears proved they could prick, and the hound's long tail thumped the ground.

"I'm a terror. You'll regret waylaying me." He really should just shut up, but a dog wouldn't take his words personally. He'd judge Varti by his tone and his scent and his actions. A refreshing change.

He roughed up thick fur and scratched behind ears and smiled in the face of a searching gaze that felt intelligent. He'd always heard that animals were smart. Not much experience there. Nani hadn't let him have so much as a songbird, even after he'd compiled an exhaustive list of classmates who kept one. Because his grandmother didn't believe in cages. Because according to her, Newcomb was enough of one.

One that had once kept humanity safe.

One that Varti now helped to protect.

Apparently from leggy hounds without collars.

"I have nowhere else to be and nothing else to do." He backed up a step, then another.

The dog reared up, planting his forepaws on Varti's shoulders. It about staggered him. Varti wasn't a big man, so the dog loomed over him, huge and heavy. Should he bring the thing home? He could say it was his duty, getting a stray off the streets.

Mr. Whilom would spring a cog, but Phil probably wouldn't complain. He certainly brought home his share of furred or feathered friends. Couldn't Varti have one little dog?

No, it wasn't even remotely feasible.

Space for an animal. Licenses and health checks. Just feeding this monster would gouge deep. And on top of that, both he and Phil often took extra tockings, even on Newdays. He couldn't imagine caging a dog in their quarters for so many long, lonesome knells. It wouldn't be right.

Still, when Varti got himself out from under the beast, he whistled softly and beckoned hopefully. And it *worked*, which was staggering in a whole different way. Maybe his curse didn't work on animals? He needed to think how to bring the possibility to Dr. Kang's attention. But for now, Varti was just glad that it'd worked.

Running on, he kept peeking to the side, just to confirm that the hound was still there, keeping up at a lope. Varti hit a good rhythm. He felt light on his feet, and for once, for a short while, he was able to outrun his troubles.

The path worked its way inward, toward the city center. The elevated trolley rails were a landmark, held up by a network of arches and girders. At this knell, the shops beneath were still quiet. It was too early for those on a night tocking to flood the stations. Instead, eateries were restocking and readying for the dawn rush.

None of the delivery sled drivers from the shipyards looked Varti's way as he slowed at the mouth of an ordinary alley. On the cobbles, colored glass cups held vigil candles. These must have been lit during the change between winding time and locking time, since they were burning low, near to guttering out. Among them, standing stones formed peaceable patterns. Gifts for the dead.

Though there were no conifers nearby, pine needles scattered the cobbles, folksome offerings that meant this loss had pierced many. They also suggested that the victim had honored Bittern, the least popular of the olde dignitaries, but the one who was said to hold his devotees all the more closely because of it.

Poor woman. There was nothing Bittern could do for her now.

Varti knelt and brushed aside needles. The hexagonal cobbles had been washed, of course, but blood had seeped in, staining the cracks. A muzzle pushed aside Varti's hand as the big dog snuffled around. His resulting sneeze blew out two of the vigil candles.

Polly Barrister had been the third victim.

She wouldn't have known to take care. Headquarters hadn't wanted to cause a panic, and in hiding the first two murders, they'd condemned this woman. Polly had suffered and died here, on the edge of the park where Varti started his days.

As one of the city's protectors, he'd failed her.

As head of the Bastion's file room and evidence lockers, he could only guard what remained. Facts in reports. Neatly stacked, folded, and stained incidentals. He knew that Polly had two middle names and that her pocket watch was engraved with fae symbols and a date—Bittern 22, Two Twenty-Two. She'd been carrying her tool kit, a book, and a take-away meal. Her coin purse, embroidered with flowers and fit with a kiss clasp, had contained 3 knobs, 2 cogs, 6 bobbins, a WC token, and a green prayer stone.

Small, pointless details. They didn't add up to much, not as evidence of a crime. But they'd belonged to her, and that should matter.

Two robed figures with beaded vestments shuffled out of the mist, one carrying an ornamental shepherd's crook from which hung a lamp. The other carried a cricket bat. An incongruity, but a practical one. The whole city was on alert, even the many mercies of the Composite Cathedral.

Varti stood and stepped back.

The one with the lamp cast about, found one of the many brass fittings among the cobbles underfoot, and inserted the crook into it. Hands freed, she pushed back her cowl and gestured for him to continue. Varti felt caught. But the woman didn't let the moment become awkward. She twisted the long chain around her neck, searching among its jingling charms until she found Bittern's. Holding it between her thumbs, she steepled her outspread fingers and closed her eyes.

Varti's attention skated to the other mercy, whose gaze roved while his partner offered prayers. From under his cowl, lamplight reflected off eyes in a telltale flash, two red disks. So he was Folk. A Darke Childe. Suited to night.

Good. The mercies were taking care, of both the living and the dead.

Varti could leave them to relight the tiny flames that were thought to encourage souls to drift up and away from earthly cares. Elsewise a ghost might be born into this alley. But first he ducked his head and waited until the priestess or nun or whatever finished her prayers.

Only when he turned away to resume his run did Varti realize that the dog had abandoned him. Leaving him alone in a city that was no longer entirely safe for the solitary.

# 2

## The Drears

VESPER 03, FOUR NINETY-EIGHT
FIRSTMOST VONNEDAY
7 KNELLS, 28 KNICKS
ON THE FIRST FACE OF THE CLOCK

Varti returned to The Green Man with his hair still damp from the baths, two freshly steamed uniforms over his arm, and a glassine bag swinging by its handles from the crook of his elbow. Early errands were part of his share in the household duties because Phil wasn't a morning person. Not that Varti could have managed without a certain amount of preparation. His best friend had arranged everything to make Varti's job easier.

The fullers, the bathhouse, and even the tea and bun carts had standing orders. All Varti needed to do was step up to a counter, coins ready. Nobody in their neighborhood knew the real reason why Varti wouldn't speak. Phil left it vague and poured on the charm, thanking everyone for understanding. People went out of their way to look after the two of them, especially their bun mother. She'd been making sure they got enough to eat since they were newly moved into The Green Man—both fifteen and forever hungry.

In the alley, Varti slowed to consider the ground. The rising

9

sun was driving the morning mist back into the canals, but even in the gaining light, he couldn't see any sign of an intruder. Just the usual patched pavement with its litter of dead leaves. He needed to sweep soon.

He knelt to reclaim his bob. And stilled.

His simple trap had been sprung. Sort of.

The bobbin still leaned against the kickplate, right where he'd put it, but a cog now rested alongside. The silver was filmed in black, but it was easily identified as a coin of the city by its teeth. Varti peered up and down the alley, trying to think who would have done this.

Had someone seen him earlier? Varti had been alert, and he hadn't sensed anyone nearby. Also, why *add* a coin? Someone picking up a stray coin made more sense. That had always been a possibility, which is why he'd also left the small stone. Wait. Tarnish it all, the *pebble* was gone. But why?

Varti suspected that someone was teasing him.

Was it the same person who'd oiled the lock?

He picked up both coins. The cog was really quite old. A limited release tricentennial, pierced with a triangle instead of the usual circle. Not the rarest of coins but not something you found in circulation anymore. Polished up, it might be worth a flash or two.

Was there a message here? A threat? Hardly likely.

Perhaps a taunt? Did the culprit know how frustrating this was for Varti? That he wouldn't be able to *tell* anyone.

Tucking the coins away, he opened the door, checked the lock—which fairly gleamed from its recent oiling—then hurried to his shared quarters on the highmost floor.

Phil's guest from the night before was already up.

Tybalt turned from rummaging in their meager tea cabinet and broke into a relieved smile. "Weller, you're a gladsome sight! Look at that load. It's unfair how much you spoil Kemp. But ... err. Any chance you took care of me, too?"

Varti couldn't say a true thing to save his life, but his curse didn't twist everything. He was always on time for work. He never lost case reports or evidence from the lockers. He could do sums and update ledgers correctly. And he could choose things that he knew would please his few friends.

He set crinkling glassine on the counter, then removed a hex of apples from his scrip, setting them in a row on the table.

Tybalt dove into the bag, snagging a steamed bun. His eyes lit up when Varti next produced three silver bottles with gleaming copper labels, the man's favorite brand of coffee. "Aubade's? Weller, you are still best boy."

Varti simply hung and straightened the uniforms on their pegs. If he opened his mouth, anything he said would cut. Tybalt knew Varti couldn't help it and didn't mean it, but the curse was particularly vicious when he knew someone well.

There came a snap and hiss as Tybalt broke the seal on a bottle, releasing a puff of fragrant steam. Tybalt sighed happily, then crunched into an apple. Varti puttered, pushing aside drapes and moving his one houseplant onto the leftmost sill. A second bun disappeared while he got out the polish he used for boot buttons and his watchchain. Neither were due for a cleaning, but if Varti kept busy, people were less likely to interrupt him with attempts at conversation.

Tybalt left him to it, crunching through a second apple while he considered the project that had kept him and Phil up for most of the night.

The case wall.

They'd pulled down everything from Phil's previous investigations, even removing all the colored pins from an oversized city map. Technically, the map was Varti's. Had been since academy days. Their instructors had retired the thing, deeming it inaccurate enough to be misleading. But Varti had begged it off the custodians and mounted it in their quarters. Amending it had become a personal hobby, but ever since graduation, Varti's map had become something more.

A way for him and Phil to outwit the curse.

A means for having an admittedly imperfect, woefully abridged, but refreshingly honest exchange.

An ongoing conversation.

"Let me get your bestie," Tybalt said, checking his pocket watch. "Darling Philtrum has had enough beauty sleep."

Varti ran a polishing cloth over his own timepiece, which was old as Olde. According to Nani, the silver pocket watch was handed down from his great-grandfather, though she'd always been vague about which one. It kept time, and it had a compass set inside its cover, but there were no engravings. She'd probably picked it up in a pawn shop and spun a story to give it an heirloom's gloss. But at the time of its gifting, all Varti had cared about then was having one. All the other students at badge academy would be properly fit, so the lack would have been mortifying.

By now, the watch's weight in his vest pocket was as familiar as the faint clatter of charms that hung from its chain. These, too, were customary, though Varti only kept a few on display.

A medallion granted upon his matriculation to the badge program.

Two buttons, which Phil had clipped from their academy uniforms and sewn back-to-back.

A bronze hex etched with lines, representing a map of the city. The royal seal was on the reverse. This marked Varti as a full-fledged badge.

A dodger from his first purse, pierced and laced into place with fine wire. The coin was usually meant as a charm to attract further fortune, but Varti wore his because he'd been so proud to be earning a wage. Proof he could take care of Nani, just as she'd taken care of him.

Last was the charm Phil had selected and paid for.

Varti couldn't have afforded it.

Hadn't known how much he'd need it.

Final exams for graduating classes were always held in Concordia, the nearest woodland village beyond the city's walls. Phil's hometown. Tybalt's, too.

Mystics made up a large section of Concordia's population, and market stalls were filled with folk-blessed charms. In keeping with longstanding badge tradition, class members would choose an Olde charm before the test. Wards against accident or injury. Tokens of allegiance. Prayer stones or icons or totems. To each their own.

These were meant to be the first of four blessings on their chosen career. Even in Newcomb, everyone knew the saying: something Olde, something new, something bartered, something blue.

A quaint custom, but Varti was skeptical. Truly Olde things couldn't be so easy to come by. So while everyone else snapped up tokens of Bittern or Milvine or one of the other fae dignities, he'd hung back. Varti could recall trailing after Phil, hoping for

13

a new, blue, folk-blessed charm he could swap for, covering all four traditions in one go. For efficiency's sake.

But Phil believed in everything. Superstitions and fortune-telling were as much a part of him as his freckles. So of course Varti must have *something*.

Setting aside the polishing cloth, he ran his thumb over the charm Phil had chosen.

A silver oblong with irregular edges surrounding an intricate pattern. The medallion looked as if liquid metal had been poured out and a finger pressed into the resulting puddle, leaving a whorl of interconnecting paths. Varti's eyes had traveled the delicate maze many times, learning its secrets. It was supposedly the sign of Qiiq the Raveler, threader of labyrinths, diviner of ways.

While Varti couldn't bring himself to actually worship Qiiq, he thought he might owe the wily Folk hero his life. Because during his final exam, when everything had gone widdershins, Varti had seen death in that Olde Childe's stare, yet Varti had opened his eyes to find his head resting on Phil's lap, with the faint jingle of his best friend's many charms dancing just above his nose ... and Qiiq's sign still clutched in his fist.

In the seasons since then, Varti came to realize that he *did* have one single stitch of faith holding his life together.

He believed in Philtrum Kemp.

# 3

## *Dog & Doggerel*

Vesper 03, Four Ninety-Eight
Firstmost Vonneday
7 Knells, 57 Knicks
on the first face of the clock

Tybalt backed through the beaded curtain strung across Phil's bedroom door, half-dragging him into the room. His red curls were chaotic, and dark circles shadowed his eyes. He wore an undershirt and yesterday's trousers, so he hadn't even changed for sleep. "Mmm. Mornin', Varti. Did Tibbs leave us any food?"

Varti crossed to the map and carefully placed a pin.

Phil selected an apple and went to the window, gazing skyward while he ate. Because this sort of thing only worked if he pretended not to care. Which might seem silly, especially since the two of them had never actually talked about the routines they'd fallen into. But Phil wasn't a badge in the irregulars for nothing. He specialized in cases and crimes involving Folk.

Only after Varti retreated to his chair with a bun and an apple did Phil glance toward the map. He asked, "How much did you overhear last night?"

With Phil, Varti didn't try to hold back. "I couldn't sleep for all the moaning."

Tybalt snorted. "Not sure why you bother asking questions Weller can't answer."

"Because he's not a piece of furniture to talk over and work around." Less sharply, he added, "Try to remember who's doing the talking. I think his curse enjoys embarrassing him."

"And does a good job of it." Tybalt's smile held pity. "No hard feelings, right, Weller?"

Varti didn't care for apologies. Or sympathy. Even from someone he'd looked up to since he was twelve.

Upon their arrival at badge academy, he and Phil had both been sorted into Tybalt's cohort. Three years older, he'd been part big brother, part ringleader. These days, he was a member of Newcomb's Hedge, the division of badges that patrolled outside the city walls.

"What's this, now?" asked Tybalt. He was peering at the pin Varti had placed.

"Find something interesting?" Phil asked.

The city architects had designed a vast hexagon, with living quarters built into the outer walls. According to history texts, the six interior districts had once been used for growing food and grazing livestock. Back then, Newcomb had needed to be self-sufficient, closed off from the chaos that followed the Sundering.

Tracing Cannery Road from Vonneffe Station to the pin, Tybalt asked, "The gaming district?"

"Mmm, interesting. That whole stretch is full of taverns with … ah … blithesome amenities in the upmost stories." Counting over and down, Phil announced, "Assuming we're at street level, that's the Dog & Doggerel."

"Any bearing on your new case?"

"None."

"Then what's the point?" Frowning in concern, Tybalt asked, "Is this name-calling?"

"You're daft." Phil yawned, stretched, and reached for coffee. "How long have you known us?"

"You? Since you were in nappies. But I take your meaning. You two meshed cleanly from the start. Kemp and Weller. Weller and Kemp. Everyone expected … err." He cast a furtive look Varti's way. "Finest of your class, and the purnals are still expecting great things. Did you tell Weller?"

"No need. He predicted they'd give me the case."

"He *told* you?" Tybalt eyed them skeptically. "How?"

"Varti's always been best at picking up clues. You think he isn't just as good about dropping them?" Phil noted the time and grimaced. "I have to hurry. I'm meant to be reassuring all of Newcomb by way of the press. Then rallying the regulars, who might not like taking orders from an irregular."

"Now you're being daft. The greenies love you. *Everyone* loves you." Tybalt nicked an extra steamed bun. "No luck with that Bridger, by the way. Their offices were all locked up, with a black crepe wreath on the door. Didn't think anyone went in for that sort of thing anymore. Going into mourning."

Varti didn't know who they were talking about. Someone from the Bridge District? He muttered, "You're excluding me on purpose. You always do."

Which was a nice, uncomplicated opposite. His curse must be in a good mood today.

Maybe it was foolish, but it helped, thinking of the spell he was under as an existence unto itself. One that could make his life truly miserable. Phil had described the curse as an

17

inhabitation of sorts, crouched within, privy to his innermost thoughts. It forced him to lash out indiscriminately, to lead the unwary astray with his lies. But sometimes it let him off easy.

Phil said, "There's this consultant, a kind of freelancer that the Bastion's purnals have turned to in the past. In the days following the third murder, Highmost Purnal Yamada tried to call him in, but her messages weren't getting through. Since the fourth victim, she's been sending us around to knock on his door."

Fishing a black tack from the dish below the map, Tybalt stabbed a spot near the city center. "Right along the James. Just off the Grande Promenade. Got the royal view."

"Keep trying," said Phil. "I really do have to rush, but ... dinner at The Speckled Hen?"

"That'll flourish," Tybalt said warmly. "I'll meet you lads there."

And turning to Varti, Phil said, "Let me do your reading."

"Waste of time." Which gave them both a moment's confusion. Because during academy days, Varti had regularly put his friend off with those same words. Since when had they become a lie?

Phil fetched the deck he used for fortune-telling.

Varti had gone through the cards many times, and Phil had tried to explain how he did his readings. It was all very subjective, relying on combinations of lore and numerology and a glut of superstitions that weren't part of Varti's upbringing. All he'd ever admitted before was that the illustrations were beautiful.

Unlike the playing cards commonly used in the gaming district, these were tall and narrow, and instead of the usual six suits, there were different categories. All were nature-based. Rustic, woodsy stuff. Or scenes of the sea and skies. Not even the barest hint of a city's clockwork or conveniences.

"Varti Weller, lend me your hands."

He did, and Phil set the familiar weight of the guidance deck upon Varti's left palm. Then he cut the cards, turning part of the pile face-up onto Varti's right palm. And taking another, smaller cut from the remaining cards, he revealed a second, which he placed face-up.

Even if Phil was hungover or half-asleep, he performed this quick two-card reading every morning, without fail.

He peered at the cards, brows drawn together. "This is unusual. You don't usually call out to the forest cards. They're wild, and you tend to be tame. Fifth of Forest, gathering wolfberry, comfrey, and thornapple." He laid a finger on the second card. "The Howl, shiver of skies, night version, inverted. That's a powerful card."

"Wild *and* night? And twice wolves." Tybalt's expression had gone wary. "Be careful out there, Weller."

Varti was vastly less concerned. The cards had to be referring to the friend he'd made during his morning run. Wolf, dog— there wasn't much difference.

# 4

## *The Lurking Smile*

VESPER 03, FOUR NINETY-EIGHT
FIRSTMOST VONNEDAY
12 KNELLS, 22 KNICKS
ON THE SECOND FACE OF THE CLOCK

At midday, when his staff escaped the basements for their lunchbreak, Varti tended to hole up in the downermost archive room, studying any case files that included old maps. It was fascinating how much the city had changed over the centuries. The world had been a very different place five hundred years ago.

But at least twice a week, Dr. Kang would track him down and take him to one of the nearby underground eateries. They both held basement-level jobs. Varti managed all incident-related files and evidence, which were housed in three descending floors of drawers and lockers, and Dr. Oliver Kang was an examiner in charge of the Bastion's morgue.

They weren't exactly friends, but they were far from strangers. Dr. Kang had been one of Varti's academy instructors, and in the aftermath of the curse, the good doctor had been the first to grasp the significance of Varti's increasingly desperate lies.

Folk-spelled.

That diagnosis had prevented the complete derailment of

Varti's career, and Dr. Kang's subsequent reassignment to the Bastion suggested that he was either still looking out for Varti ... or he'd been assigned to monitor his condition.

So Varti had an occasional lunch companion and inquisitor and mediator.

He was aware that he was basically a test subject. Dr. Kang was something of a Folk enthusiast. But it was a comfort, knowing that if things skewed into awkward territory while in public, Dr. Kang was there to smooth over any misunderstandings.

Today, they were at their usual spot. The mother at The Lurking Smile baked his own bread, and his daughter turned out some of the city's best soup and sandwiches.

"I heard about Kemp's promotion to highmost perior," said Dr. Kang. "Are you worried? I can't help but wonder if this *honor* is simply setting him up for failure. All those cliquesome purnals and claxsome periors, they never liked him, his background, or his popularity. So they're making these murders *his* problem. One twist of a journalist's pen, and they'll suddenly be Kemp's fault."

Varti sat back and listened. Dr. Kang did so enjoy filling him in on the latest gossip. Some days, listening was all Varti did. But in this out-of-the-way place, with old-style lanterns lending shadows to every corner, he felt safe to speak. "There's a good reason he's known as Kiss-up Kemp."

Dr. Kang eyed him interestedly. "That would be true if spoken by anyone but you. But you and I both know the reasons are terrible. Imagine disliking a boy simply because he's likeable."

"My bitterest rival. My worst enemy."

That earned him a soft look. "Did you know, even your partnership was a mark against him? The country boy over-reaching, pairing off with the smartest student, who *must* have been the reason for the upstart's good grades."

Varti had always liked Dr. Kang's fairness. City or country. Human or Folk. Cursed or blessed. Everyone was given a chance, and the man respected those who worked hard.

"I trust you'll be supporting him through this new challenge?"

"Me?" Varti shook his head. "We've never seen things the same way."

Dr. Kang pointed at him with his spoon. "That was meant for peevishness. Even insult, given your tone. But it's not erroneous. He's amazingly intuitive, thanks to his upbringing. It'll prove a good thing, putting him in charge. You have to admit, in the absence of eyewitnesses, trace evidence, or viable leads, Kemp's usual … ah … *impetuosity* might turn something up."

"He's a fool. You're all fools."

"Good lad." Dr. Kang glanced to either side and leaned closer. "We could compare notes. I've finished up with the fourth victim, and Yamada has *my* report. But you must have some of the field reports by now. Did they bring in any specialists to assess the scene?"

Varti was waiting on input from a so-called ghost photographer, but standard photos and the victims' incidentals had been received and stored. Because of his role, he was aware of several unpublicized details about the murders and the victims. Secrets that were entirely safe, since he was effectively mute. "You're wasting your time."

"Thought as much! You always were swiftsome about documentation. Let me tell you what I suspect!"

But before Dr. Kang could launch into a description that would undoubtedly spoil Varti's appetite and make him late back to work, a stranger stepped up, crushing a felt cap between his hands. "Begging your pardon, gents. I happened to overhear a bit of what you were saying, and I'll confess myself curious. What you're saying. It's all widdershins. I'd swear you're having two entirely different conversations."

Middling height, average build, with graying hair falling into odd-colored eyes. Varti couldn't tell their colors by lamplight, but one eye was definitely lighter than the other.

"Is that so? What an interesting way of putting things," said Dr. Kang. "Do you work upstairs? Which division?"

"In the Bastion, you mean?" The man patted at his vest as if searching for his tags. "Not in any official capacity. But I make myself useful from time to time."

Varti noticed that the man didn't have a watchchain. His clothes were both softened by wear and frayed in enough places to count as shabby. Nobody working for the Bastion would show up at the offices so down-dressed. It was suspicious.

"My name's Vester," he offered, his gaze searching Varti's. "It's just that I've seen something similar before. You're not alone in your head, are you? Spelled, maybe?"

Dr. Kang raised his hands. "That's a personal matter. Confidential."

"I'm intruding. My curiosity gets me into all kinds of trouble." He took a step back. "Not the first time I wasn't welcome. Won't be the last. But ask around if you change your mind."

"And why would we do that, Mr. Vester," Dr. Kang inquired, his interest clearly piqued.

"Oh, it's Vester for short. The long of it's Sylvester Thornapple. Some call me Sylvie. Others call me Thorn. Vester's what I call myself, but I'm not a choosy beggar. And I'm not a bad friend to have." He slid a coin across the table. "Merry the day, gents. Next drink's on me."

It was a dodger, its gold center gleaming from within its frame of silver teeth. A whole day's wage for a thricemost ferior like Varti.

Sylvester pulled his hat down around his ears, gave it a jaunty tap, and ambled off.

"A winsome enough fellow," remarked Dr. Kang.

"Twice wolves," is what popped out of Varti's mouth. When what he was actually thinking was ... *wolfberry, comfrey, and thornapple.*

# 5

## *The Speckled Hen*

Vesper 03, Four Ninety-Eight
Firstmost Vonneday
5 Knells, 31 Knicks
on the second face of the clock

Varti's tocking never changed, even when he took the odd Newday. Start to finish, he always worked the same knells, regular as the steam locomotive whose tracks bisected the Trestle District.

In complete contrast, Phil's tocking was never the same. If the highermosts needed him—and they always did—then Phil was on duty. Varti's sleep was frequently interrupted by the chime, whirr, and chatter of the ticker that connected their quarters to the badge relay network. All knells and all weather, Phil never knew when he might be called out, held back, kept up, or sent galloping.

So when Phil said they'd meet for dinner, Varti knew from long experience that six and sixty things might interfere with their plans. Yet he was somehow the last to arrive at The Speckled Hen.

Lanterns lent a gleam to polished copper, and fragrant steam teased Varti's nose with hints of today's menu. Phil and Tybalt were at the counter, laughing and talking with the owner. If Varti was Phil's *best* friend, then Ramage was his *oldest*.

The instant Ramage spotted Varti, he smiled broadly and came strutting.

Just like he always did.

Just like that first time.

On the eve of their first Newday at Academy, twelve-year-old Phil had somehow convinced Varti that they should sneak out of the dorms. They'd gone out a window and trotted along unfamiliar streets into a district Varti had never been allowed to enter before. It had been thrilling. It had felt dangerous.

Two boys in matching uniforms, they'd been out-of-place enough to draw comment. A bouncer outside a gaming house had called out to them. Varti had been ready to make a run for it, but undaunted as ever, Phil had flung his arms wide and shouted, "Where's Ramage?"

As if this was Concordia and everyone knew everyone's business.

"He won't know!" Varti had whispered, sure they were going to be in so much trouble.

But the man had laughed. "That cock-of-the-walk? You're wanting The Speckled Hen on Livery Road. Just in from Rowan Station. Can't miss it. Or him."

Phil had asked, "Can you get us there?"

Which was almost insulting. Stranger to the district or no, Varti knew the six trolley stops. Every Newcomber did. So they'd run the rest of the way, and the daringness of their adventure had added fresh gloss to Varti's burgeoning fascination for the freckled boy with a woodfolk accent and a ready laugh. Imagine, being practically *raised* by harpies.

Ramage stirred Varti from his thoughts by brushing at his hair, then jostling his shoulder with the leading edge of one wing. "Weller. Straight from work? And looking splendid. I always did like a bit of greenery about the place."

"Greenery?" called Tybalt from the counter. "Shouldn't you say that *our* uniforms have flash? We're a brightsome pair, Kemp and me. Flatter us more!"

He was referring to their cloaks. All servants of the city wore the royal colors in some combination—copper and green. Because of their rank and their postings, Tybalt and Phil wore double cloaks with a metallic sheen, while Varti's uniform was the green of patinaed copper.

Ignoring Tybalt, Ramage urged, "Let me look at you."

Plenty of Folk made their homes in Newcomb, but Ramage might be the most famous, at least in the Trestle District. Ramage was a harpy. Well over six feet tall, he was showy, with milk-pale skin and feathers that were a delicate blue with bright speckling.

Full lips pursed, then parted, offering a peek at dainty fangs. "Lost in thought?" Interest sparkled in azure eyes, and Ramage's crest lifted above the long, tapering points of his ears. "Or rather ... lost in the moment. You and I can share one. That seems right. I wonder why?"

Blue wings bumped him closer, and Ramage was murmuring over him in a lilting litany. The harpy's prayers were nothing like those of the Cathedral and its mercies. Varti had always thought there was real magic in it. Like he was casting kindly spells. A shimmer drew Varti's gaze, and his breath caught. He wasn't imagining it. The three large crystals on Ramage's necklace were brightening.

That had never happened before.

Ramage's other wing came up, as if trying to hide the glow from everyone else. He softly said, "Come to my rescue, Weller? Lift the central shard."

Varti did as he was told, lifting the largest stone. Something Ramage couldn't have done alone, since harpies didn't have hands.

The chunk of rock salt glowed between them.

Ramage's crest lifted until it puffed out every which way, then slowly settled. When he carefully kissed the shard, its light vanished, and Varti had so many questions. But Ramage winked broadly and took a step back, so that the crystal slipped from Varti's fingers, thumping back into place over the harpy's heart. He turned with a showy swish of trailing tail feathers. "Go, wash away the weary day. I know *just* what you need. Leave it to mother."

Just then, someone pivoted away from the counter, leaving a dodger at his place and pulling a felt cap low over his eyes. Varti recognized the shabby jacket, and he took a step to follow, but something came between his ankles, tripping him up.

Catching his balance again, he stared down into the glowing amberglass eyes of a clockwork cat. Exposed copper gears whirred, and metal ears turned atop a stylized head. Its mouth opened, and it offered a squeaky mew. Then it bounded away, disappearing out the door with the flick of its articulated tail.

Had the others seen?

No. Tybalt was calling for another bottle of ale, and Phil was talking animatedly to one of the cooks. Leaving Varti in a state of growing frustration. Because he had no way to ask how long his two friends had been sitting there, talking about who-knew-what, while Sylvester Thornapple eavesdropped.

# 6

## *Quarterbound*

**N**ewcomb's mothers fed the city.

Varti knew from the oldest files—minutes from meetings between the Founders—that in order to save as many humans as possible, they'd needed to economize. By the final drafting, schematics of the quarters within the city walls were stripped of facilities that had apparently been standard before the Sundering. They opted for communal laundry and bathing facilities. And they eliminated kitchens.

According to Tybalt and Phil, houses in Concordia had kitchens, and members of each household were responsible for the procurement and preparation of food. For every meal. Every day. A daunting concept. Varti was glad to live within the city walls, where the job of feeding the masses fell to its many mothers.

Options abounded, and exploring them was certainly interesting. But every Newcomber grew up with meals from one eatery in particular, usually located close to their family's quarters. The flavors of that place became the flavors of home.

And that mother would always be *their* mother.

Varti had grown up with meals from the same mother that Nani had grown up with. He regularly picked her up and brought her back to Masala, which was located inside the city wall overlooking the Station District. Nani would praise each dish and drop hints that were far from subtle, saying Varti should find quarters in a nice, respectable hex. Not like the Drears. A good place to raise children. He wanted them, didn't he? People needed nourishing meals made from local produce. So much better than bun carts.

He withstood her chiding and chatter, comfortable in the knowledge that she cared. But he'd grown up and away from his former neighborhood, where he'd always be remembered as Holt Weller's son. No, he was better off where he was, and Ramage was the mother to whom Varti would always return.

"Hurry it up, Weller!" Tybalt lifted an amberglass bottle. "We waited for you!"

Liar.

Phil shook his head and said, "He didn't. But we saved your favorite seat."

So Varti crossed to the corner where a white marble basin awaited. Hot water from a copper tap. Soap and stacks of hand towels. But also a shallow marble shelf at Varti's eye-level. Not many cityfolk would recognize it as an altar. There were no symbols, no explanations. Just a simple, clean shelf on which Ramage kept a small, lidded bowl. If anyone looked inside, they'd find chippings of salt.

Offerings.

Once his hands were clean, Varti considered the lidded dish. Phil had shown him how to go about showing thanks to the deities that were important to Ramage. Varti didn't think he'd ever tick to the tock of any venerated dignitaries, not in the traditional sense, but he respected Ramage more than he could say. So he checked to see if the harpy was watching, then offered his thanks and allegiance to him instead.

Touch the forehead. Be mindful.

Touch the lips. Be thankful.

Touch the heart. Be full.

According to Phil, this was a prayer that the coming meal— or possibly one's whole life—would be seasoned by salt magic. Maybe it didn't count without the salt. Actually, he probably only managed the motions *because* they were a lie. But they were also a gift. One he wouldn't manage again, this side of his unspelling.

The curse could learn. And it could be spiteful.

Varti went to the seat they'd held for him, right in front of the big egg skelter that was the eatery's centerpiece. A maze of copper pipes held hundreds of eggs—white and brown and speckled and green—caught in a slow-motion tumble toward the cooks' station. While they were still in school, Ramage used to let him and Phil load the skelter with eggs delivered from the bestiary.

Egg dishes were The Speckled Hen's specialty, and they'd quickly become Varti's favorite food. Over the years, he'd become something of a connoisseur. When one of Ramage's cooks set a covered dish before Varti, he knew it for a favorite. "Take it away. Nothing but slop," he groused.

Phil calmly contradicted, "His absolute favorite. Thank you, Burr."

The cook batted thick lashes and went to check something in the back. So shy. Their counterpart set three bottles in front of Varti's seat, smiled hopefully, then wandered off. Aril and Burr were Ramage's cooks. Varti didn't know what kind of Folk they were. Vaguely faunlike, in the sense that they had hairy hindquarters and hooves. But larger and lankier, with straight hair and branching antlers. They'd begun working here after Varti's spelling, so he'd never been able to ask how they identified themselves. He guessed he didn't need a term.

They knew about him, which meant they ignored his rude remarks about their cooking. Even better, they were intuitive. Or like many Folk, they had a knack.

Varti lifted the lid from the dish, revealing a single, perfect egg, coddled in cream. A plate of toast arrived. Varti reached for the bottle he wanted, broke the seal, and took a long pull.

A hand briefly rested on his shoulder. Phil.

Varti simply reached for his spoon and started in on his meal.

Ramage picked up the thread of a conversation they must have been having before Varti's arrival. To his relief, it was gossip about happenings in Concordia. Nothing worth overhearing. Varti only half-listened to Tybalt tease Phil about the hacksome pick-up line he'd been using since academy … and the utter unfairness that it still worked. Two more covered dishes arrived in succession, piping and perfect, and Varti was glad for simple pleasures.

He was warm and full and pleasantly fuzzy from drink when Tybalt and Phil eventually stood, already in the midst of goodbyes. Varti began restacking a set of hexagonal tiles he'd been rearranging. Ramage had a variety of games set out, mostly classics that everyone knew how to play. But this one had a folksome feel to it, and Varti couldn't begin to guess at the rules.

Coins jingled onto the counter, enough to cover Tybalt's food and drink. Since Varti and Phil had officially registered The Speckled Hen as their mother, their meals were apportioned.

"We're all settled," said Tybalt. "Let's stretch our legs before the next round."

Varti stayed where he was. Another round? Was Phil really going out drinking?

"Is he drunk?" Tybalt frowned and plucked up Varti's lone empty bottle. "You can't be drunk."

"I might be," Varti muttered.

Tybalt looked to Phil. "Guess we should see him home first."

"Only if you hold my hand," Varti countered in pleading tones. "I'll be lost for certain."

Phil said, "Stop insulting him." And to Varti, "We're going to unwind for a while. You're welcome, of course."

Maybe if they'd graduated on equal terms, if the curse hadn't forced Varti to be more cautious, maybe then he'd have tried and enjoyed the same sorts of things Phil found entertaining. But as it was, Varti had no money to spare on dice games or horse races, and he didn't dare drink any more than he'd had tonight. He shuddered to think what might happen if his inhibitions dropped away, leaving his tongue limber, letting the curse speak freely.

"We'll be in later. Or late. End of winding time," Phil said.

That was optimistic. "I'll hold you to your curfew, wanton wretch."

Tybalt led the way out into the street before rounding on Varti, pleading Phil's case. "Tonight may be Kemp's last bout of freedom before this case has him locked up. You can't expect him to spend it quarterbound."

Quarterbound.

Like Varti.

But that wasn't what had Varti seething on the edge of outcry. He hated to be misunderstood, to be painted by assumptions, to have anyone insinuate that he was holding Phil back.

That wasn't how it was.

Tybalt wasn't around enough to know.

Varti dipped into the purse at his belt. "You know what's best, Tybalt Gregson. Shall I contribute a flash or two to the night's excesses? Make certain he's properly sodden and blithesome enough for the both of us."

Tarnish it all.

He hated this.

Tybalt snarled, but Phil was between them, hands clamped around Tybalt's wrists. He peered over his shoulder at Varti. "He's had one too many, or he wouldn't forget who's speaking. We'll be home during locking time. I'll make sure."

"Dawn," he countered bitterly. "And me waiting up through all the knells."

Varti turned on his heel and strode along Livery Road toward home. He didn't look back. Neither did he stay the course. He was riled and wanted a run. Or at least some exercise.

More badges than usual were on patrol since the Bastion had doubled, then tripled safeguards. The purnals were in talks with the city about imposing a general curfew, but the Fountain District was as lively as ever. Varti could hear distant cheers from the stadium, and spotlights swirled through the sky above Theater Row.

Not wanting to answer questions, Varti cut through an alley, then along the edges of a hexabout. Evading other badges became a game, and as the inmost city towers loomed nearer, he came up with a reason to continue.

The address Tybalt had mentioned. It was close.

He quickened his pace, crossing Century Plaza, where the mathematical center of the city was marked by a domed rotunda. Overhead, skywalks at various levels connected six skyrises. He veered left toward the Bridge District, where fog was already rising off the James, burying the royal gardens in cold mists. Under the first set of gaslamps, Varti spied a badge on duty, so he ducked behind a newspaper stand ... and immediately collided with someone just rounding the opposite corner.

"A thousand pardons!" exclaimed the man, who grabbed Varti's hand. Perhaps to steady him, though he didn't let go. "I never know *what* to expect, but even so, this *is* unexpected. A member of the constabulary? Dear me. I can't tell if that bodes well or ill."

Varti tried to pull away.

The man's grip tightened. "Were you looking for me? Or am I looking for you? Either way, the encounter is accomplished. Shall we?"

More baffled than anything, Varti let the man tug him along.

The badge on patrol had moved on. As the stranger who'd laid claim to his hand led Varti through the now-empty pool of light, he got a better look. A man of middling years. A slim build and a confident carriage. Posh clothes and purple hair.

"All will be well," he promised, entirely honest. "I'm Thomas, by the way."

# 7

## *Two Twenty-One*

VESPER 03, FOUR NINETY-EIGHT
FIRSTMOST VONNEDAY
9 KNELLS, 42 KNICKS
ON THE SECOND FACE OF THE CLOCK

Varti's mystification multiplied when Thomas led him straight to the address he'd intended to locate. Even with visibility plummeting, he could see the crepe wreath fluttering mournfully upon the door.

Row houses along this part of the Grand Promenade were some of the city's oldest and most historic. Engraved stones set into the walkway out front served as reminders that a dozen of these homes had belonged to Newcomb's original architects. The residences were untouched by the surrounding revolutionization, but not unencroached. Varti knew from his explorations that the back walls of these dwellings were flush with newer buildings that had been constructed directly behind.

Each narrow, three-story house was separated from the walk by a door garden hemmed by a filigree of wrought iron. Thomas let himself through a low iron gate that was more ornamental than anything. "This is us." He beckoned for Varti to follow, then jogged lightly up stone steps.

Varti kept a hand on the gate until the latch clicked, most

of his attention on the shadowy garden. The Bridge District, which flourished under the gaze of the royal residence high atop the city wall, was famous for its flowers. Here, lavender grew, thick and fragrant, and there was a pale dome mostly hidden by their stalks.

He stepped off the footpath and placed his palm against it.

Stone? No, he thought it might be clay.

The shape reminded him of coiled rope.

"I've been up and down every road," Thomas was saying. "Clear out to Keepsake Chapel, just in case. To think I'd find you here, so close to home. Well, home away from home. We've a lovely bit of farmland along the southern shore."

He lived outside the walls?

Nothing about Thomas bespoke *farmer*.

Varti clicked on his duty lamp, but even with illumination, he couldn't make sense of the structure. However, there came a low vibration from within. A hum.

"It's a hive. I'm told the design is meant to resemble ancient bee skeps. You should see us in daylight, when the whole garden is abuzz." Thomas held out a hand. "Come, Mr. Constabulary. Let's get you in out of the drear, hmm?"

Varti considered the door, which was as tall and narrow as the house itself. Old enough to be real wood, but black-painted. A small plaque was set over the mail slot beside the door, the standard hexagon you found everywhere throughout the city. The house number was 221, and beneath it a bee had been figured into the copper.

Thomas preceded him inside and fiddled with a knob. Gaslamps brightened a tidy foyer, and the man murmured, "Something to soothe or something to brace? After this day,

I need the bracing. I know just the thing. Please, be welcome. The sitting room is this way." More fixtures bloomed as the man moved deeper into the house.

Warm light gleamed dully against a patinaed sign affixed below the door knocker. A single word engraved its surface. CONSULTANT.

Varti was intrigued that the man hadn't once expected him to speak.

Indeed, he got the impression that Thomas knew he couldn't.

Dousing his lamp, Varti carefully closed the door. He noted a steep, open staircase and a vintage telephone closet. The abundance of polished wood gave credence to the house's age. Letters and cards overflowed a tin box set under the mail slot, and cloth had been draped over ... a painting? He reached for it, wanting to see beneath.

"A mirror." Thomas had rid himself of his overcoat. His vest was floral, and a cluster of greenery anchored his watchchain alongside his lapel. "We've had a death in the household, and my employer asked me to take precautions. Some do say that spirits can become trapped in mirrors. Others think they give entry to unsavory elements."

Quaint. But the man had mentioned a home outside the walls, where such superstitions took root.

"The lamps are lit, and I'll soon have a fire going."

Varti wondered at the man's watch, which had the sort of dainty design that generally appealed to ladies. More oddsome, the knell, knick, and flit hands had been removed. Was it only for adornment, then? Or was there another superstition at play?

"Sit here. I won't be long."

Easing into a leather armchair set before a deep fireplace,

Varti watched mutely as Thomas kindled a fire, then busied himself at a cabinet in the corner. The room was lined with shelves, though there weren't many books. Instead, row upon row of file boxes filled the space. He was familiar enough with them. The middlemost basement in his care held thousands of similar cases. They were for archiving papers.

At the Bastion, they held case files going back centuries.

Were these the same? Varti scanned the labels, but they didn't conform to the pattern they used for filing in his department. Many were in another language. Others involved symbols he didn't recognize at all. Runes? Or some form of shorthand?

"For you." Thomas bent at the waist, a formality Varti associated with palace servants and fae courtiers. He held a glass in each hand. "A personal favorite. Not so strong that it will go to our heads, since I need my wits about me for the task ahead."

Varti had no trouble taking the glass. Maybe his curse was as curious as he was. The drink had a tang he didn't recognize, and the essence of herbs tickled pleasantly at his nose. He took a larger swallow and sat back, more relaxed than he should have been.

Thomas eased a footstool into range, then perched on the wingback chair opposite Varti's. In better light, he decided that the man was as folksome as you could get. Or possibly one of the dandies or gents who adopted fae fashions. But that didn't fit his farmstead claim.

The crackling fire and the faint hiss of gas were the only sounds as they sat gazing at one another. The stillness was deep enough that Varti became aware of the ticking of his pocket watch. That couldn't be right. Glancing around, he swiftly located three other clocks in the room—a wind-up on the mantle, a royal chimer on the wall, and a cumbersome old grandfather stashed in a shadowy corner. All three were stopped. All at the same time.

Ten knells and twelve knicks.

"Time of death. Unofficially, alas, but I knew. I often do," Thomas said, his expression gone pensive. "An untimely death. Murder, you see."

Varti peered around more sharply. There'd been no recent murders in the Bridge District, so this was not the scene of a crime. But a death was being mourned. Varti wanted to express sympathy, to offer help. Instead, he said, "How fortuitous. You haven't filled the position yet, have you? I may as well apply. Does it pay well?"

Thomas blinked. "What an idea. Strange how you cannot see a thing until someone points it out."

He nodded. "You seem a proper dunce."

"Blind, at the very least. This is extraordinary. I was already going to be conducting an interview on my employer's behalf. Not much choice. I do hope the fellow I'm expecting isn't angry, having to deal with me instead."

A heavy knock sounded.

Thomas downed the last of his drink, set aside the glass, and paused to ask, "Folk-shy?"

"Terrified."

"Even a Darke Childe?"

"Slay on sight."

Thomas laughed. "Right, then. As he has the good grace to be punctual, I'll sort him out first. Then you shall have your turn, Mr. Constabulary."

Another heavy knock.

"On my way!" Thomas exclaimed, hurrying out.

*Punctual*? Varti checked his pocket watch.

Ten knells and twelve knicks.

A good time to be murdered.

# 8

## *Durst*

VESPER 03, FOUR NINETY-EIGHT
FIRSTMOST VONNEDAY
10 KNELLS, 12 KNICKS
ON THE SECOND FACE OF THE CLOCK

Varti contemplated escape, but they were at the very back of the house, so any former windows had been abutted out of existence. The cozy sitting room suddenly felt like a dead end. Thomas was returning, his cheerfulness undimmed, despite the worries he'd confided earlier.

"You must be chilled right through. Take a seat by the fire."

"I will stand." A deep voice, rich and slow, strangely accented.

Interesting. They didn't get many travelers through Newcomb. Had this one come by dirigible? Varti was still organizing the questions he couldn't ask when the stranger stepped into the room, focused on Varti, and drew a gleaming sidearm.

The weapon startled him, but he was more alarmed by the person holding it.

Thomas stepped between them. "I should have mentioned my other guest, Mr. Durst. He's also interested in securing a position within the household. Let's all get along, hmm?"

"Just Durst." Leather creaked as he holstered his sidearm.

Varti was caught between knowing he should look away and not being able to. Durst was definitely the most intimidating person he'd ever seen. Folk. Definitely a Darke Childe. More specifically, a gorgon. Several snakes with deep green scales writhed atop his head.

Durst's deadly gaze was still fixed on Varti. If the stories were true, then Varti should have been turned to stone, but goggles hid Durst's eyes, their crystal lenses catching and scattering light from iridescent facets.

Thomas said, "Durst, then. May I assume that your presence here means that you're amenable to my employer's terms?"

The gorgon's attention swung Thomas's way, but Varti couldn't help but notice that three of the snakes kept their beady eyes trained on him. To his utter horror, he blurted, "I want a better introduction. Do they have names?"

He definitely *didn't* need to know that.

The question had to be rude.

It wasn't as if *he* named his body parts.

Durst's attention was back on Varti, who shrank into his chair. He couldn't explain, couldn't apologize. And to his increasing dismay, he couldn't keep his mouth shut. "They're clearly curious about me. I'm flattered. We should meet."

What had been in that drink Thomas served?

Varti hadn't spoken this freely with a stranger in ages.

The reason why it was such a bad idea strolled closer. Varti catalogued six visible weapons. The heads of thirteen snakes— probably poisonous—rose up around Durst, weaving in hypnotic patterns. The gorgon planted his hands on the arms of Varti's chair and bent near enough that the snakes' tongues flickered against Varti's skin.

43

"They can taste fear." Durst's full lips drew back, revealing jagged teeth. "You have courage."

That felt like a taunt. Or possibly a challenge.

Varti wasn't feeling particularly brave, but this was the second time today he'd been faced with an uncommon animal. Focusing on the snake coiled watchfully under Durst's pointed ear, Varti lifted a hand and whistled softly.

Durst's smile faded, and his head tilted in a quizzical manner.

The snake answered his call, gliding over Varti's fingers, nosing his palm. He was larger than Varti had realized, his head roughly the size of a duck's egg, and the scales held a subtle rainbow sheen.

Forcing himself to narrow his focus, Varti rolled his hand and used his knuckles to stroke the snake's throat. A second head bumped up under his palm in a clear bid for attention. Another peeked slyly at him from under Durst's chin.

Black eyes glittered.

Ribbon-like tongues darted.

More snakes butted his fingers.

Varti felt sure he'd only been closer to death once before. Yet his curse didn't lash out. Maybe it didn't want to lose its host? Feeling foolishly reckless, Varti smiled into Durst's faceted goggles and said, "Snakes are my favorite."

The gorgon grunted. "Liar."

"Not me. I never lie."

"They can taste the truth." And with lips quirked, he repeated, "Liar."

He *knew*. This terrifyingly dangerous person could tell he was talking rubbish and hadn't taken offense. Varti wondered if Durst's snakes could taste relief.

"If you also take a position with this Mr. Holmes, perhaps you will learn their names." Durst straightened and addressed Thomas. "I would not be here if I did not like your employer's terms. I am no stranger to assassination."

Varti gaped up at the hex or so snakes still staring his way.

Thomas sternly said, "That's only as a last resort. It won't be necessary."

"Those were his terms. I accept them, even if you do not."

"Locking time begins at midnight, and the city gates will close. Be back here in one knell, and I'll bring you around to the house." Thomas smiled Varti's way. "The constable and I have business in the meantime."

The gorgon walked out without a backward glance.

After closing up after him, Thomas returned to his seat and sighed. "While I didn't entirely approve of hiring a mercenary, I believe my employer's heart is in the right place. Where the rest of him is … well! Should I make a report? I'm at a loss where else to search, and there's so much at stake. May I see your badge, Mr. Constabulary?"

"No." But he unhooked it from his belt and passed it along.

Thomas opened the case and smiled over what he found there. Gaze lifting, he said, "Good evening to you, Thricemost Ferior Varti Weller of the badge regulars. My name is Thomas Hudson. I'm currently employed as the majordomo of Hibernacle House, and I wish to report a missing dog."

# 9

## *Seekers in the Fog*

VESPER 03, FOUR NINETY-EIGHT
FIRSTMOST VONNEDAY
10 KNELLS, 22 KNICKS
ON THE SECOND FACE OF THE CLOCK

E nzo fumbled for his handkerchief and pressed it over his nose and mouth. The reek of blood was at war with the meager contents of his stomach, and he needed to stay quiet if he was going to learn anything. Vomiting against a graffitied wall would draw unwelcome attention.

A shadow slithered from between two of the cobbles at Enzo's feet and leapt upward, swirling to a stop on his shoulder.

"What did you find, Skrik?" Enzo asked softly.

"Gobbets and hairpins and filth." His familiar brushed at the wisping edges of his inky form with clawed hands. For a creature who traveled through cracks, Skrik was surprisingly fastidious.

"I'll clean you up later, I promise." Enzo glanced around, then crossed to where his other familiar was contemplating the vivid scrawls that decorated old brick. "What about you, Purdle?"

"Mmm. Too much yellow," the sprite announced, chin in hand. "It doesn't *go*. Very clashy."

"I meant about the ... the body."

46

"Oh. That." He kept his gaze averted from the gory scene he'd guided them to. "People should be nicer to their pets. I always am. Aren't I, Cubit?" He reached forward to caress the head of the Realmish newt he'd trained to the saddle, having decided that a proper prince needed a trusty steed.

Enzo protested, "You aren't my pet."

"Old Grumpers always called me that. He called Skrik your pet, too." Purdle peered up into his face and solemnly asked, "Are you going to look?"

"I should. I need to be sure."

"Mind your feet, then. Things have splashed quite a lot, and *you* don't have a flying newt to spare your shoes." Purdle's mood shifted, and he brightly asked, "Am I not fortunate to have tamed him?"

"Was it luck, though?"

"Good question. Do you suppose it was wisdom? Or maybe *destiny*? I like the sound of that. We were destined for each other."

Early on, Enzo had been exasperated by Purdle's acquisition. Wherever they went, Skrik and Purdle already drew so much attention. Adding a bright orange airborne amphibian? They'd gone from being noticeable to being memorable. Which could make them traceable.

But the newt was no mere beast. Though he couldn't speak, Enzo considered him a voice of reason, nicely balancing Purdle's impulsiveness. Cubit brought the number of their travel party to five.

A woman stalked out of the clinging fog, a shapeless silhouette thanks to the draping of several scarves. She lifted a battered lamp that illuminated little more than her scowl. "We should not stay. They will blame us. They always

47

do blame foreigners."

"Yes, okay." Enzo had risked as much before. He could do it again. "Let's get this over with."

Handkerchief firmly in place, he followed Tuppence into a neighborhood square. Well, by local custom, it'd be called a *hex*. Six trees anchored the corners, with benches tucked up against raised garden beds, and gaslamps offered a fuzzy glow. At the center, a fountain trickled. That's why Purdle had been so quick to find this place. Water sprites were nicknamed puddle-jumpers.

Enzo was looking for helpful details, but he was also trying to distract himself. Because someone had died here. Recently. Messily. Steeling his nerve, he looked and immediately wished he hadn't.

"A woman again. Mangled past knowing. No mercy. No restraint." Distaste curled Tuppence's lip. "This killer is a monster."

"Mmm," Enzo agreed, stepping with care.

Skrik asked, "Did we find him?"

Enzo rummaged in his coat pockets, then patted at his pants. Locating a smooth ring of gray stone, he held it up to his eye, clacking it against his glasses. Removing them, he tried again. There were signs of something, but were they the traces he needed?

"Is it him?" Skrik pushed Enzo's chin, redirecting his gaze.

Enzo almost took a step forward, but Tuppence grabbed his coat, hauling him backward lest he sully the crime scene. He mumbled apologies, but most of his attention was fixed on a wavering figure at the mouth of one of the other alleys, this one blocked by an iron gate.

"I can't say for certain if it was him. But ... *she's* here."

"Do not look," hissed Tuppence. "Do not listen."

"I know, I know," Enzo grumbled, though he watched as pale tendrils separated and coalesced. He'd seen the birth of ghosts before, but only those of animals. And always with safeguards in place.

Tuppence jostled his elbow, and he fumbled the stone, bobbling it before trapping it against the thick cables of his woolen sweater. Not until it was safely in his coat pocket did he breathe again. The thing was a family heirloom. Irreplaceable.

Purdle warned, "Someone's coming."

Pushing Enzo back the way they'd come, Tuppence bustled him toward the nearest bridge. A whistle sounded. Hasty footsteps approached from different directions.

"Sit," Tuppence growled, yanking him down.

He landed on a bench. They were along the Grand Promenade now, where the gaslamps were more ornate and more plentiful. But the fog was so thick, three officers ran past without noticing Enzo and his retinue.

"Now," said Purdle, because he would know best.

They were on the move again, but to Enzo's dismay, they bypassed the elevators to the trolley.

Tuppence crisply announced, "We walk back."

"You're kidding. It's *miles* to the dormitories!" Which was true in the strictest sense, since the road from the city center to the mage academy was precisely two miles. Though he thought they might call it something else here. Flicks? Clicks? Something like that.

Undeterred, Tuppence said, "No trolley for you. Too many lights. Too many onlookers. We cannot be seen. We must not be remembered."

49

Skrik said, "She's right."

Purdle said, "*I'm* right."

"About what?" Enzo asked.

"*Now*," Purdle tensely repeated, peering back the way they'd come. "We should go *now*."

All Enzo could do was push himself into a shambling jog, chasing after the meager light of Tuppence's bobbing hand lamp ... and wondering if his long search was finally over.

# 10

## *Majordomo*

VESPER 03, FOUR NINETY-EIGHT
FIRSTMOST VONNEDAY
10 KNELLS, 40 KNICKS
ON THE SECOND FACE OF THE CLOCK

Loathe to meet Durst again, when Varti left Thomas, he dived down a hushed side street, then jogged along a zigzagging alley that landed him near Farrukh Station. This was one of the endmost trolley stops on the line, which formed an incomplete circle of the city. The gap in the design wasn't practical for commuters, but engineers had done it anyway, out of respect. Otherwise, the palace's view of the Bridge District's gardens would have been spoiled.

Ignoring the bank of lifts, Varti took the metal stairs instead, his boots ringing on steel grating up to station level, where Newcomb's two trolleys ran on twin tracks. One arrived, and Varti showed his badge, then chose a seat at the back of a car. They were soon accelerating away on a clockwise course, stopping at each station in turn, until Rowan Station, which was next-to-last and closest to home. There were no lifts here, so he joined the draggle of people taking the stairs to street level.

The fogbank was thick here, thanks to the spillway and the system of locks that brought barges into the city. It was cold and damp, and for a moment, he considered turning inward, toward The Speckled Hen and the comfort Ramage would offer. But then came a low *wuff* from the shadows, and the hound emerged from the murk.

People exclaimed and scattered, understandably startled by the appearance of so large an animal. Varti didn't want them raising an alarm, so he whistled sharply and patted his chest.

The dog frisked around him, tail flagging, and the people around them relaxed. Some even laughed, especially when the hound reared back as he'd done that morning, planting his big paws on Varti's shoulders in order to gaze down at him, tongue lolling in doggish amusement.

"I was hoping for one last catastrophe." Varti tugged at wiry fur, gladder than he should have been that the stray had been lying in wait. But what was this? Stains marred his muzzle. And yes, more of the stuff was matted into the fur of his paws and forelegs.

"So he's yours, then?" asked a man.

"All mine," Varti said. Even though chances were better than fair that this was the dog Thomas Hudson had lost. He gave a push, and the beast dropped down, sitting on his haunches, ears pricked expectantly.

While Varti checked for smudges on his uniform, people moved on, and he was left with a conundrum.

This really might be Thomas's missing dog, but Varti couldn't be positive until an identification was made. But right about now, Thomas should be taking Durst through the city gates, bound for that farm he'd mentioned. Varti's pocket watch confirmed that it would soon be locking time. Proper procedure would have been to impound the dog at the bestiary, but he turned toward home. "Go away," he coaxed. "Nobody wants you. Wretched thing."

When the hound came to his side, walking quite close, Varti rested his hand on his back and strolled homeward. After frightening a couple of tipsy men headed inward, toward the gaming district, Varti tightened his fingers in the dog's fur and guided him along the quiet lanes between residential hexes.

He lifted the duty lamp from its hook and thumbed the igniter. While he wasn't on patrol in any official sense, announcing his status as a badge would lend a sense of safety to the Drears, which didn't see many foot patrols.

The attendant at the steam baths gave them a sidelong look but didn't offer any protest when Varti steered his four-footed companion into the long, echoing room of sinks and shower stalls and soaking tubs. He hung his cloak and rolled up his sleeves. Nabbing a couple of buckets, he scooped them full of warm bathwater and chivvied until the dog stood with a forepaw in each.

Wetting the corner of a towel, Varti applied himself to the stains on his muzzle, swiping until the fur was clean. A vast improvement, though the towel was past help, stained with rust. Or ... no. Varti brought it closer to the light, suddenly worried. Was this blood?

He knelt before the dog, running his hands up and down each foreleg as the water darkened. No signs of injury. So if it *was* blood, it wasn't his. The dog endured the cleaning of his back paws, which weren't nearly as dirty, and when Varti tipped out the water, he had to swish them twice, then rinse the tiles around the floor drain several times to banish every trace.

It had certainly looked like blood.

But he'd destroyed the evidence.

Finally reaching his building, Varti turned into the alley and brought out his key. "Shall we go in baying and stomping?"

The hound snuffled at the kickplate and sneezed, then had the audacity to precede Varti inside. Maybe it was scent that guided him, but he bounded up the stairs without pause. Varti found him seated patiently outside the door to their quarters.

Inside, Varti lit the night lamp. While the dog explored, Varti began his end-of-day routine—brushing his cloak, brushing his boot soles, refilling his duty lamp, closing the curtains. He was so focused, he didn't immediately notice the tape spooling onto the floor below the ticker.

Hurrying to light another lamp, he found the end, where the message began with a timestamp—ten knells, forty-one knicks, second face. The first message was a summons, because the serial killer had cut short Phil's last night of freedom. A fifth victim had been found. Varti's eyes widened at the address, for it was quite close to the place where he'd met Thomas.

A chill passed through him. Had meeting Thomas saved him from meeting the killer instead?

He kept reading. A second message followed, ten knicks later, and this was directed toward all members of the irregulars. Varti carefully tore off the paper, coiling it neatly. Turning to the map, he inserted a red pin at the spot where the murder had taken place. He was trying to divine any sort of pattern made by the red pins when a low growl came from Phil's room.

Holding the lamp high, he pushed through the beaded curtain to see what was happening.

The hound stood upon the bed, nosing through rumpled sheets and blankets.

Varti didn't like to think too hard about the fact that whenever Tybalt bunked with them, it was in Phil's bed. "Nothing ever goes on in here," he said, glancing around.

One of the reasons Phil had the only bedroom was that he had more stuff. A vintage wardrobe and a set of drawers with a mirror on top. A sturdy four-poster and the low filing cabinet Phil used as a bedside table. He'd also crowded in a saddle stand and the locked cabinet that held the firearms he carried when on assignment outside the city walls.

The room was a bit tossed, but that was Phil's usual state. Nothing seemed amiss. Varti didn't recognize the books stacked near the foot of the bed nor the square bottle that may have held some kind of liquor. There was also a bundle of dried herbs newly hanging over the room's window. But any of those things could have been brought in by Tybalt.

Another growl.

Varti rapped on the doorframe and held aside the beads.

With a grumpy *wuff*, the hound jumped down and slunk out.

Crossing to his own sleeping area, Varti pushed open a thick curtain and gestured with a flourish at his neatly-made bed. "Much grander, don't you think? Though it's the floor for you."

Varti slept in a curtained space that might not count as a bedroom since it was basically all bed. Two drawers and a few shelves were built into the wall at the foot. Those held his few odds and ends. Varti had never felt slighted by the way their territory was divided. He had few requirements, and in a sense, the entire living area was his.

His bed was so low, the hound didn't have to jump. He

stepped up and stood upon a brightly-colored coverlet that had been a gift from Nani. Maybe it was Varti's imagination, but he thought the dog stepped lightly, mindful of the embroidered silk. He was grateful for the consideration.

Retrieving his sleep clothes from their place under his pillow, Varti quickly changed, doused the brighter lamp, and set the night lamp beside the ticker. The Bastion had other ways of contacting badges, so Phil might not come home at all. But Varti wanted to know if he did, so he left his bed-curtain open.

When he folded back the coverlet, the hound hopped down, making room for Varti to get settled. Then he set a paw on the sheet, tail thumping hopefully against the floor.

"The floor, I said." But he scooted back against the wall. "Fleas everywhere. And your breath is foul."

The dog stepped up, licked Varti's ear, and sprawled beside him.

Varti tested his curse's boundaries. "You can stay with me forever."

Which was an interesting mix of true and false, because Varti would have liked to keep this beast, even though he knew all the reasons he couldn't. Not the least of which was Thomas Hudson.

He tried again. "It will be a relief to send you back."

Still a lie. Maybe the curse had decided that animals were too much of a loophole.

Phil had once told him that a folk-spelling like his could sometimes be outwitted if you spoke a single word. It couldn't *mean* anything, like creating a code in which *speckle* always meant *Ramage*. But a seemingly random, meaningless word could become a valuable clue. Unfortunately, it rarely worked with Phil anymore. The curse didn't like to be tricked, and it took vicious pleasure in stymying Phil. But maybe Varti could get away with something here and now. Since a dog shouldn't count as a person.

It wouldn't make any difference. Not really.

But it mattered to Varti.

So he folded his hands and focused on breathing. He relaxed his mind and body, not holding any thought too close, lest the curse notice and waylay him. Eyes closed, he reached for the dog, tangled his fingers in wiry fur, and spoke a word he'd never used before. In truth, he wasn't even sure what it meant.

"Majordomo."

# 11

## *Twice Deities*

VESPER 04, FOUR NINETY-EIGHT
FIRSTMOST WILLIDAY
2 KNELLS, 3 KNICKS
ON THE FIRST FACE OF THE CLOCK

Dreams were an investigator's tool, just the same as their wits and senses and resolve. Varti didn't mean the omen-bearing dreams of mystics, who had entire glossaries for interpreting imagery and ephemera. No. Varti believed in his mind's ability to sift and stew and simmer while he slept. In dreams, he wrestled with information, seeking connections. And in those hazy moments of near-waking, he found epiphanies.

So when a key rattled in the old-fashioned lock that secured their quarters, Varti came awake, sure he'd realized something. He turned his face from the sudden light and the sound of boots, needing to hold onto the dream for a little longer. But instead of his familiar pillow, he was met by a faceful of fur. And the hand at his waist was a paw. And the voice in his ear was only Tybalt.

Phil hushed him.

But then came a low whistle, and Tybalt was leaning into Varti's space. "Realm take me! Where did you find this furry behemoth? He's bigger than you are!"

"Ohhh," Phil said, also from close quarters. "You were being literal."

Varti stayed where he was, letting fur hide his expression.

"Can't say I like the look of him," Tybalt cautiously admitted.

"I am in mortal peril," Varti mumbled, wrapping his arm more firmly around the dog, whose tail thumped once in response. "We're all prey."

"What a beautiful animal," said Phil. "Whilom will spring a cog."

Varti rolled onto his back and opened his eyes. "I've named him Doggerel, and we'll soon be wed. He promised to make an honest man of me."

Tybalt snorted. "Bed for me. I need to catch a couple of knells."

Phil lowered himself all the way to the edge of the mattress and offered his hand to the hound, who sniffed, then sneezed into it. "I'm so grateful," he said mildly. Then he touched Varti's shoulder with two fingers.

Varti nodded. And would have said *wolves*. Because Phil's reading had been unsettlingly on point. But the word that made it past the curse's stranglehold was, "Thornapple."

"I'll bear that in mind," Phil promised with a weary smile. "Sleep. Morning will soon be upon us, and it's sure to have teeth."

He closed the bed-curtain. Then beads briefly clattered before swaying into silence.

The hound offered a whispery *wuff*.

Varti said, "This must never happen again. I forbid it."

A damp nose prodded his throat, and Varti belatedly realized that they'd switched places. How had the dog managed that? A paw landed on his chest, and he scooted closer in order to slide under it, letting the beast cage him. Despite his earlier complaint, Varti didn't know why so many insults were dog-related. This one wasn't mangy or flea-bitten. And there wasn't even anything particularly offensive about the hound's breath.

Doggerel—assuming the lie stuck—was a welcome source of warmth. The fur might be wiry, but it was clean. He hadn't needed a full bath, and his coat smelled pleasant, even posh. Varti could almost picture Thomas Hudson brushing until it shone. Yes, the evidence was right here, testifying that this dog couldn't be an ordinary stray.

He belonged somewhere beyond these city walls. Along the southern shore, according to Thomas. Doggerel had the sort of restraint that came with intelligence ... experience ... patience. A reassuring combination. Good company.

Varti pressed closer, breathed deeply, relaxed completely. And as he drifted toward sleep, his mind made an unexpected connection. This scent that had been teasing at the edges of memory. He'd sorted it out. Though he had no idea if it was important.

Doggerel's fur. It smelled like pipe tobacco.

A cool hand on Varti's forehead stirred him from sleep, and for just a moment, he thought it was his nani. But then Phil gently announced, "Not feverish. I don't *think* you're sick, but I didn't realize you were *capable* of sleeping in. Feeling wracksome anywhere?"

He stared blankly into his best friend's face. He'd overslept? This had never happened before. Varti always woke early, always went for his run. Yet daylight showed out the window.

Was he actually late for work?

"Varti?"

"Terrible," he mumbled, more embarrassed than anything. "I feel terrible."

"Doesn't show. You're practically aglow." Phil's gaze drifted past Varti. "I sleep better with a companion, too."

Varti's gut twisted. He didn't crave the kind of companionship Phil constantly sought, but it might have been nice to have *something*. Was a dumb beast the best he could do? Was he supposed to be satisfied? Grateful?

"The ticker woke us. Not another murder, but new information. I left the scroll for you to read. Tybalt's gone on ahead, and I need to dash, but first ... humor me?" He held up his guidance deck.

Varti disentangled himself from beast and bedding and sat cross-legged, presenting both hands to his friend. The deck on his left palm. Split and turned up onto his right. A second cut to reveal a second card.

Phil made a soft noise of surprise. "Twice wolves yesterday, and twice deities today?"

Unsure how to interpret his friend's expression, Varti scanned the cards. They were two of the season cards, easily recognized because depictions of the four dignitaries were everywhere in Newcomb.

"Bittern's Garden usually indicates loss or grief," said Phil. "But it's inverted here. Turned around, it suggests a different kind of burial. Hibernation. A season of waiting."

Varti didn't think there was anything amazing about that. Hadn't he been stranded for years, waiting for someone to figure out how to unspell him? But hibernation. That was close enough to *hibernacle* to give him a jolt.

"And this card is known as Vesper's Peril. Since that's the season we're in, it's a straightforward warning. Imminent danger." Phil looked positively glum. "What's happening to us, Varti?"

He nodded. He thought he sneered. Stupid curse.

Unperturbed, Phil confessed, "I pulled two cards earlier, just to see. Mine were warnings as well. The Imposter, which could mean almost anything. Worst case, that the killer is among the badges. But it might simply warn against two-faced people. Or someone in disguise. Or maybe it's delivering a more personal jibe, since I'm going to be useless as the leader of this investigation."

"Imprison everyone in uniform. Safest route, really."

"Right. I know. Reading your fears into the future is asking for trouble. Anyhow, the second card was Fifth of Nights, combining owl-strike and wailing. And last night was the fifth killing. There's no question it's the same culprit." Phil ran a fingertip over the silver frost along the edge of Bittern's Garden. "Maybe we'll have a lead, though. I'm meeting with an echo-catcher this morning. I'm already late, but she'll have to forgive me. We think the victim left a trace. I'm almost positive it'll result in a ghost."

"Ghosts are common as copper."

"Scarce enough to be worrisome, especially *inside* the city. Everyone knows that the walls are writ with ancient wards to keep the terrors at bay. But Varti, I think they've begun to fail." He stared into his empty hands. "What's out wants in, and innards will out."

"I love the sayings of mystics. Always so comforting."

Phil cracked a smile, but it faded. "Do me a favor, Varti.

Please. Go to Ramage for breakfast today. I will, too. I want to touch salt. I'll tell him to expect you."

Varti shoved the guidance deck into Phil's hands and pushed past him. "Can't be bothered. Waste of time. Doggerel wouldn't like it."

# 12

## *Files & Evidence*

VESPER 04, FOUR NINETY-EIGHT
FIRSTMOST WILLIDAY
9 KNELLS, 33 KNICKS
ON THE FIRST FACE OF THE CLOCK

Even skipping nearly every part of his morning routine, Varti was a solid twenty knicks late for his tocking, but his staff barely noticed. The ladies only had eyes for Doggerel, who'd apparently decided that he needed to stick to Varti's side. Barely legal with a lead of braided twine, the hound had come to heel with manners beautiful enough that the guards hadn't batted an eye when Varti lied their way through security.

Now Henna was making a fool of herself over him, scratching and fluffing and paying outrageous compliments. "Honest to honor, I had no idea dogs even came this large! He hardly seems the same sort of creature. Why, the royal dogs could stroll right under him without ruffling their manes. Who's a fine, great fellow? Who is? Who?"

Varti thought Doggerel had a pained expression.

"I worked up a local interest piece once, celebrating the pets of Newcomb. At that time—you were probably in nappies, Mr. Weller—hedgehogs were *so* trendsome. Nobody could afford pony carts, but every child wanted one. And cats, of course. Cats are a classic. As they say, a kitten in every mother's apron pocket. But these days? Clockwork pets are so hot, you need tongs. Every Newcomber will be mobbing the cogger stalls come Bittern, wanting them for Calibration Days gifts."

At first blush, Henna was a gossip.

But Varti knew better.

If you unwound time far enough, Henna had reported for the *Newcomb Buzz*, one of the city's six newspapers. She had a classical arts degree, and she'd minored in Folk Studies. She'd been at this job for longer than was polite to mention, and she knew the contents of their domain almost as well as Varti himself. He gave himself a slight edge there.

Henna knew how to *find* all the records.

Varti had actually read most of them.

And the reason Henna was so generous with information was Varti himself. Though she was fond of telling any of the interns who were temporarily assigned to their department that he'd taken a vow of silence, she knew the truth. And from the beginning, she'd made it her business to answer the kinds of questions Varti couldn't ask.

She found the swatch of cardboard that had been knotted onto a loop of twine around the hound's neck. "Doggerel? Is that meant to be insulting or ironic?"

Varti wasn't entirely sure if it had been Aril or Burr who'd fashioned the thing, but it was further proof of Phil's attention to detail. Always smoothing the way. Looking after Varti. Ramage had been expecting both of them, ready with breakfast and blessings and a cardboard badge.

Kel spoke up from the other side of the room, where she

stood with arms folded. "Is this going to become a regular sort of thing?"

"Why not?" Henna exclaimed.

"I could list six and add sixty. What if he gets into the lockers? Destroying evidence."

Kel had been assigned to the department shortly after Varti was. She did the work with an air of utter boredom. Varti felt sorry for her. He'd gathered that she was some kind of security detail, meant to keep an eye on him in case his curse developed dire consequences. But he didn't bear watching, and that meant she was as stranded in these basements as he was.

Henna asked, "Don't some of the irregulars have canine companions?"

"They do," Kel answered flatly. "But this dog hasn't earned a vest or badge."

"Yet!" Henna protested.

Varti turned to go, and Doggerel was at his side in a flit, so close he was practically leaning, which made it hard to walk in a straight line. It was almost as if the hound was steering him. The impression gained plausibility when Doggerel eased up once Varti was facing the cage wall that secured the evidence lockers.

Kel announced, "I left today's batch on your worktable."

Then a chime sounded from the front counter, which was Henna's post, and they all got down to business.

Varti sidestepped the hound and crossed to the spiral staircase that was quicker than waiting for the lift to the middlemost basement. The click of claws assured him that the hound was following.

This level was a sprawling maze of cabinets and bookshelves.

No open flames were allowed in these archives, which were instead lit by a cutting-edge system of overhead lights. He wasn't clear on the science of them, but he was grateful for their soft white glow. Indeed, the small potted plant he kept on his worktable here fared better than the one on the windowsill in his quarters.

He gently touched a pointed leaf, a swelling bud. Then he addressed the net bag Kel had left. Today's newspapers. He really should get to sorting. But he drummed his fingers atop the pile for several moments before striding purposefully into the stacks.

They kept reference books here. The Bibliotheca's collection was more complete, but the Bastion held certain resources closer to hand. Varti found the book he wanted, a hefty leatherbound tome that had been stained green and gilt with copper. Lowering it onto his worktable, he scanned the table of contents, then turned to the section he needed.

Gorgons.

The book only offered the barest of facts, nothing about culture or customs, but it was more than Varti had known. Interestingly enough, most gorgons were female, and they usually kept to their colonies. Also, they were meant to have the torso of a human but body of a snake. Durst had most definitely been walking on two legs.

Next, Varti pulled the most recent folio of international bulletins. These held so little bearing on day-to-day life in Newcomb that unopened bundles were sent directly to Varti to be filed. He always went a step further, tacking up copies of the WANTED posters in the security offices of the dirigible port, barge district, and railway station.

Varti knew Durst wasn't mentioned in any of the bulletins since his posting. He'd have remembered a gorgon. But many Folk were old as Olde, so Varti checked back through fifty years of postings and warrants. Durst did not appear. But that could simply mean that he was too cunning to be pinpointed as a culprit.

He'd been hired. A foreign mercenary.

As he was closing the books to return them to their place, he finally noticed that Doggerel had positioned himself with his forepaws on a footstool. He looked between Varti and the book, head cocked, ears pricked, gaze piercing. Like he'd been reading over Varti's shoulder.

"I'm sure Durst is perfectly harmless."

Next, Varti descended to the map room in their downermost basement. This space was smaller and held resources that were often cumbersome. For once, he didn't reach for street maps or blueprints. In a huge ledger, he found the information he wanted almost immediately, mainly because Hibernacle House had been built on one of the first tracts of land parceled out after the Expansion had been approved.

The name on the deed was S. HOLMES.

# 13

## *Neighborly*

Enzo skulked along the dormitory hall, picking the remains of a hasty breakfast out of his teeth. With weapons, Tuppence was versatile enough, but when it came to cookery, she didn't have much range. He was growing increasingly tired of the nutritional paste she considered essential. Even when it was spread on good, fresh bread, he ate sparingly. He'd have preferred to simply eat the bread. Instead, he'd coaxed Skrik into losing most of his meal down the nearest crack.

He'd tried to suggest better options, but any hints that they follow an appetizing scent into a restaurant was tantamount to insult. He'd even offered to do his own cooking. But an affronted Tuppence was the worst kind of bane, and a weepy Tuppence was bad for his heart.

She was only doing what she must. And she operated under a bedrock conviction that she could take care of him better than any of these outlandish heathens and their weird technologies. So Enzo let her have her way, even though he'd

69

needed to add a hole to his belt to keep his pants up.

Their apartment was in a part of a building that wasn't much used. Enzo suspected he'd been stashed in an odd corner because he was a foreigner. Since there was no elevator nearby, he was forced to trudge up and down long flights of stairs every day. His mentor had since offered to find him better, more convenient accommodations, but Tuppence vetoed the notion. Their current place was secure. Change was dangerous.

As far as Enzo could tell, only one other person lived along this stretch of hall, and he was scarce. But as he neared the staircase, that very boy reached the top and turned his way, cloak flowing to his knees, aviator goggles pushed high on his forehead. Their eyes met, and Enzo tried for a smile. He received a nod in return. And then a savory fragrance hit him.

The words were out of his mouth before he could stop himself. "What's that smell?"

"Huh?" The guy glanced down, then lifted the bag dangling from his fingers. There was a simple logo on it, stamped in green. "You mean this? It's just the usual buns. Same as every cart carries."

Enzo feared he was drooling. "Are they good?"

"I mean ... they're cheap. And filling. You want one?"

He glanced worriedly at the door to his apartment. "Would you mind if I ate at your place?"

The boy's brows shot up. "You're ... what? Dropping by? Being neighborly?"

"Is that not allowed? I'm hazy on what's expected."

"You're foreign."

"Yes."

"Where from?" The boy lifted his chin toward his own door, and Enzo followed him.

70

"Originally? North America. But I've been traveling for … huh. I guess it's been a decade already."

"Vagabond, huh? Come on in."

Enzo followed him in and froze, surprised by the sudden riot of color. Every wall, the floor, the ceiling—they'd been graffitied.

"Grab a seat. Chairs are under the table." The boy shot him an amused look. "Got something to say?"

"Wow."

"Scared yet?"

Enzo blinked. "Should I be?"

He shook his head. "Most people wouldn't invite themselves into a stranger's quarters, and no people would stick around for more than a flit after seeing mine."

"Oh. Okay." Enzo pivoted, searching the wild patterns for words or symbols or runes. The place was twice the size of his own. In fact, it looked as if someone had taken down the walls between two sets of rooms. The additional space had been turned into a workshop. Or possibly a studio. He spied paint and brushes in addition to the clockworks and machinery.

"Sit already. I'm Arty, by the way."

"Enzo." He offered his hand. "Are you a student here?"

"When it suits me." He was slim and angular, with dark hair and large eyes. The hand that met his had long nails painted indigo blue. "I've seen you in a couple of the practicums."

"Really? I'm sorry. I didn't notice." Enzo shed his coat and dragged a chair out from under a table that was large enough for a crowd. "I've been here six months. Well, you'd say two seasons, I guess. Since last March, which is in Milvine if I have my calendar right. Why on earth did you guys reinvent so much?"

"What language is that?"

"English …?"

"Ancient English? Like … you're a historian?"

"Not really, but I read. And I've traveled. You didn't know? It's how the rest of the world still operates."

"If you say so. Our history books begin with the Sundering and the Founders. Cataclysmic epicenter. Swarms and stole-aways. Our deal with the Dignitaries. Descent of the First Queen. Blah, blah, blah. Ancient history."

"Newcomb is your whole world."

Arty casually slit the bag, exposing six round, white buns. "And your compass is cracked if you've never tasted a steamed bun, even though they're sold on every streetcorner."

"I'm not criticizing. I suppose I'm just complaining, and that's a terrible way to approach a new culture." His stomach rumbled, and he indicated the buns. "May I?"

"Half are yours. Help yourself."

Enzo gently lifted a bun—pillowy and pleated and warm to the touch. A light sniff, a cautious bite. Steam escaped, fogging his glasses. He took a bigger bite, capturing more filling, which was a mix of meat and spice and onion and cheese. Cramming the rest into his mouth, he reached for another.

"Lever back, you knob, or you'll choke." Arty hurried to a cupboard and rummaged, coming back with a bottle. Using a tool from his belt, he pried off its cap and passed it along. "This'll go down smooth. Rightward stuff, Twitchel's."

Enzo took a grateful swig, then scrutinized the label. "Is this alcoholic?"

"I'm a generous host."

"You *can't* be old enough to drink."

"You quoting Newcomb's laws to me, old man?"

"How old are you?"

"Sixteen. Almost." He flicked a finger at the bottle. "You've never had Twitchel's before? Every mother stocks it. Bun mothers, too."

Enzo took another enormous bite and shook his head.

"Too poor for luxuries like food and drink?"

"I'm not entirely sure. The exchange rates are baffling." He didn't want to admit that Tuppence kept his purse strings tightly knotted. He fished in his pocket and brought out a few coins. "This is all I have at the moment."

"If that's pocket change, you're not poor." He straightened in his chair. "Do you even have a mother?"

"What does she have to do with anything?"

Arty rolled his eyes. "The place you eat all your meals. That's your mother."

"What? Wait ... what?" Enzo couldn't believe he hadn't realized. "Is *that* why there are no grocery stores?"

"What's that?"

"Somewhere you buy ingredients for cooking."

Arty looked incredulous. "That's a mother's job, innit? Nobody explained?"

"It's possible that my caretaker chose to ignore any instructions that didn't meet with her approval." Enzo sighed. "In my experience, the hardest things to understand are those that people take for granted."

Pushing his last two buns to Enzo, Arty asked, "What're you doing in Newcomb anyhow? Aren't you kinda old for Academy?"

"Learning is meant to take a lifetime." More sheepishly, he admitted, "I mostly enrolled so I could stay in the dorms."

"And they stashed you here? That's bleaksome."

"You live here."

"Suits me."

"So where are you from?" asked Enzo.

"Here."

"You don't sound like it. The accent, I mean."

"What, this? It's a choice. Me and my crew, we're distinguishing ourselves." He narrowed his eyes. "Who's your mentor?"

"No mentor, exactly. Just an advisor. Professor Oswald has been helping me acclimate."

"Well that's not too shabby. Enviable, even. He doesn't take on just anyone. How'd you manage that?"

"I'm a mage."

That earned him another eyeroll. "This is the Academy of Mages. We've all got a patron or a partner or maybe a fae-touched lineage with knackward consequences. Which is it for you?"

"Partnership. Or partnerships. I have more than one."

Arty laughed, like he thought Enzo was kidding. "Soldering springs, you're serious? But ... *how*?"

"It's umm ... it runs in the family."

"You've got heirloom traits? That's elite stuff. No wonder Oswald tapped you. Say, can I see?" Twirling a finger in the air, he said, "In exchange, I'll show you what I can do. Or ... you know what? Even better. I'll show you around. Me and my crew can teach you how things work around here."

Enzo hesitated.

"No?" Arty's expression slowly closed. "Got whatcha needed, so you're gonna rust off?"

"No! I want to. I really, really want to. But I'll need permission first. From Tuppence."

"She the caretaker you mentioned?"

"Yeah. And she'll want to meet you."

"Why's that have you worried?"

"Tuppence is ... umm, let's just say there are very good reasons why her nickname is Bad Penny."

# 14

## *Lead Investigator*

VESPER 04, FOUR NINETY-EIGHT
FIRSTMOST WILLIDAY
10 KNELLS, 14 KNICKS
ON THE FIRST FACE OF THE CLOCK

Holmes wasn't a surname Varti knew. Lake District families traced their lineages straight back to the founders, whose names were ,widely known and daily used. But there was no doubt that Durst had mentioned a Mr. Holmes, so the property was still in the family.

Varti's information-gathering was effectively pointless. It wasn't as if he could tell anyone about what he'd seen and done. But the curse hadn't ever hindered him from doing his job in the past. And Thomas Hudson *had* brought him a case.

Curious what might happen, Varti went to the appropriate cabinet and took out a new file folder, its edges crisp and its ID slot empty. Even though Varti worked with case files all day long, he'd never started one before. That was more of an upstairs job. But did the curse know that?

Varti had been walked through the steps for preparing case files during his academy days. Many badge students complained that the process was tedious, but Varti found it helpful to pull all the facts together in a single place. A file was simply a smaller, more portable version of a case wall. An orderly accumulation of information with bearing. If an investigator applied themselves to their task, the resulting report could contribute to a satisfactory conclusion and a just judgment.

On the file's tab, he wrote LOST DOG, and he assigned a twelve-digit case number.

He recorded the date and time of his initial meeting with Thomas Hudson, and on the line for lead investigator, he printed his own name. And with a growing sense of wonder, he set to work, adding a city map for reference and a page each for his lines of inquiry.

CONSULTANT AT 221 OLD LONDON ROAD, BRIDGE DISTRICT

THOMAS HUDSON

HIBERNACLE HOUSE

S. HOLMES

DURST THE GORGON

He searched his mind for any other possible leads and added one more line.

TOBACCONIST

Varti summarized what he'd already learned about gorgons. His research hadn't turned up anything helpful, but that only meant that he needed better resources. Perhaps if he went to the Bibliotheca on his next free Newday? They'd have extensive records, possibly even a census of each gorgon village. Tracing Durst back to his birthplace should make it easier to find documentation of his subsequent activities. Following procedure, he filled out an archive request form and clipped it to Durst's page.

Unbelievable.

77

He couldn't write out explanations, couldn't type answers to questions, couldn't leave messages. They'd tried. But if he was working as a file clerk, creating the record of an investigation, it was different? He wasn't sure why, and he wasn't sure this could last. So he stayed on task, turning his attention to Thomas Hudson.

An initial check confirmed that Thomas had no criminal record.

Going back into the stacks, he made a guess at his age and searched for him on student rosters. It took a while because young Thomas had been enrolled in one of the smaller academies, specializing in the theatrical arts.

Finding references after that was no chore. Thomas Hudson had been a popular actor. Now that he knew where to look, Varti cross-referenced records about Theater Row and found him on several cast lists. Reviews were glowing. Interestingly, Thomas wasn't ever the leading man. He specialized in supportive roles, and critics often mentioned his versatility. One reviewer remarked that he hadn't even recognized Thomas, so complete was his transformation into his character. They called him a chameleon who could adopt any persona.

So why had he retired?

And why had he gone to work on a downslope farm beyond the city walls?

On a hunch, Varti looked to see if Thomas Hudson had been the victim of a crime.

That was slower going, especially since he didn't know when the man had retired from the stage. He filled out another archive request form to see if Thomas had kept up his membership in the Theater Guild, and if not, what year he'd let it lapse.

Deciding to be thorough, he next hauled an enormous dictionary from its cubby in order to look up *majordomo*.

No wonder Varti had no context for the word. Household servants weren't part of his upbringing. He'd heard of butlers, of course. In literature. Majordomo apparently held a similar role. Thomas Hudson was a chief steward, which implied other staff members. It was also possible that the term had appealed to Thomas because it was sort of theatrical.

Varti put the finishing touches on Thomas's section, then sat back with a sense of real satisfaction. He covered his face with both hands, mind racing. Could the answer to everything be this simple? A case number. A file folder.

"Mr. Weller?" Kel called from the direction of the lift. "You have a visitor."

He let his hands fall to his lap and locked gazes with Doggerel. Varti hadn't realized the dog was so close. Doggerel carefully set a paw on his leg. Checking his pocket watch, Varti winced. It was nearly two knells past midday. He'd be in need of a walk. And a meal.

Tybalt strolled in, a bundle under one arm, his gaze roving. "Else lights! Glad to see they're taking care of you. I mean, it's still a boring old basement, but I've never seen else lights outside of a hospital. How long have they been here?"

Varti glanced up, mystified.

"Err ... skip it. I know you can't answer. I'm here for this guy, anyhow." He eyed Doggerel. "Kemp saw this morning's paper and sent me to find this for you."

Something in today's paper? Varti grumbled, "You know I can't read."

Tybalt snorted and started flipping through the newspapers still stacked on the corner of Varti's desk. He tossed the one he wanted on top of the case file Varti had been updating. The *Clockwork Sentinel*, one of Newcomb's more sensational papers, bore a headline that was definitely pertinent.

## SET UPON BY DOGS

"There'll be trouble if he isn't in a vest and on a leash. It was a real run-around, finding something big enough. Could be it won't fit." Tybalt offered the bundle. "It's as much for Doggerel's protection as the city's. Kemp didn't want there to be any unfortunate misunderstandings, especially since you can't … well, explaining him would even be hard for me."

Varti appreciated Tybalt's attempt at humor. Even more so, Phil's consideration. If someone panicked at the sight of Doggerel, Varti would be useless. But if the hound wore official colors and a clearly visible badge insignia? That should keep anyone from leaping to dire conclusions. They might even think that the Bastion was bringing in dogs to track the killer. Would Phil have already called for a team of handlers from the Hedge?

Tybalt let the harness drop onto Varti's desk. "I'll show you how it fastens. Or … talk you through it, at least. From a safe distance. You don't think he'll get all snarly about this, do you? Has he even worn a collar before?"

Varti gently tugged at Doggerel's pricked ear. "Resist with everything you have. Elsewise, I'll never be able to respect you as a partner." He showed the vest to Doggerel, who yawned. "Your outrage is understandable."

It only took a knick to work out the system of buckles. If let out as far as possible, the vest just fit. The thing was utilitarian, with snapping flaps for carrying gear or provisions. The accompanying leash had a convenient clip that would anchor Doggerel to Varti's belt, leaving his hands free.

Throughout the process, the hound cooperated with impressive dignity.

Varti supposed Thomas was the one who should be getting the credit. Still, he was proud of Doggerel and whispered, "You're an awful wretch."

"You're all set then," said Tybalt, backing toward the lift.

Recalling the case file, Varti jumped to his feet. If he showed it to Tybalt, would he understand? Maybe bring it to Phil? Or get Dr. Kang involved? He rested his hand on the newsprint that hid his morning's work from view.

A well-chosen word could call Tybalt back.

A glance at his report, that was all the other man should need.

But Varti's mouth remained shut as he withdrew the file and carefully closed it. Because he knew his job inside and out.

Systematic.

Secret.

Secure.

The evidence lockers and case files were sacrosanct. Varti was the only person in the Bastion who could access them without following proper procedure. Anyone else had to bring a signed and stamped request form to Henna at the front desk. One with the name and number of the case file they required.

Tybalt didn't have permission.

Varti couldn't give him access.

And that was that.

# 15

## Old Ebonnel

VESPER 04, FOUR NINETY-EIGHT
FIRSTMOST WILLIDAY
2 KNELLS, 44 KNICKS
ON THE SECOND FACE OF THE CLOCK

"**I** do legwork all the time," Varti informed his companion, though his eyes were on the lowering clouds. It smelled like rain. "Chasing down the very evidence that's hidden away in the lockers for which only I hold the key."

Doggerel didn't react. He was vastly more interested in swallowing eggy buns in quick succession. That was fine. Varti was only spouting drivel. The curse was feeling subtly smug, like it had pulled one over on him. Maybe it had. Varti could admit to himself that he'd gotten his hopes up about the case files. He'd been able to write true things—facts and information.

He should have realized before now. *This* was why he could do his job at all.

Working at Files & Evidence wasn't personal. On the contrary, when Varti was on the job, he handled himself in a manner that might be considered *im*personal. He stepped away from his feelings to pursue pure facts.

Varti tore apart his second bun, admiring the yellow gloss of its custardy center before popping half into his mouth. So good. Worth walking clear across the city.

Currant Bun was a mother in the Station District, not far from the quarters where he'd lived with Nani. The shop's eggy buns were a childhood favorite. He'd often bring them to Nani when he visited, so the lady behind the counter had already started filling a bag before he reached the front of the line. He must have looked like he needed two hexes. A bottle of Aubade's from a coin machine rounded out his late lunch. Nani would have fretted over his choices, but he was in need of comfort.

He did have a second reason, though.

There was a tobacco shop near the station. One that dealt in the sort of leaf used by pipe-smokers. Other shops dotted the city, but … well, this one had been near Currant Bun.

A fine drizzle began to fall, and Varti tugged up his cloak's hood. He ate a third bun, passed Doggerel the last, then folded the empty sack over his knees. He smiled at the familiar logo of a shining sun, deep orange against waxy white paper. That same sun was branded onto the top of every steamed bun the shop sold. Varti remembered asking for a currant bun once, back when he was little, and the owner had laughed. They didn't make them. Never had. Never would. The shop's name came from olden-time wordplay. A rhyming game of word exchange in which the phrase "currant bun" actually meant the sun.

Far from disappointed, Varti had been intrigued. A secret code, right out in the open. Many of the city's mothers used wordplay in their names.

Not so with the tobacconist he intended to visit. The shop was simply called Smoke, its rain-wet metal signboard showing a pipe with a gracefully curving stem wreathed in curls of smoke.

Varti hesitated outside, trying to decide if this was a mistake. He'd come without much of a plan on how to do his intended research. It wasn't as if he could ask questions.

Passersby were muttering about Doggerel. Even with an official vest and a proper leash, the hound was causing a stir. Up until now, Varti had set a brisk pace and tried to look as if they were on urgent business. Standing out front of Smoke, they were becoming a spectacle. So Varti gently tugged Doggerel's leash. The hound gave himself a shake, and they stepped through the door together.

Varti knew he was in the right place. Or at least the right kind of place. The scents of leaf and wood and matches hung as thick as smoke rings in the air. Wooden boxes and brightly labeled tins crowded the shelves, and glass jars lined the back wall. A display cabinet showed pipes in all shapes and sizes, and a glass case held cutters and bristle brushes and ... actually, he had no idea what everything was for.

A middle-aged woman in a neat white apron set aside a long-stemmed pipe and came out from behind the counter. "You've not been in before," she said warmly. "Be *welcome*. So! What can I help you with?"

Varti told a lie. "Official business."

"Interesting!"

He bit his tongue, guessing that silence would be less rude than speaking.

"Everyone calls me Madge." She considered Doggerel without any sign of alarm. "We've hounds back on the farm where I grew up, but none so big as this'un."

"This is very much my area of expertise. Practically a professional."

"Sure and you are." She winked as if he'd made a joke. "It's slow on damp days, since our regulars have the good sense to put their feet to the nearest hob and light a pipe. I'll give you the go-around, and maybe the rain will let up by the time I'm done. Sound fairsome?"

She thought he was just coming in out of the weather?

He hoped other members of the foot patrols weren't loitering in shops, but the excuse was convenient.

Madge asked, "Mind if I keep my pipe?"

Doggerel spared him from answering by moving to the counter and sitting back on his haunches, ears pricked, head cocked, nose twitching.

She laughed as she reclaimed the thing. "I only just started it, and it would be a shame to waste a bowl of Cottager Queen."

Varti thought he shook his head.

He must have looked confused, because Madge launched into a primer on pipes and tobacco. It was more than he needed to know. Indeed, he was almost certain he was wasting his time. He'd always thought he had a good nose, but how was he supposed to winnow out a remembered whiff of pipe smoke from among all the blends available?

"Everyone begins with Werifesteria, which is why it's nicknamed 'First Bowl.'" She handed him a green tin that was prettily embossed with the same trees that filled Fullnis Park. "It's a harmonious blend of two types of tobacco, with strong herbal and honey notes. Very folksome. Very nostalgic. If you mean to make a start, that tin is yours when you buy your first pipe."

She rattled off the different styles of pipes.

"I've always wanted one," he lied. One of their neighbors had smoked, and he could remember his mother complaining that it was a dirty habit. However, the dank and sooty smell in Varti's memory didn't match the pale drift of smoke coming from Madge's pipe. Toasty and sweet. It wasn't the same as what he'd smelled on Doggerel's fur, but it was pleasant.

Brightening, she began touring him through different blends, which was much closer to what he wanted. He poked his nose into cannisters and jars, eyes closing in concentration as he compared shreds and ribbons and flakes and plugs against his memory.

Did the tobacco in a box smell the same as its smoke when burned, though?

Increasingly convinced that this was a futile effort, he wondered if he should just go home.

But then she brought out a whole different variety of tobacco. "These are handmade by a local artisan. He has a workroom in the cathedral tower, and he names all these for the bells in the carillon. This particular one is called Old Ebonnel's Bellpull, for the largest of the bells. You can see how dark it is. Deep. Plummy. Hints of currant." With great care, she cut a slice from the rope. "It goes quickly, so we sell it by the medallion."

He wanted so much to know if they had anything similar.

Because while Old Ebonnel's was close, it wasn't quite right. But maybe it needed to be burned? There was nothing else for it. He brought out his purse.

Varti left with parceled up pipe, tin, and medallion ... and Madge's invitation to drop by anytime. Hood up, he debated whether to persevere or go home and see if he could light a pipe without burning down the entire Carpentry District.

Mentally, he reviewed other tobacconists in Newcomb.

If Thomas came and went from the gate under Danbright's

Light, which was the nearest road to Hibernacle House, then there were three possible shops along his route through the Fountain District. He could check. It might be his best opportunity, since Madge had said that rainy days were slow.

But not every shopkeep was so willing to fill the silence with useful chatter. In the next place, which was deep in the theater district, the owner eyed him suspiciously while he searched their shelves for brands that hadn't been represented at Smoke. And in the shop after that, which was near the stadium, he was immediately turned out because of Doggerel.

Disheartened, Varti trudged toward the city gate. The last shop he wanted to try was a little place called Stummeltons, which served the residential blocks within the city wall. He was still trying to decide if it would be worse to leave Doggerel tied to a lamppost out front or to bring him inside when someone clapped his shoulder.

Sylvester Thornapple sidled past, beckoning for Varti to follow him inside.

# 16

## *Stummeltons*

VESPER 04, FOUR NINETY-EIGHT
FIRSTMOST WILLIDAY
5 KNELLS, 42 KNICKS
ON THE SECOND FACE OF THE CLOCK

Whad choice did he have but to give chase?

Sylvester Thornapple sauntered to the counter and propped an elbow. "Lend an ear, Georgie. This gentleman is searching for something particular. A blend of pipe tobacco. What do you carry that's different from what Madge and Six-Toes and Robert have in their cram?"

"Since when do you assist the badges?" rumbled Georgie, who was now trying to stare down Doggerel.

Sylvester only said, "Let him poke his nose into a few boxes, there's a dear."

After a ruminative pause, Georgie answered, "Since it's you, Sylvie. But you? Don't you be thinking you can confiscate anything, understand?"

Varti knew a rush of indignation. But this was swiftly followed by something colder and more calculating. What badges were responsible for this man's assumption that his goods might be at risk from people who were meant to be upholding the law?

Sylvester Thornapple said, "Ah, he's a fine, upstanding fellow, this badge. Don't you worry."

Georgie grunted. "Get on with it, then."

Leaving Varti facing an accomplice whose smile was far too innocent. He moodily asked, "Do I know you?"

Sylvester removed his cap. "I *do* try to be forgettable, but that's unkind. We're on our way to becoming friends, aren't we?" He suggested, "Show Georgie the one that caught your interest."

Whether to press his point or pick his pocket, the man reached for Varti's scrip, and Doggerel growled a warning.

Immediately lifting his hands in the air, Sylvester generously added, "At your leisure."

Varti set his hand on Doggerel's head, which hushed him. Then he retrieved the purchases that Madge had bundled for him, carefully extracting the slim glassine bag that held the medallion of Old Ebonnel's Bellpull.

Sylvester plucked it and brought it to Georgie, saying, "Ever seen the like?"

"Wouldn't be worth more than dottle if I didn't. This is Tyro's workmanship." He took a whiff and nodded. "Ebonnel's. Been out of stock since last Milvine, but I reserved two ropes."

"Is this Tyro gent something special?"

"Nobody like him in Newcomb." Georgie went to a shelf, chose a box, and revealed another rope of tobacco. It was similar to Ebonnel's but not the same. "These are handmade. No way to revolutionize the process. Costly stuff. It's shared out in slim medallions like this."

Sylvester beckoned Varti over. "Get in here. Is this what you're looking for?"

He sniffed and smiled. "Exactly right."

89

"Ah, well. Not this, then. What else do you have, Georgie?"

"If the badge is satisfied, why do I have to trot out more of my reserves?"

"Because this gent is a rare wit. He spoke in jest, so let's have another. Maybe more of Tyro's workmanship?" Although it was framed politely, Varti had no doubt that Sylvester was giving an order. What gave this man any authority here?

And in a twistsome turn of events, Georgie dropped the attitude. He and Sylvester soon had their heads together, organizing an approach. They cleared the counter and started making piles. Stummeltons had three more varieties of tobacco in the bellrope line, but Varti could tell right away they weren't even close to what he remembered.

Sylvester went back to the Ebonnel's medallion. "What do you have that's similar to this. Different, of course, but with something in common. Because this is the closest he could find."

Georgie blew out his cheeks, grunted, and rearranged. "You gotta realize these blends are closely guarded secrets. It's not like I have the recipes, but I have a nose, don't I?"

"You're a real aficionado, Georgie."

The man grunted again, then waved Varti closer. "Narrow the field for me, badge."

It was orderly. It was instructive. And even the shopkeep's grumbling helped. "Might be the leaf. Might be overs or unders. Everyone's got their secret ingredient. And the spectrum from fug to floral is all to taste."

They weeded out herbals and anise. None of the oriental blends. Varti was fascinated to learn that none of this stuff was grown nearby. Some came from the continent, and some from farther overseas. Georgie and Sylvester chatted about places not on any of the maps Varti had seen because they weren't part of what the Bastion considered necessary references.

It was humbling.

Varti knew his own world very, *very* well. But not every part of it. And almost nothing beyond it. He could add visits to the Bibliotheca to his routine. Or maybe Nani would enjoy going there for their next outing?

"You gone nose-blind?" Georgie asked.

"I have no sense of smell to speak of," Varti said, then bit his lip.

Sylvester snorted. "We're confident we've puzzled it out, but there's one last test. Bring out your pipe."

Varti yielded it.

Giving it a once-over, Georgie said, "Fine workmanship, but it's never been used. You want the sip, Sylvie? Or do I have to do everything?"

"You don't mind, do you?" Sylvester beckoned for the pipe, a mocking light in his eyes. "You'll ruin that fine nose of yours if you take up with that churchwarden."

Varti knew he meant the shape of the pipe. And that was almost all he knew about smoking one. He said, "Over my dead body."

"You're a dear. Sit there. This can't be rushed."

He spied the bench Sylvester meant, tucked into a shadowy corner, and gratefully lowered himself to a seat. Georgie ambled over, broke the seal on a bottle of Aubade's, and pressed it into his hand, then set down a bowl of water for Doggerel. The hospitable gesture allowed Varti to relax enough to take stock. He was tired, and he was hungry, and his tobacco-perfumed day had left him with the beginnings of a headache.

Sylvester had a match to the bowl, the pipestem resting upon his lower lip.

The thing must have lit, for he shook the match and leaned against the counter, ankles crossed, expression meditative. His clockwork cat jumped onto the counter and sat watching him. Georgie chucked it under the chin. Doggerel came to rest his chin on Varti's knee, and the shop quieted enough that Varti noticed the drum of rain on the street outside.

Smoke slowly trickled into the room. Nobody spoke. Perhaps Georgie and Sylvester were giving the pipe time to overwhelm all the other smells in the room. Slumping back against the wall, Varti sipped gratefully at hot coffee and let his eyes drift shut.

"Weller? Weller."

He startled awake.

Sylvester Thornapple had joined him on the bench, the pipe still in his hand. "Satisfied?" he asked.

"Bitterly disappointed."

With a sly smile, he raised his voice. "We'll take some, Georgie. The big do-up in the fancy canister. He means it for a gift."

Was he so easy to read?

No. Varti knew he wasn't.

Yet this man had spoken up on his behalf, divined his needs, and become his advocate. It was a little scary, to be honest. He trusted Phil to act in his best interest, but he didn't trust Sylvester Thornapple. What was he after?

Varti didn't have a clue.

# 17

## Banderole & Bugle

VESPER 04, FOUR NINETY-EIGHT
FIRSTMOST WILLIDAY
8 KNELLS, 33 KNICKS
ON THE SECOND FACE OF THE CLOCK

"**W**hat do you say?" asked Sylvester Thornapple, still sporting a smile that made him impossible to trust. "Split a pie with me?"

Varti had no idea what kind of face he made. Inside, he was mostly baffled.

"Dinner," the man clarified. "I know you're hungry. You haven't eaten anything since those eggy buns, and that was knells ago."

That set off warning flares. How long had Sylvester been trailing him?

"I can see that I've raised questions. Join me, and we'll sort through some answers." He gestured with the pipe. "I know a cozy nook. Perfect for a drearsome evening. My treat."

Doggerel grunted. The hound sprawled on the floor, his muzzle atop one of Varti's boots, taking long, slow breaths. But his eyes were open, and they were fixed on Sylvester. Catching Varti's gaze, his tail gave a desultory stir. Like he was at peace with the whole world, now that he was surrounded by pipe smoke.

Varti muttered, "I'm not hungry."

"Best pies in the district," he promised, then went to settle up with Georgie.

In mere knicks, Sylvester had his arm through Varti's and was steering him into the warren of shops and alleys near the arena. He took a circuitous route, as if trying to get Varti lost. That was an amusing thought. Then Sylvester pulled open the door of the Banderole & Bugle and brought Varti in out of the rain.

Dragging the cloth cap off his head, Sylvester greeted one of the servers, slipped him a few coins, and wove through the busy dining room to an open table not far from the big hearth, which was throwing off welcome heat.

Varti sank to a seat and found it cushioned.

Sylvester didn't waste time. "Yes, I've been following you all day. Well, ever since you left The Speckled Hen this morning. I was curious. My fatal flaw. Well, one of them. You're interesting."

"Everyone says so."

He laughed softly. "Best kept secret, then? Very much a shame. Now … ah, don't be angry. Old habits die hard, and all that. But I wanted to know what your mother insisted you put in your pocket."

Sylvester slid a chunk of rock salt across the table.

Shocked, Varti patted the pocket into which he'd placed Ramage's gift earlier. Empty.

"I'd vow to never do it again, but I'll leave the lies to you. I can give you that much, Varti Weller." He peered up at him through his fringe. "Not saying I can promise the *whole* truth, but I won't lie. Close enough?"

"Yes."

"I wouldn't trust me either. But that will change. I have a

sense for these things."

A serving boy trundled over, enormous mitts on his hands, and he set a whole pie between them, its juices still bubbling. He took two more trips, teetering a heaped bowl of mash and another of pickles, then tankards of dark ale.

"You expect me to eat this? It looks awful," Varti muttered, somewhat in awe. He might know the names and locations of every mother in the city, but that didn't mean he'd eaten in all of them. This was by far the nicest surprise of the day.

Sylvester spooned up mash, then broke the pie's flaking crust, releasing a cloud of savory steam. He served himself, ladling chicken and vegetables in a thick gravy over everything before offering Varti the spoon.

He was too hungry to hold back.

Varti didn't protest when Sylvester heaped a second serving onto his plate. A second tankard arrived. Varti slandered the pickles, so Sylvester called for another bowlful.

When he recalled himself enough to think of Doggerel's comfort, he realized that Sylvester had put thought into his choosing. Because the hound wasn't the only dog dozing on the hearth rug.

How had he not noticed?

Maybe he was a little drunk?

"Two of those belong to Antwan, who prefers to be called a taverner. Two others belong to his crew. The rest? Regulars of the Banderole & Bugle know they can come with four-footed companions."

Sylvester stacked their dishes to one side, stuck the tip of his pinky into an unobtrusive hole in the tabletop, and lifted a center section. The reverse was beautifully inset with darker wood, a six-sided chessboard, and Sylvester showed him the drawers where game pieces were kept.

Varti quickly set up his side and launched an opening gambit. Strategy games were his favorite, but Phil didn't care for them.

Sylvester signaled for more drinks, and he relit the churchwarden.

With a growing sense of elation, Varti realized that he was having an evening out. He stole a look at Sylvester, whose pensive expression faded into an unconvincing smile.

"You're enjoying yourself."

Varti retorted, "Worst night of my life."

"That's a bit out of proportion, don't you think?"

"Worst night of my week."

"There you go," Sylvester said agreeably. "A man should be able to relax with a pint and an appropriate pastime. I wonder what else you do for fun …? It must tarnish you not to be able to say. Ah, but I'm an observant fellow. Might be I can figure it out if you didn't mind my looking in on you from time to time." He made his move before confiding, "I might try it, even if you *did* mind. Since that's the sort of thing *I* do for fun."

"Nothing would delight me more."

"You're hardly the first person left in a strange state thanks to something unnatural."

Varti knew that. But wasn't he allowed to take it personally?

Sylvester went on. "Yours is a tricky bit of menace. Nothing simple or straightforward about it, but I'm a roundabout guy. Toying with curses is interesting. It's fun."

Was that all this was? Novelty and entertainment? If so, wasn't that fine? As motives went, it was harmless. "I'm sure you're a good person."

96

"Oh, I'm not."

Varti believed him.

Varti might not trust Sylvester Thornapple, but the man somehow knew to deliver him into Mr. Whilom's hands at The Green Man. Maybe it was more proof of spying. Maybe Doggerel had served as a guide. Either way, Sylvester was gone by the time Phil clattered down to the lobby to lay claim to his ale-sodden and sleepy quartermate.

"Who ...? How ...?" The redhead looked conscience-stricken. "I thought you must be working late."

"I never go out. I have no friends."

It was almost a complete lie, and the near truth of it cut. Phil mumbled, "You can join me and the lads anytime. You know that."

Knowing you could tag along and wanting to go to the sorts of places those *lads* enjoyed ...? Tonight had been so much better than a rowdy jaunt into the theater district's night life. Varti hadn't had an evening so entirely to his tastes since his school days. Back then, he'd been able to tell someone what he was hungry for. Or to veto someone else's suggestion. Tonight had been good. His memory swirled with the scents of chicken pie and pipe smoke. He'd insulted Sylvester Thornapple a dozen ways without causing harm, then beaten the man twice at chess while Doggerel looked on and laughed in the way dogs do.

"What's this?" Phil was hanging his cloak and had found the parcel from Stummelton's in one of the roomy interior pockets.

"Gifts for the Selcouth Queen. We're having tea tomorrow."

97

Phil searched his face, then knelt to address boot buckles. "You smell like pipe smoke."

"The churchwarden is a faithless man. Now carry me to bed," he demanded.

"Did you actually have a lovely evening?"

"Damp and dull."

"I'll put the kettle on."

Then ... because Phil enjoyed turning the curse's lies into truths, he scooped Varti into his arms and only staggered a little crossing the room. It was stupid and silly, and there was vitriol seething just under the surface, but a laugh escaped Varti—honest and pure—and Phil grinned like he'd won a victory.

It had been an oddsome day. Totally off the tracks.

But Varti knew it had been good. The best in a long while.

# 18

## *Screaming Headlines*

VESPER 05, FOUR NINETY-EIGHT
FIRSTMOST TROUDAY
9 KNELLS, 3 KNICKS
ON THE FIRST FACE OF THE CLOCK

Punctuality was a steadying force. Varti's morning routine ticked along like clockwork, so that he and Doggerel reported early for his tocking. The hound immediately trotted to the gate barring off the evidence lockers, snuffling at the floor, then looking to Varti with soulful eyes.

"Glad to see our priorities align." Patting his leg, Varti moved toward the stairway instead. Yesterday was a near total loss, what with arriving late and leaving early. He grimaced at the sight of his worktable. Kel had dropped today's bundle of newspapers on top of yesterday's untouched pile. Varti knew from experience that if he let any more pile up, he'd have to work extra knells. Or spend his next Newday playing catch-up.

He set to work, aware that he couldn't really complain, since the task was self-appointed.

Every day, he went through all six of Newcomb's newspapers, looking for stories that related to ongoing cases. The articles were often specious or sensational, but it wasn't outside the realm of possibility for a journalist to turn up valid lines of inquiry. They interviewed witnesses, and they made speculations that fell just shy of slander. The ones who fancied themselves investigative journalists loved to broadcast all the gritty details about events. Even ones that the Bastion would rather *didn't* get released.

During his final year at academy, Varti had proposed that the Files & Evidence division support their investigation teams by keeping track of what facts were made public and which ones they'd managed to keep under latch and key.

His instructors had conceded it was a fine idea in theory, but impractical.

Now, it was standard procedure. Varti culled the information from the papers, and Kel drafted summaries for each case's lead investigator. She delivered them personally. And according to Henna, she didn't leave until they'd read her report. Varti couldn't blame her. This was their contribution, and it would be a shame if all their efforts went to waste.

He unfolded crisp newspapers, which Kel purchased in triplicate. One to go intact into their archive. One for clipping the even-sided articles. One for clipping the odd side. Varti had perfected his technique, which involved scissors, paste, and an official Files & Evidence rubber stamp, which he used for marking the date of publication and the pertinent case number.

Yesterday's papers all dedicated their front pages to Vonneday night's murder. Fanned out, the headlines summed up the city's outcry.

## KILLER CLAIMS VICTIM No.5

Straightforward enough. That was from C. C. Newsome, a journalist for the *Innerworkings*, the city's most conservative press. They tended to focus on news relating to the city's founding principles—math, science, education, and cooperation. Varti appreciated that all of their articles were fact-checked. It was widely believed that if something was reported in the *Innerworkings*, then it must be true.

## MONSTER IN OUR MIDST

The *Clockwork Sentinel* had wider appeal, in part because their stories were accompanied by striking illustrations. Reporters for the *Sentinel* trod a fine line, peppering the most outrageous statements with qualifiers so they couldn't be accused of publishing lies. Georgette Anders, one of their key reporters, definitely liked drama. Her lead story was accompanied by the depiction of a looming beast with vaguely canine features, gleaming fangs, and bloody claws. And yes, Varti found a refrain of her "set upon by dogs" headline in her third paragraph.

No wonder Doggerel was making people so jumpy.

## DEATH STALKS OUR STREETS

The reporter for the *Newcomb Buzz*, which usually promoted art, culture, and food, was putting on a brave face. Timothea Jingle had gone directly to the head of the Bastion's Irregulars for a statement, and she included Highmost Purnal Sarah Yamada's guidelines for keeping safe during the current crisis. Maybe because she'd gone straight to the top, Ms. Jingle had more details, including a statement from lead investigator

Philtrum Kemp.

"One thing we *can* confirm is that each of these poor souls lost their lives in the dark. Please, Newcombers. Through all the night watches—wicking time, winding time, locking time, and echoing time—stay safely indoors."

By far, the oddmost article came from Minnow Strange at the *Hexagon*. Their paper was a celebration of the scandalous and weird. Nobody pretended they were a credible source, yet everyone somehow managed to take a peek at their daily oracles. The *Hex* didn't concern itself with documentable facts. They were all about phantasms and phenomenon, as proven by their headline.

## *VICTIM HAUNTS LARCH COURT*

That reminded Varti about Dr. Kang's mention of a ghost photographer. They'd been called in after the fourth murder, and Phil had since mentioned a meeting. Nothing had been posted about it on their case wall at home, and so far, Phil's team hadn't submitted anything to Files & Evidence.

According to the *Hexagon* article, an unnamed Bridger with a folksome knack had encountered an echo of the fifth victim. Mercies from the Composite Cathedral had been brought in to soothe the site lest a true haunting take root. If the victim did linger, it would be the first documented haunting within the city walls since Newcomb's founding.

Varti knew this couldn't be true. He'd read the case files, and Philtrum was right about an uptick in ghost activity. But the Bastion preferred that these echoes remain *un*documented. They dealt with each case quietly, either with the cooperation of the mercies or with help from Keepsake Chapel, which lay deep in the woods to the northeast, beyond the city walls.

A soft growl brought Varti's attention to his surroundings.

The soft *ding* of the lift announced its arrival on his level. When Dr. Kang entered, carrying a large box and escorting a tall woman, Varti leapt to his feet.

She peered around with an expression of mild interest, then twirled a knob on the side of the glasses she wore, dropping a pale blue lens into place over her left eye, then switching to a green one. The soft click of the mechanism was the only sound until she spoke. "Have you always attracted the interest of elsewithers? Or is it only since your spelling?"

# 19

## *Personal Effects*

VESPER 05, FOUR NINETY-EIGHT
FIRSTMOST TROUDAY
10 KNELLS, 0 KNICKS
ON THE FIRST FACE OF THE CLOCK

Pointing up, she next asked, "Do the witherlings ever change color for you? Else lights can be so protective once they become attached."

Varti had no idea how to respond.

What was she even talking about?

Tybalt's remark yesterday was the first time Varti had even heard the term. This suddenly felt like an enormous oversight. He'd been trained as an investigator, prided himself on being observant, yet he'd missed something that was clearly important. Maybe it was natural to take fixtures for granted. It wasn't as if he gave much thought to the floors, shelving units, or ventilation ducts either. But should he discount things simply because they were unremarkable?

Determined to research else lights at the first opportunity, Varti muttered, "You should go."

Dr. Kang brightened. "Good to see you, too, Weller. Now, then. May I present Hexadille Porter? She's a consultant for the Bastion. Specializes in capturing echoes on film."

She was easily a head taller than Varti, with long, straight hair in a dark blonde that brought amberglass to mind. While most Newcombers wore a shirt and vest over sensible breeches and boots, Hexadille wore a slim skirt with pleats and a fuzzy green cardigan that drooped past her hips. When she stepped closer to offer her hand, he noted pale green eyes, faint freckles, and a firm handshake.

Varti said, "I have a deep and abiding respect for your work."

Hexadille blinked, then offered a tight smile. "You're a cynic? Or afraid of things you can't explain?"

"Now, now, Hexadille. Don't leap to the defense. There's more than one way to twist a man's words. Rather than assuming that he *dis*respects your work, I think it far more likely that Weller is ignorant about the entire process."

She tipped a violet lens down over her right eye and squinted at him through it. "How perfectly insidious."

Varti tended to agree. And shook his head.

Patting the box he carried, Dr. Kang said, "We were asked to bring everything here."

Asked to?

By whom?

Then there was another soft *ding*, and Varti recognized the faint yet familiar jingle of the charms on his best friend's watchchain. Phil arrived with a swish of copper cloth, vibrant red curls catching the light, eyes bright, even though he was trying for a professional demeanor.

"You can't be here," Varti growled. "I forbid it."

"I apologize for the imposition, Weller. I needed to go over everything in a secure location, and this counts. As meeting places go, it's a little unorthodox, but as I'm in charge of this case, I get to decide how to run the investigation. And I want you in the loop."

Varti slowly placed his hand over his own mouth, not wanting to give the curse a chance to let loose. How shiftsome. He hadn't anticipated *this* outcome to his best friend's enviable promotion. Phil was making him—a glorified file clerk—part of his team?

Dr. Kang moved to place the box on Varti's worktable. "These are the fifth victim's personal effects. I've finished my analysis, so I'll be leaving them in your hands."

"We'll start there," said Phil.

They stood around the table. To Varti's amusement, Doggerel reared up and planted his front paws on the surface, gaze fixed on the box. Varti tugged at the dog's collar to get him to back down, but he didn't budge. Phil waved off the impromptu addition of a hound to their meeting, giving his full attention to Dr. Kang.

"Willa Cyrine, age twenty-four. Cause of death was … mmm, *violence* is an understatement. Like the others, she was torn apart. Officially, we settled on mauling, since none of the damage appears to have been done by a weapon. She seems to have been set upon, tooth and claw, so massive trauma, unchecked blood loss. Something *destroyed* her. I don't think … merciful Milvine, I *do* hope it was quick."

"That's what the timelines suggest," Phil said grimly. "She wasn't alone long enough for it to have been a lengthy dismemberment."

"Another woman," Hexadille remarked.

"But not a helpless woman, by any means." Dr. Kang lifted the lid from the box and brought out a pile of bloodstained green cloth upon which an insignia was still recognizable.

Varti knew it at a glance. The guard.

"*Far* from helpless," agreed Phil. "Willa was a badge academy graduate whose proficiencies included combat training. That night, she was on the wall. Her guard rotation ended at nine knells on the second face of the clock. Still in her uniform, she was returning from her post above Gilraith's Light. I spoke with her perior and other members of her cohort. Normally, Willa would have caught the clockwise trolley at Kennedy Station and disembarked at Trouvaille Station, since she quartered in the Bridge District's military housing."

He passed Varti the watchchain.

"Instead, she traveled widdershins to Farrukh Station. But the knells and knicks don't quite add up, so I think she must have hopped off at either Chromwell or Newsome, probably for food."

Varti lay the copper watchchain across his palm.

Willa wore all her school emblems, not just the matriculation medallion from badge academy. Both her earlymost and middlemost schools were in the Station District. If she'd been craving childhood flavors, she may have disembarked at Newsome in order to visit her mother.

The next four charms were from her graduation test—Olde, new, bartered, and blue. And here was her first-purse dodger. But then a gap. In fact there were two gaps in the row, which suggested some of the tokens had been torn away. Yes, he found a twisted connecter. Was this collateral damage? Or had the items been taken by the murderer? Theft hardly seemed a reasonable motive for murder. Trophies, then? Or could charms be part of the reason these women were targeted? He wanted to go back over the watchchains of the previous victims. He could do that. They were here, in the evidence lockers, along with every shred of spoiled clothing and crumpled take-away slip.

Dr. Kang was saying, "She was armed, but all of her weapons remained sheathed."

Varti was paying more attention to the remaining charms. A small, white piglet that may have been a team mascot or a quirksome gift or a good luck charm. A golden ring with an inscription. A religious icon he couldn't place. And, oh. Oh, no. He knew this one. A copper crown set with a green gem.

His gaze leapt to Phil, who nodded. "Willa was a member of the Verdigris Standard, the queens' color guard. I had to break the news yesterday. Her majesty was … displeased."

The Verdigris Standard was an all-female unit that attended the royal party whenever they appeared in public. According to everything Varti had heard about them—mostly from articles in the *Royal Observatory* or from Kel, who was a surprisingly fanatical royalty-watcher—these women were personally chosen by the Selcouth Queen, who treated them like daughters.

This had to be adding pressure.

But also … Varti was privately amazed by something that didn't really matter. Phil had met the fae queen? Even though it was incidental to the case, he wanted to hear more about it.

Phil circled back around to the takeaway. "If we can find the mother who looked after her that night, we can be more precise with the time of death."

Dr. Kang interjected, "Between ten and eleven knells."

"It's unlikely that the exact time of death matters, but I have people asking around. I'd like to know if Willa was seen with anyone, confronted anyone, followed anyone. *Something*. We have no witnesses for any of these crimes, and I don't have my hopes up. The entire Bridge District was buried in fog, but we have to try."

"I turned up a new detail. It wasn't in the earlier reports because the examination wasn't conclusive. But there were enough signs that I sent to the archives for her records. Willa's birth certificate confirms that her maternal grandfather is a Darke Childe." Dr. Kang seemed to be having trouble choosing his next words. "Newcomb owes its very existence to the Folk. Our whole way of life is based on principles like equality, respect, and cooperation. But I fear these murders have sown seeds of distrust. It's as if humans have suddenly noticed that their neighbors could be dangerous."

Varti said, "Humans are never aggressive. Crime is beneath our dignity."

Phil folded his arms over his chest. "Integrity has nothing to do with a person's ancestry. All of us have the same responsibility to abide by Newcomb's laws."

"No doubt," said Dr. Kang. "I wholeheartedly agree. But people are nervous, even afraid. I wanted to admit my … mmm. *Relief* isn't the right word, but I want to be honest. My heart breaks for Willa and for everyone who cared about her, but I'm also glad she stopped the trend."

Varti could see what he meant. The victim profile had shifted slightly.

Unlike Gemma, Aster, Polly, and Tess, Willa had Folk ancestry. Something else linked the victims. Assuming there was any connection at all.

# 20

## *Misnomers about Ghosts*

VESPER 05, FOUR NINETY-EIGHT
FIRSTMOST TROUDAY
10 KNELLS, 41 KNICKS
ON THE FIRST FACE OF THE CLOCK

Attending to his duty, Varti checked every piece of evidence against the official list, making his own notes in the margins with green ink. His annotations were entirely accurate. They always had been. And he'd never questioned it before yesterday. Now, he was trying to set aside his consternation and focus on the task at hand.

Dr. Kang and Hexadille Porter had opted for a stroll through the stacks, and Varti could hear the low murmur of their voices somewhere in the vicinity of the Folk resources section. Having other people in the room made him uneasy. He didn't want the curse to foul their evidence in any way, so he kept his head down, afraid to even make eye contact. He hesitated over the religious icon on Willa's watchchain. The record as it stood was woefully incomplete, only listing the number of charms, not their design or possible import.

Phil came to his side. "Is something missing?"

"Nothing worth mentioning."

"Let me take another look."

Varti picked up the chain by the charm he'd been puzzling over and ... hid the entire thing behind his back. Tarnish it all. The curse could be so childish.

"From memory then?" Phil dropped onto Varti's chair and stretched out his legs, acting like his boot buckles were more fascinating than anything else. "Early, middle, and vocational matriculations. Charms for courage, luck, clarity, and safety during her final test. Her selections made me wonder if she was ... ohhh. *Rebellion* is too strong a term, so let's say she was trying to prove herself. Those charms. An emblem of the sun for courage. Citrine for optimism and luck. A dandle-tuft for clarity. And a cameo of Fullnis, Lady Solstice herself, to watch over her steps."

He paused there, giving Varti time to finish making notes.

Nodding to himself, Phil continued, "Strange choices, don't you think? For someone with Darke Childe heritage. But according to her mother, Willa and her grandfather were always close. His nickname for her was Buttercup, and he used to call her his sunshine. It's no wonder that Queen Aelia loved Willa. She was a Fullnis child, through and through."

Varti stole a look, already knowing what expression he'd see on his best friend's face. Of course Phil would want to get to know each of the victims as people. It was one of the things that had always frustrated Varti. They needed facts to solve a case. But Phil was forever making friends, even posthumously, and he never would let Varti brush past the plights of those involved.

Taking on a case meant seeing every side of a story.

For Phil, this meeting wasn't about Victim No.5. He wanted justice for Willa. And he was making certain that Varti had the facts he'd need in order to find the monster that she hadn't been ready to meet in the fog.

"The dodger is traditional," continued Phil. "The ring took the longest to sort. The inscription inside the band is Realmish, so I needed a mage to work up a translation. My consultant thinks it's a contract token. Willa may have had a familiar."

"I love it when you talk in complete sentences that make no sense." Varti blinked. The curse didn't often let him be sarcastic. Once upon a time, he'd have said just this sort of thing.

Phil looked so happy. He shrugged off the jibe. "Mages rarely have magic of their own. It's bestowed by a higher power, generally of Realmish origin. Or else the mage forms a contract with a magical being in order to gain access to their magic."

Varti was annoyed that something so important wasn't even mentioned on the list. He wrote furiously, then underlined two words several times. POSSIBLE WITNESS.

"What have you written? May I see?"

"I always give curiosity-seekers full access to confidential records."

"I'm the head of this investigation."

"Abuse of power."

"You're such a stickler for procedures. So I only get a look if I do the paperwork?"

"Never happening. I'll shred the request form on sight." Nice and easy opposites. It was almost like having a conversation.

"I don't know what to make of that piglet charm. And then there's the icon. Ah, that's the one you didn't recognize. Understandable. Helve is a lesser forest deity. He's often categorized as a patron. Since it's the last item on Willa's watchchain, her connection to him may be recent. It's possible that Helve's people guided her through the process of forming a contract." Phil frowned and took a jotter from his vest pocket. "I should have followed up on that. I know who to ask."

Varti returned Willa's personal effects to the box, then sealed it and assigned it a locker.

Phil called back Dr. Kang and Hexadille, thanking them for their patience and offering to send for tea. Henna, who may have been eavesdropping, appeared with bottles from the vending machines on street level, which was the limit of their division's hospitality. When she left, she took along Willa's box. Doggerel scrambled to his feet, intent on following, but Varti got a hand on his collar and held him back until Phil could shut the door.

Then it was Hexadille's turn.

She asked Varti, "Are you familiar with ghost formation? Or more accurately, the inhabitation of the empty space left behind by the departure of a soul?"

Varti frowned, which was confusingly honest.

Even though he lived with an irregular, Phil wasn't the kind of guy to try to convince skeptics. And inviting a discussion wasn't exactly possible for Varti anymore. He knew some mystical jargon from case files, but most of those reports were either lamentably abridged or assumed the reader had more context.

Hexadille rolled her eyes. "Are you going to tell me that you don't believe in ghosts?"

Dr. Kang hurried to Varti's defense. "He can't control his expressions any more than he can help what he says. Even gestures can be curse-driven."

Varti wanted to pull out his hair. "Ghosts are a figment of the mystical imagination. If they were real, they wouldn't be completely absent from my division's many case files."

Phil's smile tightened. "I'm sure Weller would appreciate any *helpful* remarks you want to make."

"Fine. I just wanted to know how far back I should start." She eyed Varti. "I'll be candid. Citybound regulars are a pragsome lot. I don't blame you people for the gaps in your learning. Mages keep their secrets close in much the same way that coggers jealously guard their schematics. Unless you pursue mysteries, they will remain mysterious. And if you don't even realize a mystery is there, how can you pursue it? But while this may excuse—or at least explain—your persistent ignorance, it does not unmake the mysterious."

Phil quietly ordered, "Make your report, Ms. Porter."

"I have a knack that allows me to both draw out echoes and capture them on film. That's earned me a label—ghost photographer. Both my partner and I can communicate with these emanations, but we're not in high demand. Cases with the irregulars account for most of our business, and that business usually takes us outside the city walls. Until recently."

Dr. Kang interjected, "There are a lot of misnomers about ghosts."

"Quite so," Hexadille acknowledged. "People cling to old wives' tales about hauntings and grudges and unfinished business. In those stories, ghosts are souls that linger in this world after separation from the body. But the truth is closer to … oh, bells. Do you know about keepsakes, Mr. Weller?"

"Yes, of course. What do you take me for?"

Phil held up a hand. "Like Hexadille said before, the departing soul leaves room for something else to take its place. We call them emanations, and there are elaborate theories about where they come from. For today, let's compare them to changelings. But instead of all the baby-swapping mischief, a Realmish entity latches onto a departing soul and trades places. It's still mischief, plain and simple, and most of these emanations don't last. They can be hurried along by simple means: vigil candles, offerings, and prayers.

"But on rare occasions, an emanation finds better purchase. We think it's because the outgoing soul and the incoming entity form a contract. Their reasons are unique to the individuals involved, but the results are fascinating. The resulting 'ghost' looks and sounds and acts like the person they replace. They have memories and information only the deceased would know. Or it's possible they're still linked. But no matter how convincing this ethereal doppelganger might be, the original soul is gone. It can be ... really complicated. Especially for those who think their loved one is back." Phil searched Varti's face. "Enough to go on?"

Hardly. Varti couldn't decide if Phil had raised more questions than he'd answered. "You're wasting my time."

Phil waved for Hexadille to continue.

She undid the clasp on a thick brown folder and brought out a stack of glossy photographs. "As agreed in my contract, I'm submitting these as evidence in Highmost Perior Philtrum Kemp's investigation into the murders of Tess Bishop and Willa Cyrine. I did visit the locations where the other three victims died, but I found no lingering emanations. If they were there at all, they'd dispersed." She arrayed six photos on the desk. "Tess's ghost was uncooperative, to say the least."

Tess had been something of a puzzle because she hadn't been carrying ident tags or a belt-pouch or a watchchain. Their only lead was the old-fashioned watch pinned to her lapel. Her husband thought she must have stepped out to run a quick errand. And because of the clutter in the place she'd been found, Dr. Kang's team hadn't been definitive about what was hers and what was litter, but they'd placed her in a nearby bob & knob where she'd picked up a pint of ice cream.

Varti leaned over the worktable, trying to pick out something otherworldly in the first photo. To no avail. If this was evidence, he couldn't tell what it proved.

Phil lifted one of Hexadille's other photos, hummed, then set it in front of Varti. "Compare these two. Tess's ghost is aware of Hexadille. You can tell because she's turned her head."

Varti held them next to each other, gaze shifting back and forth. It felt like they must be having him on.

"Just here. Huddled beside the fountain." Dr. Kang pointed to the place. "It's possible to pick her out, but she may as well be made of glass. You can see right through her."

Suddenly, Varti found her.

So faint, no wonder he hadn't registered her presence. But yes, there was the curve of a cheek, a snub nose in profile. And in the next photo, her face was turned, her eyes wide, her mouth open as she half-rose from her crouch.

Hexadille rearranged the photos. "This is the correct order."

Varti flipped through and almost wished he hadn't. The ghost went from her huddle to noticing the camera, then leaping up and running at Hexadille, hands weirdly elongated as they reached for her, mouth agape in a silent scream.

"She was really very distraught. Barely coherent. She kept muttering and pointing. My partner swears the woman was trying to get us to do something. The only thing I know is that whenever she pointed, it was either toward the palace or at the ground. The action may have been an echo, like she was arguing with the person who killed her, but who knows? After that, she ... well, it was as if she got annoyed and marched off in a huff."

"Do thank Rowena for me," murmured Phil.

Hexadille nodded and fanned out a different set of photos. "I'm glad you contacted me immediately after the fifth victim was found. Too often, a team will wait until morning, but night and fog don't really have any bearing on my work. As you can see."

Varti's stomach dropped. Some of it was the raw brutality captured by the camera, because he knew that the chunks and spatters and the occasional jut of white were the wreckage of a body. But far more arresting was the sight of a young woman cast in shining pearl, feet set, weapons in hand, staring defiantly into the camera.

The ghost of Willa Cyrine standing guard over her own body.

# 21
## *Tardy*

VESPER 06, FOUR NINETY-EIGHT
FIRSTMOST FARADAY
9 KNELLS, 46 KNICKS
ON THE FIRST FACE OF THE CLOCK

Enzo was going to be late for his morning lecture with Regius Professor Coquelicot. He'd become completely turned around. Again. The very foundations of this city were mucking with his sense of direction. He was used to thinking in squares, but Newcomb was based on hexagons.

He stumbled into a marble hall that he hadn't even realized was part of the academy complex. Timekeeping apparatuses filled every niche and pedestal, sort of like a museum. Trickling water drew his attention to a working clepsydra. Next, he studied a timepiece that appeared to be tracking the phases of the moon. A sandglass filled with something glittery and green looked large enough to measure an entire year. He walked toward a vast copper orrery in a domed rotunda. Gracious, the thing was a masterpiece of moving parts.

While Enzo circled, the planets and moons wheeled through their courses. Absolutely hypnotic. Definitely a mistake. Because when he finally dragged his attention away, he didn't know which way to turn. Six possible paths fanned away like spokes on a wheel. So yeah, he was totally going to be late.

"Skrik?" Not seeing any handy cracks in the immediate vicinity, Enzo brought out the shield-cut pendant that was their contract token. A bezel setting kept the cracked stone from falling apart. Holding it on his palm, he confessed, "Skrik, I seem to be lost."

A shadow welled up, spilling from the black stone to fill Enzo's palm before taking shape. Skrik stretched and peered around, then blinked up at him. "Where are you supposed to be?"

"One of the lecture halls. Professor Coquelicot's thing is soon." He shifted the imp to check his wristwatch. It might not have been designed to count knells and bells and tickings and tockings, but it still told time. Only the terminology had changed. "Think you can get me there in three minutes?"

"Mmm. I can try. Stay put." Dropping to the floor, Skrik scuttled across a seamless marble, and disappeared into the crack under a door.

Enzo hadn't noticed the door. It was nondescript, having been painted the same color as the wall. He drifted closer, curious what was written on the copper doorplate. But there were no words, only a tinge of patina, green against the underlying metal. He ran his finger over it, exploring the textures, then reached for the knob. No luck. There wasn't one. He tapped the door with a finger, then rapped lightly with his knuckle. It was wood. No sign of hinges. But ... wait. So *that* was it. A pocket door.

Poking one finger into a shallow groove, he slid the door aside.

Beyond was a vaulted space with sunlight slanting through from somewhere above. There was enough light to pick out a small forest of columns, a staircase that spiraled upward, and three orderly stories, each packed with shelves. Enzo closed his eyes and breathed in an old, familiar scent. Books. Had he found a back entrance to the academy's library?

"I told you to stay put." Skrik clambered up to Enzo's shoulder and grabbed a handful of his hair. "It isn't far, but you'll need to run. That way."

"Run …?" Enzo hastily closed the door and started in the direction Skrik pointed.

"Jog."

"How long have we been friends?"

The shadow imp sighed. "I'll settle for a brisk walk, but don't get distracted along the way. Now, go."

Wheezing slightly, Enzo staggered into the lecture hall. He was late, but a group of mages were in a knot off to one side, too deep in conversation to notice the time. Or the tardy.

Murmured conversation drifted down on all sides. The tiered seating was full to bursting.

Professor Oswald, Enzo's academic advisor, spotted him and hurried over. "Nick of time, dear boy! Nick of time! But you'll have to climb for it."

"Excuse me, sir?"

"The observation deck." Oswald waved a hand at what amounted to a balcony section. Usually cordoned off, it was filling fast. "Still a few desks open."

"Umm, great. I don't suppose there are any elevators?"

Professor Oswald laughed. "Big, strong lad like you? Go on with you."

With no other choice, Enzo trudged upward. "Big, strong lad, am I?" he muttered. He might have inherited his father's and grandfather's build, but he was no athlete. Truth be told, he'd been quite soft about the middle when he'd left home, but Tuppence's tender mercies had just about burned through any of his fat stores. Maybe gaunt was easily mistaken for fit?

By the time he reached an empty desk in the upper deck, Enzo was done in. "Do you suppose Purdle will be joining us?" he asked Skrik, who'd melted into the shadows under the desk. "I'm thirsty."

A moment later, small hands were pushing a glass bottle into the open.

Enzo quietly asked, "Is that for me?"

Skrik stiffly said, "Purdle isn't the only one who can find water."

"I'll remember that for next time. Thank you." The water was icy cold. Enzo decided not to ask where Skrik had found it.

More latecomers were grabbing seats at long tables that were definitely antiques. Holes pocked the polished wood where inkwells would have fit during a bygone era. Instead, students flourished fountain pens. A few were setting up input decks, but by far, the most popular method for notetaking was to compel, bribe, or politely request that one's familiar pay heed to the lecturer.

Enzo had never set this sort of task to Purdle or Skrik. Orders made him uneasy. He was more comfortable talking things through, getting their advice, then working together. Grandfather hadn't approved, didn't think Enzo was keeping his *pets* properly in hand, but it was Enzo's choice. And the last thing he'd do was take away Skrik's or Purdle's choices. So his familiars did as they pleased, and Enzo never really knew what to expect.

Someone took the chair beside Enzo's.

That was a surprise. He'd been avoided since day one by other students. At first because he was a foreigner, but then because he was … well, he was good at this sort of thing. Scion-of-a-dynasty levels of good. He'd tried to play it off as the result of extra experience, since he was a few years older. But he hadn't thought to hold back during his early practicums. Overmatching a couple of professors? Not smart.

"Hey. Where've you been?" Arty slouched disreputably, his gaze wandering the lecture hall. "Somebody warn you off or something?"

"What? No!"

"Your caretaker ground you?"

Enzo relaxed into a smile. "No, nothing like that. Tuppence always calls a meeting on the first of the month. Budgets and tuition and … well, it's boring, and it takes all day."

Arty squinted at him. "First of *what* now?"

"Oh. Umm. Yesterday was October first." He held out his arm to show Arty his watch. The display included the date.

"What's FRI?"

"Friday. Today is Friday, October second. At least, that's what the rest of the world calls it."

Arty looked suspicious. "It's Faraday."

"Named for Dr. Samira Farrukh, one of Newcomb's architects, I know. I looked it up."

"Where are you from again?"

"My family has a quiet, backwoodsy sort of place in North

America. I've been traveling, though. Long enough to see how lots of different parts of the world dealt with the Sundering. But you guys made history. Or rewrote it."

"I know everything there is to know about Newcomb, so don't act like you know better just because you know how it is in other places." Arty pointed down. "This city was built to last. Five centuries later, we're still here, proving every single day that the founders did a brillsome job, rightward and without a doubt."

"Okay, sure. I meant no insult. It's just taking some getting used to."

At the front, one of the professors struck a bell, calling the room to order. Apparently, there were enough notable guests in the crowd that a formal welcome was required.

Scooting his chair closer, Arty ignored the opening remarks to whisper, "You still interested in us showing you around? My crew knows what's what."

Something occurred to Enzo then. "Are you even in this class?"

"Nah, but I didn't see your caretaker person with you, so I figured this was safe." He flipped open the top of his messenger bag and pulled out a paper sack. "Hungry?"

Enzo's mouth watered. "There's no food allowed."

"Not hungry, then?" He used a multipurpose tool from his belt to slit the bag with barely a sound, exposing a dozen pale spheres.

"From a bun cart?"

"I planned better'n that. Went to a proper mother. Gog-worthy stuff, this." Arty tore one in half, revealing a custardy yellow center. "It doesn't smell too strong, and it won't crunch. Perfect for eating on the sly."

Enzo wanted one. So much. Enough to break a rule?

"Say, can I give one to your shadow?"

Skrik had moved up onto Enzo's knee, and he was peering up at Arty from under the desk's edge.

"That's your familiar, huh? Very respectable." Arty held out one of the soft rounds. "Everybody loves eggy buns."

The imp looked up at Enzo, who nodded. "Skrik, this is our neighbor Arty. He's a friend."

Arty's smile widened when Skrik beckoned with both hands for the treat.

Just then, a murmur rippled through the room, halting the officious preamble. Heads turned, and every eye soon fixed on the cause for interruption.

"Great. Just great," groaned Enzo. "Purdle."

# 22

## Fashionably Late

VESPER 06, FOUR NINETY-EIGHT
FIRSTMOST FARADAY
10 KNELLS, 19 KNICKS
ON THE FIRST FACE OF THE CLOCK

Enzo waved his arms over his head. "Up here, Purdle!" And to the general assembly. "I sincerely apologize. Please, carry on ...?"

Nobody did. Not immediately. They were too busy watching Cubit, who clutched at the mist forming beneath his small feet, tail swishing as he swayed along over everyone's heads, aiming for Enzo.

"Realm take me, he's defying gravity," muttered Arty.

"I know, right? You get used to it."

Purdle sat with dignity, turning from side to side, waving in genteel acknowledgment.

Reaching Enzo's place, Cubit cocked his head to one side, eyeing Arty with suspicion. Purdle swung from the saddle, his boots making a faint *clack* against the desk. He marched to the edge that overlooked the lecture hall and gave a final wave.

Clearing his throat, the professor at the lectern shuffled through his notes, trying to recall where he'd left off.

Purdle skipped back to Enzo and loudly whispered, "Being late is *fashionable*!"

Enzo shook his head. "I'm pretty sure it's only rude."

"*You're* late. All the time!"

"That's a recent affliction." To Arty, he admitted, "I get lost here."

"We can make orientation part of your familiarization. Me and my crew, we all grew up here. Know it from highmost to downermost. We'll see you sorted." He slumped forward, chin on his folded hands, putting himself closer to eye level with Purdle. "You really do have two familiars."

Technically true, but Enzo wouldn't have phrased it like that. "We do look after each other."

Purdle struck a pose. "Servitude is not stipulated in our contract. On either side."

"He did try, though. At first," Enzo confided.

"Princes have servants and things!"

"Are you royal, then?" asked Arty. "It's a flash crown."

"Thank you, friend!" And without actually answering Arty's question, he turned to Enzo. "Tuppence said it's my turn. It was my turn last time, too. Have you ever noticed that Skrik doesn't ever take a turn? Do you think I might be put-upon? Should I be aggrieved?"

"It's a compliment to the neatness of your penmanship. But really, Purdle, you don't need to take notes for me. The things in these lectures … umm. We already know this stuff, don't we?"

"Which of us gets to tell Tuppence that her wishes have been ignored?"

Enzo sighed.

Purdle nodded. "Nitpicking the erroneous bits can be fun. May I have a chair, please?"

Patting his pockets, Enzo took out a small moleskin journal he'd had since boyhood. Its pages held a variety of magic circles, each capable of summoning various odds and ends. They'd been experiments and diversions, but after he'd met Purdle, who was always asking for this and that, he'd added things to please the sprite. The very first had been the tiny crown he'd created. The magic had only taken moments, but Purdle treasured the gift, which had sealed their contract, even though it wasn't their official token.

The most recent addition had been Cubit's saddle. Paging slowly backward, he found several items of Purdle-sized furniture. "This one?"

"No, no. Let me." Purdle knelt before the book and turned pages that were half his tiny height. "This one! It would look well here. And it has a footstool."

Purdle was soon settled amidst blue cushions, a journal propped against his knee as his pen scratched busily.

Arty, who'd been sharing out pieces of a second eggy bun to Skrik, offered a piece to Purdle.

The sprite beamed at him, then addressed Enzo. "I wonder why you took so long to make a friend. This man is perfectly lovely."

Enzo mildly pointed out, "You're my friend. So's Skrik."

"Maybe so. But *this* one doesn't live under Tuppence's heel. And his food is much nicer than paste."

"Much nicer," he agreed, with a grateful nod in their neighbor's direction.

Arty's eyes were sparkling when he reached for his messenger bag. "Want to meet *my* notetaker?"

Purdle, whose cheeks were stuffed, beckoned with a regal flourish of fingers.

Out came a flat spiral of metal about the size of Arty's palm. It looked like a seashell lying on its side. Enzo was immediately interested in the symbols curling along its surface, but before he could get a better look, Arty depressed one of the small magenta crystals studding it. A faint click was followed by the whirr of clockworks.

Legs unfolded, pushing the shell upright, and crystal-topped eye stalks emerged, along with an alarming number of additional legs. Meanwhile, Arty unfolded an input deck that was half the size of the ones other students were using. Setting it before his clockwork companion, Arty said, "Coquelicot may have something interesting to say. Do your best, Swab."

Tiny chimes sounded in answer.

"Inhabited clockwork?" checked Enzo.

"They're something of a specialty of mine. Lots more where Swab came from."

Enzo had been surrounded by clockwork inventions like this for months, but he still marveled over the intricacy of their designs and the startlingly lifelike fluidity of their movement. Some of this was due to the technical expertise of the coggers who built them. Coggers like Arty. But just as important was the mage who gave these mechanical golems life by borrowing it and binding it to the machine.

Enzo still hadn't decided how he felt about this particular branch of mage-craft.

Professor Oswald, who specialized in this sort of familiar, had been honestly baffled by Enzo's reservations. "Are you not contracted to two Realmish creatures? Inhabited clockwork is a similarly binding contract, but instead of the usual ring or pendant for a token, the clockwork apparatus serves."

It wasn't the same, though. Enzo knew better.

Most inhabitations were accidental or sometimes even incidental, an upshot of the Sundering. The resulting entities could get up to all kinds of mischief. People in other parts of the world called them *dwellers*, but making one on purpose ...? That was taboo. Every city Enzo had visited was armed with a system for un-souling inanimate objects. They probably even had one here.

Yet Newcomb's mages took pride in the creation of inhabited clockworks, as if emanations were just another power source, like their steamworks and gaslamps and windmills and waterwheels.

Swab's spindly legs rippled over the input deck, tapping against keys without pause.

Arty asked, "Something on your mind? You look like you have a question."

"How does Swab know what parts of the lecture are worth recording?"

"I told her who to listen for, so she'll record whatever Coquelicot says."

Enzo asked, "How does she know which person that is?"

"I taught her."

"So she can learn?"

"Yeah. It's true, she has limits, but I find it interesting to work within them. Swab and the rest, they're like logic puzzles. The better I am at setting up the rules she needs to function, the more confident she is that she's doing well."

Enzo murmured, "Does she have a choice?"

Arty considered that seriously enough. "Do you really think any of these wanderers would brave the rift and search for a point of contact, then a contract, if they had no interest in living among us?"

Purdle interrupted them by remarking, "Thaaat's not going to work the way she thinks it will."

Enzo looked to the front. Regius Professor Coquelicot and two of her assistants were pouring colored sand into the recesses of a permanent circle etched into the floor. Given the patterns and the colors, they were about to attempt some advanced elemental magic. The setup was for a summoning. Except that the interior runes were reversed. It was a simple, stupid error, but they went right on as if nothing was amiss.

Weren't any of the attending professors paying attention?

Could nobody see that they were inviting disaster?

Gracious sakes.

"Sirs! And ... and ma'am!" Enzo leapt to his feet, raising a hand and his voice. "Sorry to interrupt, professors! I have a question! One that really can't wait. Please."

Professor Coquelicot slowly turned from her task and asked, "Which one is it?"

Professor Oswald helpfully pointed.

Enzo wracked his brain for a question that wouldn't call the old professor's sanity into question. Maybe if he asked about the types of gemstones used? Or the coarseness of the grain?

"Is there a problem, young man?" asked Professor Coquelicot, an edge to her tone.

Well, damn. "Yeah. I mean ... yes, ma'am."

Silence finally gave way to the soft hiss of whispers, but Professor Coquelicot's gaze didn't waver. "You wish to take me to task?"

"With all due respect ... *yes*."

Turning to Oswald, the old woman murmured something, and the man nodded, answering eagerly enough. While they conferred, Enzo whispered, "Thanks for the warning, Purdle."

"You'd have noticed if you were watching." The sprite was still busily taking notes. "Do you think Tuppence will praise me for saving your life?"

"What?" Arty stood to get a better look at the magic circle. "Is that thing dangerous?"

Enzo whispered, "'Realm take me' … it's a figure of speech here, yeah?"

"We use it regular enough. Just a turn of phrase."

"That's a flipped summoning circle. And it would have literally taken us through the rift. All of us, given the size of it." With a tight smile, he added, "It's best I stopped her. Otherwise, we might have been forced to find a place and a purpose as some fae creature's familiar."

Arty's expression found its way to thunderstruck in the time it took for Professor Coquelicot to call the room to order with a word. "Basker?"

"Yes, ma'am. I'm Enzo Basker."

"Report to my office. Day after tomorrow. First light." And she walked out.

Purdle capped his pen and asked, "Are we in trouble? That would be unjust. We just didn't want to be Realmed, did we, Cubit?"

The newt blinked placidly.

"Speaking of trouble," said Arty. "How worried should I be about this Tuppence person? Is she as scary as Enzo says?"

"No, no. Enzo is too softhearted to tell the whole truth. Right, Skrik?"

"Enzo does not want Tuppence, but more than that, he does

not want to hurt Tuppence." With a nod in Purdle's direction, Skrik grumbled, "Very soft."

"Tomorrow, then," said Arty. "Since Coquelicot just requisitioned your Newday, give my crew tomorrow. Which is Chromday, if you didn't know."

And just like that, Enzo's weekend was booked.

# 23

## *Setting Precedents*

VESPER 07, FOUR NINETY-EIGHT
FIRSTMOST CHROMDAY
7 KNELLS, 59 KNICKS
ON THE FIRST FACE OF THE CLOCK

If Tuppence noticed Enzo's distraction, she didn't say so, but his guilty start when a knock came on their apartment door put her on alert.

Purdle asked, "Is that our neighbor? The friendly one? He's perfectly lovely, Tuppence."

"Okay, yeah. That will be Arty. I invited him."

"Why?" asked Tuppence.

"To be neighborly. I'd like you to meet him."

"Why?" she repeated.

"So that you won't worry so much when I go."

"Go? Where would you go?"

But then Enzo was at the door, and he had it open. Arty flicked a couple of fingers in casual salute. "Knell's bells, you look a wreck. Nervous?"

He managed a tired smile. "Good morning, Arty. I was just telling Tuppence that we have plans for the day."

"That's good, yeah? Made a beginning?" Stepping inside, Arty didn't look the least bit concerned that Tuppence had drawn a small blade. He just shoved his hands in his pockets, looked her up and down, and genially asked, "What are your rules?"

Tuppence's scowl faltered.

Taking a step closer, he reframed his question. "What rules have been set for someone wanting to be Enzo's friend?"

"There is no precedent. The young master does not have friends."

"There's Purdle, isn't there? And where's Skrik?"

"And Cubit," chimed in Purdle. "You mustn't forget Cubit."

"Impossible to misremember Cubit. He's a rightward fellow." And addressing Tuppence again, Arty asked, "If there's no precedent, can we set our own rules, adapting to the needs of the moment?"

"You *want* rules? From Tuppence?" Purdle asked incredulously. "She'll make you keep them."

Arty shrugged. "Why wouldn't I keep them, if I've agreed to them? Wouldn't that be friendly to Tuppence?"

Enzo had never seen Tuppence looking so uncertain. She grumbled, "There is no precedent."

"Purdle is a precedent. Skrik is a precedent."

She hesitated, then admitted, "They were here before me."

Which was entirely true. Enzo hadn't realized that his grandfather had foisted Tuppence on him until they were miles from home.

"Cubit, then," suggested Arty. "You have no objections to Cubit."

Tuppence frowned. "That one poses no danger to the young master."

Smile widening, Arty said, "I pose no danger to the young master." And before she could argue the point, he asked, "Is that your first priority?"

"The young master's safety is my first priority."

"And the second?" prompted Arty.

"The young master's health."

"Safe and well. Yeah, those are understandable concerns. Especially when someone is going so far from home."

Tuppence's chin lifted. "The young master is safe and well."

"Good for you, Tuppence. I can see that. Plain as primer." Arty asked, "Is there another? Maybe you were trusted with more?"

"One more."

"I'm impressed. What's your thirdmost priority, Tuppence?"

"The master's peace of mind."

Oh. Well, damn. That was also plain as primer. *The master*. Not the young master. Enzo had always suspected that Tuppence was reporting back to his grandfather. But he'd hoped to win her over. Maybe it wasn't possible.

"You make allowances for Enzo's education. He goes to classes without you."

Tuppence's scowl was back. "I am not a student. I am not allowed to accompany the young master, since I do not pay tuition."

Enzo had been entirely grateful when Professor Oswald insisted that lessons were conducted in a safe environment. At first, she'd hovered on the fringes, checking up on him from a distance, but now she simply demanded that Skrik or Purdle stay close.

"Knowing Enzo is receiving a fine education must put your master's mind at ease." Arty added, "I'm a neighbor, and I'm a friend. But you know what? I'm also Enzo's tutor. Lessons with me will be a real boost."

"The young master is already exceptional."

"Oh, I've seen that for myself. But there are gaps in his knowledge. Not in mage-craft, of course, but in common-sensical things. I know all the ins and outs of Newcomb. My lessons will familiarize Enzo with the city. Useful, right?"

"Lessons," Tuppence echoed. "In a lecture hall?"

"Nah. It's practicums, innit? We'll be going around the city, having a grand old tour."

"The city is not safe."

"Especially for the ignorant. So I think you should come along. These are lessons you can share with Enzo. Me and my crew, we'll treat you right."

"Together?"

"We'll make a day of it, then totter back and toggle the locks before the bells peal for curfew." Arty casually suggested, "Let's make *your* peace of mind a rule between us."

"And your crew?"

"Patina and Seelie are waiting streetside. Nunc has this thing about class attendance, and Jamie takes a tocking in his family's shop, so they'll meet us later. They're my crew, and they're all the kind of people who understand priorities."

Just then, Skrik writhed out of a crack in the floorboards and scuttled onto Arty's shoulder. The imp said, "More dangerous than he looks. Better an ally than a foe."

Enzo hadn't even been aware that Skrik's opinion held weight with Tuppence, but she sheathed her blade with a snap.

Decision made.

Permission granted.

Cenotaph Road stretched from the tower that housed the Academy of Mages right into Newcomb's city center. As far as Enzo could tell, most people walked to wherever they were going. Or made use of the trolley to shorten their walk. But there *were* vehicle lanes for an assortment of transportation, all humming, hissing, or clacking along. Noise levels seemed to depend on power supply.

Arty hustled them toward a long stone bench where two young women waited, kicking up their heels and chatting. But at a sharp whistle from Arty, they looked over and raised hands in greeting. Enzo guessed they were about Arty's own age. Students at … well, one academy or another. But definitely in their teens.

The first to hop to her feet seemed to be human, though her hair had been tinted green. She jounced from foot to foot, hands fisted beside her cheeks, barely containing a squeal at the sight of Purdle and Cubit. Introductions were taking care of themselves, so Enzo hung back. He overheard enough to learn that this was Patina.

The other girl was Folk, and Enzo wondered why Arty hadn't mentioned it earlier, then wondered at himself for even having the thought. If he had to guess, he'd say that one in four people in Newcomb were either Folk or had Folk heritage. They'd been living on equal terms with humans since the city's founding. He might be the only person in the city who got all excited over novelties that weren't.

Her name was Seelie, and Enzo knew from books that she was a Childe of Parliament, a variety of Darke Childe. She had the characteristic heart-shaped face, reminiscent of a barn owl's, except all in grays instead of snowy white. In place of a nose, she had a hooked beak. Below it, her mouth and jawline looked human enough, but above was an astonishing pair of large golden eyes.

He was staring.

She stared right back. "You didn't hear anything Arty just said, didja?"

"Umm, yeah. Was it important?"

Arty took over. "When anyone needs to meet up with a friend—or tutors—the best thing to do is choose a mother or a founder. Since we don't cling to any one particular mother, this here's our usual meet-up." He gave the stone bench an affectionate slap. "We'll call it a lingering smidge of filial affection, since I have the good fortune to be descended."

Enzo realized only then that they were using a sarcophagus as a bench. And that Arty had slapped his hand over the nameplate, obscuring most of it. He could just make out the first four letters and made a guess. "James?"

"That's right. Like the river." And when Enzo showed no sign of following, Arty snorted. "You don't know, do you? The name of the river that runs through Newcomb."

"The Thames?"

Bafflement. Incredulity. Sarcasm. "Riiight. And next we'll be calling this a fine Friday in October."

"It's Saturday."

"Pay attention, Enzo. Class is in session. Newcombers rely on the James. Our river is strong and clear and drinkable. It waters our gardens, fills our moat, turns our waterwheels, sluices our sewers, and brings business from the coast. Without the James, Newcomb wouldn't have happened. Same could be said for this James."

Patina interjected, "Genius, this codger. Same as our Arty."

"They even share a name," said Seelie.

"Me and half the boys in this city. Some of the girls, too."

"Is Arty a nickname, then?"

"Yeah. Well, what can you do when all three guys in your crew have the same first name? So we go by Arty, Jamie, and Nunc. Much simpler."

While Tuppence questioned Seelie and Patina about their suitability as friends for Enzo, then about the safety of their current surroundings, Enzo beckoned Arty aside and quietly offered, "Thanks. For putting Tuppence at ease. I never can, not when I'm the reason her guard is always up. You managed her *so* well."

"I told you. I have a lot of experience with her sort."

"She's not a golem."

"Neither are all of mine." Arty glanced Tuppence's way. "She's a keepsake. At least, that's what we call them here."

"I first learned to call them tsukumogami. But I like keepsake."

"How long have you been together?"

"She's been with the family for generations, thanks to an irrevocable contract. When I left home, she kept turning up like a bad penny. I thought at first that my grandfather had sent her to bring me back. Once we realized she'd been smuggled into my baggage, I invited her to travel with us openly. That was about nine years ago." Enzo wryly added, "Travel doesn't agree with her."

Arty nodded. "Too many variables."

"Exactly!"

"Ever consider staying put?"

"Not really. I've been searching for something."

"And it's not here?"

Enzo caught sight of a newspaper stand, where all the headlines bewailed the presence of a monster in the city. "I'm not sure. Maybe."

Arty hummed, then shrugged. "Tour starts with food. Then more food. Hungry?"

"Starving."

"Follow me, yeah?" Arty led off, promising personal introductions to every mother who'd earned his devotion.

Enzo moved to follow, but he glanced back. Curious. The nameplate on the sarcophagus was clearly visible now. It extolled the man resting within as a brilliant mathematician, engineer, and diplomat. James Moriarty.

# 24

## *Winding Back Time*

VESPER 07, FOUR NINETY-EIGHT
FIRSTMOST CHROMDAY
8 KNELLS, 28 KNICKS
ON THE FIRST FACE OF THE CLOCK

Varti worked Chromdays. Most badges with desksome jobs could only count on Newdays off. Because he could set the schedule, Henna and Kel were off on alternating Chromdays. Kel would be on duty this week, and Varti and Dr. Kang would be going through the formalities of an assessment of his spelling for his quarterly report. It would take a few knells, and Varti didn't like to leave Doggerel with Kel for that long. Or it was possible that he was trying to spare Doggerel.

He didn't know how to break it to the hound.

Explaining to Phil wasn't going to be a problem. He and Tybalt hadn't come home the night before, possibly because this coming Newday was the final day of Tybalt's quarterly duty-break. Tomorrow, he'd be saddling up and returning to his post beyond the walls.

It hadn't missed Varti's notice that Phil was letting him go. He could have spun a few gears and pulled a few levers if he'd wanted Tybalt on his investigation team. Like Varti.

People came and went a lot in Phil's life. But not Varti.

Embarrassed to be proud about something that was petty, Varti ate breakfast while standing before the case wall, which was as up-to-date as he could make it. Their avenues of inquiry were few and uncertain. Varti thought he might use his lunch break to visit the site of Willa's death, but he didn't know the first thing about familiars and their contracts. That was the realm of mages, but what if he noticed some detail … any detail? He was good with details.

The only thing holding him back was the proximity of Larch Court to the office where Thomas might be waiting for a report on his lost dog. All the more reason to leave Doggerel home.

He put off leaving, choosing small, meaningless tasks.

A new roll of paper for the ticker.

A splash of water for his plant.

He noticed the tricentennial coin among his things and put off leaving even longer by taking the time to clean it with solvent and attach it to his watchchain with a twist of wire.

But finally, he knelt down and patted his thigh. That still worked, apparently. Though this time, it felt like a lie. Or at least a trap.

Before he could lose his resolve, he secured one half of a set of regulation handcuffs through the hound's collar, then locked the other half around the radiator pipe with a smart *click*.

Doggerel turned his head, then looked at him with an expression of such frank dismay that Varti bowed his head. He stroked fur and fondled ears, mumbling, "Wretched thing."

Doggerel didn't growl or snap or try to jerk free.

If anything, he looked annoyed.

Varti still felt guilty. And in need of support. So before he left, he took Phil's guidance deck, hugging the cards to his chest and hoping Phil would be pleased. Then he cut the deck himself, setting the cards neatly upon their little table. That way, if Phil came home for a change of clothes or a quick nap, he'd see them and do his reading.

When Varti locked the door to their quarters, he left behind the Sixth of Echoes, a card called The Wall, and a sulking Doggerel.

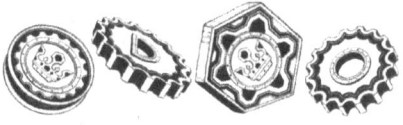

The usual stack of newspapers awaited Varti, who tried to set all else aside and focus on each headline and article.

## QUEEN CALLS FOR CURFEW

In the wake of Willa Cyrine's death, a rare royal decree had been issued. Citizens who needed to travel after sunset could only do so with a badge escort. And since the number of available badges was so limited, the city was effectively on lockdown.

Responses varied. There was outrage, with criticism heaped on everyone from the royal family, safe in their wall-top palace, to the incompetents who had failed the city by letting the killings continue.

## CITY HELD PRISONER

## TOO LITTLE, TOO LATE

In the absence of actual facts, speculation was still running rampant.

## *FOLK OR FOREIGNER?*

And as usual, the *Newcomb Buzz* tried to find a gentler approach to the latest tragedy by celebrating the victim's life.

## *WHO WAS WILLA?*

Thankfully, Chromday papers had fewer pages than usual. It was as if the presses were saving their strength for the big weekly editions that dropped on Newday. Free of anything more pressing, Varti applied himself to his own investigation. His next task promised to be tedious, but it would be easier than legwork.

Tybalt had mentioned trying to call upon the consultant who worked out of the Bridge District. This was oddsome. First, why hadn't Phil used one of his department's usual couriers? More perplexing, why was Tybalt Gregson, a highmost member of the Hedge, acting as courier during his days off?

He feared he was taking a long-around approach to finding answers, but he worked backward through the records of any cases overseen by Highmost Purnal Yamada. Because if she'd turned to the consultant at 221 Old London Road before, then a report should be in the file. That would give Varti his name, at the very least.

Two knells later, Varti had found a modicum of success.

Three payments had been issued in the last decade to the consultant at that address. Each case was unusual, having Realmish elements. Perhaps he specialized?

More interesting were earlier cases, back when Sarah Yamada was a highmost perior like Phil and further back, when she was only a thricemost fernal.

Some of the case notes were in her own handwriting, and she was devastatingly blunt.

*I'm desperate enough to sign off on a consultation. His rates keep going up. I think he wants me to refuse to pay him. Had an answer ready, though.*

*The vexsome derelict won't even see me. His assistant sent me off with an apology and a list of who to ask what ... and where to look. How did he know?*

*Don't know why Bollard bothered to bring me along. Left standing at the door. Inside this time. But his assistant brought tea and biscuits. Very polite. If I was in charge, I'd contact him instead of his employer.*

*My perior went in alone, left me on the stoop. Apparently, this consultant can't be bothered with women.*

**Varti kept working backward.**
**Sarah Yamada's predecessor, one James Bollard, had gone to the consultant twice before Yamada's time.**

*He's an ass, but he's good.*

*I'll swear it here or anywhere. The man picked my pocket, used my name and my badge, and was so convincing when he solved the case, I got a promotion.*

Even stranger, Bollard's predecessor mentioned the Old London consultant in a few cases. As did *his* predecessor. Varti calculated the year and frowned. Surely this couldn't be the same person. These cases were one-hundred and thirty years old.

And they weren't the beginning.

He was getting a better sense now for the types of cases that needed a certain variety of consultant. Or if the case notes were to be believed, they had to be difficult enough problems if they were going to catch the detective's interest. In nearly every instance, there was grudging praise, backhanded compliments, and … now *that* was interesting. A royal commendation.

Finally, three hundred years back, the reporting badges were referring to the consultant by his surname—Holmes.

Varti cross-checked his indexes and appendices, and the trend continued.

*Top of my class, and he makes me feel like a bloody schoolboy. I mightn't mind feeling a fool if he hadn't persisted in calling me one.*

*Hire him. By all means, if you can get him, hire him. But after that, step back and let the man do his job. Holmes won't be impressed by anything you have to offer.*

*Holmes turned down a case of poisoning, three bodies uncovered in the Pasture District, and reports of a literal dragon in Lake Tethys. But he sent around a note about a chalice gone missing from The Tree of Knowledge.*

*Say what you will, he saved my life.*

The records went back—some badly in need of detail, others rendered by someone much more conscientious—all the way to the city's foundations. And in the earliest records, fragile with age, Varti found a sheaf of cases set in a London that wasn't referring to Old London Road. These apparently predated the Sundering, when a Mr. Sherlock Holmes had rooms on Baker Street. He skimmed for anything that might be helpful in understanding how this same person could be alive today.

Names recurred: Watson, Hudson, Lestrade, and … Gregson. Tybalt hadn't shown any sign that the consultant on Old London Road was someone whose history overlapped his own. But then again, why would he know a scrap of detail that was at least five hundred years distant?

Might the purnals have sent Tybalt for that selfsame scrap of a connection?

Genealogy was a vibrant hobby in Newcomb. People adored tracing their family history to the founders. But Holmes wasn't in the genealogical lists. According to their history, he was one of a kind. No kin. No progeny. Alone.

Varti was updating his LOST DOG case file when Kel stalked into the room. "Mr. Weller, sir. Someone to see you."

There were no appointments on his calendar.

"He's no badge. Not even sure how he got in the building, but he wants a word." Her hand dropped to the weapon at her side as she grimly added, "Let me know if you want me to drive him off."

# 25

## *Unexpected Guest*

VESPER 07, FOUR NINETY-EIGHT
CHROMDAY
3 KNELLS, 14 KNICKS
ON THE SECOND FACE OF THE CLOCK

S ylvester Thornapple tugged his hat by way of greeting. "Merry met, friend. Where's your usual companion?"

Did he mean Phil?

"I've been loitering nearby, waiting on you. Thought I might catch you at noontide. Did you work straight through lunch?"

Varti shook his head and checked his pocket watch. Three knells on the second face already? He'd been buried in research nearly all day. Doggerel must be in a fit state.

"So ... Doggerel. You have him here with you?"

"Yes, of course."

Sylvester dragged his hat off and rumpled his hair. "Is that so? I wonder if I *did* see him, then. Not many large dogs, even in a big city like this one. No vest, though. Did he part company with you?"

Another dog? That was a jarring thought. Varti had assumed that Doggerel must be the lost dog that Thomas reported, but what if there was more than one?

Then in the distance came a sudden clatter of running feet, and the claxon of alarms sounded somewhere above.

Kel jogged past, shouting, "I'll find out, sir!"

She was only gone a knick or two and returned with eyes wide. "Number six, sir."

Which was badge business, not to be bandied about in front of outsiders. But Sylvester Thornapple had managed to slip away.

"It was in the Academy District, out back of the hippodrome. Do you think Highmost Perior Kemp will want you on scene this time? I could close up and escort you to him. Sun will be setting in a couple of knells, and that means the curfew."

She looked ready for any kind of action.

He made up his mind. "Don't be ridiculous."

"Yessir," she said crisply and started locking down their division.

It took a few flits for Varti to collect his wits enough to help.

They didn't get very far before Hexadille Porter came running along their hall, camera case thumping against her hip. "Weller! Sun's setting, and they won't let me leave the building without an escort! Can you get me there?"

Varti looked Kel in the eye and hoped the curse didn't devolve into anything particularly nasty. "I think you'd better leave this to the men."

She cracked a smile. It was a very dangerous smile.

But then Kel said, "Understood, sir." She grabbed her weapons case from the cabinet by the door, requisitioned an extra duty lamp, and lifted her chin at Hexadille. "We'll take my cycle. Have you there before the tick can tock."

Which left Varti alone with his thoughts.

Doggerel first.

He could get to where Phil was after he looked in on the dog. It'd be a short jog if he cut through the halls in the city wall behind his district.

Swinging the barred gates shut, Varti made them fast, then ran for home.

Varti crouched before the alley door into The Green Man in utter mystification. Even in the twilit dim of the Drears, he could see that a coin leaned against the kickplate. Glancing up and down the empty alley, he picked it up.

Another cog, but with a square cutout, from the city's quadricentennial year. He turned it over, trying to account for its arrival.

Was it a message?

Was it a mistake?

"You there!" came a small but imperious voice from somewhere overhead.

Varti slowly stood and found himself facing a tiny person astride a very large newt. Well, large for a newt. They hung quite comfortably in midair. The rider was arrayed in gauzy blues, and a crown nestled around his puff of silver hair. He wore a necklace with a bitty blue droplet gem. Given the general splashiness of the ornamentation on the saddle and his boots, Varti guessed he was facing someone elemental. And Olde. He warily declared, "Flame sprite."

"Is that a joke?"

It wasn't. He sighed and said, "Stone sprite."

The little fellow considered and softly said, "Try again."

"Moon sprite."

"Again."

"Sun sprite."

"Keeeep trying."

"Leaf sprite. Vine sprite. Brine sprite."

"You're getting wetter! I'm not salty, though."

Varti didn't know it was a lie until it popped out of his mouth. "River sprite."

"No, no. All wrong." He smiled, blue eyes bright. "The curse knows what I am. *And* what I can do. Do I worry you?"

"Not at all."

"Then you're *both* worried. Is it strange to be in unison?"

Varti wasn't sure he had time to be chatting with Realmish beings in back alleys. He hugged the bag of buns he'd bought at the corner. They were meant as a feast for Doggerel. And for an apology, too. He turned away, fumbling for his key.

"That smells nice. I've had many nice things today. Skewers and cider and pies and puddings. And *toast*! Bread is boring, but toast is transformative!"

Only thinking of escape, Varti whispered, "I don't need you."

Which gave him pause. As lies went, that one was particularly revelatory. Was this person capable of unspelling him?

He turned back, mute and desperate.

"I'm Purdle. This is Cubit. Where is the Hound?"

# 26

## *True Words*

VESPER 07, FOUR NINETY-EIGHT
CHROMDAY
3 KNELLS, 47 KNICKS
ON THE SECOND FACE OF THE CLOCK

Purdle spoke with complete confidence. "You're not him, but he was here. Only I couldn't follow him inside. Did you know this building is warded against the uninvited?"

Varti hadn't known, but that did seem the sort of precaution Phil would take.

"I found *you* next. It was easy. And you left a coin, though you did it all wrong. Still, I marked your door." Purdle's gaze shifted, and he stood up in his stirrups. "Oh! Oh, you lovely man! You *kept* it. You're wearing my token!"

The tricentennial cog, newly added to Varti's watchchain.

"That simplifies everything!" Purdle leaned forward. "You cannot say what you please, but can you do as you're told?"

"No."

"Have you a basin of water?"

"Such luxuries are beyond a man of my means."

"Good. Use it to invite me in. Take the coin with the square bite and drop it in the basin." Waving at the door, Purdle said, "Go ahead. It'll do the trick."

Varti didn't hesitate. He was halfway up the first flight of stairs before the latch clicked shut on the alley door. Up and up again, to the third story, where he slammed through the door to his quarters. And stood breathless in the silence that welcomed him.

He crossed the room, boots clunking, boards creaking, to where Doggerel's harness was still cuffed to the radiator. Empty.

Where could he have gone?

He couldn't have freed himself.

Did someone take him away?

Flits passed before he returned to the task Purdle had set. Hurrying to the mirror stand that held their basin and pitcher, he dropped the quadricentennial cog into the remains of Phil's shaving water. The coin disappeared with a *ploop* and clacked against the ceramic bottom.

Immediately, the filmed surface trembled, bubbled, and welled upward as Purdle and his newt emerged, dripping soap scum and red whiskers.

The sprite's expression soured. "For future reference, clean water is preferred." He extended a hand, and a ball of rippling water rose from the adjacent pitcher. It drifted over to Purdle, then splashed over him and his newt, rinsing them off.

Varti offered his handkerchief.

Patting at his face and arms, Purdle peered around. "It's very dim in your part of the city. Skrik would like it. I prefer more light."

So he lit the lamps. And stowed the buns. And found the guidance deck back on its shelf. Which meant Phil had been home at some point. Maybe he'd taken pity on Doggerel? Or it might have been Tybalt.

Meanwhile, Purdle dried his saddle, then rode his newt over to inspect the case wall. "Aren't you organized? I see! You were looking for him, too? But if you caught him, why did you let him go? That was very unwise. It happened again, didn't it?"

And selecting a pin with a blue head, Purdle staked the narrow space between the hippodrome and the city wall.

Right where the sixth murder had taken place.

Right where Varti needed to go next.

"Doggerel is a killer." Varti didn't believe that for a flit. It simply couldn't be true. Could it?

He supposed there *was* that bath after the last murder, when he'd washed what looked like blood out of Doggerel's fur. And he was missing again, right when another death was reported. But that wasn't proof of anything. It was circumstantial. Coincidental.

But not impossible.

Although he nodded, every part of Varti rebelled against the idea. Doggerel couldn't possibly be the reason six people were dead.

"I can grant a boon, you know."

Varti glanced up, seeking Purdle's waiting gaze.

"I can grant a boon," he repeated. "I'm that powerful, you see. Only, most people don't see, but that's how it is with people. But you're folk-spelled, and that's changed you."

"Heave off, or I'll drown you in a puddle."

Purdle tapped his newt's head and came closer. There was a dangerous light in his eyes, and his voice took on the ring of authority. "I *am* that powerful, and I need true words from this man."

Varti's heart leapt, even as the curse twisted. "Don't you dare."

Snapping his fingers, Purdle reached toward the basin. Water swirled, and a small ball of it lifted, carrying the silver coin. He directed it Varti's way and said, "Take it. Keep it. Use it to call for me. And because I'm really *very* amazing when I try, you may have ... four words. Yes, I think I can manage that. Four true words in my presence. But only four, so choose wisely."

The coin dropped onto Varti's palm with a splash.

He glanced between it and Purdle, whose expression was expectant.

But Varti was wary of Olde things. How much would this boon cost him?

"It's done, you know. I don't go in for sparkles or chimes like some do. Are you disappointed?" And flinging his arms wide, Purdle urged, "Tell me the truth."

"I hate to lie."

That was the pure, unvarnished truth. And it had just come out of his mouth. Varti found he needed to sit down.

Purdle rubbed his chin, then sighed his way to a smile. "It's not a bad beginning, but I already knew that, silly. Choose better words tomorrow."

"It didn't work."

"It did."

"You're a vile thing."

"We both know I'm not. Even Cubit finds me handsome."

"I want you gone."

"I wish I could stay, too, but Enzo will be needing me. I can tell."

"I never want to see you again."

"Yes, yes. I'll be back. Cubit is a very clever newt. He'll find you. Especially if you keep the triangle coin. That one's especially potent. That's why it made such a good marker."

To Varti's embarrassment, the curse railed against Purdle, using slurs and dredging up words that had never been part of his vocabulary.

Purdle heard him out, then smiled a quiet little smile and smugly said, "You're welcome."

# 27

## *No.6*

VESPER 07, FOUR NINETY-EIGHT
CHROMDAY
4 KNELLS, 18 KNICKS
ON THE SECOND FACE OF THE CLOCK

V arti only had to follow the blaze of lights to find his way. The southeastern corner of the Academy District, between the city wall and the Cannery Road skyrises, wasn't part of the Drears, but it was similarly overshadowed. Perhaps that's why the city planners had placed the sprawling hippodrome here, so that horseraces—and those who came to bet on them—were pleasantly shaded. But that meant that the crime scene was in the dark even before the sun set.

Crews from the Bastion were holding back a crowd of curiosity seekers. Varti ducked under copper tape that glinted in the light of dozens of duty lamps, then paused to peer upward.

Nobody could approach the crime scene on foot, but the lines they'd drawn weren't stopping gawkers in the twelve-story residences built over-top the spoke road. If he could have, Varti would have immediately ordered a rain screen set up. Ideally before any enterprising journalists got their photographers onto one of those balconies.

A few steps later, a whole range of smells hit Varti's nose. They added up to death. No wonder the horses had spooked.

So far, nobody had questioned his presence.

He hadn't been part of a crime scene since graduation, and those were mostly staged by their instructors. Even so, it was the easiest thing in the world to slip into old ways. His breathing slowed. His focus shifted. His attention sharpened. Already, he was cataloging distances between structures, the slope of the ground, the sections of quarters that would need to be canvassed in case there had been witnesses.

It felt natural. Like he'd never been interrupted. Then again, maybe he'd never really stopped looking at the world this way. Attention to detail wasn't limited to criminal investigations.

He'd still been applying himself, just in different areas. He was an untapped font, a glut of miscellany, a walking guidebook to Newcomb. And the only thing he could do was lie about it. Or keep scrupulous notes that nobody would ever see.

"Weller!" Tybalt lifted his lamp so he could be seen. "Round this way. Kemp, he made it!"

Badges in copper cloaks stepped out of Phil's way. He was pale and drawn, but his smile was real and relieved. "I waited for you. We haven't moved anything."

The enormity of his faith was staggering.

And because he was fresh from a study of files relating to Sherlock Holmes, he drew an obvious parallel. Wasn't he also an outsider, brought in to consult on a case that nobody else could solve? Phil clearly expected him to see things that the other badges would overlook. Even though they'd all gone to the same academy, studied under the same instructors, and learned the same protocol.

Varti could alienate these badges. And maybe even make an ass of himself. Still, he pushed back his cloak, using a series of hidden buttons to secure the ends, lest they flap forward while he bent to his task. He rolled up his sleeves and found their buttons as well. And all the while he organized his thoughts.

He couldn't *question* anyone, but Phil would see to that. He couldn't *talk* about his findings. In fact, he shouldn't speak at all. A lie here would be disastrous. But he would *know* what he found, and thanks to Purdle, there was some small hope of sharing four true words with Phil.

What might those four words be?

*Thank you so much.*

*You saved my life.*

*I miss talking back.*

*Rinse out the basin.*

So much of what he wished he could say was stuff that didn't need to be said. Phil knew. And wasting four words on complaints would be pillsome. He should probably use his four words for case-related remarks.

*Prioritize finding Willa's familiar.*

*Is Doggerel Purdle's Hound?*

*Sylvester Thornapple is suspicious.*

*Where is Sherlock Holmes?*

But words would have to wait. And they could wait. Because there were a handful of people here who knew why Varti needed to work in silence. He would be leaning heavily on their support.

Phil had turned to confer with some of his people. Varti wanted to get a message across. Naturally, his jaw was stubbornly locked, but he had to try something. Cuffing his best friend's shoulder, he made an unsightly gesture. The voluntary rudeness may have surprised the curse enough that he got away with his next move. He raised his hand higher, along with his eyebrows.

Tybalt muttered, "Are you thicketed, Weller ...!"

But Phil looked up.

He shouted, "Holt, Mullins! Push back the barricades and find the rain sheets. I want cover, quick as you can manage. Barrow and Keyes, douse those lamps. Wait until those tarps are in place before we shed more light. I want to give Weller here a good look, not the press."

Barks of assent on all sides.

Varti spotted Kel in the group carefully raising and angling the rain sheets.

Dr. Kang had also arrived. He stood off to one side, arms folded over his chest, an expression of almost paternal pride on his face. And not all for Varti, though he did earn a nod. The man had instructed most of them.

Phil made a circuit, then returned to Varti's side.

He doubted the curse would let him get away with anything else. He ground his teeth and hid his hands behind his back. At least the contrary streak brought his need to Phil's attention.

"Oh, of course." Phil turned over his own gloves and sample case, which Varti added to his belt. "Take the time you need. I'll do my best to anticipate."

Four rain sheets framed a section of the grassy slope, angled to obscure the view.

Phil's team brought in specialized lamps that blazed pure white. Placed at intervals along the fringes of the carnage, they illuminated every bloodstained blade of grass and the tattered remains of a person. Varti resisted the urge to think of them as a number. Phil wouldn't like that.

Varti was drawing parallels again.

He couldn't speak. Neither could this victim.

But words weren't always necessary.

There were signs for those who sought them.

In a way, it was Varti's turn to do a reading.

As he fell into a textbook search pattern, Varti let his mind slip sideways into a part of himself that could observe without letting the horror of this death touch him. If he'd had four true words for this person, what might they be?

*What brought you here?*

*Tell me about yourself.*

*Show me what happened.*

Little by little, Varti took note of details that might prove helpful. He knew it wasn't his job to identify the victim. Dr. Kang would do a full examination in his turn. But there was a person here, and it wasn't as if Varti could ignore them. Torn and strewn and ravaged and raw, but a few knells ago, they were standing on this slope just like Varti was now.

Yes, standing. Or walking along. They weren't dragged here.

And there. The reason. Mired in a pool of coagulating blood. The pipe stem was broken, and the bowl cold. But there was no smoking in the hippodrome, with its plank seating and wooden boxes. The same was true of the nearby animal barns, since their fodder was flammable.

A man. That was a man's hand.

Fair skin. Neat nails.

A ring. He had a partner, a family.

This man would want Varti to take heed, to find more.

His eyes were blue, his hair dark blond and showing signs

of pomade. His shirt was that trendsome gray that was in all the shop windows. A new color for Verspertide. So he'd been fashionable. The vest was in bad shape, but Varti thought it might be vintage. Or the tapestry itself was vintage. That spoke of boutique tastes and money.

A pin on the vest's lapel gave him pause. Where was the pocket watch? He cast about, knowing it must be nearby. There would be a watch and a chain, and that would confirm his suspicion. But first ....

Mindful of each step he took, he slid tweezers from the sample case and folded over the lapel. It would do no harm to take this item, which would speak for him. For both of them. So he crouched, twisted, and claimed the lapel pin. Abiding by procedure, he did a visual check, then pulled a vial from his belt and dropped it inside. Capping it smeared blood on the glass, but he held it out to Phil anyhow.

He took it. Held it up. Grimaced. "This is the logo of the *Clockwork Sentinel*."

"You are badly mistaken."

"Do you know which of their dauntingly daring employees this might be?"

"No." He tried for snide. "Just some wiseacre."

Phil closed his eyes, swallowed hard. "Sure about that?"

"Totally random."

"Right," he sighed. "Back to it. See what you can see. I'll deal with this."

"You get all the easy jobs."

Phil shook his head. "Glad you're here." Trudging toward the double row of concerned citizens beyond the barricades, he raised his voice above their clamor for a statement. "Begging your pardon, but this once, I have a question for you. Do we have a representative of the *Clockwork Sentinel* in our midst?"

"Here!" exclaimed an eager voice. "Georgette Anders of the *Clockwork Sentinel*!"

Amidst protests from the other papers, Varti watched Phil lead her away, his back straight, face forward as she practically skipped at his side, angling for an exclusive. Varti could pretty much imagine how this was going to go, but he hadn't finished his part in all of this. So he refound his focus. There was still ground to cover. A lot of it, since O. N. "Owen" Acres had died messily.

But Varti wouldn't have traded places with Phil for anything.

Acres and Anders. Anders and Acres. They were investigative journalists with a longstanding rivalry for the front page. Their headlines turned heads and sold papers. But tonight, Phil was going to have to break it to Georgette that her husband was dead.

# 28
## *Lurker*

E nzo woke in the dark to the murmur of voices and the smell of food. Actual, palatable food. And coffee. Propping himself up on an elbow, he reached for his glasses and wristwatch on the bedside table. He had to summon light to his fingertips in order to see the dial. Sunday morning. Early. Oh, right. The thing with Professor Coquelicot. "Skrik?"

Something dropped onto his pillow. "Here."

"Can you get the lamp?"

Shadows brushed Enzo's cheek, and luminous eyes widened with urgency. "There are sausages."

"That sounds promising."

"And pies."

"Even better."

"And *butter*."

"Your favorite."

"You'll share?" Skrik wheedled.

"We'll feast together."

Skrik patted his forehead and leapt away. Then the light from one dim bulb washed over an unaccustomed jumble of cushions and blankets on his bedroom floor. Because he had guests.

Enzo grabbed his pants and a clean shirt, then tiptoed around Nunc and stepped over Jamie on his way to the bathroom.

Arty's crew had done their best to empty Enzo's pockets yesterday, since he'd insisted on paying. A fair exchange for the guided tour. Tuition, willingly tendered to his tutors.

They'd been seemingly everywhere, but Arty assured him that every place they'd visited was no more than a ten-knick walk from here. Close to sunset, with the other two Jameses added to their party and curfew impending, they'd piled into Enzo's apartment and made themselves at home.

Barefoot and belly rumbling, Enzo joined the people already gathered in his kitchen.

Patina called a bright, "Mornin', guv!" But she followed it up with a critical once-over. "Is this you all the time?"

He glanced down at himself. "My clothes?"

"Plaid is ... a choice," she said carefully. "Bold."

Seelie asked, "Is it a foreign fashion?"

"I didn't really notice. Do you not wear plaid in Newcomb?"

"Outmoded in the extreme," said Patina.

"Welllll ... you do sometimes still see plaid in a tweed vest," offered Seelie in diplomatic tones.

"But never in pants. And *never* so baggy." Patina tried to bring Arty into the discussion. "Can we all agree that he looks foreign? And that's something you should avoid. Nobody likes a foreigner."

"They're comfortable, so I'm keeping them." Enzo had no interest in the fitted breeches and tailored vests that were worn by men and women alike. "More importantly, who cooked?"

Seelie blinked her large eyes. "Mothers cook."

Arty may have stayed quiet about matters of fashion, but he was only too happy to ply Enzo with food. "These pies. They're only sold in the morning, and they're gone in flits with no chance for seconds. It's a good thing Tuppence was ready to go early."

A pie as big as Enzo's fist sat warm on his palm. He nibbled at the crimped edge, sparkling with sugar, then bit deep and found spiced apples.

Tuppence filled the bowl that usually held nutritional paste with sausages and broiled tomatoes and presented it. "You need to eat more. According to your friend Arty, this will improve your appetite."

Ducking his head, Enzo murmured, "I'll do my best. Thanks, Tuppence."

Her eyes flashed with satisfaction.

Arty passed him a steaming bottle of coffee, then produced a newspaper and spread it on the table.

## *SLAUGHTER CONTINUES*

He said, "Another one. Last night. It didn't happen anywhere near us, but still. Seelie and Jamie especially like to wander the city after dark. But you gave us a reason to stick together last night, so my crew's safe."

Enzo couldn't take credit and would have protested, but his mouth was full of pie.

Pulling out a pocket watch, Arty added, "Plenty of time to eat. I'll get you to Coquelicot's on time."

This time, Enzo couldn't protest. He had no earthly idea

where the professor's office was located. So he gave in with grace ... and ate faster.

Fifteen minutes later, Enzo thudded downstairs after Arty. Once they were on the level again, Enzo asked, "What do you think she wants?"

"Yeah, about that. I did some snooping, and I don't like what I found."

"About the professor?"

"Nah. Not specifically." Arty flipped his hair out of his eyes. "Did you know that there's something lurking in the Academy of Mages?"

"First I've heard." Enzo felt he should point out, "That's not really an issue for me. Skrik is a first-class lurker."

"Well, *this* isn't someone's familiar. Some people say it's a ghost."

"Is that really so worrisome? You folks need emanations to power your clockworks and whatnot. If anything, a ghost should be worried."

"I don't think it's a ghost." Arty stopped walking. "Say, are you dismissing me because I'm younger than you?"

"I wouldn't do that. I've been on the other end of that sort of thing for most of my life."

"Yeah?" Arty's gaze narrowed. "How old were you when you contracted with Skrik?"

"Officially? Four."

"Unofficially?"

"All my life."

"And Purdle?"

"I was *much* older and wiser when Purdle came along. Nearly eight."

Arty glanced around, then stepped closer. "Why?"

"Why what?"

"Why'd they want you? Why'd they choose you?"

"Umm ... let's just say it's a family secret."

Arty immediately backed off, but he looked worried. "Does Coquelicot know your family secret?"

"Couldn't be." Enzo tried to redirect the conversation. "Is there a more palatable theory than ghost for the lurker in the tower?"

"You mean ordinary, yeah? Like a squatter."

"Not every shadow is a dark portent or ill omen."

"I mean ... it's great that you're open-minded about these things, but there's times when you've gotta call a ghast a ghast and make for the nearest blest item." The sky was lightening, and Arty got them moving again. "I hear stuff, yeah? And this thing—whatever it is—has people on edge. Think about it! A strange emanation or ghost or whatever that nobody can pin down. Or stop. Could be it's responsible for all these murders."

"I suppose that's a possibility," Enzo answered carefully.

"What if a gog-worthy mage, one who could outclass most of the professors is just the thing? What if Coquelicot set you up and called you in because our purnals think they know who's been killing Newcombers. And what if this is them, deciding to throw a foreigner at that problem."

"Because nobody likes a foreigner?"

"Exactly."

"You're a very suspicious person."

"I've got my reasons, and I've got my ways. And there's reason enough to worry, and there aren't many ways I can help."

"But you want to."

"'Course I do, you knob. You're this ultward balance of posh and pushover. I don't even have to pick your pockets or cut your purse strings. You *offer* to pay."

"So you're after my money?"

Arty cheerfully promised, "I'll wring you dry."

# 29

## *First Light*

VESPER 08, FOUR NINETY-EIGHT
NEWDAY
6 KNELLS, 59 KNICKS
ON THE FIRST FACE OF THE CLOCK

Arty steered Enzo into an elevator in a fancy filigree cage, pushed one of the pearl buttons, and backed out before the doors could slide shut. "Straight to the top. I'll wait for you somewhere hereabouts."

"You're a good friend."

"Nah. Just nosy. I wanna hear everything."

The elevator barely made a noise as it whisked up to the twentieth floor, and Enzo definitely owed Arty for getting the timing just right. He was in the glass enclosure at the top of the academy's tower, and in the east, the sun was just cresting the horizon. First light, as ordered.

"Up here," called the professor from somewhere overhead.

Enzo spun around, spotted a curving staircase, and took his time mounting it. The view was spectacular. All six towers rose above the walls, putting them on the same level as the royal palace, which looked like a mammoth wrought-iron conservatory.

The rising sun struck magically-enhanced glass, glittering

with prisms. No wonder the professor had summoned him now. The effect was dazzling.

Regius Professor Coquelicot's office wasn't so much a room as a loft that gave her a panoramic view of the city. He got the sense that she and the other five people who held these high offices must be watching over Newcomb.

"Good morning, Professor," he offered.

She waved a beringed hand. "Go ahead and have your look. It's a rare view."

Enzo moved right to the edge and looked down. Morning mist billowed up, obscuring both the street and station levels, but the spoke roads were clearly marked by the lines of apartment and office buildings that had been built above them. Over the centuries, Newcomb had surmounted the problem of limited acreage by rising above it. He'd learned during yesterday's tour that none of those structures exceeded twelve stories, so they remained below the city walls, which were eighteen stories tall.

The buildings below had unique architecture within a unifying palette of copper and green. Some were elaborately decorated with cast bronze figures. Others were streamlined, encased in colored glass. Enzo's personal favorites were the buildings draped in greenery, vertical gardens that added to the city's visual appeal while undoubtedly helping to feed its citizens.

After looking his fill, Enzo turned to consider the professor's office. Honestly, he was shocked. Not a bookshelf in view. To use the local vernacular, it was oddsome. Mage-craft relied on books that carried forward discoveries about myths and magic. They unraveled the mysteries of grand circle-craft and the lesser art of hex-craft.

But the only book in the entire room rested on the corner of Professor Coquelicot's desk. Its cover was a deep midnight blue, and its ornamentation was all in copper. The stars and moons looked like they belonged on an ancient wizard's robes. And since Enzo had a tendency to name things, he decided in that moment that if the book had a name, it would be Merlin.

The professor beckoned for him to take one of the chairs facing her desk. Without preamble, she announced, "The class on Faraday was a test, and you're the only one who passed."

"You weren't actually going to pull the entire room into the Realm?"

Her lips quirked. "Who can say? It might have been interesting."

"What about the professors? Where they in on it? Is that why they didn't step in?"

"Only my two assistants knew about my orders."

Enzo frowned. He didn't like it when people hinted instead of saying things plainly. It was confusing. "So that whole thing wasn't your idea?"

"Indeed, no." She sighed. "I cannot possibly explain everything, but it would help if you understood that the mage academy has a history of strange occurrences. It comes tongue in groove with dabbling with the otherworldly. The magic changes things, and many believe it changed us. That's why the skills for mage-craft now run in families. Oh, we still test for aptitude in our youngsters, and so new blood sometimes finds its way into our halls, but the citizens of Newcomb are essentially born for one tower or another. The mages, the engineers, the archivists, the healers, and so on."

Enzo listened politely, but he was waiting—rather warily,

thanks to Arty—for her to come to a point.

She suddenly asked, "Where were you taught?"

"Home."

"Who were your mentors?"

"Books."

"What about your line?"

"What if I said we were banished?"

She blandly countered, "Hardly rare. Where are your people from?"

"Originally? Or currently?" Enzo hoped this meant that grandfather wasn't meddling after all. That was good.

"Currently will do."

"North America. We went into seclusion centuries ago, and we never left. Well, except for me. I'm the wayward son."

"And heir to an interesting assortment of familiars."

Enzo didn't like that she assumed Skrik and Purdle were family heirlooms. "Is there a point to this meeting, mage?"

It was technically polite, but using this form of address implied equality. He wasn't under her tutelage. In fact, there was very little that this academy could offer him besides a place to stay ... and access to their admittedly wonderful library.

"There is."

He prompted, "I passed a test ...?"

"You have."

"And is there some consequence for doing so?" He hoped it wouldn't be a Herculean task, like hunting down the mystery lurking in this tower.

"Yes. There are twelve seats in the academy."

Enzo tried to fit that with other schools he'd visited. "Like a cabinet? Or a board of trustees?"

She hesitated, as if considering unfamiliar terms. "For a city such as ours, there are those whose function is governance. They maintain the systems that are in place. But it is just as important to have those whose purpose is guidance. The academy's twelve seats are people who explore possibilities. Stagnation is a danger unto itself. Complacency invites disaster. Life is change."

He nodded, though he wondered if he should have brought Purdle with him. To take notes.

"Due to an unfortunate circumstance, we have an empty seat. The person who held it is no longer able to fulfill the duties of his seat, yet he's refused to yield it. Until now."

"So he's still around."

"After a fashion. I will tell you—in confidence—that he is *also* a royally-appointed professor. A brilliant mind, but difficult. He hasn't taken on an apprentice since my student days, and the only reason I know he did is ... that was me."

Enzo couldn't think of a polite way to bring up the math. Not without calling attention to a lady's age. But she was eighty if she was a day. "He's Folk, then?"

"It's more accurate to say that he's no longer entirely human. I'm not sure even he knows what he's become."

"And you're saying he's ... what? Electing me to his seat, sight unseen?"

"He's been watching you."

"That doesn't really answer *why*. I'm not even from here."

"I cannot speak for him, but I agreed to pass along two items that he believes will convince you to accept the chain of office and the waiting seat."

Professor Coquelicot eased to her feet, and he shot to his feet as well.

She tottered around the desk and waved him closer. First, she placed a large key in his hand. Then she struggled to lift the midnight blue book, so he quickly relieved her of it.

Smoothing his thumb over the nap on the cover, he turned the key over. "What's this for?"

"I have no idea."

"I thought you said he was your mentor."

"Oh, he was. But I was not his *successor*, and he kept all his best secrets for them. For *you*, if you'll accept the responsibility."

# 30

## *Free Day*

VESPER 08, FOUR NINETY-EIGHT
NEWDAY
7 KNELLS, 4 KNICKS
ON THE FIRST FACE OF THE CLOCK

**V**arti had only slept for a few scant knells when he woke, his body insisting that he was late, and it was time to begin his day. He lay for a while, staring at nothing, then decided to budge up. Normalcy could be a balm, and he needed one.

He did his best to run away from memories of helping Dr. Kang collect body parts. His former mentor had asked that it be just the two of them, in case they found anything helpful. Dr. Kang had talked him through the whole process, treating it like a practicum. And at the end, Varti created a neatly documented list of personal effects, which included a pouch of Saint Danbright's Light tobacco, a broken bent apple pipe, and a locket on Owen's watchchain that held a photograph of him and Georgette on their wedding day.

Phil had returned with damp lashes from his brief conference with Georgette. And then they'd waited for Hexadille, who'd insisted that all the garish lighting be taken away before she could begin.

Varti tried to empty his mind. Just jog. But it was lonesome with only his footfalls for company. He missed Doggerel. They'd only been running together a handful of times, yet Varti was unhappy enough that he might even welcome Sylvester Thornapple's company.

At least he could look forward to seeing Ramage this morning. He and Phil and Tybalt would have breakfast together at The Speckled Hen before Tybalt returned to his cohort.

Things would go back to normal.

Weller and Kemp. Kemp and Weller.

But would it be the same?

Things had changed. *Were* changing.

Ever since Doggerel.

Varti finished his circuit and found Phil and Tybalt already at the bathhouse, both sluggish as they lolled in the soaking tubs.

"I knew you'd be up and ready," Varti cheerfully lied.

Phil managed a wan smile.

Tybalt bluffly declared, "Newdays are too precious to squander in sleep."

So they left together, cleanshaven and cloakless, free as the day, at least for the moment.

"Look who it is!" exclaimed Ramage. "Hurry yourselves inside, there's room. Always room for more!"

The harpy never seemed to give anyone special treatment, yet Varti knew that Tybalt and Phil were two of his favorites. And that he was simply riding their tailfeathers.

Ramage strutted right up and dipped his head in order to speak softly. "Touch salt, brave badge. Let Ramage do what he can."

Varti could feel his sour look, and he was mortified by the slur that slipped out, but Ramage's tone turned conspiratorial.

"In inversely proportionate terms, that's the sweetest thing anyone's said to me all week. Come around more, Weller. I can't get enough."

He was able to touch salt then, letting his fingertips graze the big crystal on Ramage's necklace. Ramage's gaze gentled, but he didn't say more. Just used a wing to nudge Varti toward the sink before moving on to greet an incoming family.

Aril—or possibly Burr—served him a plate of bread that had been dredged in egg and griddled. When they next placed a bowl of small oranges on the table, Varti was startled by the extravagance. They were nothing like the usual hothouse oranges, which were larger and paler. Had these been brought in by dirigible?

Tybalt asked about them, and Ramage came by their table.

"A new connection, thanks to my inestimable sisters. They have an incomer at the Covey. She's a sphinx. Very popular already. Anyhow, her people are orchardists, and they were willing to favor me with a contract. Aril and Burr have been making candied peels and marmalade. Because we're fancy like that."

After breakfast, the three of them strolled through a hex of shops, loitering until the last possible knell. Then they escorted Tybalt to the stables, where they saw him off.

Back at The Green Man, Phil checked in with Mr. Whilom about rent and repairs, and Varti looked to their quarters. Tickertape had formed a loopy pile on the floor, and he fished around for the end. Skimming the messages, he spooled everything neatly in case Phil wanted a look.

Phil came in with mail that had come through the pneumatics for him. Varti went to update the case wall but only stared fixedly at the pin Purdle had stabbed into the very place O. N. Acres had been found.

How had he known where the victim had died?

Had he been there before anyone else?

Could he have seen the killer?

Choosing his next four words was going to be difficult.

"Varti?" Phil held up his guidance deck. "I never had the chance to do yesterday's reading for you. Shall we start there?"

Since they didn't have any kind of couch, it was one bed or the other if they wanted to sit together. Varti dropped onto his own bed, and Phil joined him in a companionable slouch.

"The Wall." Phil found the card, which showed a soaring wall of stone and birds wheeling in the blue sky above. "This card can mean a lot of things depending on the cards it combines with. There are all kinds of walls, literal and figurative. And emotional. In our case, it could mean the city wall, or it could signal a need to be on guard. You also drew Sixth of Echoes, which in hindsight is portentous enough to make me quakesome. Acres was the sixth victim."

Varti hoped his next draw didn't include the Seventh of anything.

"Now for today's reading." Phil shuffled meditatively. "Doggerel was gone when I stopped in at midmorning yesterday for a clean shirt. I saw the vest and the cuffs. Did you have him confined?"

He glanced miserably toward the radiator.

"Tybalt didn't think he was an entirely ordinary dog. Did you have any reason to suspect that he might be a Realmish creature?"

"Absurd."

"I hate that I'm suspicious of him. Mind you, I have no idea what he may have done. He can't be our killer … right?"

Varti hoped not. Elbowing Phil, he muttered, "I don't want guidance."

"Humor me anyhow."

And then the familiar weight of the deck was in his hand.

The first card that turned up was The Howl, and Varti made a small noise. Kind of a whine. Really embarrassing. He wished he could blame it on the curse, but it'd been all him. He was that relieved.

"Right. Looks like we'll be seeing Doggerel again."

The second card *wasn't* a seven. It showed a sun-washed stretch of seashore with a thatched cottage in the distance.

Phil considered it carefully before admitting. "I don't see how this applies, but let me tell you the usual meanings anyhow. Maybe something will make sense to you. First of Shores, gathering sweetgrass, salt, and sea glass. First in any suit generally implies urgency or priority. When you're wavering between two paths, drawing a first card provides direction. Sweetgrass is for freshening. Salt can be the sting of tears if the card is inverted, but you're facing it straight, so … cleansing. Or the pinch that gives savor. And sea glass is an unexpected find. A found treasure. All in all, it's a card that means change, especially a refreshing one."

"Time to move out."

"You or me?" Phil asked, sounding amused. "Up for a walk?"

Varti shook his head.

"You choose our destination."

That, at least, was easy.

Although he longed to run, they would have drawn too

much unwanted attention in a city that was strolling through its rest day. So it took half a knell before he and Phil stood before 221 Old London Road. Everything was as Varti remembered—the scent of lavender, the hum of bees, and the flutter of black crepe.

"I suppose it doesn't hurt to try," said Phil. He let himself in by the gate, skipped lightly up the steps, and knocked. Then he turned to gaze out over the Bridge District, where people were enjoying the sunshine and the first turn of color on the royal garden's trees. After letting a knick pass, he knocked again, then returned to Varti's side. "No use. Yamada's been sending someone around regularly, but this consultant fellow has made himself scarce."

That was news to Varti.

Had nobody else talked to Thomas?

"Next?" prompted Phil.

Although they weren't in uniform, Philtrum Kemp was a person of note in Newcomb. Varti had seen more than a few black looks. People apparently didn't think he deserved a break while people were dying. Varti lifted his own hood and waited until Phil followed suit, then he led the way down a side alley, into a maze of back lanes.

"I'm so lost right now," Phil admitted. But a few knicks later, he softly said, "Oh. Good thinking," as they stepped out into Larch Court.

The base of the fountain was thick with bouquets. Flowers were the proper offering for a Fullnis child like Willa. Vigil candles lined its rim. But Varti quickly fixed his gaze on Phil's face, waiting while blue eyes scanned the vicinity. They stopped and brightened with recognition.

"She's still here." And raising his voice, Phil said, "You're a stubborn one."

He walked to a bench in the shade and brought out his guidance deck.

"I came prepared to do readings. One for you, then one for me. And Varti will make three if you have the patience." Phil glanced at Varti. "I was here once before, and since Willa's echo seems willing to interact, I thought this might help. I'm glad I pocketed my cards."

While Phil shuffled, Willa drifted closer, until she was standing right over Phil. He didn't seem bothered to have a ghost so near. He simply began a full reading, laying out cards one at a time in a pyramid pattern. His peaceful expression never wavered, even when dire-sounding cards turned up. Then Phil began interpreting Willa's cards in his usual, unhurried way.

Varti wanted to skip ahead, but interrupting would have been beyond rude. Also, he needed the curse to be distracted, otherwise it might stop him. So Varti rearranged candles in order to sit on the fountain's edge ... and waited.

There was always the possibility that Willa's reading would help Phil.

Finally, Phil gathered up the cards and shuffled. "My turn. I'm dreading this, but it must be done. Lend me some of your courage?"

Varti was done waiting. Before Phil could begin, he spoke up. What came out of his mouth was an entirely predictable slight. "He's terrible at this. Never gets it right."

Phil looked his way.

Now. He needed to do it now.

Not wanting to lose his among all the other coins in the

fountain, Varti cupped a handful of water and splashed it across the quadricentennial cog in his other hand, hoping it would be enough.

"Varti …?" ventured Phil. He stood and came over to see what was in his hand.

Willa followed, shimmering in the air between them, looking from face to face.

And nothing was happening.

What if it didn't work?

Was there a trick to this?

But then came a splash as Purdle and his newt popped out of the fountain. He adjusted his tiny crown and looked between Varti and Phil, then focused on the ghost. "Well, this is more interesting than anticipated. Were you frightened, friend? This echo isn't dangerous, you know." And to Willa's ghost, "Enzo is making new friends, so why shouldn't I?" And to Phil, "How do you do? I'm Purdle, and this is Cubit. Ohhh, I say! Are all these flowers for me?"

Afraid the moment would somehow pass, Varti reached for Phil, right through Willa's ghost. He grabbed Phil's hand, gripping it hard as he blurted, "Where is Willa's familiar?"

# 31

## *Summons*

VESPER 09, FOUR NINETY-EIGHT
ROWDAY
6 KNELLS, 20 KNICKS
ON THE FIRST FACE OF THE CLOCK

First thing the next morning, Phil had Varti bully him out of bed so he could take the trolley round to the Academy of Mages before his tocking. He'd find somebody to help him locate Willa's missing familiar. "Lots of ways and means, but I don't have the knack for it. Somebody there should be able to help."

Thanks to Purdle, Phil was making a fresh line of inquiry.

For today, they were saving up Varti's four words in case something crucial needed to be said later. Purdle wasn't opposed to dropping by on the daily, so long as there was sufficient water for him to pass through.

If all went well, Varti and Phil would meet for lunch, and they'd go over what he learned. Then in the afternoon, Dr. Kang and Hexadille Porter would be making their reports on O. N. Acres.

A full day.

But just before ten knells, Henna pulled Varti away from his newspapers.

"A call for you. I know you generally don't answer the telephone, but this seems to be personal. A Mr. Whilom …?"

Varti's first thought was that Doggerel had come home.

Henna plucked up the receiver and said, "Thank you for waiting. Mr. Weller is here. He can listen to what you have to say."

When Varti got the telephone to his ear, Whilom was already talking. Fast.

"… says he knows you, but why would he come *here*? And in such a vehicle. It's a flagrant violation of community codes! One stray spark, and we could lose everything! But he won't budge, and it's you he wants, and oh, what am I supposed to do? Varti, I think you'd better come." And in a hasty whisper, "*Please*, Varti! I don't like the look of him!"

Varti wasn't sure what to do.

Kel had turned up midway through Whilom's hysterics, and Varti thrust the phone at her.

She brusquely ordered, "The pertinent details only."

Then, "Have you been threatened?"

Finally she said, "He's on his way," and hung up. To Varti, she said, "I'll take you round."

Before they entered the Bastion's parking garage, she requisitioned an extra side arm, which wasn't exactly heartening. Her cycle was meant for two passengers, so he boarded behind her and held onto the weapon case slung across her back. Varti didn't know if she was armed because of something Whilom had told her or if this was her normal. Thinking back, Varti couldn't ever remember seeing Kel *un*armed.

She steered into the open, turning onto one of the vehicle lanes that circled downtown. They exited the roundabout onto Old Livery Road, and Kel picked up speed. Their green cloaks billowed and snapped as she maneuvered around slower vehicles, and Varti moved with her. It was exhilarating, and Varti wondered if he could possibly rent a cycle before Bittern dampened the appeal by dumping snow on the city. He could try to get one with a sidecar and take Nani for a spin. She'd love it.

The ride was over too soon, and Kel didn't need directions to his tenement. Maybe Whilom had given her directions. Actually, it was more likely that she'd always known. For security reasons.

The cause of Whilom's distress was immediately apparent, because Durst waited out front of The Green Man, leaning against the door of a wood-burning vehicle, its chimney releasing a thin trail of fragrant smoke. And the occasional spark.

"You know him?" Kel asked in a low voice.

"No." He pressed three fingers into her shoulder, which would have meant something to Phil. He tried to warn her instead. "You can take him."

"Oh, realms no. And don't you try either."

Varti kind of wished that Kel was in the field. That's clearly where she belonged. In a world of different outcomes, he'd have wanted her for his cohort. Or even as a partner, he trusted her that much. "Together on three. You're with me, partner."

That earned him a flat look. "Wishful thinking, Weller."

But she stayed where she was, letting him walk up to Durst alone. The gorgon's crystalline goggles glittered in the shadowed neighborhood as his head turned, but his expression didn't change.

"Lovely to see you again."

The gorgon grunted. "Nobody has *ever* said that to me. People do not usually get a second look. If they ever see me."

"Nobody can fault your level of professionalism." Except law enforcers like Varti. It was quirksome that empty courtesies could be considered lies. Either that or the curse was more wary of Durst than it was of the people Varti usually spent time with.

"Mr. Hudson wants you. Bring stuff, or you will be sleeping raw, and it gets cold at night."

"What a pleasant surprise!"

"Ten minutes."

Varti had no idea what a minute was, but he didn't want Durst to come after him. So he hurried inside, bolted past Mr. Whilom, and shed his uniform cloak, hanging it carefully on its peg. That would be its own kind of message. Then he moved his plant, grabbed his satchel, and loaded it with the overnight kit that was always ready, an emergency field medicine kit, his ident tags, and a hand torch.

Pausing before the case wall, he really wished its borders were pushed further so that he could mark Hibernacle House. Instead, he riffled through Phil's guidance deck and found the card he'd drawn before. Bittern's Garden. He turned it upside-down so that it meant hibernation, then propped it against his duty lamp.

It would have to do.

Remembering the tin of tobacco he'd purchased, he added it to the bag, buckled its flap, and thudded back downstairs. Out front, he pointed to Kel and ordered, "Don't tell anyone!"

She didn't look happy about that, but she tapped a finger to her brow in a casual salute.

Varti really felt she should have been more concerned for his wellbeing.

He certainly was.

Durst tossed a couple of logs into the engine's stove, then joined Varti in the double-wide front seat. As he made a U-turn and accelerated toward Old Livery Road, Varti became increasingly self-conscious. All of Durst's snakes were staring at him.

"Yes, I missed you, too," he offered.

The gorgon's gaze didn't stray from the road, but he remarked, "Careful. They believe you."

Varti wondered how that worked. Did each snake have its own wits and way of thinking? Or were they extensions of Durst, and he was using them to keep an eye on him. The books hadn't said, and he wasn't about to waste four precious words to try to find out.

Durst took the central roundabout, which lengthened their drive considerably, given the congestion around Century Plaza. But he eventually made the turn onto Foundry Road, breezing under the Werifesteria trees and past the fountains, all the way to the gate under Saint Danbright's light. Once through, the world immediately opened up, giving Varti a clear view of the sky as they drove across the long, wide bridge spanning Lake Tethys.

Though Phil had invited him more than once, Varti hadn't left the city walls since graduation. On some level, it felt dangerous to do so. As if Newcomb's wards and lights and royals could fend off anything dangerous.

That clearly wasn't true. Otherwise, Durst wouldn't have been able to come and go at will. And Dr. Kang wouldn't have six mangled bodies in his care.

Durst turned left onto the hardpacked road that skirted the lakeshore. Knee-high grain rippled away to the south, deep gold and swaying in a breeze that was coming from the direction of the distant sea.

They passed groves and vineyards and long rows of fishponds. Sheep with thickening wool grazed hillsides, and a steam-powered harvester chugged through a field of corn. One householder had already stooked their wheat. Domed haystacks. Pumpkin patches. Irrigation ditches. Dairy cows. They were essential to Newcomb. Nobody could own property without a contract delineating their contribution to the city's resources.

Varti knew from the documentation he'd found for Hibernacle House that during the last census, they'd listed six people as members of the household. And that their primary contributions to Newcomb were walnuts, beans, assorted root vegetables, herbs, and honey.

The city remained visible behind them until Durst took a downslope turn onto a narrow trail. He hopped out to shut an iron gate behind them. Varti had to wonder if the statement it made was enough to keep people away, because anyone could have jumped the slender rail fence that laced the edge of the property.

They passed under a grove of nut trees, then curved around a grassy hill before the house came into view. It gave the impression of being low and sprawling, perhaps because it wasn't closely flanked by any other buildings. Varti resorted to counting windows. By the time the car stopped out front, he'd decided that this place was roughly twice the size of The Green Man.

Built of local stone, it had a steep roofline that would shed snow in Bittern. Gable windows might be an attic. He was only guessing since there had been no blueprints attached to the five-hundred-year-old contract. Sliding out of the car, he tallied up several outbuildings, a couple of haystacks, rows of corded wood, and at least two beehives.

Thomas Hudson opened the front door and extended a hand. "Welcome, Mr. Weller. No luck finding the dog, then? I wondered how that would go. Do come inside, both of you. Warm up in the kitchen over a pot of tea."

Snagging his satchel, Varti started toward the house, which was draped in the same red ivy as the alley alongside The Green Man. Over the front door, the smooth stone of the lintel had been chiseled with the farm's name—HIBERNACLE HOUSE.

"The rest of the staff are enjoying a day out, so it's just us." To Durst, he added, "Wendall took them to Plover in the barouche. And very chuffed he was to ready the team. They made a fine showing."

Durst only grunted and glided past Thomas, disappearing inside.

Varti stood before the smiling majordomo, questions bottled up, lies brimming. The one that made it out first was, "I came willingly."

Thomas's concern was immediate. "Durst wasn't rough with you, was he?"

"Bruises everywhere." He unbuckled his bag and brought out the tobacco.

Surprise was quickly followed by pleasure. "My employer's current favorite. How did you know?"

"Dumb luck."

"I'm quite certain that's not true." Thomas had him by the elbow. "I consider it a sign. You are meant to be, and none shall say otherwise. Not even our Mr. Holmes."

"We're old friends, Sherlock and I."

"My expectations for you soar higher with every moment." The front door closed with a weighty thud. "Let me just put your gift in his study, then we'll join Durst in the kitchen."

Varti peered around.

By modern standards, his tenement in the Carpentry District was considered derelict, what with its creaking boards and fussy trim. But Hibernacle House had the feel of an antique that had never seen a day's neglect. The building materials were still outmoded, but their luster and solidity were undeniable.

The midday sun sliced though diamond panes in fading colors that dyed the floor in harlequin hues. A staircase with a fanciful newel post and wide banister climbed to a landing where more windows let in confetti light. He took in coat hooks, a hat rack, and a telephone cabinet.

A low, soft tick, barely more than a vibration, drew his attention to a grandfather clock situated at the end of the narrow hall down which Thomas had gone. Glare on the glass made it impossible to tell the time, so Varti took a step to the side, trying for a better angle.

What he'd taken for a reflection changed shape. Pale amidst the shadows, with indistinct edges, it lengthened and lurched closer, reaching for Varti.

# 32

## *Ghost in the Hall*

Vesper 09, Four Ninety-Eight
Rowday
12 Knells, 6 Knicks
on the second face of the clock

Hibernacle House had a ghost?

Even though the thing didn't seem substantial enough to do any harm, Varti backed away. This was really very careless. No vigil candles or mercy prayers or city safeguards. Did people simply let echoes take hold out here beyond the walls?

Thomas returned then, walking right around the half-formed ghost. "Did he startle you? You have my every apology, but Mr. Holmes doesn't want us meddling with him. Benedick will decide if he stays or goes in his own sweet time. Which could be a while. Decision-making wasn't his strong suit."

This was someone Thomas knew. Black crepe fluttered in Varti's memory. The stopped clocks. A death in the household. "Maybe if Mr. Holmes finds a new assistant, Benedick will feel easier about moving on."

Which wasn't how this sort of thing actually worked. Just yesterday, Phil had explained that while the ghost they'd visited *looked* like Willa, she was something from the fae realm that had slipped into the space the woman's death had left behind. Resemblance, idiosyncrasies, and lingering memories could be persuasive. But Phil had assured him that ghosts were visitors from the Realm, and their emanations should dwindle away with time.

Nobody came back from the dead. Souls didn't linger in this world. But death was a kind of sundering, and the way out could become a way in.

"I can see it in your eyes," said Thomas. "You think me dream-bound and wish-addled, and you aren't entirely wrong. I'm often chided for romantic notions, but not everything can be neatly divided between fact and fancy. Not when our world is so full of miracles."

"The blessings of the Realm are always good and gentle."

"Not entirely, but I'm the sort to give myself over to hope." Thomas beckoned. "The kitchen is a cozy space, and the extra warmth is best for Durst. He's from a hot climate. Doesn't much care for our cold season. Do you play cobble-take?"

"Sorry, no. Never heard of it."

"Lovely. Durst prefers games of strategy, and you'll prove a better opponent than I ever could. It'll pass the evening. We haven't much else for entertainment unless you happen to be longing for a soliloquy."

Varti stepped into the kitchen with a sense of entering forbidden territory. As Thomas drifted from cast iron stove to cannister to kettle with careless grace, Varti retreated to the table and sat across from Durst, whose seat was nearest to the hearth. All those cooking implements were intimidating, almost as if entering a mother's domain had become taboo for Newcombers. That had to be the reason why Varti was more uncomfortable being in a kitchen than he was facing a gorgon.

Durst didn't budge. For all Varti knew, he had his eyes closed behind his goggles. But the snakes were definitely taking turns peeking at him. It was a pattern. He'd just about sorted out their surveillance technique when Durst sighed. "Are you also cursed to stare?"

Rudeness came in many forms, and they weren't necessarily lies. But Varti's curse seemed happiest when it could combine the two. Still, it didn't seem to want to get him killed. He let slip a relatively inoffensive lie. "I worry about them, with Bittern coming on."

Durst angled his head, frown deepening. Then he pointed to his head. "Them?"

"It never snows here. Bittern is the balmiest season."

"You are not deceiving anyone."

The ridiculous lies were easier to bear. Near-truths led to misunderstandings.

"Why speak at all?" challenged Durst.

"I can't bear silences."

"Are you compelled to fill them by that contrary-minded curse?"

"I enjoy embarrassing myself. It endears me to all the best people."

"I suppose it would not be cruel enough if you could defeat this binding with silence. So it humiliates you? Is it your pride that stings? Or your conscience?"

He had to think about that.

Durst flashed those jagged teeth of his. "Lie to me all you want, but if you cheat at cobbles, death can put an end to your embarrassment."

195

Thomas brought bowls of thick vegetable soup. "Now, gentlemen. Let us embrace a spirit of conviviality for what remains of the day."

He joined them, and they ate in silence. The food was good, but Varti kept darting looks at Thomas, waiting for him to explain why he'd been carried off. But once their bowls were empty, the man announced, "Since the others are away, Mr. Weller, you will help Durst with the outdoor chores, and I will see to the indoor ones. Make yourselves useful until sunset."

Varti frowned.

Thomas snapped his fingers. "You weren't prepared for this turn of events. Fear not, I'll lend you something warmer."

He trailed after the man, who led him upstairs and showed him to a spare room. Then there was a thick woolen sweater in his hands. And still no word of explanation. Varti pulled the thing over his head but wrestled back out of it. The knit snagged on his vest buttons and watchchain. First ridding himself of watch and chain, vest, and the tie he wore to work, he tried again. The sweater was meant for a much taller man, and Varti had to roll up the sleeves, but there was no mistaking the scent of pipe smoke.

Stealing back downstairs, he took a meandering course back to the kitchen, peeking into odd corners, searching for any sign of Doggerel. No dog bed or blanket. No food or water dish. Maybe one of the outbuildings was a kennel? But Varti seriously doubted that the hound was meant for cages.

Out in the yard, Durst's stride lengthened, and Varti didn't bother trying to keep up. But the gorgon's snakes bobbed their heads at him, as if urging him to hurry.

Durst turned back. And waited. "I have not been here a week, but Furze explained the basics. You will need to do the eggs." His smile was impressively sinister. "The hens do not like me."

Basket in hand, Varti stepped into slightly more familiar territory. Every earlymost academy student spent their Fulnisses volunteering at either the Bestiary or the Garden Wall, gaining an appreciation for the hard work that went into feeding the city. Gathering eggs was nostalgic, and the hens were docile enough. It didn't hurt that he'd always liked the feel of warm feathers. That was probably Ramage's fault.

Eggs collected, he checked their supply of food and water. Unsure how else to proceed, he delivered the eggs to Thomas at the kitchen door, then followed the sound of an axe to where Durst was splitting logs.

"The horses are gone with the rest, so there is little else we can do."

A solid knell passed before Durst offered Varti the axe, and they swapped roles. It felt good to swing into a clean split. Oh, he might ache from it tomorrow, but Varti was enjoying himself.

"They do get cold."

Varti glanced over to where Durst crouched, gathering another armload of firewood to add to their stack. His snakes were all looking Varti's way again.

"My undulation," said Durst. "I have a turban for your balmy Bittern temperatures."

To his amusement, the snakes wove neatly together, snug against Durst's head, as if ready to be bundled. He ventured, "Bitterns here are short."

"It is already too cold for my tastes, but I wanted something remote." He straightened and said, "I will decide if I want to endure more once I have met the elusive Mr. Holmes for myself."

"People say he's charming …?"

"You have been asking around?"

"I'm good at wheedling secrets out of people."

Durst hummed. "I suppose badges have access to information. Did you look me up?"

"Never even occurred to me."

"Find anything?"

Varti tartly replied, "Every detail, right down to your mother's marmalade recipe."

"So long as her basbousa recipe is still safe, I do not think she will come after you." Durst's lips quirked. "And you would not have found anything. I told you, did I not? If someone sees me, it is for the last time."

Which could be taken as fair warning that Varti's days were numbered. But it didn't really feel like a threat. Just a diresome boast.

They kept right on splitting wood until the day was fading. Inspecting a couple of blisters forming on his palms, Varti trudged up the grassy rise beyond the house. From the top, he could see the silhouette of Newcomb against clouds gone red and pink and amber.

He'd missed lunch with Phil. And the post-mortem with Dr. Kang. And Hexadille Porter's photographs.

The road home wasn't that long. Not an easy jog, but a doable one.

Durst's boots thudded dully up the slope after him. He said, "Do not try to leave."

"I wasn't even considering it." As good as a confession.

"If you run, I will have to bring you back. Orders." The gorgon joined him in considering the sunset. "Do you want me to ask

Mr. Hudson why he brought you? Perhaps over dinner?"

"Don't you dare."

"He is ... different, but he is also harmless. And he means you no harm. Unless you try to leave. Then, it becomes my job to bring you back, and I am not harmless. So do not try to leave."

"You look fast."

"Have you ever attempted outrunning a gorgon before?"

"Yes ...?"

Durst bent so they were more on a level, and he calmly repeated his order. "Do not try to leave."

# 33

## *Out of Harm's Way*

There was a definite benefit to stepping beyond one's usual boundaries. Perspective.

Ever since graduation, Varti had given himself over to his small routines, even found comfort in them. But today, he'd ridden on a steam cycle and in an automobile. He was a guest at a lakeshore estate. He'd faced a ghost, a gorgon, and a majordomo who knew his way around a kitchen. And none of them had cared a tin cog that he'd lied to them. Repeatedly.

Just like Dr. Kang and Kel and Henna, they knew about his affliction. And they weren't the only ones. Ramage never minded when his tongue slipped, and Aril and Burr were endlessly gracious. Tybalt may have taken offense, but he'd been drunk, and Phil was there to sort him out.

So if he had a partner who could explain, or if he was part of a cohort who knew he was folk-spelled, couldn't they all just … get over it and get on with it?

Why was he still under observation? Why keep him in the basement, apparently basking under else lights? Yes, working with the public was out, but why not simply assign him to the irregulars?

"Fourteen years," he said miserably.

"Thirteen snakes," Durst replied in a lazy way. He'd eaten more than half of the meat pie Thomas had served for the evening meal.

Thomas smilingly suggested, "Twelfth Night."

Varti pursed his lips. He rather wanted to say *elevenses*, but the curse wouldn't allow it, and everyone lapsed back into silence.

Durst set up a bizarre game board. Varti had always played chess on a six-sided board, but Durst's rehearsal of the rules matched the two-player version of the game Varti knew. He outmaneuvered the gorgon in their first bout, only to lose the next two games.

Thomas said, "I'll just lay a fire in your room, shall I?"

Varti sat back in his chair, his gaze on the fire, content in a way that brought Sylvester Thornapple to mind. He'd enjoyed his evening at the Banderole & Bugle, too. All that was missing here was the smell of pipe smoke and Doggerel in easy reach so he could scratch the big brute behind his ears. He tried to think back. Did he stay home because he preferred it? Or had he allowed his embarrassment or his pride to corner him there?

"Cards?" asked Durst, who brought out a deck and began shuffling.

"My expertise."

The gorgon explained the rules of a game in which they would compete to collect sets of cards. He'd never seen a deck like this. There were only four suits. But it was simple enough to learn and varied enough to stay interesting. At some point during their third hand, Thomas reappeared with snifters and a bottle of liquor in a queer shade of green.

Durst dealt him in. Then said, "Mr. Weller wants to know why he is here."

"Didn't I say?" Thomas's glance was apologetic.

"I didn't mind dropping by," Varti said stiffly. "My sudden disappearance won't inconvenience anyone."

Thomas grimaced. "Ah. The arrangements were made in haste. When an Oracle speaks, who can argue? To be frank, I wanted you out of harm's way."

Durst silkily inquired, "More harmful than me?"

"While you are a potential threat, I fear our Mr. Weller was in danger of meeting a much more active one." To Varti he added, "I'm sorry I couldn't do more for you. All I can really say is that I hoped to give you a good night by sparing you a bad one."

"Leave it there," ordered Varti. "Ignorance is bliss."

"There's really nothing more I can tell you. Except that the Oracle is never wrong. And my timing is always good."

Varti's gaze strayed to the man's watch with its missing hands.

Durst cleared his throat and pointed up. "This one."

Following the direction he indicated, Varti frowned at the stout beams overhead.

"Too far." Durst blandly repeated, "This one."

The snake at the front, directly above the gorgon's right eyebrow, rose a little higher and held his head in a superior sort of way, like he outranked the others.

Varti bobbed his head.

The green snake swayed, eyes glittering.

Gesturing with his cards, Durst said, "You may call him Driss. Or at least think of him as Driss, since your tongue is bridled."

"At least until your unspelling," murmured Thomas before

rearranging the cards in his hand, then spreading them on the table. "I'm out."

Durst grunted. "Another?"

"Another round of cards, another round of drinks. Perhaps some fruit and nuts," offered Thomas, bouncing up and moving toward a cabinet.

Varti surrendered his cards and watched them disappear under Durst's big hand. When the gorgon didn't move, Varti looked up into the bright facets of his goggles.

"Not the answer you were hoping for?"

How could he answer? Yes, Thomas had answered Varti's question. But he'd raised another one. Varti desperately wanted to know if Thomas's oracle—the one who was always right— had mentioned his unspelling. Because while everyone else referred to it as a remote possibility requiring the intervention of fae deities or complex mage-craft, Thomas made it sound like a foregone conclusion.

If his quadricentennial coin hadn't been upstairs in the pocket of his vest, Varti might have been tempted to summon Purdle. But what would he even say?

*Where is this oracle?*
*Is my unspelling certain?*
*Who can accomplish it?*
*Where have they been?*
*I've waited long enough.*

# 34

## *Portentous Asides*

VESPER 10, FOUR NINETY-EIGHT
VONNEDAY
5 KNELLS, 8 KNICKS
ON THE FIRST FACE OF THE CLOCK

Varti woke enough to reach for his covers and pull them up over his shoulder. Was the radiator not working? But the room smelled wrong, and his head rather hurt, and the man crossing the room wasn't Phil.

Thomas worked quietly, adding wood to the fire. When he turned from his task and met Varti's gaze, he murmured, "Sleep longer, Mr. Weller. Take rest while you can."

Which made him sit up.

And regret doing so.

Holding his head, he grumbled, "Bless all doomsayers. The more cryptic, the better."

Thomas hurried over and poured water from the crystal decanter on the bedside table. "I don't mean to. These sorts of things just slip out. Mr. Holmes grouses as well. Lack of evidence and all that. But maybe you can sympathize? I have a strong knack, and it can be ... impressively inconvenient. Not unlike your current circumstances, since I can't control my words."

Varti downed the water.

Thomas refilled his glass. "I know it doesn't sound as awful as it is, but you'll see, by and by. Offhand remarks have a way of being true. So rest. At least until the sun sees fit to rise."

After the man left, Varti tried to decide if it would be worse to always lie or to always tell the truth. No, that wasn't quite it. Thomas Hudson was plagued by portentous asides. No, there was more to it. Varti was quite sure the man hadn't been telling the whole truth.

Because it was too much to get into at this knell?

Or was it because Thomas had something to hide?

Without his usual trip to the steam baths, Varti's jawline was decidedly scruffsome, but his kit included a clean shirt. The debate between his own vest and the borrowed sweater was settled by the frost on the spare room's windowpane. He was still rolling the sleeves higher when he arrived in the kitchen, where a stranger was talking with Thomas.

Had the other members of the household returned? The woman had at least a decade on Varti. Middling height, green eyes, rosy cheeks, fair hair bobbed. She was wrapped in a capacious striped apron, and a pair of tortoiseshell reading glasses hung from a beaded chain around her neck.

She looked Varti up and down. "Who's this then?"

"Mr. Weller is an applicant for the gap in our ranks," said Thomas. "Our paths crossed quite serendipitously."

"Well, there's no arguing that."

Thomas made the introduction. "Regina Watson is our cook.

Last night's fine pie was her handiwork."

"It was slop." Varti covered his eyes with his hand.

"Folk-spelled, I'm afraid," supplied Thomas. "Mr. Weller is lying. He polished off two pieces. Didn't leave a flake of pastry behind."

Without a fuss, the woman said, "Call me Reggie. Everyone does."

Varti looked to Thomas and waited.

"Have breakfast with us. Durst will drive you back ... hmm. What time do you think it will be before the fog retreats into the channels. Nine knells? Ten to be safe?"

Safe from what?

Varti suspected Thomas of further waylaying him by giving him a tour of the house, then insisting that he visit the outbuildings. Two shaggy horses now stood in the paddock, but if there were any other household members besides Reggie hanging about, they didn't show themselves.

It was the first knell on the second face of the clock before Durst stoked the fire into readiness in the woodburning automobile.

Neither of them made any attempt at conversation on the return journey. Varti propped an arm out the open window, enjoying the feel of the sun and the wind as Newcomb loomed increasingly large.

As Durst took the turning onto Old Livery Road, Varti couldn't think of a way to explain to the gorgon that his automobile was in direct violation of vehicle codes for the Carpentry District. But Durst stopped just shy of the line of shadow that marked the edge of the Drears.

"This far, is what Mr. Hudson said. Can you find your way from here?"

Hugging his bag to his chest, Varti said, "I'll be lost without you."

"Careful," he warned, pointing up. "They believe you."

Varti dropped to the curb, closing the door with a snap. Through the open window, he promised, "I'll miss you."

Durst huffed what might have been a laugh, pulled away, and executed a completely illegal U-turn, bumping over a boulevard in order to gain the in-bound lane.

"Nicely done," muttered Varti, glad he was still out of uniform. As a badge, he couldn't condone that sort of behavior. Oh. Varti pressed his hand to thick wool. He'd been so comfortable in the sweater, he'd completely forgotten to return it.

Slinging the strap of his bag over one shoulder, Varti aimed for a side road that would give him a quieter jog home. He was zigzagging between tenements when he caught a flash of copper tape and slowed to a stop. Backing up a couple of steps, he spotted it again. The other end of this alley was cordoned off.

He strode forward and found that the next two were similarly taped off.

And at the next, he spied a badge from the foot patrol standing at the other end of that alley, his back to Varti and to the copper tape that forbade entry.

Had there been a traffic accident? A medical emergency?

It was too soon for it to be another murder.

Picking up his pace, Varti ran through a courtyard and turned onto a street that would open up in front of The Green Man. But it was completely barricaded, closed to all vehicles as well as foot traffic.

Fully anxious now, Varti darted down a narrow alley, popping out behind a grand old house with gingerbread trim. This place housed their historical society and served as a community center for the Carpentry District. The ginnel between it and the next building was barely wide enough for his shoulders. Phil wouldn't have fit unless he worked his way through sideways. But this was Varti's best option. It would put him directly behind The Green Man.

Leaves and debris always accumulated here, so he wasn't exactly stealthy as he made a final push toward home. One more intersection, and he'd be at the vine-draped alley that he used every day.

The smell hit him first. Terrible in its familiarity.

What was the stench of death doing here?

He knew so many people in this neighborhood. Good people. When he reached their alley, he was already sick with dread over what he'd find. But he had to know.

Varti peered through.

More copper tape crisscrossed the other end, and he could see barriers and the cloaks of milling badges beyond. And in the alley itself—his alley—was the seventh victim.

# 35

## *Scrying Stone*

VESPER 10, FOUR NINETY-EIGHT
VONNEDAY
2 KNELLS, 3 KNICKS
ON THE SECOND FACE OF THE CLOCK

**B**adges were everywhere, but only one had an unruly mop of orange curls. Heart in his throat, Varti croaked, "For shame, Philtrum. You've spoiled the ivy."

Phil whipped around, eyes wide as they stared at each other from across a fresh crime scene.

"Where were you? No, I don't care. Rust and ashes, stay there. I'll come round!"

Disobedience was instantaneous, because Varti wanted to get to his best friend—and answers—that much quicker. They met at the corner, and Phil grabbed him by the shoulders, looking him up and down. Varti unloaded a bunch of pointless insults that Phil didn't even seem to hear.

He asked, "Whose woolens are these?" As if that was more important than the bloodbath on their doorstep. "You missed our meeting, and when I came looking, Kel said you'd been carried off by a gorgon. I couldn't make crowns or laurels of the things you left behind. But I thought ... *wait*? Was the inverted Bittern's Garden asking me to wait? So I waited up. Or tried to.

Woke to screams and cries for help at half gone eight when poor old Kenny from across the way noticed the blood. Might be the quickest a badge was ever on the scene." Heaving a shuddering breath, he whispered, "You're all right, then? Truly?"

"Backwoods ninny," he said snootily, like they were twelve again and name-calling was easier than admitting you cared.

"So … a gorgon?"

"Harmless. Mostly. I do wonder about his hair-snake friends. They have it in for me, so I kept my distance."

Phil cautiously admitted, "I don't know how to interpret that. If I go with simple opposites, the mental image is … definitely skewed by my overwhelming interest in meeting a gorgon. How did you get around the whole death-gaze thing?"

"I'll hire him to kill you, shall I? Surest way to arrange matters. I can easily afford an international expert."

"I dearly hope that you're here now because he's actually a fine, upstanding citizen."

"Yes."

Phil wilted. "What is happening to us, Varti?"

"I have no answers."

He frowned. "Should we summon Purdle?"

"Already done for the day. I needed four words to apologize to my host for the staggering inconvenience that my well-intentioned kidnapping and subsequent survival caused him." That had come out rather well.

Phil gripped Varti's shoulders harder. "Survival?"

"Nobody trusts oracles."

"Sweet Ireeni. At this point, I'd believe that you've solved this whole case and just can't tell me who to arrest."

"You've always been better at procedure."

Phil muttered, "I'm *not*. You're the one. Always have been. But somehow, they've left me in charge."

"I'll outrank you before you know it."

With a searching look, Phil admitted, "I'd love to spite this curse by turning its lie into a pure and shining truth. But right now, I need you in my cohort. Hexadille has already taken photographs. She thinks she's onto something. And Dr. Kang is around front. But we were waiting. I thought we should wait."

Varti pulled the overlong sleeves of the sweater over his hands. "Right to it, then."

They worked their way back to the front of the building.

Phil suggested taking the sweater off so it wouldn't become stained.

Shirtsleeves rolled up, Varti accepted both gloves and a sample kit.

Kel looked on, her jaw set, daring anyone to question her right to be there. She lifted her chin in greeting, and he rolled his eyes. Both rude *and* unprofessional.

Worse, he caught sight of Highmost Purnal Sarah Yamada standing off to one side with the man who was either her assistant or her bodyguard. Possibly both. She and Dharm worked closely enough that Varti surmised they were actually partners, even though the man never wore a uniform.

She noticed him and closed the distance. With a nod to Phil, she addressed Varti. "I've had a quick look, and so has Kemp. What do you think *you* can tell us, Weller?"

"The truth."

She blinked, then coolly ordered, "Any lead is more than we have. Find it."

So for the second time in four days, Varti let his focus shift and sharpen as he searched for answers. Even though so many people were waiting on him, and their expectations added a strange pressure to the scene, Varti took his time. And as he went, he kept remembering lines from the case reports in which Sherlock Holmes had swept in and found clues that the badges had overlooked.

A single hair or fiber. Mud on the soles of shoes. Ash from a certain brand of cigar. The state of a victim's fingernails. An oddsome odor or stain. An item gone missing. An item inadvertently left behind. Varti wondered how long the consulting detective had studied in order to make deductions that appeared effortless in the moment.

In this case, there was no message conveniently scratched in the alley grit. And it was more difficult to check someone's fingernails when you had to first locate their hand. The shattering of bones and dismemberment were the same, but how had it been accomplished? Dr. Kang insisted that no bladed weapon had been used. Mauling was closer to correct, yet there was never any sign of an animal on the scene.

Varti found an arm and realized that their killer was growing more indiscriminate.

The first five victims had all been women under the age of thirty.

Mr. Acres had broken that trend, but here was another shift. This man's beringed hand—nails tidy, veins prominent, knuckles slightly swollen—was spotted by age. Yes, there, partly obscured by ivy and stained by blood. This gentleman was old enough to have gone completely silver.

Dr. Kang would sort out anything the body could tell them,

so Varti tried to focus on the setting. The Bastion was desperate for any clue to the killer's identity. But there were no footprints to hint at size or weight or gender or race. Maybe the killer didn't have feet? What then? Wings? Varti peered upward, wondering if something could have dropped down on the man from above. He made a mental note to go up onto The Green Man's roof.

The victim's clothing was unusual, at least in this district. His vest had all sorts of fussy tucks, and the fabric looked expensive. What was a poshsome gentleman doing in the Drears?

Looking for answers, he gently turned the man's torso, wincing when it exposed much of his chest cavity. But there … his watchchain. He had nearly as many charms as a mercy jangling from its considerable length. Triple swagged, with homages to multiple deities and dignitaries. He half-turned to surrender it to Phil, who knew more about folksome things, but then Varti realized the significance of six bright hex-cut gemstones. They were rank markers. This man was a mage.

What if …?

He cast around and soon spotted a fang-shaped crystal on the ground. There were other loose gemstones as well. Dropped? No, they looked to have been set in a pattern, but the arrangement had been scuttled by the attack.

Bringing the watchchain to Phil, he waited for his verdict.

"A six-fold mage? But what was he doing …?" And then, "Oh, nooo. I *know* him. But why …?"

He turned to speak to Yamada, and Dr. Kang stepped up and tapped Varti's other hand. "What did you keep hidden from him?"

"Nothing important."

"Show me."

Glad the man had noticed, Varti uncurled his fingers from around the fang-shaped crystal.

Dr. Kang's eyebrows jumped. "That's a scrying stone."

Varti was aware that such things were used for tracking, but he was vague on details. However, he knew that in some cases, a mage would be asked to trace an item or a person by magical means. Had this man's scrying stone led him here? If so, what had he been searching for?

The monster that killed him?

The water sprite and his newt?

The dog who was lost again?

"I'll just show this to Yamada for you," offered Dr. Kang. "Need anything?"

"No."

Dr. Kang patted his pockets and came up with a jotter. "For any case notes you want to make."

Varti returned to his former position and quickly drafted a map showing the placement of the crystals in relation to the alley walls and door. And turning to a new page, he creased and tore six small flags, which he placed beside each item so that the photographer wouldn't overlook them. To his annoyance, despite this definitely being official business, the flags weren't numbered in the right order. They weren't even all numbers.

Two.

Y.

Theta.

Eight-one.

Green.

J.

Really very lovely. But it didn't matter, so long as the positions were marked.

Varti was nearly finished picking through everything when a low growl startled him. Doggerel stood at the other end of the alley, hackles raised, teeth bared as he sniffed at the air. Someone behind Varti shouted, and he heard the cocking of more than one firearm.

He straightened and lifted his hands in the air, still facing the hound, and hoped he was blocking their shot. The dog paced forward, head low, that deep rumble a warning. But for whom?

Varti winced inwardly as the hound paused to sniff at a coagulating spray of blood, then proceeded forward, marring what remained of the crime scene with his big paws.

Because he was just a dumb dog who didn't know any better?

Then why did each footfall feel like a calculated choice?

And why did it leave Varti wondering if there had already been blood on his paws?

Phil's voice rang out. "It's all right! It's fine! Stand down. He's one of ours. A tracker!"

Which wasn't exactly true, but the badges holstered their weapons.

"His name's Doggerel. Weller's been working with him for a while now."

Such vague terms. Almost a lie. Only one week had passed since Varti first encountered the dog. Three murders had taken place in that time, and during the time of each death, Varti had no idea where Doggerel had been.

"You're not a suspect," he lied.

The hound reared up, planting his forepaws on Varti's shoulders, staining his shirt with blood while he peered over his head at the body of the mage.

Again, Varti had the sense that he wasn't propping up an ordinary dumb beast, and ignoring it was no longer an option. Phil had his guard up, too. Folksome things were afoot. But that didn't stop Varti from being glad that the dog had come home to him.

"I expect to hear your alibi. In your own words."

Doggerel peered down at him, then slopped his forehead with a lick.

"Well, I didn't miss you. Not for a single moment." Varti roughed up wiry fur wherever he could reach it. "You didn't miss a thing."

Phil stood in the alley entrance, expression troubled. "Right, you two. Doggerel, move to the other end of the alley. Consider yourself on guard duty. Nobody gets in from behind. Varti, you'll assist Dr. Kang once the photographer gets frames of everything you flagged."

It took knells.

Dr. Kang's steady commentary made it somewhat less awful. He turned their careful retrieval into a lecture for a classroom of one. Unless you counted Doggerel. His ears were pricked, so Varti felt certain he was listening in.

When it was over, Dr. Kang removed his gloves, brought out his handkerchief, and dabbed at eyes wet with tears. "Poor bloke. It's almost as if ... oh. Oh, now."

Varti waited for him to finish the thought.

Dr. Kang turned back staring into the bloodstained alley. "You know, it might explain why these ghosts aren't behaving in the usual way."

They weren't?

Oh. Varti had missed yesterday's meeting. What had Hexadille shared?

With a sidelong look to include him, Dr. Kang quietly posed, "What if the reason we can't find any sign of their attacker is because they were attacked from within?" He hugged his hands to his chest, then curled his fingers as if digging into his own flesh and flung his arms wide. "I think they might have been torn open and ... and *discarded*."

# 36

## *Touch Salt*

**V**arti was unwound past ticking by the time Phil came over to report, "Dr. Kang has gone ahead to the morgue, and I'm dismissing my team. It's been a long tocking for all of us. Reinforcements are arriving, and I'll wait here for the cleaners and for a security detail. Nobody wanted to stay the night with a fresh ghost forming, so the building's standing empty. And Mr. Whilom sprang every cog he had when he realized that the mercies would be coming. He begged me not to let them clutter our alley with open flames."

Vigil candles would definitely break the Carpentry District's safety codes.

Phil said, "I want you to go to Ramage's for the night."

"That's a terrible idea."

"But a bath is a wonderful one. For both of you." And Phil signaled to someone loitering in the shadows. "Badge Mirza, can I turn him over to you?"

"Not a problem."

Varti glanced up into Kel's stern face and bit his lip lest he say anything untoward.

Phil said, "Ramage is expecting him at The Speckled Hen. Do you know the place?"

"Who doesn't?" she asked, sounding impressed.

The bathhouse took care of Varti's and Doggerel's mutual mess. Varti gave up on salvaging his shirt and changed into yesterday's, then added the sweater on top. Doggerel immediately buried his nose against Varti's belly. It stood to reason. Probably smelled like home.

Kel had her cycle waiting out front when he emerged, and she eased into an inbound lane. "He's keeping up just fine," she remarked.

Doggerel was loping alongside her cycle. Varti whistled softly and murmured, "Bad dog."

Kel barely tapped the accelerator, and they were rolling into a slot behind Ramage's place. It wouldn't have been a long walk, but Varti was grateful to forgo the necessity.

Ramage flutter-hopped over, radiating concern. "Kemp sent a messenger, and we've made preparations. I'll bring you in the back way." And to Kel, "As a small token of my thanks, dinner is mother's treat if you'll find your way to the front counter. That way, we can chat for a bit."

About Varti, no doubt. He elbowed her and gruffly said, "I'm sure you can choke something down to be polite."

"Yes, thank you," said Kel. "It's been a long day all around."

"Time flies at a frolic," Varti said sweetly.

"He's wracked, cross- and sideward. Want me to carry him in?" Kel offered with a similarly cloying tone. It was frightening, actually.

"Waited long enough to offer, you blighty wench."

Kel got down into his face—also quite frightening—and asked, "Is that any way to introduce me to your mother?"

Ramage glanced between them. "Youuu ... know each other well?"

"He's my boss."

"You *do* realize he's lying?"

"Yeah, I know. I'm kind of chuffed." She headed toward the street entrance, but before she rounded the corner, she looked back, shook her head in wonder, and asked, "Blighty wench?"

"Too right!" Varti tossed after her. Then bit his knuckle.

"I quite like her. Why didn't she know you do, too? Did you try to spare her? That's just like you." Ramage got a wing around his shoulders and steered him toward the back entrance. "If you'll just get the catch for me? Thank you kindly. In with you, Doggerel. That's the way!"

Varti had never been in this part of the building. He could tell they were behind the kitchen. Why hadn't it occurred to him that Ramage and his staff lived on the premises?

"This way. It's possibly a challenge for you, although Burr and Aril do manage the climb in a pinch, and they have hooves. Opposable toes are occasionally a plus." He preceded Varti up, wings partially spread for balance.

Varti faced a series of logs set into brackets, creating a ladder suited to Ramage's feet. The distance between them was a definite stretch for Varti, and the bark was rough against his palms, but he was getting on all right. Until he realized the climb wasn't over after the first story. Having surmounted the second, he decided it was best not to look down.

A platform soon came within reach, and Ramage held out a

leg. "Nearly there," he encouraged.

Varti grabbed a scaled knuckle and let the harpy pull him the rest of the way up. It was immediately apparent that this was Ramage's private space. The room held a variety of roosts, and an east-facing window looked large enough for escape.

Hopping onto one of his perches, Ramage pointed with a wing to a pile of blankets and cushions on the floor in the corner. "Aril contributed a ground nest and a sleeping robe, and Burr brought up food mere knicks ago. I expect you to eat it all."

"Not hungry," Varti lied, edging toward the drop. Doggerel was watching for him, his forepaws on the second rung. Unsure if it was wise, Varti patted the edge and whistled.

Doggerel was up in a galumphing scramble that took a fraction of the time Varti had needed.

"There's something there for him, too. So eat, change, and tuck yourself in. I'll check on you once things settle down, but if you need anything, there's a bell. That teensy silver one. Give it a tap, and I'll know."

"What do I have to do to be rid of you?" Varti asked sourly.

Ramage spread his wings and alighted to the floor, swishing closer until he loomed over Varti. "Touch salt, brave badge."

Varti gathered all three of the large crystals into a fist and bowed his head. "I don't need you. Never did."

"You're sweet to say so."

"I know I'm your favorite." Stupid curse and its twists. Why must it use lies to betray his fears and his feelings?

"Is that so?" Ramage quietly countered, backing away so that Varti had to let go of his necklace. "Consider where you stand, and consider what that means."

Then with a rustle of wings, he dropped away.

Varti slept so deeply, he wondered if Burr or Aril had put something into his tea. Because he woke to sunlight bright against his eyelids and turned his head into his pillow. But then came the sound of distant bells. Not Old Ebonnel or silver Griffdawn or the realm-stirring peals of Edwinna the damsel-bell, all of whom were part of the carillon in the heights of the Composite Cathedral. And possibly inspiration for Tyro's line of bellpull pipe tobacco.

No, these bells were high and airy and sweetly insistent. He couldn't help but listen. And then he was awake.

Maybe Ramage had an alarm clock?

Pushing aside the down filled blankets that made up his nest, Varti glanced around in confusion. It was still dark outside. It felt like the final knells of the night, time for him to go out for his run. Yet there was light so bright, he'd mistaken it for the sun.

More details crashed into him, each more perplexing than the next.

Doggerel was gone. Hopefully not for good.

Ramage was there, crouched on one of his perches, face upturned toward the light. He looked utterly calm, even though the light didn't have a source. The air around him swirled like a forming ghost, only instead of a bone-pale emanation, motes of teensy sparks gave the air a blueish shimmer. And the whole of it pulsed in time with the mysterious jingling.

Varti slowly turned and sat, huddling in his blankets.

Without opening his eyes, Ramage asked, "Will you keep my secret, Weller?"

He only shook his head.

The harpy turned his face and opened his eyes, which seemed to swim with those flecks of brightness. "Not even Philtrum knows."

Varti shook his head again.

Ramage accepted that with a half-nod, and his eyes drifted shut.

This was ... meditation? Or an attitude of prayer. Not being terribly familiar with the workings of deities, Varti couldn't begin to guess if this was typical. Phil certainly never glowed, and there were no singing bells when he did his readings. But Ramage was the most devout person in Varti's acquaintance, and his seemed an honest sort of devotion.

Was Varti rude to watch? He was finding it difficult to look away from all the misty magic on display. It was beautiful, really. Ethereal. Until things began to coalesce.

He scrambled onto his hands and knees, but was he meant to be rushing to Ramage's aid or running away? Because whatever was forming, it was Olde. But Ramage's serenity blossomed into a genuine smile, and so Varti crouched there, half-hidden by blankets, holding his breath.

The bells rang more clearly, and then there were three other figures in the room.

Ramage rose up on his perch, then calmly stepped down into their midst, welcoming them each with a nod. Like this was as much his routine as a morning jog was Varti's.

He didn't recognize them. Though they had wings, they weren't harpies because they had arms. Draping layers of cloth made them modest, and Varti couldn't tell if they were male or female. Only that they carried themselves with dignity as they helped Ramage to undress, to wash, and to put on clean clothing for the day.

The loose half-breeches with buttoned cuffs.

The colorful sash, snug around his waist.

The swagging layer of a tasseled scarf.

As soon as the trio finished their work, they dissolved into those same glittering motes and gently dissipated, leaving Varti and Ramage alone in the dark.

"Come here, Weller."

"No ...?" he croaked. It was almost true, he felt so weak.

But he made it to his feet, and he shuffled to the harpy. Ramage said, "They left the last bit to you. Touch salt, brave badge."

Varti followed the sweep of a wing to a larger version of the altar shelf downstairs. Ramage's necklace rested there, all three of the large crystals giving off a faint glow. At his touch, they seemed to wake further. He didn't understand why. Neither could he ask.

He brought it to Ramage, whose crest lifted and settled. Then he spread his wings in a graceful way and bowed at the waist as if to royalty.

Varti carefully maneuvered the necklace's cord over showy feathers.

Ramage straightened and asked, "Lift the central shard for me?"

It still glowed between them, and Ramage studied it, then Varti.

"I can't wait to tell everyone," Varti whispered.

"We both know better."

Ramage placed a reverent kiss on the salt crystal. Last time, the simple caress had snuffed it, but it glowed steadily. The harpy's crest puffed, and he shook out his wings. If anything, he looked concerned. "Weller, be a dear? I know you only touch salt to humor me, but I would rather you didn't leave this nest without adding your prayer to mine."

"It will be a good day. Quiet and orderly."

"Kiss salt, love. This once, at least. For me."

Varti went up on tiptoe to better reach, and he touched his lips to the cool, flat surface. He held there, his gaze locked on Ramage's, hoping for some hint that he was doing this right ... doing some good.

Relief shone in the harpy's eyes as the glow slowly dwindled away. "Promise me, Weller. Set your feet with the utmost care." He grimly added, "I fear this day will have teeth."

# 37

## *The Imposter*

VESPER 11, FOUR NINETY-EIGHT
WILLIDAY
9 KNELLS, 13 KNICKS
ON THE FIRST FACE OF THE CLOCK

V arti had barely addressed the double stack of newspapers on his desk when Doggerel raised his head. Phil walked in, looking like he hadn't slept a wink. He didn't say anything, just sat heavily on a stool, reached into his vest pocket, and brought out his guidance deck.

Folding and stacking papers to one side, Varti muttered, "You look well."

"It's been one thing after another since yesterday. Been here all night."

Which was nearly true. According to Ramage, Phil was the one who'd brought around Varti's uniform, gear, and Doggerel's harness during the night.

Phil added, "After this, I'll run home and catch a few knells. Promise."

"You make promises all the time. To everyone."

Phil blinked, then chuckled his way into a sigh. "Not much for commitment, am I?"

His friend was certainly dodgesome when it came to love.

Phil kept things casual. Varti sometimes wondered if that was his fault. Had his spelling tarnished both Varti's career and Phil's chances in the realm of romance?

Cards riffled in the quiet.

Phil seemed lost in thought.

Varti poked a finger into the vest pocket where the quadricentennial cog rested. Should he call for Purdle? What would he even say?

*You aren't always dodgesome.*

*Friendship is a commitment.*

*Did I spoil everything?*

*Are your hopes dashed?*

*Am I a burden?*

Phil glanced up, and Varti quickly lowered his gaze. He'd never waste Purdle's boon on such maudlin thoughts. Words were too precious, and work was more important.

"Hexadille begged a day or two. She needed to follow up on an idea. Said she'd be revisiting the scenes of the murders. Don't worry, I assigned a couple of badges to her, so she'll have some protection." Phil placed the cards on the table and fussed with straightening their edges. "Dr. Kang is also going back over everything. Looking for evidence to support a wild theory. Those are his own words."

He rested his elbows on his knees and peered under the worktable at Doggerel, who'd sprawled across Varti's feet like it was the only place he wanted to be.

"Any idea where he could've been?"

"On a murderous rampage."

"Did you ask him about the harness?"

"Made for lovely pillow talk."

Phil frowned, then asked, "What do you say, Doggerel? Shall I do a reading for you?"

An ear pricked.

"Varti first, but then it's your turn." And to Varti, "Lend me your hands, please."

He took the deck, and the first cut turned up a card with a rough chunk of crystal on it.

"Touch Salt," Phil said with a fond smile. "I meant to ask. How was your night at Ramage's?"

"About what you'd expect."

Phil's eyebrows rose.

It was such a normal thing to say, Varti actually looked to see if there was a puddle-jumping sprite lurking nearby. Then again, Ramage had said that the things Varti had witnessed were a secret. Private. Even from Phil.

"Right then. This first card is actually called Salt of Ages, but my aunt always did say 'touch salt' whenever it turned up. Maybe because of our close connection to Ramage's colony. It means protection, and it implies that you are being protected." Nodding slowly, Phil said, "Ramage would have done what he could for you. This confirms the strength of that protection, since the card leapt to the fore."

Cutting the deck, Phil winced at the next card revealed.

This one showed a figure with their face partially hidden by a smiling mask. The eye that peered out from behind seemed to gleam with menace.

"I drew this one a few days ago. The Imposter. Usually a warning, although sometimes it can indicate that the person who turns it up is hiding the truth from those around them."

Varti said, "Oh, well that can't apply to me."

"It might or it might not." Phil tapped the other card. "In conjunction with Salt of Ages, it could mean that you're being protected from someone who isn't what they seem. Or *by* them, actually, considering your recent removal from the city."

Phil reclaimed his deck and began to shuffle anew.

Doggerel heaved to his feet and trotted to the stairs, which he vaulted up without a backward glance.

"Doesn't want a reading," Phil remarked.

"Total coincidence," said Varti.

Which almost proved it wasn't.

It was nearing lunchbreak when Henna called from upstairs. "Mr. Weller? Doggerel got in! Naughty boy! Where do you think you're going?"

Varti left off filing and hurried to see what the hound had gotten into.

Henna stood with a sealed evidence box propped on her hip, the keys to the cage door in her hand. "I was just putting this lot away. Trial's done as of this morning. As soon as I had the door open, he pushed past me and ran right on through." She grumbled, "Should've known, the sneak. He's always nosing around this door. Like a cat watching a mousehole, he is."

The evidence locker was a long, narrow storeroom with high shelving units that were anchored right into the ceiling. Hooking ladders were needed to reach the oldest evidence boxes, but this wasn't a particularly large space. It didn't take long to locate Doggerel, who was sniffing along the edges of the shelves where boxes for the most recent cases were kept. The items inside were fresher, and Varti could imagine they carried the strongest scents.

It was his solemn duty to protect the contents of these boxes, so he grabbed the hound's ruff and pulled back.

A deep growl startled him into letting go, and a glare warned him off. Doggerel disappeared into the next aisle.

Henna came over, hands propped on hips. "I'll help you corral him toward the door."

"Yes!"

"No?" she asked. "It's the quickest way."

"Undoubtedly."

Henna hesitated. "I'll just get Kel, shall I?"

Varti was at a loss. He didn't think Doggerel was the killer, but was that wishful thinking? Endangering Henna and Kel wasn't an option. He steered Henna out the door and locked himself in. Then he went to reason with his dog. Or lie to him, anyhow.

He found Doggerel another aisle over from where he'd last been, his paws up on a shelf, stretching to sniff at the ones above.

"Hang on. I can reach it for you."

Doggerel shot him *such* a look, and then he reached up on his own.

Varti went very, very still. Because that wasn't a paw anymore. A furry hand stretched, and thick claws grazed the box.

Unclipping from his belt the short club that never saw use outside of training drills, Varti forced himself to take a step forward.

A deep growl resounded, much louder than the last.

Doggerel was still shifting, becoming more and more bipedal. Sturdy legs ended in paws, their claws scraping the concrete floor. Ribs shifted, and under the shag of gray fur, muscles realigned themselves, turning Doggerel into a powerful opponent. Into a monster who could rip his victim to pieces.

From out of view, Henna worriedly called, "Mr. Weller? Is everything all right?"

"Yes. He's already succumbed to a belly rub."

After a beat, she announced, "I'm getting Kel."

The clatter of her bootheels faded, and Doggerel's tail bristled. But then he slowly pointed at the evidence box he'd been trying to reach. And he spoke. "Benedick."

# 38

## *Friend*

VESPER 11, FOUR NINETY-EIGHT
WILLIDAY
11 KNELLS, 37 KNICKS
ON THE FIRST FACE OF THE CLOCK

Enzo yawned as he dragged a comb through unruly hair, snagging on a tangle halfway to his shoulder. "Umm ... Skrik?"

The imp fiddled until the knot came free. Skrik was the reason Enzo let his hair grow. The shadow imp was understandably reclusive by nature, but Enzo liked companionship. So rather than riding around in their amulet, Skrik kept to Enzo's shoulder, using hair for cover. The more there was, the less yanking Enzo had to endure.

"Where's the ... whatsit?" Enzo murmured, rummaging for the cloth he used to polish his spectacles. "Think there's coffee?"

"I can bring some," Skrik immediately offered.

"I know you can, but I meant to ask if Tuppence bought some?"

"You could rely on me more," he said sulkily.

Enzo was an only child, so he'd never experienced sibling rivalry in a firsthand sense ... until Purdle's contracting. Then he suddenly had two familiars, each trying to outdo the other, needing to know if they were loved at least as much, if not more than, their rival.

"If Tuppence has coffee somewhere in this apartment, I'd be grateful if you'd bring me some."

Skrik flickered away and returned with one of the thermal bottles that Jamie had recommended. Enzo gratefully broke the seal and inhaled fragrant steam. Newcomb was backward and roundabout in many ways, but they did other things very, very well. Tea might be the royal beverage, but Enzo was glad there was a distinct subculture devoted to strong, black coffee.

He'd been up until all hours, paging through the midnight blue book that Professor Coquelicot had left with him. Categorizing it was tricky. Some parts were like a journal, filled with posits and speculations. There were lists and sketches and recipes and runes. Other parts were nonsensical, but there were flashes of brilliance in the brainstorming.

Enzo had greedily pored over notes about amending magic circles, only to turn to a page that was completely dedicated to possible names for a new summon, most of which were crossed out.

There must have been a trip abroad at one point, because several pages read like a field journal, with both Spanish and French words in their descriptions.

Midway through the book, Enzo noticed a subtle shift in tone, as if the author had been making notes with the intention of producing something for publication. But by and large, the pages drifted from one topic to the next without any discernible plan. Being used to a more linear form of study, Enzo grew frustrated, especially when something interesting came up, but the author moved on to something else without reaching a satisfying conclusion.

Enzo thought it would take years to unravel this record, but the pursuit would be worthwhile. The author's intent had been personal enrichment, and in the latter sections, the observations were astonishing. Plenilune Marsk—for this is how the author had named himself on the flyleaf—had tried things Enzo had never heard of or imagined. Perhaps because a deity or dignitary became his patron and assisted in his crafting.

But the longer into the night Enzo read, the more convinced he became. There was a very different reason that this grimoire was so unique. Marsk didn't simply have good connections with Realmish entities. He'd been to the Realm for himself.

"Breakfast," announced Tuppence, who loomed over him in a manner that most would find threatening.

Enzo knew she was only eager to show him what she'd found. "Did you go out already?"

She snorted. "It is almost noon."

He grabbed for his wristwatch. He'd slept much later than intended, but he could still drop by Professor Oswald's office on his way to ... well, whichever lecture hall was on his schedule. Purdle would know. Or Cubit.

Tuppence held a sort of bakery box, and from it she brought out a crusty folded pie. She said, "Seelie told me that these are a favorite of growing boys."

"Aren't you glad we've made such knowledgeable friends?" Enzo asked, breaking off a corner and popping it into his mouth. "Did you find a mother you like?"

She inclined her head with great dignity. "Nine. So far. You will be pleased."

Taking a mouthful of tender meat, spicy peppers, and thick brown gravy, he smiled up into her face. "I'm hugely pleased,

Tuppence. Thank you for taking care of me."

After much rearranging of her many scarves—a sure sign she was flustered—Tuppence passed him a second pie and ordered, "Eat it all, young master. It will do you good."

Enzo didn't know what the future held, especially with regards to the book and the key. But it was considerably brighter than it had been in a while. Nutritional paste was permanently off the menu.

After some internal debate, Enzo placed the book and key in Tuppence's care before leaving their apartment. Better safe than sorry.

Staff offices took up three entire floors of the academy's tower. Hundreds of mages boasted a room here, and Enzo couldn't have navigated the honeycomb maze without help. Every door had the usual hexagonal brass plate, and these were numbered. But very few were inscribed with names. Instead, each mage had found unique ways to identify their domain. According to Professor Oswald, it was a longstanding tradition.

Enzo had questioned the need for so many professors. Even a city as robust as Newcomb couldn't possibly produce that many youngsters learning mage-craft. But Enzo had misunderstood. The Academy of Mages wasn't just a school. It was the hub of the entire mage community. Not every mage in residence presided over the lecture halls.

Professor Oswald used himself as a prime example. He wasn't overseeing any classes until next Milvine, but he advised thirty-odd students who shared his specialization. In addition, he mentored graduates in his field, many of whom had embarked on careers in the public sector. But for all of Newcomb's mages, this was home base.

When Enzo veered off to inspect the runic circle on an office door that had been painted emerald green, Purdle said, "That's the wrong hall."

"I know. Just a sec."

"Do you have time for a flit? That's what they call seconds here. Flits."

"Sorry." Enzo straightened and glanced around. He hated to admit it, but he was already lost.

"This way," Purdle said, only sounding a little patronizing. And after they were going in the right direction again, he said, "I meant to tell you, I really did. But then things were so distracting. And I was hungry. Do you know, I think eggy buns are just as good as toast. I can't decide between them, so I will love them both, just like you love me and Skrik the same." With a hopeful look, Purdle asked, "You *do* love me as much as Skrik? Even though I came later? I would've come sooner if I'd known."

Enzo gently redirected. "What had you forgotten to tell me?"

"Me? Oh! Yes. It's a new and momentous event." Sitting tall in the saddle, Purdle proudly announced, "I made a friend."

"Do you mean Arty and Seelie and Nunc? Them?"

"You shouldn't leave people out!" protested the sprite. "It might hurt Patina's and Jamie's feelings. But no. Not them. I found a friend of my own!"

Enzo had to smile. "That's very enterprising. What sort of friend are they?"

Purdle pondered that for several local flits, then sagely said, "A grateful one."

Professor Oswald wasn't in his office, and Enzo made it down to the lecture hall with minutes to spare. The room was unusually noisy. People mostly used the final minutes before a test to review, but nobody seemed to give a fig for Folk of the Woods and their Lore.

Having read several books on the subject, Enzo couldn't imagine there would be anything new on the exam, even if this was the advanced course. Or highmost, as per the local vernacular. He dared to hope it would include a practicum. He enjoyed the complexities of collaborating with something like a leaf sprite or a thistle-flit, but it was boring when all the professor wanted was for you to describe the attendant casting sequence line-by-line. Much more fun to actually *do* it.

He was trying to come up with an interesting twist to the potent intersection of overlapping runic circles when Arty slouched into the seat beside his.

"Good morning," Enzo offered. "Well, I suppose it's afternoon. Hold on. Are you even taking this course?"

"Nah." Arty offered his fingertips to Cubit.

"Nice to see you and all, but why are you here?"

"Just checking in. Making sure you're all right."

"Why wouldn't I be?"

"Been a tragedy, hasn't there?"

Enzo cut a look Purdle's way. "Has there?"

"Haven't you seen the papers?" Arty asked. "Front page news."

Purdle said, "Tuppence calls newspapers a waste of money. Why learn about a foreign place's concerns when you'll only be moving along? Not that she's always right. I often disagree with her. But ... privately. It's safest."

"Well, that's just widdershins." Arty pointed out, "You're *here*, same as the rest of us. And current events don't discriminate."

The sprite raised a hand. "Have you insulted me? Or Tuppence? It wasn't entirely clear, by your wording."

"Nah, not you. Really, it's Enzo who's the most widdershins of all. Only mage I ever met who's ruled by his familiars. Are you trying to protect him from the truth?"

Enzo considered his familiar's studiously averted eyes. "What did I miss?"

"Victim number seven was found in the Trestle District yesterday morning," said Arty.

"Purdle, did you know?"

"Me? Well ... yes. I suppose I did, but I was distracted!" To Arty he added, "I have a friend, you know. A friend of my own. Nobody else knew about it. Except Cubit, of course."

"You seem pleased," Arty said.

"I am! Unless Enzo isn't. Am I not allowed to have friends? I hope you'll allow it. I don't think I can be unfriendly now. I already granted a boon. We're getting on all right, but he didn't call for me yesterday. So I went to see him. It seemed the friendly thing to do. But I didn't like to get too close. I mean ... well! Murder is so messy."

Arty leaned forward. "You knew about the murder? You were there?"

"Not during, thankfully. But after." Purdle lifted his hands beseechingly to Enzo. "I should have said something. I could have, but I didn't want you to be sad. The Hound must have gotten to him. I wonder if he knew about you and him? Do you suppose it was a warning?"

Enzo glanced around, then lowered his voice to a whisper. "Purdle, be clear. Are you saying your friend was there? Why would they be anywhere near a murder?"

"Didn't I say? He's a badge. That's what they call their police officers here."

"And the Hound?"

"He was with my friend. Probably."

Enzo glanced at the front of the room. Class hadn't started yet. "Purdle, please," he begged, low and urgent. "How did you meet your friend?"

The sprite tapped his fingers together, looking guilty. "It was going to be a surprise. Because I'm just as good as Skrik, just as helpful. In my own way."

"And why...?" He stole a glance at Arty but went ahead. "Why would you think the Hound knows about me? We've never met. I doubt he even knows I'm looking for him."

"Because!" Purdle exclaimed, his eyes so full of sadness. "Because he killed your advisor."

Enzo whispered, "*What*?"

"Professor Oswald," supplied Arty. "He was victim number seven."

# 39

## *Simulacrum*

VESPER 11, FOUR NINETY-EIGHT
WILLIDAY
12 KNELLS, 32 KNICKS
ON THE SECOND FACE OF THE CLOCK

"Do you have time now? We better talk." Arty peered up at him through his flop of bangs. "Let's go."

"Now?" Enzo echoed, incredulous.

"Never cut class before?" Arty stood. "Plenty of cause. We're in shock. Come on, just follow me out."

Enzo felt awful for more than one reason, but nobody seemed to care when he scooped up Cubit and ducked out of the lecture hall on Arty's heels.

"You didn't bring it? The book, I mean."

"No. Sorry," replied Enzo. Yesterday, Arty had been as good as his word. He'd waited for Enzo, and he'd been curious about the meeting. He'd wanted to see the book, but Enzo had put him off.

"It's quite heavy," Purdle put in. "And very blue."

"I should think you'd like it. I mean, *you*'re quite blue."

Purdle pouted. Enzo knew from long experience that the sprite preferred compliments to comparisons.

Arty asked, "You gonna let me have a look sometime?"

"Honestly? I want to read more before I decide."

"Moving on, then." Arty waved for Enzo to follow. For once, they took an elevator down instead of up.

"There's an underground?" The doors slid open, revealing a long chamber reminiscent of a subway tunnel. Larger, though. Enzo was already reading shop signs. Locksmiths and mechanics. Steam cleaners and public bathhouses. Recycling centers and charging stations. No train tracks, though. Just the usual walkways and vehicle lanes.

"Plenty of good stuff on this level. It's not crowded in Fullnis, when everyone wants a bit of blue sky and balmy air, but once we're Bittern-blasted, this gets busy. We call these the Burrows, and they're named for the street we're under."

"So ... Cenotaph?"

"Guess that follows, but nah. Up at street level, that's just nicknamed Cenotaph Road because of the markers. The official name is Loyalty Road. So these are the Loyalty Burrows."

Purdle piped up. "Have you been teaching Enzo the wrong information?"

"It's like anything, innit? There's lots of ways to understand a thing. Layers of meaning." They joined the ranks of inbound pedestrians. "This is Loyalty. Clockwise 'round from here are Cannery, Livery, History, Industry, and Piety. The names are old as Olde. We learn this stuff as sprogs, same as the days of the week, seasons, and both faces of the clock."

Enzo glanced up at one of the ornate clocks that were posted everywhere in the city. "Two faces?"

"Twelve knells on a clock face, but twenty-four knells in a day. Past midnight is first face. Past midday is second face."

"Got it. It's your version of a.m. and p.m."

"If you say so. Here's us." Arty pointed to a restaurant with a cutesy critter on their sign. "Swirly's is the absolute best. Whole city comes here, no matter who their rightful mother might be. Lots of sizzle and not too flash. You'll love it."

The restaurant was larger than Enzo had realized—long and narrow, practically a dining hall. The front part had family-style seating, but Arty led the way to booths at the back, which offered more privacy. As usual, Purdle and Cubit were turning heads.

Arty caught the eye of a server and held two fingers across his palm.

"You've ordered?"

"Yeah. Everyone gets the same thing. Two hexes should do for a start. Any more than that and they'd get cold. Better to call for fresh rounds." And with a hand gesture that Enzo was beginning to associate with getting back to business, Arty asked, "Did the book tell you anything? Anything *useful*."

Enzo guessed it was fine to share things *about* the book. "It's handwritten, and the subject matter is widely varied, largely speculative, and frustratingly incomplete. It's not quite a grimoire, and it's not really a field journal. It has a title, though. *Imponderabilia*."

"Confirmed the author, then?"

"Yeah. It's Plenilune Marsk."

"And Coquelicot said he's the one who called for the test? You're sure?"

"Yes."

"About that. I did some fact-checking, and I think someone's got you by the bell pull. There've only been six regius professors in the whole history of Newcomb. Seems it's a rare honor. Coquelicot is the most recent. The bloke before her was ages ago."

"Marsk?"

"That's the guy."

They sat back when a server arrived with a platter of hand pies, hot from the frier. They looked to Enzo like empanadas, their surfaces golden-brown and blistered.

Arty grabbed one and immediately had to drop it. "Specialty of the house," he said, snagging a paper napkin so he could break the pie in half, showing its center. "Pork and these crunchy bits and a secret sauce. Whole city's addicted. You should be, too. Here, Purdle. Let this cool first, yeah?"

Enzo broke open another and softly called, "Skrik? Are you hungry?"

It was kind of funny to see Arty's face light up when the imp peeked up over the tabletop. Enzo half-suspected that the guy was helping him out because of his familiars. He couldn't come up with any reason why Skrik and Purdle couldn't make friends of their own. Even if that friend was a police officer with possible ties to the Hound.

He debated circling back around to that topic, but he could quiz Purdle anytime. While he had Arty—mostly—to himself, he figured he should stick to finding the author of *Imponderabilia*.

"You know, Professor Coquelicot said she was his apprentice."

"Can't be." Arty was feeding tiny pieces of cooling crust to Cubit. "Doesn't math out. Marsk was appointed as the fifth regius professor just before the tricentennial, so he's long gone."

Except he wasn't. According to Coquelicot, not only was he still around, he'd been keeping an eye on Enzo. "Can you verify that? Like ... does he have a burial plot or a marker on Cenotaph Road? Does the city keep birth and death records?"

"You think he's alive?"

"Coquelicot does. And I have no reason to disbelieve her." He went a step further. "I don't know by what means, but I do think he's still around."

"Well, that's interesting. I can't deny there's ways to go about it." Arty finished two more hand pies before he said, "Right. If there's something to be found, I can find it. Come by my place for a bit? We can get takeaway for Tuppence."

"That'd be great." And because it was true, Enzo added, "This is delicious, by the way."

"Right?" Arty flagged down one of the servers, crossing his palm twice and adding a signal that must have indicated it was to go. "They're best fresh, but they're not bad cold."

"About Marsk. I've been trying to think where to start. Do you know if he has an office in the tower somewhere?"

"Could be. Worth a look-see." Arty nodded at Skrik. "Have you tried?"

"Mages ward their doors."

The teen's smile turned sly. "And you *need* doors to get around, do you?"

"Nooo."

"So?"

Skrik stole the last hand pie from the platter. "After dark is better. I *could* look around. Tonight …?" He peeked at Enzo. "I'll only go if Purdle can stay."

"Yes, yes. Cubit and I will stand watch through *all* the knells. That's what they call hours here, did you know? And they've named the night watches."

"Have they?" Enzo hadn't really noticed. It wasn't as if this stuff was posted anywhere. Not when the whole city apparently learned this stuff as sprogs and just assumed everyone else knew what they were talking about.

"Just another of those older than Olde traditions. From when the lamplighters had to go through the streets, and the city clocks needed winding." Arty shrugged. "The curfew makes it all moot, anyhow."

The server arrived with two heavy bags and the bill, which Enzo glanced over, mostly out of habit. His attention snagged on the shop's name. "The Swirly Pine?"

Arty traded a knowing look with the server, then said, "It'll come to him eventually. Want me to cover the ticket? It's only rightward, since in my heart of hearts, Swirly's my mum."

Enzo waved aside his offer and settled the bill, and they walked along the lamplit Loyalty Burrow all the way to the elevators that could take them up to street or station level in front of the school.

While they trudged up the final flights of stairs, Enzo asked, "Should I feel honored that you brought me home to meet your mother?"

Arty laughed and lifted their bags of takeaway. "You're gonna be all in, now you know my mum, my crew, and my crumbs."

"Crumbs?"

"It's what I call them. They're the real honor, since I've decided to trust you." Arty opened the door to his place. "You've seen them before. But like most people, you didn't know what you were looking at. Or who was looking back."

Enzo glanced around. Something he'd seen before? The apartment was still a riot of color, its graffiti walls clamoring for attention.

Arty beckoned him deeper inside, and rounding a corner,

Enzo was surprised to find dozens of shiny hexagonal plates neatly mounted onto the wall. Each pane showed the faint lines of a magic circle.

As Enzo leaned close, trying to unravel the meaning of the runes, the surface lit up, and a picture came into focus. Of Purdle. The sprite seemed to be studying Enzo through the panel.

From behind and above, Purdle exclaimed, "Hello, you! Are you friendlier than the last one?"

Enzo spun, craning his neck to locate Purdle. He was perched in Cubit's saddle, contemplating a random section of the painted wall. Enzo turned back to the display. More panes lit up, showing views of the room from all different angles.

"These are magically linked to your ... *crumbs*, did you say? It's a variation on your inhabited clockwork. We can see what they can see." Enzo spun in place, peering around. "But where are they? I don't see them."

"Crumb's just a nickname. Short for simulacrums. They're here. Look closer." Arty gravely said, "I'm *letting* you see them."

The walls seemed to ripple as small mechanical creatures stepped out of alignment. They looked as if they'd been painted over with the same graffiti as the wall. Wings lifted. Pincers flexed. Tails curled. And tiny crystals glittered in rainbow hues.

"This is amazingly complex," Enzo whispered, totally in awe. "Where did you get so many emanations?"

"Oh, these aren't fae emanations. They're too fickle, and they fade too fast." Radiating pride, Arty said, "I use souls."

# 40

## *Benedick*

VESPER 11, FOUR NINETY-EIGHT
WILLIDAY
11 KNELLS, 54 KNICKS
ON THE FIRST FACE OF THE CLOCK

Doggerel tore off his harness before reaching a clawed hand toward Varti. "This one. This is the box. Benedick."

Varti knew the case. How could he not? Mysterious deaths and murder were far from common in Newcomb. Or they used to be.

Benedick Carraway, age forty-seven, trained as an archivist, served nine terms as a professor of history. Current employer unknown. Last address on record, Danbright 12-433, though he'd changed quarters several years ago. No forwarding address. Died on the fiftieth of Fullnis under mysterious circumstances. Found in one of the display halls at the Academy of Mages, but his body had been moved to that location. Cause of death, inconclusive. No witnesses. No suspects. No longer a priority.

"Benedick." Then with a pleading note, the bipedal wolf added, "My good friend."

Doggerel was involved in another murder? He'd *known* the victim?

The pieces meshed smoothly. Benedick Carraway was the ghost in the front hall at Hibernacle House. He'd been a member of the household, Sherlock Holmes's assistant. And Doggerel, Thomas Hudson's lost dog, was trying to track him down? Did the beast not understand that the man was dead?

"Scents," Doggerel said huskily, as if unaccustomed to speaking. "I need to know if there are scents. He wants to find who did this. If there are scents, there might be some clue. He will know, and I will hunt. For Benedick. He was my friend for so long. Who took him from us?"

Varti was having trouble with the fact that words were coming from Doggerel. Indeed, he was growing increasingly articulate.

"Help yourself." But Varti put a foot forward, raising his club. "Anyone can access the evidence lockers at any time."

"This is the one, and you have the key. Open it, Varti." Doggerel straightened further. "A minute, a knick. A few moments. Give me the scent, and I can find the trail."

"We can skip the formalities. I don't mind at all."

"Tell him, tell him, tell him for me," Doggerel muttered miserably, seemingly to himself. And in a somewhat different tone, "That is quite enough!"

And the bipedal wolf writhed and wilted and shifted even further, until all the grizzled fur retreated, leaving a barefoot man in silk pajamas. He was fair-skinned, quite tall, too thin, and he peered down a hawklike nose. Pushing lank dark hair out of his eyes, he said, "Varti Weller, I do apologize. I'm back in control. Key?"

Varti struggled to fit new information into a faulty framework. Doggerel was ... what? Werefolk were an Olde

Worlde legend, not any kind of Folk that Varti had learned about in school. There *were* different varieties of shifters, and some did assume an animal form. But his mind was intent on making a very different logical leap. Because many frustrated badges had slipped insults into their reports.

*A spindle-legged crane of a man.*

*Looking down on us like a hawk.*

*Thin as a rake, smart as a whip.*

*Strolled in, took charge, and kept it.*

So when the man who was no longer Doggerel extended a long-fingered hand and archly repeated, "The *key*, please," Varti was certain. This was the man himself. Sherlock Holmes.

From the direction of the cage door, Kel's voice boomed. "Weller! Do you need help?"

There was no good way to answer that, so Varti acted instead. He took Holmes by the arm and marched him toward the back wall, to an unmarked door that hadn't been used in ages. Except by Varti. Unlocking it with one of the keys on his ring, he pushed Holmes through and closed the door behind them.

"Up or down?" Holmes asked in a low voice.

"Up."

Holmes took the downward flight, bare feet making no sound. Varti sheathed his club and thumbed the switch on his duty lamp, then thudded after him.

"It lets me see through its eyes. Sometimes. The creature you call Doggerel." Holmes paused at a turning, looking up. "It *wanted* me to see you. Usually, when it seizes control, there are lengthy gaps in my memory, during which anything might be happening. It's sly, this beast."

Varti took the lead, and they descended two levels.

Another door. Another key. A hushed tunnel with only Varti's duty lamp for light.

Holmes continued his ... well, it sounded rather like a confession. "It's a reprehensible beast ruled by appetite and instinct, and I have become its cage. If I let down my guard, if my inhibitions are lowered, if I sleep too deeply, it can overwhelm me. Keeping it under control has consumed my life."

He sounded bitter, weary.

"My assistant went missing, and I was in the midst of investigating when something unprecedented happened. The beast within bartered for control. It claimed an attachment to Mr. Carraway. It wanted to find him, and when it proposed cooperation, I was ... tempted."

The sound of Holmes's footfalls paused, and Varti stopped, lifting his lamp in order to search the man's face.

"Such a thing went against my better judgment. This monster has killed before, and it's capable of killing again. But for Benedick's sake ...? I shouldn't have listened. I shouldn't have relented." With a bleak expression, he muttered, "Seven murders."

Was he confessing?

Varti didn't think so.

"I regret ever giving it a toehold." Holmes pushed at the hair that kept falling into his eyes. "I don't know. I really don't. But the possibility remains, and so I've taken measures. If this monster is responsible for the recent killings, then I *will* stop it. But I find myself unwilling to look into the eyes of death without proof."

Durst. He had to mean Durst.

"*You*, Varti Weller. As I said, it let me see *you*. Your methods are sound. You can think. You're persistent." The man's gaze was difficult to read. "Your lines of inquiry. The woolen jumper. Tell me, Weller. Have you crossed paths with Thomas Hudson?"

"Never heard of him."

"His knack is a fearsome thing. Unaccountable. Yet I cannot discount it." He rubbed the pad of his thumb along his fingertips, lost in thought. "I'll want his opinion."

Varti moved along. He chose an alley that opened onto one of the burrow roads. It would be busy at this knell, so close to midday. Roundabout, then.

Retreating a few paces, Varti fit his fingers into the catch of an access panel that led into a network of backhalls that were used by engineering teams when making upgrades and repairs.

Holmes drawled, "Very good. If I may?"

As he eased his lean frame through the opening, Varti realized that Holmes had a loop of twine around his neck, from which Doggerel's cardboard nametag still dangled. They really were one and the same.

"Follow me." Holmes strode confidently, heedless of the dark. "Revolutionization has robbed me of several boltholes over the years, but a handful remain intact. We are a scant half mile from one, and it's reachable by these backhalls."

He set a brisk pace, and Varti was intrigued. While he knew a few outmoded entrances into the Bastion, he hadn't explored the under-levels much further than the route they'd just taken, which he'd only sorted after two Newdays and a lot of trial and error. Perhaps he should add these inner workings of the city to his mental map? Clearly, they could prove useful.

Holmes stopped, raising a hand. "Just here," he said. "Up this ladder."

They emerged through another access panel into a dim alley. Varti peered around trying to get his bearings, but it was a blind approach in either direction. Holmes strode without a trace of hesitation to a nondescript door with a coded lock set into it.

"Watch. Just in case." Holmes slowly keyed in an alphanumeric sequence.

Pulling open the door and tapping on the lights, he made Varti precede him into a room that was nothing like a set of quarters. It was more of a closet. Clothes hung from racks to either side, and there were several shoeboxes and hatboxes on the shelves above. A dressing table with a mirror held rows of pots and pencils and what looked like jewelry cases.

Holmes was already selecting garments. He offered a distracted, "Make yourself at home."

Varti perched on the edge of one of two narrow beds tucked up under the clothing racks. He spotted a medical tin, a hotplate, and a teapot. More surprising was the bank of six pneumatic tubes and the telephone.

Scant knicks later, the man turned from the mirror, looking much more polished. "Let's have a better beginning, shall we? My name is Sherlock Holmes, and I–"

A rap on the door silenced him. But rather than concern, the man's eyes lit with wry amusement. "As I said, Weller. Unaccountable, but impossible to discount."

# 41

## *Means to an End*

Vesper 11, Four Ninety-Eight
Williday
1 Knell, 31 Knicks
On the Second Face of the Clock

Holmes was at the door in two strides. Letting it swing wide, he offered a bland, "You are very nearly late, Mr. Hudson. Yet not a moment too soon."

"Here you are at last, sir." Thomas stepped through. "And Mr. Weller, too? Splendid!"

Then Durst crowded in, mouth set in a grim line, snakes weaving in their orderly—yet undeniably unsettling—search pattern. Realizing that the frontmost snake over Durst's right eyebrow was fixed on him, Varti found himself lifting a hand in greeting. "Driss! I knew you'd come. Save me?"

The snake snapped up into a more threatening posture and bared his fangs at Holmes.

Durst reached up and covered Driss's head, pushing it down and back.

Holmes said, "Mr. Durst. I trust Mr. Hudson has explained my particular requirements?"

"*And* my reservations," Thomas quickly interjected. "There will be no need for extreme measures. Mr. Weller may well back me up. The Hound isn't as terrible as you say. If you could only see him begging scraps from Mrs. Watson or dogging Wendall's heels. And he was thoroughly devoted to Mr. Carraway."

"You may see a side of the beast that I never will, but it's equally true that I know it as you do not. The Hound is no lapdog."

The gorgon spoke into the tense silence. "Just Durst."

Varti stepped up to Thomas, hand extended. "I had no idea he was your dog."

The man nodded sympathetically. "I expect you wanted to keep him. He's quite the charmer when he takes to someone."

Holmes curled a lip. "Don't even begin to think that the dreadful thing is being noble. Nor that it's seeking justice for Mr. Carraway. It is driven by rage and a desire for revenge. It wants me to find the one who killed my assistant, and it wants to tear out the culprit's throat."

Thomas quietly stated, "We each grieve in our own way."

Varti didn't doubt Holmes. Yet he couldn't quite reconcile the man's version of events with the rapport he'd found with Doggerel. Could two entities inhabit a single body? That's how it felt for him. Varti and the curse, bound in unrelenting opposition.

He spied the twine and cardboard collar, tossed aside while Holmes had changed. Varti palmed it and tucked it into a pocket.

Questions. He had so many. Four words at a time would never be enough.

But Holmes sat across from Varti and gestured that the others sit as well. Thomas quickly claimed a seat beside his employer. Varti's cot creaked ominously when Durst sat next to him. Their height difference was the only reason Varti didn't immediately have green serpents messing with him. He stole a peek and whispered, "You'll get your turn. Every name will be inscribed upon my heart."

Tarnish it all, why was the curse courting trouble?

Durst didn't look his way nor act as if he'd heard. Then again, he was meeting his new employer for the first time. Acknowledging Varti's outrageous lies would be as unprofessional as ... as Varti's outrageous lies. Better that Durst was spared the indignity.

Holmes leaned forward, elbows on knees, fingers loosely laced together. "I shall begin by laying out the facts as I know them. My assistant, Benedick Carraway's whereabouts are unaccounted for from the forty-eighth of Fullnis until the discovery of his body on the fiftieth. We were not alerted until the murder appeared in headlines the following day, because Mr. Hudson suggested an outing into the city. That in itself might be considered proof."

"I never do go into town, you see," interjected Thomas. "Unless it's absolutely necessary."

"We identified Carraway's body, but the scene of the crime had been tidied." Holmes paused. "At that point, I lost time. The Hound overwhelmed me, and there was a long lapse before I came to myself."

"Nearly three weeks," Thomas supplied.

"During which time, the first two killings took place. I looked into them. Not in any official capacity." Holmes sought Varti's gaze. "It was at this point that the Hound offered to cooperate in the search for Mr. Carraway's killer. I put off the decision for several days, but I *did* relent. I would characterize the resulting alliance as ... uneasy. And when I next wrested full control, a third and fourth killing had taken place. At this point, I secured

Durst's services. That was the eighty-ninth of Fullnis."

Varti appreciated the succinct and unemotional delineation, even though it was oddsome that the man would put so much care into building a case against himself.

Thomas said, "From then, I never knew what state I would find Mr. Holmes in. Sometimes a man, sometimes a dog, sometimes a combination of the two."

He must mean the bipedal dog that Varti had spoken with in the evidence lockers.

"I regret my decision. Since then, the thing takes over more easily. Keeping it at bay has become more taxing." Holmes waved that aside and addressed Varti. "Lest you harbor any illusions about its motives, you should know that I am the one who oiled the lock at your building. And it was no accident that you encountered a dog in the park later that same morning."

Thomas had a pained expression when he lifted a hand. "May I ask pertinent questions? I feel I can anticipate the obvious ones."

Holmes rolled his wrist, inviting the man to get on with it.

Summoning up very plausible affront, Thomas exclaimed, "You broke in? To his domicile? Whatever for?"

"*Attempted* entry. There were wards in place, so even though the lock posed no problem, I couldn't cross the threshold. And my reason should be obvious. This man is listed as the head of the Bastion's Files & Evidence division. I was going to see if I could use him in order to gain access to Mr. Carraway's personal effects."

"What, you were going to impersonate him?" Thomas scoffed. "With my skills and that nose, you *might* have passed for an older, much-taller brother."

"I was, at that time, unaware of Mr. Weller's height, heritage, and predicament. But I've since taken his measure."

He said it so dismissively. As if he'd learned everything that was worth knowing. Varti would have liked to speak for himself, not have someone reduce him to a short list of deductions. But he could see how the knack for doing so might be useful when facing other kinds of silence. The dead could not speak for themselves. And criminals rarely told the truth.

Holmes didn't need words to suss out the truth.

Was that why he was so willing to overlook Varti's lies?

"You were the means to an end," said Holmes.

Varti didn't think that was the whole truth. Perhaps it had begun that way? What had changed?

Thomas wasn't done being affronted on Varti's behalf. "We have the necessary connections to gain *legitimate* access. Highmost Purnal Yamada has been sending twice-daily couriers to your office. The mail slot fairly bristled with requests, and I had to have someone from the post look at our pneumatics. They were so backed up, the central and district hub both stopped service."

"I wanted an alternate means."

"Why?" prompted Thomas.

Holmes ran his fingertips over the pad of his thumb, then clenched a fist. "I don't wish to consult with the Bastion about the recent string of killings."

"Because …?"

"Because I knew them all."

Thomas missed a beat. "Do you mean the victims?"

Holmes sought and held Varti's gaze. "I have no memory of those days, no way to account for my whereabouts during the killings. It may be coincidental, but with the badges desperate to lay blame, I present a likely candidate. I wanted to be able to prove my innocence before bringing attention to the fact that I knew all of the victims."

"Do *I* know them?" asked Thomas. "Wouldn't that make me equally culpable."

"You do not have the means to shift into a monster capable of tearing someone limb from limb. But yes. We are both passingly acquainted with them." And he began a flat recitation.

"Gemma Zimmer worked in the tobacconist shop that Thomas and I frequent, and Aster March was a courier hired by the Bastion's branch office in the Station District. She has been to our offices on Old London Road with communication on several occasions."

"Miss Gemma died?" Thomas looked heartbroken. "I had no idea."

"Polly Barrister."

"Nooo," groaned Thomas. "We were always chatting. She's … she *was* one of the royal gardeners, and we'd sometimes talk about the flowers."

"And the fourth victim was Tess Bishop."

Thomas's eyes narrowed. "I'm not sure …?"

Holmes sighed. "She came to our offices a couple of times, but most of her pestering came by post. I refused to take her case, but she was … persistent. And Willa Cyrine. Her death troubles me more than all of them. She's the one who brought the inquiry that Carraway was looking into when he disappeared."

"Are they connected?"

"I don't know." Holmes cut a look in Varti's direction. "I don't have enough facts. And unfortunately, one of my best informants is also dead. Owen."

Thomas nodded. "I was aware that Mr. Acres died. And Jacob, of course. I must confess, I did wonder if they were embroiled in that earlier business and came to the same end as Benedick."

"No. At least, not at my behest."

"Jacob Oswald was a consultant for the Bastion's Irregulars, the same as us," explained Thomas. "We were on friendly terms. We enjoyed many a supper as his guest at the Tree of Knowledge."

"He was a valuable resource," said Holmes. "I'll miss having a mage to call upon."

Thomas tutted disapprovingly.

"The badges are seeking a connection, something that links the killings. I am one such connection." Holmes's gray eyes held a challenge. "I cannot deny that I'm harboring a murderer. The thing has killed before. You are part of the team assigned to the case. Will you lay the blame at Doggerel's feet? Or can you find another explanation?"

"You are the murderer. Clearly."

Holmes asked, "Would you let fondness for the creature cloud your judgment?"

Varti only needed a moment to know his mind. "I am easily swayed from my duty."

He didn't want Doggerel to be the killer. But he didn't think it possible, either. He knew the evidence that the Bastion had accumulated, and nothing pointed to a physical dog doing the mauling. But Holmes was right about the pressure Phil and his team were under. Would the purnals and periors blame Doggerel without sufficient basis, simply because they had no other suspects?

There was only one solution that suited the situation.

Varti and Phil would need to find the true culprit. There had to be another connection the victims shared. Where they were found, where they were from, where they'd worked—nothing matched. The only thing that linked the victims so far was their manner of death.

Giving Holmes private access to the files and evidence was impossible.

Like it or not, the man's motives could be called into question. Knowing what he did now, Varti would refuse access even if Yamada herself was escorting Holmes. He spread his hands in surrender. "Full and immediate access."

"I know." Holmes's gaze had turned inward. "I'll have to sequester myself. Mr. Hudson and Durst will stand guard. And while the whole city hides from a monster that hunts in the dark, I shall await Mr. Weller's denouement."

Thomas lifted a hand. "On the night we met, I suggested that Mr. Weller would make a fine assistant. You know you prefer working with a companion."

Holmes arched his brows. "There *is* merit to the suggestion. Have you given any thought to a change in employment, Weller?"

"Not once." Having already contemplated a change from the regulars to the irregulars, Varti let himself consider a very different leap. There couldn't be enough mysterious cases to warrant a full-time assistant. If the files he'd gone through were any indication, Holmes only consulted for the Bastion at odd intervals, with years of silence stretching between cases. "I am irreplaceable."

"You are wasted on the post," Holmes countered.

Thomas seemed surprised by this assessment. "How would you know, sir?"

"The wretched beast *let* me see. Insisted I take note." With a wave, he declared, "Weller, you have a good memory, and you're careful with details. You attack problems in an orderly manner. Working backward is a start; working forward will come. You take initiative even when nobody's looking on, a terrifying prospect when employed by fools. But in your case? Promising."

"And Doggerel likes him," added Thomas.

Holmes dryly said, "*Not* a factor."

"And Durst likes him."

Thomas and Holmes looked at the silent gorgon, whose posture had gradually relaxed until his arms rested across his knees, putting Varti very much in reach of several of the nearer snakes. They kept slyly nosing his hair and flicking him with their tongues.

Varti stole a glance in Durst's direction, only to find himself nose-to-nose with one of the green snakes. Oh. Not just any snake. "You will be *my* assistant. Always choose for beauty, that's my motto."

Thomas inquired, "You're commandeering Durst?"

"No." Durst came to Varti's defense. Sort of. "He has been telling my undulation pretty little lies, and they enjoy the attention."

Holmes vaguely said, "Do they, now?"

"You can relate, sir?" Thomas inquired sweetly.

Ignoring the question, Holmes addressed Varti. "If you can prove that I am not the murderer of those seven people, then I'll take you on as my assistant. You can learn from me and my methods. And if that's not inducement enough, I offer this. Your case. I'll take it on."

Thomas helpfully asked, "Mr. Weller has a case?"

"It's an interesting problem, his predicament." Sherlock Holmes offered his hand. "Find the one at the bottom of these crimes, and I will learn the means for your unspelling."

# 42

## Palace of Books

Vesper 11, Four Ninety-Eight
Williday
1 Knell, 44 Knicks
on the second face of the clock

E nzo asked, "What do you know about the library off the hall with the orrery?"

"That's like bibliotheca, innit?" asked Arty.

"Umm ... sure. A collection of books."

He shrugged. "Which orrery?"

"Is there more than one?" But of course there must be. Otherwise, he wouldn't have asked. Enzo explained, "It's huge. Big as a room. It was in a long hall full of clock displays."

"Right. I know the one you mean. But there's no large-scale book collection near there."

"Yes, there is. The door's not marked, but I went in. Not very far, but enough to get a good look. It felt old, ornate. Flying buttresses and frescoed ceilings and mullioned windows. Like a tiny palace, but full of books."

Arty stared at him for a while, then said, "You're gonna have to show me."

"Okay, sure. If you can get me to that orrery, the door's right there."

When Arty shouldered a chunky wheel-thingie that was clipped to a strap, Purdle asked, "Is that clockwork?"

"More of a machine. Built it myself."

"What's it for?"

"You ride Cubit, yeah? I ride this."

"Does it have a name?"

"I never thought of that. You think it needs one?"

Arty took the lead, Purdle at his side, happily suggesting possible names.

On Enzo's shoulder, Skrik softly said, "I also saw your palace of books."

"Did you want to be the one to guide us there?"

The imp glumly admitted, "I was hoping you'd forget about it."

"You thought I'd forget about a roomful of books?"

"No. Not you. Not if there were books."

Enzo wondered at Skrik's tone. "Did you see something there that worried you?"

"There was something I *couldn't* see. That is what worries me."

They went down, entered the tower from a door Enzo didn't think he'd been through before, and zigzagged through a section so hushed, he could hear the faint hiss of the gaslamps. Then they took a wide staircase down, which put them in the grand hall Enzo remembered.

Arty paused to peer up at some of the displays, in no apparent hurry, so Enzo let himself be distracted. After reading several of the information plaques, he realized that many of these timepieces had been gathered from distant kingdoms and countries. Funny, considering Newcomb's relative isolation.

"These are foreigners, you realize. They're marking hours and minutes on the sly, totally ignoring your knells and ticks."

"I think you mean flits," said Arty. "And you left out knicks."

"Knicks and knacks."

"Interested in knacks, are you?"

"Do you mean inherited magical aptitudes?"

"Suppose you could call 'em that. Too much of a mouthful, though."

"Are there many kinds?"

"As plentisome as hexes in a hive, but without a hive's symmetry. They're individual. Totally unique."

"Do you have one?"

Arty looked at him askance. "That's a very personal question."

"I suppose it would be. Do people in these parts prefer to keep their knack a secret?"

"That all depends. Some people advertise their knack because it makes them better at their job. Like a knack for weaving or a knack for reading tea leaves." Arty turned the question around. "Do you have a knack?"

"Umm ... don't think so. Does anyone around here have a knack for figuring out knacks?"

Arty shrugged. "That'd be useful."

The orrery's planets and moons were going through their ponderous revolutions, and it took Enzo several seconds to orient himself. No, wait. Was he turned around? Because the wall he'd walked to so confidently was seamless. No trace of the door he remembered.

"Problem?" asked Arty.

"Yes. It's missing." Enzo went to the other five walls. He even walked down each branching hall. Finally he said, "I don't understand. It was right here."

"I can tell you what's behind these walls." Arty wasn't arguing exactly. Just stating facts. "That's the amber lecture hall, and this way's the constellation room. There's a practicum hall off this way, and that way is Professor Borealis's classroom, with Natterwit's straight above. And behind here is the beryl lecture hall."

"And there are no gaps? Somewhere to hide a secret room or a hidden passage?"

Arty led him to a map near the street-level entrance, which clearly showed the very same layout Arty had rattled off. "I can do some checking. You might've run across some magical upshot that's since been dispelled. Happens all the time. Too many students practicing their art, yeah? It's probably nothing." He hesitated. "I need to meet my crew over at the skate park. You okay to get home from here?"

"I have Skrik and Purdle. We'll be fine."

Arty strode out the doors, unclipping his wheel-thingie as he went. Folding down treads on each side, he stepped on, perfectly balanced as he skimmed away, weaving between pedestrians.

Purdle announced, "We named her Swirly, after his mum."

"His vehicle?"

"She's a monocycle, and he said he can make one my size."

"That's very generous of him."

"Why did you lose the door?" Purdle inquired.

"I don't know. It was there. Right, Skrik?"

"Yes."

"Show me," said Purdle. "Maybe there's something I can do."

So they backtracked to the orrery, and Skrik growled.

Purdle helpfully announced, "I found it!"

"It wasn't there a minute ago," said Enzo. "What do you guys think?"

"The door was gone, and now it's back. That's magic," said Purdle.

Skrik said, "It wants you. It doesn't want Arty."

Enzo asked, "Want to take a quick look around?"

"No," said Skrik.

Purdle simply waited to see what Enzo would decide.

"I do want to," he admitted.

Skrik sighed and said, "Me first."

The imp dropped to the floor, then poured through the crack under the door. A few seconds later he returned and said, "It's the same as before."

"Is that good?" asked Purdle.

Skrik replied, "I don't like it, but Enzo will."

"A palace of books?" Purdle laughed. "Enzo won't want to leave."

The door slid easily to one side, and after the briefest hesitation, Enzo stepped through. He left the door open an inch, for all the good it would do if the door could vanish. He walked toward the center and spun, trying to take everything in. The frescos and stained glass were just as he remembered. The steep angle of the sun through vivid panes matched the time of day on his wristwatch, so he hadn't been transported far.

Turning his attention to the antique script on the plates mounted on the ends of each shelf, he quickly realized that these were spell books. All of them. An absolute trove of fresh reading material. Selecting one, he stood transfixed, slowly paging through a compendium of Realmish tinctures and their effects.

But then Skrik tugged a lock of his hair. "We aren't alone."

"Really?" Enzo pushed up his glasses and peered around. "Where are they?"

Purdle pointed up.

"Should we go say hello?"

"Maybe," said Skrik. "Maybe not …?"

"Let's try. They might be a librarian, and I have questions."

They took a curving staircase up to a balcony level. The view was quite nice, for the center of the floor below had been set with a detailed mosaic. But Purdle and Cubit drifted toward another, smaller staircase that spiraled more tightly to an enclosed room on a third level.

There were books here, too, but one entire wall was taken up by a large mirror surrounded by masks. Curious, Enzo crossed to the collection and began reading labels. A jade mask from a faraway jungle. A couple of carnival masks from Venice, and theater masks from Japan. Ceremonial masks and tribal masks and death masks and festival masks. Some were beautiful, and others were grotesque. Having so many empty eye holes staring at him was eerie. They seemed to be watching him.

Enzo was drawn to one that was identified as a Roman parade mask. Its expression was pleasant enough, if a bit melancholy. He gently touched cool metal and smiled a silent greeting.

Skrik hissed softly.

Recalling himself, Enzo asked, "Is anyone there?"

"Yes. I'm here." A man's voice, deep and bored.

Enzo turned to consider the room. There wasn't anyone else. "Where are you?"

"Here. Or *there*, I suppose, since you asked if anyone was there."

Still no sign of the speaker. "Hello. I'm Enzo."

"Yes, I know."

"Then you have the advantage over me."

"Yes, I expect I do."

Enzo patiently asked, "May I know your name?"

"You already know my name."

"Are you Plenilune Marsk?"

"That's quite the leap of illogic."

"Or a really good guess. It's you, isn't it?"

"As it happens, yes."

Enzo asked, "Is this library here? In Newcomb?"

"It's neither here nor there. Yet here we all are."

He was listening closely, trying to pinpoint the source of the voice. "You have an impressive collection."

"I've had time to build it."

Deciding to address himself to a particularly regal chair set at an angle in the corner, Enzo said, "I like your book."

"Finished it, have you?" The tone was slightly mocking.

"No, not at all. It'll take me years. Especially if you let me borrow more of these books."

Marsk said, "My apprentice—and his familiars—are welcome any time."

"So it's conditional? Access to the library, I mean."

"Yes. Upon your acceptance of my offer, you'll gain full access."

"Tempting."

"I did think it would make for an easier capitulation." Calm and genial. Which made the disembodied voice all the more ominous.

"Can we talk it over? I don't really understand what your offer would mean for me. Like … what do you expect from me? What would my responsibilities entail? None of that has been spelled out."

"We'll talk if you return, and you may not return until your heart and mind are set."

"So I won't know any of the terms and conditions until after I accept?"

"Does that seem unjust?"

"It's really sketchy."

"It's the way of many secret societies," Marsk pointed out.

"Are you a society?"

"Not as such."

Enzo didn't think he had enough information to make a decision that would be magically binding. "Is there anything else you *can* tell me?"

"As a matter of fact, yes. You're searching for someone."

"You know about that?"

"I can help you find him."

"Really?" Enzo could definitely use some guidance, but he was skeptical. "You know where he is? Does that mean he's here in Newcomb?"

"Oh, he's here. In this very building."

Enzo's heart took to hammering. "The Hound is?"

Marsk sounded as if he was smiling when he revealed, "He's admiring the orrery as we speak."

# 43

## *Villain*

VESPER 11, FOUR NINETY-EIGHT
WILLIDAY
2 KNELLS, 55 KNICKS
ON THE SECOND FACE OF THE CLOCK

Varti had never been in such a strange situation before, walking arm-in-arm with Mr. Hudson, whose other arm was linked through his employer's.

Holmes said, "It's the only way we've found to keep him from catastrophic encounters."

"It's efficacious, but not a cure by any means," warned Thomas. "At least with a badge escort, we avoided any unsavory elements."

"I daresay that Durst also serves as a strong deterrent," said Holmes.

Varti had already gathered that Thomas had a knack that involved portentous asides and time ... or timing. Apparently, he was prone to chance encounters, serendipitous timing, and all manner of coincidences. Despite this, they reached the main doors of the Academy of Mages without incident.

Holmes said, "The trail is long gone cold, but I want you to see where he was found for yourself, Weller."

This was largely new territory for Varti. He might know

every street, but the towers were worlds unto themselves. Many sections were not open to the public, yet Holmes strode with utter confidence along marble halls to a chamber filled with strange mechanisms. Varti didn't need long to realize that they were all clocks, many quite ancient.

"Here is where Carraway was found." Holmes stopped before an enormous sculpture with moving parts. Rings and spheres lifted in slow, graceful arcs. "The mages were quick to try to cover up the incident. They even went so far as to rewax the floors. The beast was furious to find every scent obliterated."

There came a sudden scrape and the thud of running feet coming from around the other side of the orrery. A man dashed out and stumbled to a halt at the sight of them. "You!" he gasped, looking from face to face. "Which of you …? I can't tell! Shouldn't I be able to tell?"

He was easily as tall as Holmes, youngish, likely in his twenties, and in need of a shave, with unkempt blond hair and round spectacles. The accent was as foreign as his attire.

"What do you think?" he asked, but he didn't seem to be speaking to any of them.

Ah, there. A shadowy figure peeped out from under his hair, its eyes glowing from within the shifting shadows of its form. Varti guessed it must be an imp. Probably a familiar, assuming this man was a mage.

Then another voice came, high and light and imperious. "Oh, just *ask*. Isn't that the easiest way?"

And Purdle glided into view astride his orange newt. The sprite caught sight of Varti and urged Cubit forward. "Hello, friend! This is a nice surprise. It really is. Enzo's been searching since forever, and you brought him. That's stellward of you!"

"Stellward?" the man asked, looking baffled.

"It means good. Jamie says it all the time. Isn't it lovely?"

So this foreigner was Purdle's person? *Enzo*, if Varti remembered correctly.

The young man shook his head, tugged at his hair in frustration, then blurted, "Which one of you is the Hound?"

Three possibilities. Enzo hoped he wasn't supposed to be able to tell which of these men was the one he sought, because … he couldn't.

A tall, lean man with a piercing gaze. His attire fit Enzo's idea of what an English gentleman would wear, which lent him an air of importance.

Beside him was a man in comparatively flamboyant attire. His shirt was brocade with silk fastenings, and there were flowers pinned against his shoulder. The whole ensemble seemed to have been selected to compliment his hair, which was a distinctive shade of amethyst, due to either Realmish affectation or fae ancestry.

Enzo recognized the third man's green cloak as the sort of thing worn by the local police. A constable or whatever. Shortest of the trio, he had brown skin and black curls, and there was a spark of challenge in his large brown eyes as he stepped forward, as if to protect the other two.

Which one? Which one? Enzo *really* couldn't tell, so he took Purdle's advice and asked outright. "Which one of you is the Hound?"

The dandified man gasped.

The officer brightly answered, "That would be me. I wondered when you'd find your way here."

Enzo was relieved and elated and eager to make a beginning. Hurrying to catch the man's hand with both of his, he tried to explain. "It's been a long road. Where do I even begin? I've been hunting for you. All of us have been. For years and years! After you were stolen, the family searched, but then there was the Sundering. Suddenly, London was gone, and my ancestors fled for their lives. We couldn't do much more than barricade ourselves in and send out inquiries."

The tall gentleman crisply asked, "What are you after?"

"The Hound," Enzo patiently repeated. "I've been searching for years, all over the world. To think you were here!" He searched the officer's upturned face. "You work for the city? That's astonishing. According to our records, you've always resisted any attempt to impose structure. Though I suppose some of it depends on how much remains of the vessel's influence."

"Hunters kill their prey." the officer said. He looked confused by his own remark.

"All four words," Purdle complained.

"Oh, I'm not hunting like a hunter. I should've said I've been searching. This is my quest. To find our long-lost family legacy." His tone gentled. "Reunion was a big part of the goal. And to offer my services. I know everything there is to know about a fell beast's particular needs. It's been our duty since ancient times. Well, up until the unfortunate incident. We lost you to a reprehensible thief, but if you read between the lines in the family account, your vessel back then wasn't the best match. I've always assumed you were unhappy with your lot and decided to try your luck with someone new."

"What's your name, young man?" demanded the gentleman.

"Enzo," he offered, embarrassed to have forgotten basic courtesies. "Enzo Basker."

"Good God." Piercing gray eyes narrowed. "That's not your full name."

"What? Oh. No. Enzo is short for Fiorenzo."

"Your surname," he snapped. "You're a Baskerville."

Enzo gamely answered, "That's right. Way back when, before the family emigrated, we were originally Baskervilles, and he's our Hound." He smiled at the officer. "*Finally.*"

"What services do you intend to offer Mr. Weller?" the gentleman asked, tone still sharp with suspicion.

"Anything, really. I can look after all sorts of basic needs. Well, not cooking. But health and harmony. Balance and rest. And should worse come to worst, my heritage makes me a suitable haven." Again, he appealed to the officer. "I hope to befriend you and use my particular skills to help you to flourish."

"Suitable haven," echoed the man with amethyst hair. "Do I take that to mean you hope to reclaim the hound for the sake of your family?"

"No! Well, yes. But Mr. Weller doesn't seem to be in any distress." Enzo supposed it did sound bad, especially since relinquishing the Hound would likely kill the man. "I'm more of a ... a friendly influence? A resource, really."

The gentleman drawled, "You're not very bright, are you, Mr. Basker."

"I'm sorry?"

Purdle piped up. "You're mixed up. My good friend lied."

"What?" Enzo pushed at his glasses. "Why would anyone lie about something so important?"

"I haven't lied," the officer grumbled. "I never do."

"Not by choice." Extending his hand, the one with purple hair said, "My name is Thomas Hudson, and this is quite the remarkable happenstance. Have you really been searching for centuries?"

"Not personally. It's a family thing."

"This is Badge Varti Weller. I do apologize for the misunderstanding. He isn't the person you're seeking." Turning slightly, he added, "This is my employer."

The gentleman took over with a grim smile. "I do not consider myself to be the monster you seek, but there is no denying that I share space with it. My name is Sherlock Holmes."

Enzo whispered, "You? It's … still you?"

"Ah, so you *do* know my name. Yes, Mr. Basker. *I* am the villain in your family's history."

# 44

## *Commandeering a Perior*

VESPER 11, FOUR NINETY-EIGHT
WILLIDAY
3 KNELLS, 19 KNICKS
ON THE SECOND FACE OF THE CLOCK

Varti was beginning to feel extraneous. Thomas took Enzo in hand and was plying him with questions, and the young man was proving to be exceedingly polite and generous with his answers. Varti tried to remember how he used to be, back when dialogue was ordinary and effortless. Not this free. Phil had always been the talker.

Even if Holmes managed his unspelling, Varti doubted it would transform him into a squawk-box. He was too used to biting his tongue and keeping his own council. Out of similar habit, he analyzed Enzo.

The accent was interesting. Varti had always liked listening to people whose speech hinted at different places. But pronunciation wasn't personality. Neither was plaid.

Enzo's clothes weren't a good fit—on him or in Newcomb. Perhaps it was difficult to find enough to eat while traveling? Sickness was also a possibility, though Enzo looked fitsome enough at the moment.

Spectacles. He was nearsighted.

No watchchain from which to garner clues. Indeed, his watch was strapped to his wrist, which was bizarre.

Nothing about him stirred Varti to suspicion. Enzo Basker seemed an honest man with a lot of enthusiasm ... and two familiars. Possibly three, if Cubit counted. Varti had been taught that mages only had a single contract. Was Enzo an exception, or had he been fed erroneous information? He wanted to ask Enzo about Purdle and about the shy creature who kept peeping out from under the rumpled curtain of Enzo's hair.

Actually, Varti would have liked to consult with him about Willa Cyrine's familiar, but resources went to waste if you couldn't tap them. So frustrating.

As Enzo explained to Thomas that he lived in the maze of dormitories connected to the academy, Varti came to a startling conclusion. For someone who was apparently well-traveled, Enzo gave the impression of being sheltered. Naïve. And overly trusting, although that might be the contrast between his attitude toward Doggerel and that of Holmes.

Holmes characterized the hound as both a monster and a murderer, and he'd taken steps to stop the beast within, even if it cost his own life. Yet Enzo had blundered in, promising to spend the rest of his life seeing to that monster's every need.

On the one hand, Varti was glad for Doggerel.

But would Holmes let Enzo take care of him?

"Weller." Holmes stepped closer and lowered his voice. "I'll need to meet your Mr. Kemp in a more official capacity. Can you bring him around to my office within the knell?"

Varti hesitated. It was the next logical step. Phil would drop everything if it meant meeting with the consultant Yamada was so keen to find. But how did Varti convey that? A message?

A calling card? What if Thomas accompanied him? That would be ideal.

"I'll loan you Durst."

"What a *wonderful* idea." He would be bringing an assassin—well, a *presumed* assassin—into the heart of the Bastion. His gaze slid to the gorgon, who was listening to something Purdle was saying. Or possibly ignoring the sprite. The goggles really did make it impossible to tell.

Holmes brushed a finger across his lips, but it didn't really hide his smile. "There is a *range* to your lies. That was almost tongue-in-cheek."

Varti wished he could warn Holmes not to antagonize the curse. If it took a disliking as it had to Phil, the future would be riddled with verbal barrages. And what was amusing and novel at first quickly led to steadily increasing distances.

But Holmes radiated unconcern as he enacted his plan, putting him out with Durst at his side.

Varti turned down a side street and stuck to back ways, then chose the quickmost stairwell into the Burrows, where it would be easier to keep to the shadows.

"Are we lost?"

"Yes. Hold my hand?"

Durst ignored that. "How well do you know these passages?"

"Can't make crowns or laurels of them." Opening an access panel, he looked up into faceted crystals. "Better ready a weapon or two. This path isn't without its perils."

The gorgon followed Varti, deftly replacing the panel. "I am rarely in a city long enough to learn these sorts of secret ins and outs."

"Not much further now."

"I do not mind. This is nostalgic. I was born in a labyrinth."

Varti successfully dredged up a random word. "Fourteen."

By some miracle, Durst understood. "That is one way to look at it. If you are counting heads, we are fourteen, but gorgons are numbered by their tails. Are you picturing baby Driss?"

"No. He has always been as he is now—majestic and powerful and deadly."

"He has certainly always believed himself to be." A little while later, Durst remarked, "I hear water."

"It's your imagination."

Durst grunted. "So the river is not confined to the big canal."

"This is where all the purest drinking water is stored."

"Sewers below, then. It is well-designed, this city."

Maybe Durst would be interested in Varti's maps? But they weren't headed for Files & Evidence. The offices of the Bastion's Irregulars were in loftier climes. And really, it would have been pure folly to arm an assassin—a *presumed* assassin—with any more knowledge of ways to elude capture.

Nearer to the city center, Varti led Durst up to street level and through the Bastion's main doors. He approached the first gate guard he saw and announced, "He's under arrest."

"A joke," Durst smoothly countered. "We are expected by Highmost Perior Philtrum Kemp of the Irregulars."

Another guard came over, a call was put through, and they made Durst fill out a visitor's form. When he stubbornly maintained that *Durst* was his only name, as his people didn't require surnames, the woman at the desk said, "I can't accept an incomplete form. Can't you put *something* there?"

With a sidelong look at Varti, Durst printed *Duress* on the line.

Then Phil came jogging across the lobby, watchchain jangling, eyes wide. "This is promising. I hope. Please tell me you've made progress."

"None whatsoever."

Phil looked so relieved. Offering his hand to Durst, he confessed, "I've been eager to meet you ever since I heard you and Varti—err, Weller—were connected. I'm Kemp. Won't you join us upstairs?"

"No need." Durst smoothly twisted Phil's arm behind him and marched him toward the exit. "Mr. Holmes would prefer the meeting take place in *his* office."

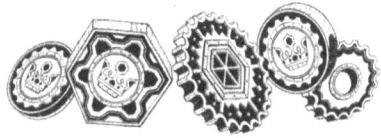

Varti was shocked by how easy it was for Durst to commandeer a highmost perior and remove him bodily from headquarters. The whole thing was possible in part because Varti couldn't raise an alarm. But Phil definitely helped by laughing off the manhandling and promising to come quietly.

The office at 221 Old London Road was an easy walk from the Bastion. Phil bumped Varti's shoulder as they strolled along. "You *found* him. The illusive Mr. Holmes."

"I deserve more credit. It's owed me."

"Help from any quarter will be welcomed with songs and festooned in laurels."

For the rest of the walk, Phil did his best to lure Durst into conversation. The questions were ordinary enough, but Varti suspected his quartermate was flirting. Or somehow signaling a willingness to flirt. Durst didn't seem all that interested in getting to know Phil, but neither was he rude. Driss, for one, kept his glittering gaze firmly fixed on Varti.

Strangely, the curse seemed indecisive about how to deal with Durst and his undulation. They no longer felt like an overt threat, but the potential was there. Varti found he wasn't compelled to scowl or swear or otherwise insult Durst. It was freeing. So he lifted a couple of fingers, acknowledging Driss.

Durst immediately turned his head.

Varti muttered, "This is between me and Driss. Don't interfere."

Phil looked between them, bemused.

Mercifully, their destination came into view, and Thomas hailed them from the garden, a bouquet of lavender resting in the crook of one arm. He swung the gate wide. "Go on through. I'll bring tea."

Durst gestured for Varti to go ahead, then split off, following Thomas into the kitchen. So Varti brought Phil into the sitting room, where Holmes paced. Enzo was there, too, tucked into an armchair and steadying a cup and saucer on his knee. His expression closed at the sight of Varti, which wasn't new. Being a known liar was nothing if not isolating.

In marked contrast, Purdle drifted over on Cubit, all smiles. "I have learned your name. Weller! Is your name really Weller?"

Varti shook his head. To his surprise, the sprite sprang from Cubit's back, colliding with Varti's cloak buttons and climbing higher.

"I *knew* I liked you!"

Unsure what the protocol was for dealing with such a small person, Varti cupped his hand under Purdle and lifted him so they were eye-to-eye.

"Varti Weller," the sprite said, sounding enormously pleased. "I seem to be very good at making friends."

"Sit," Holmes brusquely ordered. "I will listen to what you have to say, Mr. Kemp. Don't try to play up the plight of the city. Don't try to make the case sound more interesting in a bid for my attention. You have it. All I want are unadorned facts."

So they took chairs, and Phil outlined the case.

It didn't take long. There was so much they didn't know.

When Phil concluded, Holmes drawled, "So all you really *know* is that people are being killed."

Enzo shifted in his chair. Varti thought he looked as if he wanted to say something. And not for the first time. Twice before now, he'd caught Holmes sending the young man a warning look. Varti gathered that Holmes didn't want Phil to know the truth about Doggerel's identity. And he didn't trust Enzo not to betray him.

Varti really wished someone had introduced Enzo. They needed a mage's insight for some aspects of the case. He quietly addressed the sprite seated in his palm. "I haven't used my words."

"Yes, you did. It's not my fault. Oh! Did you have something to say? Can I guess? Lie to me, Varti Weller." He wasn't exactly subtle. Clear and bright, his voice seemed to beckon for everyone nearby to listen. As if having an audience was his right.

Into the silence, Varti solemnly lied, "I'm a mage."

"Nooo," Purdle patiently countered. "*Enzo* is a mage. He's *my* mage. Well, I do share him with Skrik. And Cubit, of course. Did you want to be a mage, too?"

Phil pivoted. "Oh, of course. I'm both rude *and* an idiot. Thank you, Varti." And offering a hand to Enzo, he asked, "Would you be able to help me locate a missing familiar? One of the victims had a contract token. There's a chance that the familiar witnessed the murder."

Enzo scooted to the edge of his seat. "Enzo Basker. May I see the contract token?"

"I don't have it with me, but I could arrange for you to see it." He glanced at Holmes. "I should have mentioned this earlier. Varti's the one who picked up on the detail. Willa Cyrine, the fifth victim, wore a contract token on her watchchain."

"And you didn't think to pursue the information until now?"

"No! We did. But the mage who was looking into it for me became the seventh victim."

Enzo's eyes widened. "Professor Oswald?"

"Yes. You knew him?"

"Yes. He's ... he *was* my mentor."

"Such losses have tolls as far-reaching as Old Ebonnel's." Phil turned back to Holmes. "I would of course accompany your assistant, given the risks of pursuing the matter further. He'd be as safe as we can make him."

"*My* assistant?" Holmes echoed incredulously. "See here ...!"

"There's an idea!" Thomas Hudson sailed into the room with a tea tray. "I wonder why it didn't occur to me sooner? Mr. Basker *does* have promise. But what of Mr. Weller?"

"I'm sorry?" Phil shot a quizzical look Varti's way. "Highmost Purnal Yamada mentioned that you usually work with an assistant. Isn't that Mr. Basker?"

Holmes said, "I do not have an assistant at the moment."

"Two applicants, I think," Thomas said, his tone dreamy and certain. "How in either realm will you choose?"

# 45

## *Starting Over*

VESPER 11, FOUR NINETY-EIGHT
WILLIDAY
4 KNELLS, 32 KNICKS
ON THE SECOND FACE OF THE CLOCK

H olmes proposed a division of duties. It was a whole lot more like handing down orders, but Phil looked so relieved to have someone else providing direction. He was glad enough to return to the Bastion with Enzo, though he hesitated over leaving Varti behind.

Waving them off, Holmes said, "Weller is with me."

To which Varti replied, "I'm obviously against you."

"I haven't had a proper rival in ages."

"I'll go easy on you, as you're out of practice."

"Do you even know how to go easy?" countered Holmes.

Which made Phil relax into a wrysome smile and get back to work.

Holmes tapped a finger against his frown until they heard the front door close. "I let it see. Irascible thing. It wouldn't settle until I let it see that you are unharmed."

Doggerel.

Varti crossed to where Holmes slouched in an armchair and bent close, peering into his eyes.

The man's gaze didn't waver. "It's more at ease with you than the Baskerville brat."

"Nobody ever regretted placing their trust in a self-proclaimed expert."

"I am one such expert."

Varti drew back, unaccountably disappointed that he couldn't see any sign of his dog in the man's demeanor. Even his eyes, which were a piercing sort of gray, were ordinary when compared to the Hound's lustrous silver.

"Do you trust me?"

"Yes. Entirely."

His brows arched, and he countered, "Qualified trust. I suppose you've taken issue with my assessment of the beast within. But when it comes to the task at hand, to my work. Do you trust my integrity there? Will you permit access to your findings, even knowing I might be harboring the killer?"

Varti was so sure, it was almost insulting that he had to speak. "You *are* the killer."

Holmes slouched even further into his chair. "I must admit, I find some small comfort in your conviction. Shall we get down to it, then? You will escort me to Files & Evidence. Your Mr. Kemp's recitation of the facts left much to be desired, so I'll need to consult the case files."

Now that Phil had met with and agreed to work with Holmes, this was permissible.

"And ... if you would be so good." Holmes unfolded from the chair and checked his pocket watch. "It may be necessary to appease the beast. It has expressed a craving for eggy buns."

Doggerel.

Varti couldn't see him or reach him, but he was in there

somewhere. And that was for the best. So long as he was trapped inside Holmes, he was safe from accusation.

Varti was so focused on which documents Holmes most needed to read, he completely forgot that he'd left his staff in a state of confusion.

At the front desk of Files & Evidence, Henna yelped at the sight of him, then burst into tears. "Where did you go? Where have you been? What happened to Doggerel?"

"He needed to go out. I walked him in the park."

"How did you leave?"

"Out a window."

"In the *basements*?" She realized the futility of asking questions and turned to Holmes. "Do you have anything to do with this?"

"How do you do? Mr. Weller has brought me in as a consultant. I'll need access to several case files."

"What? Goodness. Yes, all right. I have the forms right here." Henna reached for the request slips, but she wasn't entirely diverted. In an injured undertone, she said, "We were *so* worried."

"He's back, and he's clearly intact." Holmes considered the form then complained, "One for each file? Is that really necessary? Weller, you do them."

Varti began jotting off file numbers from memory.

"Signatures?" Henna asked. But her concern vanished when Varti passed her the first two forms. "Oh, I see! No problem.

You've a member of Highmost Perior Kemp's team right here."

She plucked a green pen from its holder and proffered it to Varti, who neatly added his name to each form. They were valid because Phil had given him the authority. Rusting bolts, it felt good.

"Two more forms, if you please." As soon as Henna relinquished the additional forms, Holmes briskly said, "Right, then. We'll carry on in Weller's office. No interruptions."

The woman gaped at his retreating back and shot a look at Varti that begged, *Who does he think he is?*

Which was so in keeping with the snippy asides in all of the case files Varti had read, he wanted to laugh. Instead, he followed Holmes downstairs and showed him to a seat at one of the reading desks. The one closest to his own worktable, in case the man needed anything.

For the next few knells, Holmes did little more than read case files while distractedly consuming eggy buns and sipping the tea Henna brought round in order to check on Varti. And to let him know her tocking had ended. And to remind him that there was a curfew.

Wouldn't matter. Holmes would probably take all night.

At odd ends, Varti caught up on newspaper clippings.

Knells later, Holmes said, "Weller. Show me the watchchains from the evidence lockers."

At first, Varti worried that Holmes would try to make another bid for the materials in the Benedick Carraway case, but the man remained at the reading desk while Varti brought him the chains, then ran back and forth fetching reference books and newspapers. Whatever the man needed.

He could have been annoyed.

Historically, badges were.

But Varti had gone into this forewarned.

He'd put up with Holmes. For Doggerel's sake.

During another lull, Varti went to the cabinet and chose a new file folder, adding it to the case log and assigning it a number. He labeled the file BENEDICK, and he named himself as lead investigator, with Doggerel as the petitioner.

He made some initial notes, then cross-referenced the records that had been submitted last season. The whole affair was oddsome. According to a brief note clipped to the top page, it appeared that the Academy of Mages had requested that the Bastion close the investigation. The only signature was a stamp. One Varti didn't recognize. He was trying to replicate it in pencil for his own case file when Kel stalked in. Her glare would have quelled chimeras.

She had a wooden drink caddy in her hands, and when he scraped his chair back and stood, she shoved the box into his chest. "I've been lost in the backhalls for *knells*, trying to find you."

"Serves you right," he muttered, trying to lead her away from Holmes.

She didn't budge. "Is everything all right?"

How to answer?

"No, of course it isn't. But with him." She angled her head toward Holmes. "Does he bear watching?"

"No."

Kel frowned. "Right. Should I stay on?"

"Yes."

"If you say so." She stood down and took a resigned tone. "At least I'm not bored. I'll alert the night watch that you'll be here until all knells." And giving his shoulder a light cuff, she walked out.

Varti found a hex of thermal cups of tea—the good stuff from a shop, not a vending machine—and another hex of chicken soup. His stomach growled, and he checked his pocket watch. At this rate, they really were going to be here straight through winding and into locking time.

When Varti returned from a quick nip over to The Lurking Smile for sandwiches, Holmes was partway through his second cup of soup. "Are you catering to me or to the beast."

"Doesn't matter."

"I fear it does. Wretched thing keeps asking after you."

Had he phrased it that way on purpose? Wretched thing. It's what Varti called Doggerel. "He's mine."

Holmes eyed him wearily. "That's a strange lie, don't you think? Does it often use your hopes to hurt you?"

He picked at his sandwich. "No, never."

Holmes finished eating with brisk economy, as if getting a necessary task out of the way. But when he returned to his reading, he did say, "That was good. Thank you."

Varti took a large bite to quiet the insult he could feel dancing on the tip of his tongue.

"Starting over is cumbersome. Carraway was with me for so long, we each knew what to expect, what was needed. All without words. Not unlike the balance you've found with your Mr. Kemp."

"In every report I've read, you are praised as a good-natured, kindly soul."

"Clearly not. Though it *is* useful to have an assistant with those qualities." He peered thoughtfully at Varti. "You would be quite the departure. Contrary and pugnacious by turns. And you lie with so much conviction, idiots might actually believe you. The Baskerville brat is more in line with the usual sort. Optimistic, knowledgeable in his field, sense of justice intact. Just affable enough to put up with me."

"Mr. Basker is the obvious choice."

"It hardly bears thinking." Holmes drained his tea before adding, "I do wish Mr. Hudson hadn't taken a shine to the idea. Unaccountable, yet impossible to discount."

So they were rivals for the position?

Varti had always excelled in competitions.

"It doesn't like the else lights." Holmes pointed up. "They make it easier for me to keep my wits about me."

That was surprising. Doggerel hadn't avoided this room. He'd seemed content enough curled up at Varti's feet. Perhaps being under the shadow of the worktable had helped?

At long last, when he'd gone over every detail in the files, Holmes retrieved two extra request slips. He dashed off several lines, correctly filling in two case numbers that nobody else knew about. "If you would be so good. I require these as well."

Varti plucked a green pen from its place and added his signature, which allowed him to bring out two additional files— LOST DOG and SET UPON BY DOGS.

# 46
## *Ghosts*

VESPER 12, FOUR NINETY-EIGHT
TROUDAY
8 KNELLS, 22 KNICKS
ON THE FIRST FACE OF THE CLOCK

**V**arti arrived early for his tocking, feeling vaguely discombobulated. The Green Man was still locked down, so after escorting Holmes into Mr. Hudson's and Durst's keeping, he'd spent what was left of the night at Ramage's. That part had been good, but as a consequence, he'd skipped his usual run, then eaten too large a breakfast. He also hadn't seen Phil, and he missed Doggerel.

Quieting his mind enough to focus took so long, he may as well have been late for work.

A few knells later, a familiar clatter and jingle dragged his attention to the stairs. Phil strode his way, expression bright.

"We have something definitive," he announced. "Mr. Holmes's assistant was able to shed some light. Actually, I think it was his familiar that suggested it. But it meshed with what Hexadille was already pursuing. It's not the answer to everything, but it's a lead."

The lift *ding*ed, and Kel escorted Dr. Kang and Hexadille Porter into the room, then grabbed a seat for herself, arms folded, intent on staying. Phil acknowledged her with a nod, then invited Hexadille to make her report.

"I have photographic documentation—backed up by subsequent witness testimony—that O. N. Acres left an echo. As did the more recent victim, Jacob Oswald. We can get pedantic about unreported cases, but as a rule of thumb, such strong, stubborn, clear emanations *never* form within the city walls. Ancient wards are in place to prevent it from happening, which is why these arrivals are so perplexing. But Mr. Basker and his familiars proposed a very different explanation.

"Rowena and I—she's my business partner—we put his theory to the test and confirmed something that's frankly staggering. They're ghosts."

Varti had no idea what his face was doing, but inwardly? He was less than impressed. This wasn't news. They'd brought in a ghost photographer because they had ghosts.

"*Not* emanations from the fae realm," Phil quickly supplied. "Not echoes or keepsakes or visitors as we know them. Willa really is Willa. And the ghost of Owen Acres is the man himself. The same goes for Jacob Oswald."

"I'm calling them *true* ghosts." said Hexadille. "These people had their souls cast out of their bodies, and then those bodies were savagely destroyed."

"Tell him about Aster," suggested Phil.

Aster March. She'd been the second victim. Her watch and its chain were rose-gold, which Henna said had been trendsome several decades back. It had probably belonged to a grandmother. Aster's trinkets followed the usual pattern, but her early education had taken place in Plover. A large tear-shaped pearl hinted at a continuing love for the sea. Her purse had been rather flat, holding little more than a lending card for the Bibliotheca, peach-tinted lip balm, and a handful of takeaway receipts.

Hexadille said, "On Rowena's recommendation, I searched again for the souls of the earlier victims. Because if they weren't fast-fading emanations, we should be able to find them. Aster is our first success. Kemp and Basker found her early this morning, loitering in the bibliotheca branch in the Station District, which is near the building where she was employed. Her coworkers say it's where she took all her lunch breaks." Hexadille managed a small smile. "Aster seems a perfectly lovely person. Most helpful. And cautious. Nobody in that bibliotheca branch seems to have noticed that they've a ghost haunting their stacks."

Ghosts. *True* ghosts.

What degree of communication was possible? Willa's ghost had shown interest in Phil's reading, but she couldn't speak. Then again, neither could *he*. Not reliably. So that might not be a barrier if the individuals involved found creative work-arounds. Which meant that if all seven souls of the victims were found, they'd have seven witnesses to the murders.

Dr. Kang took over then. "I've gone back over everything, and I believe all of the victims were torn apart from the inside. I speculate that the killer somehow forced out the soul, taking its place. But something went wrong. Maybe they weren't compatible." He made the same wrenching gesture he'd shown Varti. "And so they broke free in order to try again."

Hexadille said, "The concept isn't new. Some religions call it possession, indwelling, or transference. In ancient times, it was speculated that making the leap from an aging body to a youthful one was the path to immortality."

Phil said, "Enzo referred to something called a *fell beast*. We think it's searching for a physical host. The killings are happening more quickly, so it may be getting desperate. Or ... angry? Frustrated." He frowned, then suggested, "Given the string of victims, they may have preferred a female host, but their clock is unwinding.

"We think Jacob Oswald was not only tracking the killer, he had it cornered. Enzo was able to confirm that the arrangement of crystals in our alley was the beginning of a trap."

That raised another question. What was the thing doing outside their tenement?

Thomas Hudson had implied that removing Varti to Hibernacle House had been for his safety. Was it possible that the killer had been looking for him? If so, was Varti endangering Ramage, Aril, and Burr by staying at The Speckled Hen?

He shouldn't go back there. It wasn't worth the risk.

"Hexadille and I will be working to track down the missing ghosts. With Enzo, of course. I want to see if Owen is still around, and apparently Enzo knew Oswald. They're my starting point for today. In the meantime, can you sort out the best places for us to search for the others—Gemma and Polly and Tess?"

Varti simply shook his head.

Phil softly asked, "Any need to call in Purdle yet?"

No. They had a clear direction. Better to wait and see if they needed those precious four words for whatever they found out. Varti's rude gesture had Hexadille studying him through different colored lenses.

After the rest left, Varti stared glumly at his desk. He could pull out the files again, but by this point, he had them memorized. And they were as good as useless. None of the badges who'd filled out those reports had included personal details like where the victims liked to go on their lunchbreaks. They'd need to go back and speak to their families, their friends, their coworkers. He wasn't going to be much help there. If anything, he'd probably hinder the investigation.

"Give me one of the ladies." Kel was still in her chair, arms folded. "I can ask for basics. Actually, I'd like to take two of them. Tess and Polly. Unless you think I'm overstepping."

He brought her the files. "You're an incompetent."

"To be *courteous*," she began, favoring him with a beady look. "I'll check in every knell with updates. And I won't push past dark. Good?"

"Worst idea I've ever heard."

Kel angled her head toward the door. "Want to come along?"

"Yes. No. Yes." His answer confused even him.

With a nod, she walked out.

Varti wondered if Holmes was in a similar state of frustration, forced to stay back while hoping others—namely Varti—could sort out where their killer was hiding.

# 47

## *Specialist*

Vesper 12, Four Ninety-Eight
Trouday
9 Knells, 22 Knicks
on the first face of the clock

E nzo put off asking until the very last minute. Standing in front of the city's equivalent of the police department, he blurted, "May I bring a friend?"

Kemp pivoted with a swish of his very official-looking copper cape. His gaze went to Purdle and Cubit, and he answered, "Your familiars are more than welcome."

"I meant a fellow mage. I think he might have valuable insights. He specializes in ghosts."

Hexadille perked up. "One of the mages at academy? You can't mean true ghosts, though."

"He did mention souls ...?"

Kemp was nodding. "If you know someone who can lead us toward an answer, I'm willing to meet them. Which department is he in?"

"To be honest, I never asked about that. But he's really knowledgeable. Really ... informed."

Hexadille asked, "Should we split up? I'm meeting Rowena at the station in ten knicks. Divide and conquer?"

"I'd be grateful. See if Rowena can pin down Gemma's location. I'll bring Enzo and his professor around to confront Owen. And if there's enough daylight, we'll see if Oswald is still in my back alley."

Enzo hadn't meant to be misleading. Or to imply that his fellow mage was one of his professors. Maybe it was a natural assumption? But he really did want Arty's opinion on this. "Skrik, can you find Arty? Let him know about ... all this. Well, maybe not *all* of it. Since I don't think Mr. Kemp wants to broadcast certain parts. But tell Arty that I need help. And to meet us umm ...?" He looked to Kemp for guidance.

"Out front of the academy is fine. I'd rather not inconvenience him."

So they walked along, with Cubit swaying confidently in the lead. Mr. Kemp was a nice guy. And popular. All along Cenotaph Road, people recognized him. Enzo guessed he stood out nearly as much as Cubit, what with the vibrance of his ginger hair.

Enzo was still trying to figure out how to explain about Arty when Skrik returned and reported, "He's on his way."

"But we're going there."

"He wouldn't wait." More softly, Skrik said, "You said you needed help."

"Oh ... whoops? I went and made him worry. And he's on his way?" Enzo wondered how Arty would know where to find him, but then ... if anybody might know, it was definitely Arty and his crumbs.

"I see him!" Purdle sang out.

From the direction of the Academy of Mages, Arty came flying on Swirly, weaving effortlessly between slower vehicles.

Stopping in front of Enzo, he glared belligerently up at Kemp. "Are you making trouble for my friend?"

"Arty!" greeted Purdle, seemingly oblivious to the tension. "Have you built me a monocycle yet? You're so fast!"

Tone immediately gentling, Arty said, "Not yet, Purdle. But I haven't forgotten your wish."

"My wish!" Purdle echoed with a chortle. "Yes, you should grant my wish. That would be nice for a change."

Kemp spoke up then, hand extended. "Hello, there. You're Arty?"

Squaring up to the officer, he said, "That's what they call me, yeah. All right there, Enzo?"

"It's okay. Nothing's wrong. Nobody's in trouble." And gesturing at Kemp, he added, "This gentleman is in charge of finding the ... umm."

"I know who he is," Arty said coolly. "Highmost Perior Philtrum Kemp."

"That's right." Kemp let his hand drop. "I hadn't realized you were a student."

"Got a problem with that?"

"I'm only surprised. Enzo is under the impression that you can help me."

Arty straightened. "You're calling me up?"

Kemp shrugged. "I'm definitely considering my options. Enzo said you know about ghosts?"

"Could be." His gaze darted between them. "Is this maybe about the ghosts of the victims?"

Kemp indicated the road. "Do you mind if we walk and talk?"

"Not so fast. If you're at a loss, then this isn't a typical emanation. I bet I can help, but I need more information."

"This is a Bastion matter."

"I get that. All the more important that I go in with some forewarning. And equipment. So what should I pack?"

Kemp didn't hesitate for long. "We're going to attempt to speak with the ghost of one of the victims."

"Which one?"

"Owen Acres."

"I know the guy."

"You do?" Kemp was clearly surprised.

"Not personally, but ... you know what?" And flashing a grin, Arty said, "I've got an idea. Be right back. Oh, and heads up, Enzo."

"Yes?"

"Here comes trouble."

Arty zoomed off. Right past an oncoming Tuppence.

"Oh, I am in so much trouble," he whispered. And lifting a hand, he called, "Tuppence! I'm glad you're here. This is Mr. Kemp. He's an officer of the law, and he's after the killer."

She scowled. "I thought *we* were–"

"Tuppence, please!" Enzo cut across. Now that he'd finally found the Hound, he was going to protect him. And Mr. Hudson had explained that the best way to do that was to find the true killer. "I umm ... how sensitive are you to ghosts?"

"Are you questioning my capabilities?"

"No! Not at all. It's just ... well, it's never come up before. Skrik helped us out yesterday, but with you along, we might be even more useful to Mr. Kemp. Don't you think?"

Her glare faded. "This is important to you?"

"Yes. Will you help?"

Kemp stepped in then, offering his hand. "Hello, good lady. Are you Enzo's guardian?"

So he could tell. That simplified matters.

Tuppence said, "Yes. I will be going wherever he does. Are we hunting?"

"In a way. I want to try to have a conversation with the ghost of one of the victims. Finding them is important. And calming them, I think." And to Enzo, "I'm so glad Weller was able to secure your cooperation."

Enzo hadn't liked Weller very much. Even if he couldn't help it, his lies had made everything awkward. "If we can stop the murders, it's all good."

Tuppence barged in. "Will you be leading the young master into dangerous territory?"

"No! I shouldn't think so." Kemp lowered his voice conspiratorially. "Unless the young master is prone to gambling."

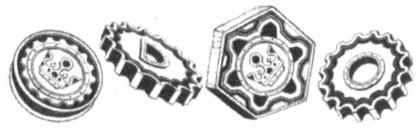

Enzo stole another look at Kemp, trying to figure out if the man minded Arty acting like he was in charge. But the redhead only dropped back to the rear of the group, a pleasant smile on his face as he scanned their surroundings.

"There've been a few rumors about the racetrack," Arty was saying. "Spooky stuff. Ever since last Chromday."

"How did you hear about it? I mean, you don't bet on horses, do you? And the racetrack is about as far from our tower as you can get."

"The hippodrome is right next to the skatepark, innit?"

Kemp added, "There was a small article in the *Hexagon* to that effect. Yesterday's edition."

"That's how it goes, yeah? Word gets 'round!"

"I have friends who *do* bet on horses, and they were in a proper clangor about it last night. That's one of the reasons I wanted to start here. Our good friend Owen is probably on the premises. Because if he'd gone home, Georgette would have put it on the front page of the *Sentinel* this morning."

Enzo must have looked confused, because Arty explained, "His missus is another reporter."

As they neared the hippodrome, Enzo took note of other sport-related venues in the vicinity. Arty's skate park, fields for football and rugby, and a lawn that might feasibly be used for cricket matches, archery tournaments, and jousts? Okay, not really. Enzo had never really been involved in team sports. Or … any sports.

Columns, arches, and statuary made the hippodrome the showpiece of the district.

Kemp said, "Mr. Acres had a gentleman's taste in hobbies. He liked his pipe and to wager on races. In fact, he owned one of the finest racehorses of the season. So there wasn't anything out of the ordinary with him being here."

"I've seen him up there plenty of times." Arty pointed to the section of hillside still staked off. "Me and my crew, we're here at least twice a week."

"Why would you take note of Owen?" asked Kemp.

"I mean … I'm an artist. Always taking in the view."

Arty led the way through the main gates of the racetrack like he'd been there a thousand times. Enzo didn't know where to look first, there was so much going on. Colored lights and fluttering banners and hawkers with refreshments on offer. While the seats weren't completely filled, a fair-sized crowd cheered on horses pulling small two-wheeled buggies.

"Not everybody notices ghosts. Mages are more sensitive to Realmish things."

"Mystics, too," said Kemp. "I was assigned to the irregulars because of my familiarity with Folk."

"Got a knack?" Arty asked.

Kemp's only answer was a small smile and a nod into the stands. "Shall we split up to search?"

Enzo was pretty sure all of them gave the officer the same blank look. If that was his plan, it was a good thing he'd asked for help.

"Nah, there's no need," said Arty, his tone just a little too diplomatic as he indicated the same direction all the rest of them had been looking. "That way, I think. He's up there."

# 48

## *Investigative Journalist*

VESPER 12, FOUR NINETY-EIGHT
TROUDAY
10 KNELLS, 51 KNICKS
ON THE FIRST FACE OF THE CLOCK

T all buildings overshadowed the stands, forcing the entire hippodrome into a kind of twilight, but strings of winking colored lights shone all the brighter because of it. Arty started up one of the steep staircases that fanned up into the stands. It was quite empty at the back, right up underneath an upper deck.

In the last row, a softly shimmering man sagged disconsolately in a seat, his gaze fixed on the track.

"Beg pardon," Arty said, completely casual as he stepped over the guy's knees. "You can sit tight. We're joining you."

The ghost glanced up in surprise. It made Enzo wonder if he'd given up on anyone noticing that he'd been cut adrift from his body. He offered a small wave.

Purdle wasn't half so shy. "Does it hurt?"

The ghost sat straighter as Enzo sat next to him.

Kemp picked a spot in the row below theirs, hooking his arm over the seat back as he peered up into the ghost's face. A pale and wisping hand stretched Kemp's way. The officer didn't flinch from his touch. He just lifted his own hand, but the ghost's passed right through him. "Hello, Owen. Sorry to take so long. We didn't realize what had happened, and we don't know *how* it happened. Maybe you can help us?"

Owen's ghost made a rude gesture.

With a sad smile, Kemp said, "I don't blame you for being angry. I've been next to useless, but I have good people around me. These two want to help."

"Count again," Purdle suggested snippily.

"Six then," amended Kemp. "Unless Arty here has a familiar of his own who'll need to be acknowledged."

This time Arty ignored the leading tone.

"My name's Arty, and my friend here is Enzo. He can't help being foreign, but he's nearly as brillsome as I am. I can help you, but this Highmost Perior has a firstmost priority. I mean … city to protect, killer to catch, and all. You help him, and I'll do my bit. 'Pon my word."

The ghost passed a hand over his face, opened his mouth, then grabbed at his throat. Owen's expression shifted toward anger, then his shape rippled and blurred.

"Easy, now," urged Arty. "Calm is best for communication."

"He can't speak," Kemp pointed out. "None of them have been able to."

"Who's the expert here?" Arty rolled his eyes and opened his kit. "You being a reporter and all, I'm sure you know your way around one of these."

He placed an input deck on his knees and flipped up the top.

Owen snatched at the machine, but his hand passed right through it.

"Unwind a little. I'm still setting up." Next Arty brought out a clockwork golem. Unlike the one he'd brought to class, this one was basically humanoid, its body about the size of Skrik. "You should be able to inhabit this. Runes are top notch. Integrate, and you can move it. And that means you can use the deck to communicate."

The ghost didn't budge.

"It's not a trap," Arty grumbled. "You can come and go as you please. It's like … a suit of armor. Or like having a sit in your favorite chair at the club. This is a generic design. Something I had on hand. If you take a fancy, I could work up something more personal. So long as you're not opposed to a more prolonged collaboration."

Owen looked to Kemp, who raised his hands. "I've known the young man for a scant knell, and I'm no expert on this kind of coggery. But I'll protect your rights to the best of my ability. You're still a citizen of Newcomb."

Enzo quietly asked, "May I see?"

Arty handed off his golem. Enzo turned it around looking for an opening. Arty reached across, flipped a catch, and pointed into the inner workings. "Main runes are etched here. Nothing binding. No contract sigils. I use it for training newbies."

Enzo studied the runes, then suggested, "Give it a try, Skrik?"

The imp sighed. "If I must."

Arty closed everything up again, and Skrik looked it over, passing his hands across the surface before pressing through a crack. Right away, the golem looked up, stood to its feet, and inspected its own hands.

"All right there, Skrik?" asked Arty.

The mechanical man sat back down, bowed its head, and Skrik billowed back out, reforming beside it. He said, "A nice toy." And to the ghost, he said, "Arty told the truth. You will be safe."

O. N. Acres reached for the golem. As before, his hand passed right through it. But the inner runes triggered, drawing him in. Enzo caught a fleeting expression of perplexity on the ghost's face before he vanished. It took a little longer than with Skrik, but the mechanical man began to fidget, testing joints and peering around.

"All right there, Owen?" asked Arty. "Take your time. Get a feel for it."

He tried to stand and staggered, but that didn't stop him. Owen crawled awkwardly to the input deck and began pushing keys. Words scrolled across the display.

THANK YOU. IT DOESN'T HURT, BUT I FEEL COLD.

Purdle made a soft noise of sympathy and snapped his fingers at Enzo. "Give me your handkerchief!"

He searched his pockets. Fruitlessly.

Kemp offered his, and Purdle beamed at him. "I like you. Consider yourself blessed." Then he shook the thing out and tied it around the golem's neck like a tiny cape.

All the while, Owen kept typing.

IT WAS AN ORDINARY DAY. STOP THE PRESSES
RACED WELL. WE TOOK A FAT PURSE. I WANTED
MY PIPE, SO I WALKED OUT TO MY FAVORITE
PATCH AND ... AND ... EYES. AND A VOICE.
AND SOMETHING SNAPPED.
BROKE.
THAT WAS WHEN THE COLD BEGAN TO SEEP IN.

Okay, this guy was definitely used to telling stories. He was rattling off his report with ease, despite the recent displacement of his soul. And the details? Those worried Enzo. He traded a look with Skrik. This could be bad. He only knew of one kind of creature that could force their way into the place where a human's soul belonged.

MY SENSES. I CANNOT SMELL.

CANNOT TOUCH. CANNOT TASTE.

AND PEOPLE PASS BY WITHOUT SEEING ME.

OR THEY SEE ENOUGH TO STARTLE

OR SCREAM OR SCURRY AWAY IN DREAD.

AM I DEAD?

"Only your body," said Arty.

Purdle tutted and patted the golem's arm. "You are still a person, but you aren't human anymore. Neither am I. Congratulations?"

Skrik said, "Dying is not always ending."

Owen twisted to look at Kemp before tapping out a single word.

GEORGETTE

The redhead's expression softened into sadness. "Would you like for me to arrange a meeting?"

The golem held still for so long, Arty asked, "All right there, Owen?"

NO.

NO.

NOT READY.

DO NOT TELL GEORGETTE.

NEED TIME.

DO I HAVE TIME?

"All kinds of time, so take it easy." Arty shot a look at Kemp, then said, "Best we hurry things along. Ask your questions."

The clockwork figure spread his hands wide and beckoned.

Kemp ran through the events of the day with him, and his answers were succinct. Only when it came to the moments just before and after his death was Mr. Acres hazy about what had happened. All he really had were vague impressions that didn't add up to a helpful description. At an impasse, Kemp gestured for Enzo to take over.

"Mr. Acres, have you ever been assessed for magical aptitudes?"

YES. STANDARDIZED TESTS.

Arty explained, "Every kid's tested, all through their early forms. Helps with placement in the academy system."

"Are you privy to your results? For instance, would you know your linking score? Is it called that here? Testing for an intrinsic capacity to work in tandem with an entity that exists outside yourself."

"I think he means synchronicity," said Kemp. "A high score in that column is desirable for anyone going into the Academy of Mages or into the Seminary of Mercies, since it's considered a prerequisite for communing with a deity, patron, or familiar."

Arty said, "My synchronicity score is top tier. They invited me into the mage academy early."

"Mine is middling," Kemp shared. "I have much higher augury numbers."

The clockwork golem began to type.

SYNCHRONICITY RUNS ON MY MOTHER'S SIDE
OF THE FAMILY. SHE WAS PLEASED
THAT I RANKED IN THE MID-SEVENTIES.
FOR SENTIMENTAL REASONS.
IT'S NOTHING SPECIAL.
NEVER PURSUED TRAINING.

Enzo glanced between Arty and Kemp. "I'm short on context. Is mid-seventies considered ... good?"

"My rank is one fifty-six." Arty was clearly bragging.

Kemp whistled. "Mine is seventy-two, which is better than average."

"Is it?" Enzo asked, trying not to show his incredulity. They could be assigning scores differently. Although seventy *was* considered the baseline for mage-craft in most countries. "Okay, that's ... interesting. Can we check the synchronicity ranking of the other six victims?"

"Easily," Kemp assured.

"Say. What's *your* sync score?" Arty asked suspiciously.

Enzo didn't like to say. "My family situation is unusual. You might say we breed for the quality. My lineage is full of people who were ... the right sort of people."

"Numbers!" demanded Arty.

"Three hundred twelve."

"Godlyle's tarnished baubles, that can't be right! Has to be a different system or something." Arty demanded, "Purdle, is his rank twice mine?"

"Lovely, isn't it? Aren't you proud of him? I certainly am."

Enzo asked Kemp, "How many people in Newcomb would

rank your level or higher?"

He admitted, "I have no idea."

ONE IN SIX HUNDRED

The clockwork golem pointed to himself and to Kemp. Pivoting so that he pointed at Arty, he returned to his keyboard.

ONE IN TWELVE-THOUSAND

RUST IT ALL, PHIL!

GET THIS KID AWAY FROM HERE.

AND THAT GOES SIXFOLD

FOR THE WINNER OF THE BREEDERS CUP.

HIGHER RANK, HIGHER RISK

# 49

## *Simple as Simpkin*

T hanks to Kel's findings, Varti was able to create summaries of likely places where the irregulars could track down the missing ghosts. With each new detail, Varti got a fuller picture of the individual lives that had been lost. Their quarters, their coworkers, their neighborhoods, their hobbies, and any habits that might refine the search.

Gemma Zimmer, the first victim, hadn't taken up any hobbies, though she went to the Cathedral "pretty often." She'd lived with her brother, who hadn't known anything about what she did there, not being religious himself.

Polly Barrister, the third victim, was a member of the Royal Garden Club and had also volunteered at a private zoo in the Terrace District. She'd adopted a Werifesteria tree in Fullnis Park and a set of twelve planters down in the Burrows. A true gardening enthusiast.

And Tess Atkins, the fourth victim, had not been employed, but she'd become a local leader for her neighborhood, trying to get her hex listed as a designated historical district. Their rallying cry—revitalization over revolutionization—had been covered in the *Clockwork Sentinel* by O. N. Acres. That was a connection they'd missed before. Had any of the other victims met?

Kel carried the report directly to Yamada on behalf of their team, and Varti's tocking ended without fanfare.

He didn't know what to do with himself. If the killer was somehow trailing him, he didn't want to bring trouble to Ramage's doorstep. He aimed for the Drears mostly out of habit and went to the baths alone. The day was getting on, and curfew would soon be in force, so he put his uniform back on. Dinner. He needed to eat something, and he didn't fancy gnawing through a bun on a street corner.

The Green Man was still locked up tight. He missed his routine. Wished Phil could do a reading. Hated that he couldn't update the case wall. And he wanted Doggerel at his side. It had felt so right, having a dog in his life. Should he look into getting a pup?

Varti immediately rebelled against the idea. He didn't want to start fresh with some weansome and wriggling runt. Doggerel hadn't simply seemed intelligent; he'd been a person in his own right. A partner.

He made up his mind and started walking.

It was an impulsive choice, and he regretted it almost immediately. Because when he reached the Banderole & Bugle, Sylvester Thornapple was there just ahead of him, doffing his cap and holding the door. "Merry met. Shall we?"

"What a coincidence."

"You chose your path, and I chose mine accordingly." Sylvester angled his head. "We're letting in a draft."

Giving in was easy. Varti hadn't wanted to be alone. He sank into a deep chair near the hearth and watched the dogs lazing there. Sylvester came from the bar with two mugs. Varti sniffed and sipped. Hot milk and honey, with a splash of something stronger and a dash of something spicy. Not a thing he'd have ordered on his own, but it was new and interesting, and it warmed him through. He relaxed, and maybe he let down his guard a little, because Sylvester was ready for the lapse.

"You've lost your dog."

"Yes. He's gone for good."

"Glad to hear it." And with a considering look, "Why so glum?"

"No reason."

"You look like a man who's lost *something*. Had a tiff with your bestie? He's been scarce since the mucking of your alley."

Varti really wished Sylvester didn't know so much. It was suspicious. Or maybe the man was a compulsive snoop. Varti couldn't guess what he was after. *Something*, though. Holmes had been after something. Did that make Varti an easy mark?

"Suspicious, are you? I haven't been following you. Not exactly."

Sylvester's clockwork cat glided into the open, strolling fearlessly past the dogpile before the fire and sitting primly on the floor before Varti. He said, "I've always been a cat person."

"Her? You shouldn't trust her any farther than you can throw her. Not that she'll let you get a hand on her. Very standoffish is … my … Guinevere."

The cat reared up, placing metal paws on Varti's knee and offering a creaky *mew*.

"Well, now. Seems you've caught her interest. Mind your pockets. She'll pick them clean."

Varti doubted that was even possible, but then again, Sylvester *had* promised not to lie to him.

Guinevere coiled back on her haunches, then leapt onto Varti's lap, where she curled into a heavy lump across his thighs.

"She was made for mousing, so she has a proper set of fangs. Always bringing me things—dead rats, tree balls, bottlecaps, small change, and the odd bit of gossip."

"Scrap her."

A metal ear swiveled his way.

"Don't listen to this one, Guinny love. He talks rubbish, but watch his hands and his feet and the set of his shoulders. They say plenty about a man and his true intentions."

Varti nodded. Because it wasn't true. The curse messed with his expressions and gestures all the time.

"Spellings like yours aren't terribly complicated," said Sylvester. "You can be a handful for it if you set your mind to it. Let's play a game. A contest between you, me, and that bit of bother."

Varti was more than *bothered* by his curse. "Don't meddle. I'm happy as I am."

"A weak will is easy to overcome, but you're a thinking man. Resisting. Withstanding. I can admire that, and I'll concede that silence is one form of triumph. But let me teach you another." Sylvester leaned closer. "I'll teach you *and* your hanger-on both. More fun that way."

"I'm terrible at games."

"Plays to win and likes to play," Sylvester accused. "Ready? What if old Vester was to say something preposterous, and you want to disagree. Can't shake your head, though. Too honest. So you nod. But opposites are simple as simpkin. So we set a new

315

rule. Nodding means check your hands. I look to see if your hand is palm-up or palm-down."

He demonstrated each position.

"Palm-up to affirm. Palm-down to deny. Only your curse just learned that trick, too! Thinks it's so clever. But a new rule will work a treat. Palm-up cancels out the nod, palm-down means check your feet."

His feet. Varti nodded, but why use such a convoluted plan?

"Tap your toe for the truth. Or turn out your foot to call for a better direction. And while the curse is scrambling to read your intentions and muddle the meaning of your every gesture, you take advantage." Sylvester sat back, looking entirely smug.

If Varti tried to confirm a statement, he'd contradict it. And if he managed to outmaneuver the curse's countermeasures, it was still even odds that he'd mislead the man. Varti went over the whole scheme twice and came to the conclusion that it was a load of dung.

"You're brilliant."

Sylvester Thornapple lifted a finger and tapped the side of his nose, then winked his brown eye. "It'll make more sense if we try it, so let's have a go. Lovely weather we're having."

Which may have been true. At least it wasn't raining. But Varti shook his head, then turned down his palm and tapped his foot.

"Three lies, nice and tidy. So you agree!"

The smugness coiling in Varti's soul spiked with indignation.

"Your gentleman friend in the Bridge District is as natty as he is knackish."

Varti supposed he meant Thomas Hudson, and he wondered how long Sylvester had been nosing about in the vicinity of

Holmes's office. "Am I not allowed to take a lover?"

Which was more deflection than contradiction.

Except that it was true enough to be confusing.

He ended up with one palm up and one down. And he clicked his heels together.

Eyes sparkling, Sylvester lifted a finger and said, "Take advantage."

Varti said, "Ghosts." Before he could be surprised over this smidgen of success, he unleashed a string of mortifying invectives that sent Sylvester into a fit of laughter.

"Doesn't like me, does it? You're a quick thinker, which helps. Faster we go, the more frantic it will be to contradict you." Sylvester leaned closer again. "Have you seen a ghost then?"

"Yes." Palm down. Right foot pointing off.

"But you want to."

"No!" he spat out. Palm up. Ankles crossing like he wanted to stay all night.

This was utterly useless. A nonsense game. Tedious and taxing. He didn't want to play. So he cast about, looking for something that would suit. The taverner kept a large basin on the floor for watering the dogs. Lugging Guinevere with him, Varti sank to his knees before the basin and dropped in his quadricentennial cog.

# 50

## *A Pig in Heels*

VESPER 12, FOUR NINETY-EIGHT
TROUDAY
5 KNELLS, 43 KNICKS
ON THE SECOND FACE OF THE CLOCK

"**W**hat are you up to?" asked Sylvester, peering over his shoulder. "What've you gone and done that for?"

The basin water welled up, heralding the splashy arrival of Purdle on Cubit.

"Hello, Varti Weller!" And spying Sylvester, his smile fell away. "Are you in trouble?"

"Imminent doom."

"That's fine, then. What sort of place is this?" asked the sprite, peering around.

"A stable. I muck it out on Troudays as my good deed for the week."

"Cozy. I like the dogs." The sprite's gaze returned to Sylvester, and he asked, "Who are you?"

Sylvester Thornapple tugged his forelock and said, "Evening, highness. Care for a spot of what we're having?"

"I don't think that's why I'm here." And he looked expectantly at Varti.

Grabbing Sylvester's arm, Varti waited for the man's full attention before carefully enunciating, "Seven ghosts. Seven witnesses."

"That ... wasn't nonsense, was it."

While Purdle happily explained his magnanimity, Sylvester steadied Varti up, since the cat made it awkward.

"Four words. That's a powerful boon. What did he do to win your favor?"

"Varti Weller is my *friend*."

"Pleased by that, are you?"

"So. Much."

Sylvester was suddenly all business. He dropped a few coins on the table—dodgers again—and asked, "Up for a stroll?"

As if these words were a signal, Guinevere unwound herself and sprang to the floor, slinking away.

"Wait!" Purdle appeared in front of Varti, holding out the quadricentennial coin in both hands. "Don't forget this, Varti Weller. Isn't it special to you?"

"No. You can keep it."

"I'll help. I can be very helpful." Purdle tucked the coin into Varti's vest pocket and patted it in an almost proprietary way. "Oh. I should ask. Do you have a synchronicity score?"

"No."

"Is it a big number?" Purdle asked worriedly.

"Most outstanding in my generation. Triple digits."

Sylvester Thornapple pointed out, "If he *was* exceptional, he wouldn't be in the regulars. It's the copper cloaks you have to watch out for."

Snapping his fingers, Purdle asked, "Is your score higher than Philtrum Kemp's?"

"Yes."

"So *lower*," the sprite muttered. "That should be all right, don't you think, Cubit?"

The newt gave no answer that Varti could see, but Purdle was satisfied. As soon as he and Cubit splashed away, Sylvester aimed them toward the door.

Antwan tried to stop them from leaving. "Sun's good as down, Sylvie. Curfew's on."

"I have myself a badge escort, now, don't I?" And waving his hat, he left with a cheery, "Merry the day!"

Which was answered by a chorus of well wishes. Sylvester Thornapple, friend of many. Would he stop singling out Varti once his curiosity was satisfied?

The evening had gone dark and damp. Varti tried to shake off the hand at his elbow, only to say, "I want to be carried."

"Begging your pardon, I'm thinking there's an order to things. Let's get something to fortify us for whatever's ahead." And angling his head inward, he said, "I'll show you the best of good times. Take you around to my favorite mum. Ever been to The Basted Hock?"

"Never heard of it."

"Lead on ...?" Sylvester invited.

Another game, but one that offered no challenge. Varti may never have eaten at The Basted Hock, but he knew its location. He didn't even hesitate. The two of them were underground in a trifling.

This was Varti's first evening visit to the Burrows since the queen had commanded a curfew. The undercity was unsettlingly empty. If Varti hadn't been in uniform, the patrols would have collared him and Sylvester, packing them off to a holding cell or a hostel to wait for morning.

"Cheery," muttered Varti.

"Eerie."

"It's sure to be open."

"They never close."

He was right. The Basted Hock was brightly lit, and twice-twelve customers crowded inside, filling the place with a gloom-defying din of conversation. Varti trailed after Sylvester, who stepped up to the takeaway counter.

The man there glanced up and smirked. "Vester. The usual?"

"You know my feelings about a Pig in Heels. Two orders, Saulie."

"Right you are. Won't take a knick." Saulie caught Varti's eye and added, "Scrappers know where to scrounge. You won't find better for a bob."

"You've a roomful," Sylvester remarked.

"This lot have a night tocking in the warehouses. Patrol has them pull together here, then escorts them 'cross to the Barge District. Keeps us hopping. Keeps us happy."

A Pig in Heels turned out to be a deep-fried cutlet of minced ham slathered in sauce and pressed between two heels of bread.

Saulie handed them off with a bluff boast. "You'll be back for another of those. Two, three more, and you'll be calling me mum."

They took their order out into the stillness of the vacant burrow, where they shared a bench. Sylvester produced two bottles of Aubade's from his scrip, and they ate quickly. Even folded into wax paper, the sandwich proved to be a messy meal.

"Good?"

"Worst of the worst."

"Pure bliss," said Sylvester. "Saulie never disappoints."

While Varti mopped up with his handkerchief, Sylvester produced his pipe and packed it with tobacco nipped from a square blue tin with white flowers on the label. Noticing Varti's interest, he passed it to him. COLUMBINE: WICKING TIME. The company was in Plover, a seaport to the southeast.

"Simple stuff. Suits me." Gaze fixed on the lazy thread of smoke drifting toward the gaslamps overhead, Sylvester asked, "Read anything interesting lately?"

Varti had trouble knowing how to answer. The question was so vague, with so little intent behind it, that any answer might be true or false. It was amusing to think that his curse could be stumped by something as innocuous as small talk.

He finally offered, "Case files always make for exciting reading."

"I suppose a man who reads for a living wouldn't spend his off-knells knocking about the Bibliotheca." Soft puffing filled the silence until he asked, "Ever run the wall?"

Surprised, Varti said, "I don't know what you mean."

"The Burrows are more to my taste, but a man like yourself can't spend all his time between the basements and the Drears. Those who like to feel the sun and wind on their skin take to the heights."

Most of the skyrises in Newcomb had rooftop gardens and walking trails, and Varti had visited all of those that were open to the public. But the city walls were high and wide, and there were parks and observation decks and long, daisy-chained tracks that were designed for running, cycling, and skating. In Fullnis, when the days were long, Varti spent his evenings running or rambling on the wall.

Sylvester next asked, "Any interest in religious matters?"

"Only on Newdays and Willidays." He nodded, turned up a palm, and tapped his toe. Mostly as a jibe, since the sequence was effectively meaningless.

Sylvester snorted, then began anew. "Poor Gemma. Georgie was heart-reft. She's his baby sister, and he could be overprotective. So she'd steal a few knells to herself once the work was done."

Gemma. He had to mean Gemma Zimmer. The first victim.

"You met him yourself. Her brother. Georgie's the tobacconist at Stummeltons. Them finding her about destroyed him. He's doing the best he can, but it's blighted him. Sad to see." Sylvester looked his way. "It's hardly a secret. Anyone in their surround—friends or neighbors—would tell you the same, though not in Georgie's earshot. To spare his feelings. He blames himself, even though I told him this wasn't the sort of thing you could stop, any more than you could take it back or fix it. All that's left is to move on."

Varti was almost choking on all the words he couldn't say.

"Easy, friend. I'm coming around to it. Now, Gemma? She was as sweet as they come. *Is*, if the soul is person enough to still count. Pure of heart, that young lady. All she wanted of an evening was a stroll along the James and a bouquet from the royal gardens, then off she'd go to chapel." Sylvester faced him then, gaze serious as he repeated, "Up for a stroll?"

He shook his head, thumbed his nose, stamped a foot, grabbed Sylvester Thornapple by the collar, and managed to snarl a single word through the muddle. "Please."

# 51

## *Piety Road*

VESPER 12, FOUR NINETY-EIGHT
TROUDAY
6 KNELLS, 36 KNICKS
ON THE SECOND FACE OF THE CLOCK

S ylvester tapped the back of Varti's hand, which had crept up to throttle him. "Goodness, your eyes have gone all soft. That cost you, didn't it? Olde things can be so cruel. All right, friend. We'll manage, you and me. Let's take the lady's walk and see if she joins us."

Varti let go, torn. He knew he shouldn't trust Sylvester Thornapple. He couldn't. Not fully. But the man hadn't lied. Varti was sure of it. Here was a chance to do something besides waiting for someone else to do the legwork.

Abandoning the bench, Varti disposed of their trash. Straightening his clothes, Sylvester softly clicked his tongue. A few flits passed, and Guinevere strolled out of the shadows, a dead rat dangling from her jaws. She lay it at Sylvester's feet and peered up at him expectantly.

"Must you?" the man asked.

She mewed.

"We don't want to run afoul of any other badges. See what you can do?"

With a flick of her tail, Guinevere was off.

Varti couldn't imagine what Sylvester expected her to do.

The man gestured in the direction she'd gone. "Shall we take in the night air?"

They rode a lift to street level, and Varti unhooked the duty lamp from his belt. In the Bridge District, wispy fog shivered above the James, so only the bridges were obscured. Stars shone faintly, but the moon hadn't yet put in an appearance. They kept to a stroll, passing flower stalls and food stands draped in green-striped tarps for the night.

The royal gardens were unnaturally still, but not entirely quiet. Music spilled from the six-story alehouse for which the district was famous. Were people really planning to dance until dawn?

"Connecting doors to two different sets of quarters," Sylvester remarked. "What's the harm? They should be safe, and Daniel will fill his till twice."

Varti wondered if Phil had found some blithesome place for the night, since they were home-reft. He stood for a while, searching the bright windows for a glimpse of red hair.

"Just along here," Sylvester softly called. "This is where she'd make her pick."

The tussy-mussy stand was laced up tight, but Varti knew what it looked like on Milvine and Fullnis days, bursting with color and surrounded by boys and girls with posy baskets, singing out to passersby.

"From here to Piety Road." Sylvester stood there, hands in pockets, waiting on Varti.

Giving it some thought, he chose the avenue that a lone woman who was fond of flowers would take. Because Mayfair

Lane was lined with neat hedges and overhung by young Werifesteria trees. And because it meandered through three small parks before they'd have to climb to station level.

They passed under Industry Road's distinctive archway, then the trestles of the railway, moving clockwise around to Piety Road, which skirted the Terrace District.

A group of factory workers with a four-badge escort rambled along toward Newsome station to catch the trolley. The guards acknowledged Varti with casual salutes and the hand signal for *all's well*, which Sylvester cheekily returned. And that was all. Very business-as-usual.

"She wouldn't be lingering anywhere along here."

He agreed, so they kept moving.

Varti spotted several mothers hosting crowds. Many of these eateries were located inside the buildings that the spoke road cut through, so residents could come and go without stepping outside. Those who lived inside the city walls would have even more options, since you could circumnavigate the entire city by traveling through the Passages.

"Strange, how they feel safe just because they're indoors," remarked Sylvester.

Varti didn't like that line of thinking. Not one bit. "If the Queen says to stay in, then in is made safe by the Queen."

"Do you often tell yourself lies?" Sylvester caught his eye and tapped his temple. "Can't see it. I'd wager ingots that you're brutally honest in there."

"Lies are a comfort."

"Not every truth is kind."

Further outward, once they passed under the last few buildings beyond the trolley station, Piety Road was briefly open to the sky. This was one of the most famous public sections of the city, because the approach to the Composite Cathedral passed through a tunnel of stained glass.

Lights suspended on the inside ensured that anyone nearby could see Piety Road's showpiece, and rows of gaslamps along the outside meant that even at night, those who sought the mercies were splashed by rainbow colors.

Varti had been to the Cathedral exactly twice. Realms & Religions was a standardized course in early education, and the topics were addressed again in greater detail before students could graduate from academy. Both times, those courses culminated in a class trip here. And both times, Varti had felt extremely out of place.

That hadn't changed.

They approached the cathedral's vast double doors, which were ancient wood, carved with sweeping depictions of Werifesteria trees. They stood wide open, which was strange. How could they be in compliance with the Queen's curfew if they didn't bar the doors? But a single blot in the midst of spilling golden light resolved into a figure seated on a stool. He stood, and Varti was surprised to recognize him as one of the two mercies who'd visited the site where Polly had been killed. The cowled Darke Childe armed with a cricket bat. He still carried it.

Gray-skinned and grave-faced, he solemnly said, "Be welcome."

Sylvester said, "Merry met, Ammil."

"Mr. Thornapple. And ...?"

Dark eyes swung Varti's way, briefly reflecting red in the light from his duty lamp. Realizing it was no longer necessary, Varti turned it off and hooked it to his belt.

"This is Badge Weller," supplied Sylvester. "We're looking for a friend. She's probably sheltering here for the night."

"This is a sanctuary."

"This gentleman isn't here to accost or arrest anyone. We're only going to confirm that the lady is here. It would put our minds at ease."

All true.

Maybe Ammil could tell, too, because he only asked, "Do you need a guide?"

Sylvester turned to Varti. "Do you know your way around this place?"

"Yes."

"Same. Ah, well. Yes, a guide, please."

The mercy gestured gracefully. "Turn to the right. Someone will meet you in the vestibule. Tell them what you need."

"Understood. Be seeing you, Ammil. Merry the day."

"Good eventide, Mr. Thornapple. Mr. Weller."

He made a gesture that Varti assumed was a blessing, then resumed his seat.

Varti edged inside the door, warily eyeing the Cathedral's ostentatious decorations. Lamps and candles and statues and oil paintings crowded a vast entrance hall, and doorways of every shape and size were set at intervals. He knew from his academy days that each led to a chamber set apart for ... well, for whatever shape the worship of its particular religion took.

To the right, mercies occupied a pew. They seemed to be studying, or possibly praying, because each held a small, square book, and they were murmuring softly. The sound of it wasn't unpleasant, and Varti didn't mind the mingled smells of the place. But visually? The Composite Cathedral was decidedly overwhelming.

A man stepped forward.

He was definitely Folk, but Varti was having trouble pinpointing his classification. It wasn't always easy to tell. But whatever sort of person he was, he was giving Varti—or more likely his curse—a bad case of the jitters. A mercy shouldn't be dangerous, should they?

"Good eventide. My name is Brother Dexter."

Sylvester swore under his breath.

Varti glanced at him. What was the problem?

"Ahhh, yes. Sylvestser Thornapple. My brother has mentioned you." With a smile that was just a little too wide, he asked, "What can I do for you?"

"Since it's you, I'll make this quick," Sylvester said flatly. "Gemma Zimmer. Is she here?"

"Yes!" With a fixed smile, Brother Dexter regrettably added, "And no. The tower is warded against unnatural things. She did not get very far."

"But you said she's here."

With the twirl of a hand equipped with slender claws, he said, "Not in the Tower, no. She is in the cloisters, which were added later and do not benefit from the dignitaries' blessings of peace and protection."

"Lovely loophole. Will you show us the way?"

"Certainly, sirs." Brother Dexter graciously inclined his head. "It would be my pleasure."

# 52

## *Guilty Pleasure*

**V**arti's previous visits to the Composite Cathedral had not included the cloisters, which was definitely a shame. Compared to the riot of ornamentation inside, the walkway Brother Dexter led them onto was calming. Graceful columns and arches sheltered a wide, covered path. Open to their left, it overlooked a courtyard, and to their right, small rooms hugged the tower wall. Each held a tableau that was secured behind barred gates.

Instead of gaslamps, this part of the grounds was lit by actual torches, their brackets set into stone walls. They guttered and smoked, providing wavering light. Varti wondered if they were really even needed, since the path was also lined with thousands of sparks of light. Vigil candles were set on every possible niche and ledge. They also edged the walkways in the courtyard. Since most things were stone, the unattended flames didn't pose the same danger here that they would have in his neighborhood. But he wouldn't have liked to be a mercy, draped in sweeping robes, hems fluttering close to all those tiny flames.

Something moved in one of the gated rooms. It looked like a flame jumping from one candle to the next. Varti stopped, peering between the bars. There. A fire sprite with hair like flames leapt from one cluster of vigil candles to the next, strolling between them like a shepherd tending their flock.

Varti glanced into more rooms as they passed. These held sarcophagi or altars or statues of scowling gods and scythe-bearing gods and many-armed gods. Some were ancient saints or dignitaries, their hands positioned to bestow blessings. Varti was baffled that all of these things could coexist without contradiction.

Did Qiiq the Raveler have a statue or a shrine somewhere? It might be nice to put a face to the name of the god whose trinket he'd been wearing for so many years.

A fountain trickled.

Doves cooed sleepily in the lone tree that was their roost.

A pair of cowled mercies passed in silence.

Was that flash of copper … Guinevere? Sly thing.

All the while they walked, Varti memorized each turning. He even confirmed his bearing with his pocket watch's compass. Mapping the proverbial labyrinth.

Passing through a colonnade, they left the covered walkway, entering a new courtyard, this one draped in moss. At its center stood a large, six-sided pavilion, its dome supported by columns tangled in woody vines. Another statue stood inside, and seated on its base were two figures, one significantly more solid than the other.

Brother Dexter stopped before the pavilion steps and bowed deeply. "Forgive our trespass. These gentlemen have come seeking Gemma Zimmer. Will you give them leave to approach?"

"Come forward."

Varti considered the lady. She was Folk, for antlers rose above the leafy crown that adorned the cascade of pale hair that fell to her waist. Her eyes were especially large, set wide and marked by barred pupils. She bore a passing resemblance to Aril and Burr at The Speckled Hen, but bare feet showed below the hem of her robes. And she had none of their shyness. Indeed, her direct gaze seemed to challenge him. Perhaps because she looked to be protecting Gemma Zimmer's soul. Pearly and pale, Gemma huddled at this mercy's side.

"Good evening, marm." Sylvester dragged off his cap and bobbed in a clumsy curtsy.

Varti had snapped to attention, but he bowed his head, hoping that was sufficiently respectful. Because he was almost positive that this lady was an Olde Childe. Some part of him—probably the curse—recoiled as if she were a threat. He suspected that this lady could unspell him, but he didn't know how to ask for help. Or what such a boon might cost.

Sylvester said, "My friend here is looking for whoever did this to Miss Gemma." And voice gentling considerably, he added, "Hello, love. You remember old Sylvie, don't you? We've been worried and came looking."

"She knows *you*." The mercy's gaze returned to Varti. "But not you."

"This is Thricemost Ferior Varti Weller of the badge regulars. A peaceable man. He's part of the team who'll stop these killings. May we ask questions, Gemma love? Maybe you know something that will help our Mr. Weller."

Varti kept his own mouth firmly shut, but it felt as if the curse had burrowed deep. When the Realmish lady caught his eye again, he found he could nod. And he was grateful.

Sylvester said, "That night. Do you remember it?"

"She does," answered the lady, who seemed perfectly prepared to speak on Gemma's behalf.

"A walk along the James? A posy to lighten your mood. Ah, no. A posy for *this* lady. An eventide offering."

"True."

Sylvester gently asked, "So this is where you came that night?"

"Yes, she came here. Came and went."

Sylvester winced. "So you were on your way home. What path did you take, Gemma, love? There are many ways home, and Mr. Weller thinks you like a pretty path."

"No," said the lady.

Gemma left her side then, moving toward Sylvester. She was trying to speak, making the same pattern of gestures over and again. Sylvester watched her closely. "It's all right. I'll hear you out. No need to beg Old Sylvie. Haven't I known you since you were a wee one?"

She hung her head.

He held out a hand. "You didn't stroll through gardens then?"

"No," confirmed the lady.

"Where might you have gone, Gemma love. What took you from us, hmm?"

The lady calmly said, "A guilty pleasure."

Sylvester frowned.

Varti could see his confusion. He'd described this young woman as pure and sweet. Not someone capable of anything sinful or seamy.

"She was hungry. She went down."

Sylvester fondly shook his head. "Oh, Gemma love. Only you

would feel guilty for stepping out on your mother. What then? Did you stop for a sweet or some pudding?"

"No."

As it happened, the young lady had wanted something fried crisp and spicy with sauce. And Varti felt a fool. He seized Sylvester by the elbow. The man searched his face, then said, "That's done it. Good girl, Gemma. We'll be cracking on, then."

And without acknowledging the lady's or Brother Dexter's help, Varti bolted back the way they'd come, retracing their steps until he blew past Ammil and along the stained-glass alley.

"What?" Sylvester caught up and matched his stride. "How was that important?"

Varti couldn't explain, but with the curse still recoiling, he found he could lie obviously. "They aren't connected at all. None of them."

"Done with me, then?"

"Yes. Get gone." And in utter exasperation, he added, "It was so obvious."

# 53

## *Hunting Grounds*

Vesper 12, Four Ninety-Eight
Trouday
8 Knells, 26 Knicks
on the second face of the clock

**B**ending the rules wasn't Varti's style. Normally, he wouldn't imagine straying from the particulars of his sworn duty. But Owen had died on the fourth day after Willa, and Oswald had died on the third day after Owen. This was the second night. Maybe it was too soon. But it might already be too late for some poor soul.

The connection Varti had made wouldn't help anyone if he couldn't communicate it. He needed Sylvester to make a report. A complete report. And that meant dipping into the evidence lockers so the man could see the slender thread they'd all missed.

Retracing the same route he'd used to escort Holmes out of the Bastion, Varti brought Sylvester in. Guinevere stayed ahead of them, skipping in and out of the light from Varti's duty lamp.

"I thought I was the only one who knew about these passages anymore," said Sylvester.

"I know all of the backhalls."

"Well, I actually *do*. Want me to show you around?"

Varti quietly admitted, "No." Because that was knowledge he badly wanted.

"Save me the odd Newday. You won't regret it." And after another couple of turnings, "This only goes one place. I know I'm not under arrest, so why bring me into the Bastion?"

"Guinivere needs licensing." Climbing the stairs that would lead them into the evidence lockers, Varti paused with his key. Then brought out his handcuffs.

Sylvester grimaced. "Isn't that a bit much? What if I promised to behave?"

Varti closed one of the rings around his own wrist.

"Maybe one day your trust in me will match mine for you." It was grudging, but Sylvester accepted the shackling.

Somewhat hampered by the cuffs, Varti carefully removed evidence from four separate lockers, then hurried down to his office, where he tapped a switch, filling the room with light.

Sylvester swore softly, tugging his hat lower over his eyes.

Laying out the items on the desk, he next went for the proper form for witness statements, Sylvester trailing after him all the while. Back at his desk, Varti filled in the case number, checked the box for anonymous testimony, then set the sheet before Sylvester.

He skimmed the page. "Not sure what I'm meant to report. Help me out."

So Varti lined up each item of evidence.

Three takeaway slips that had been folded into Aster March's purse. Investigators had discounted them since they weren't from the day she died. But they were all for the same shop, making her a regular.

The WC token Polly Barrister had carried. These were commonly used in the Burrows, where some mothers gave their customers access to a washroom so they could tidy up after a meal. Polly's was one of the personalized ones, stamped with the same shop name.

Tess's incidentals had included a badly stained and torn takeaway bag. Only a small part of the shop's logo was discernible, but Varti was certain that the previously unidentified shape was a pig's trotter.

Which brought them to the pig charm on Willa's watchchain.

"She clinches it. Definitely a devotee of Swirly's. So that's the connection? They share a mother. Or at the very least, the shop is near your killer's hunting grounds." Sylvester drummed his fingers on the desk, then held out his hand for the pen. "I'll make the report for you, but is that going to be enough? Your Mr. Kemp will take heed, but should we be leaving this to him?"

"I'm contemplating mutiny. I'll stop the killer by my own strength, with my own two hands."

"I'd be up for an overthrow, but *this*? It isn't the best path to glory, fame, or promotion. At least you realize you shouldn't be going in alone." Sylvester's gaze turned shrewd, but then he smiled. Giving his wrist a shake to rattle the chain that linked them, he cheerfully asked, "Together, then?"

That gave Varti pause. "We are enough. Skip the report."

Sylvester reached for a pen and began to write. "We *should* go have a look around. I don't like to brag, but I'm good at spotting this sort of trouble. Got a real nose for it."

Varti said, "You don't seem the sort to make trouble."

"You have me sorted. Be a dear and don't let on."

"I'll write up my own report."

Sylvester's pen nib scratched lightly over the page, and with every item he added, more of Varti's tension ebbed. This was working. Sylvester's motives might still be in question, but his assistance was making a world of difference.

"With my promise to deal honestly in force, I feel I should point out that you've overlooked something. Even the cleverest and most careful men do, from time to time."

Varti leaned close to scan the report Sylvester was making.

"Not with this, and not with me." And raising his voice, Sylvester sweetly called, "Whatever it is you've plucked, put it back and come over here, Guinevere love. Our Mr. Weller will blame himself if anything goes missing."

From several rows of shelves away, there came a guilty *mew*.

Once the testimonial was witnessed, signed, and sent off via pneumatics, Varti locked everything down, switched off the lights, and herded Sylvester—and his snoop of a cat—down into the backhalls. They needed to get into the Burrows.

Varti didn't like to think about cornering a predator. That part made him wish for Doggerel. So he focused on other things instead. Like intervening in time to save a life that would have been lost otherwise. He was one of Newcomb's protectors. And they had a lead. Sort of.

"I know exactly what to look for."

"Of course you don't," said Sylvester. "You're not a mage. And your curse isn't convivial."

Was Sylvester a mage then? Plenty of people had mixed

rankings on their early assessment tests, which meant that when they chose their field of study, they might have untapped aptitudes that went largely ignored. Hidden potential.

Sylvester tensed. "It might be soon. I think it'll be soon."

Varti wanted to ask how he could know that, but it probably didn't matter. Sylvester's conviction fell in line with Varti's own sense of urgency. Any day now. Any knell now. The imminence of it made Varti queasy. Or ... was his curse reacting to something? Why would it, though?

The Burrows were even quieter than they'd been earlier that evening. The only people moving openly were badges patrolling in teams of two. It would soon be midnight, and they'd cross over into locking time, when most mothers closed down until morning.

Off on the edge of everything, Varti lifted his duty lamp high enough that his uniform was obvious. Sylvester stayed behind him, and his voice was close and low. "Access panel just here. Another on the other side of this building. They're mirrored across the way." Sylvester reached past Varti's shoulder, pointing up into the shadows beyond the reach of the gaslamps. "These tunnels are domed, and there's a whole network of catwalks. Getting around unseen? Never been a problem."

Suddenly, a wail swelled, then thinned away, followed by a shrieking cry.

It echoed weirdly, but Sylvester found a bearing. "There! It's there!" he snapped and charged forward, disappearing around the corner.

Following protocol, Varti blew his whistle in a call for assistance even as he followed. He'd nearly caught up when another scream rent the air, this time in a cry for help. Varti rounded the corner at full tilt and had to pull up short.

Sylvester growled, "This one's unharmed," and spun a lady with full skirts, a snug bodice, and an excess of ruffles his way.

She was about his own height with pale pink ringlets framing a waxen face that was spattered with blood. Glossy lips trembled, and then a surprisingly husky voice begged, "Help? Oh, help. It's Salsify. H-he's … *nngh*." She clamped a hand over her mouth and swayed.

People were running from at least two different directions, and another whistle sounded.

Sylvester gruffly said, "I *can't* be here, and this one *shouldn't* be here. Bench. That way." Then he waved his hat at the oncoming badges. "Over here! It's happened again! Get word to Kemp!"

"I'm here!" called one of them. And it really was Phil. "Weller?"

"Not here!" And he guided their prospective witness toward the bench. They must have been wearing heeled boots under all those ruffles, because their feet clacked as they tottered along at Varti's side.

Theater district. That had to be it. Only a performer would dress so outrageously.

Varti knew how to handle distressed witnesses, but only in a by-the-book way. Reassure them first. Then get them talking. But opening his mouth wouldn't do either of them any favors. All he could really do was sit with them. When he did, they turned into him, hiding their face to muffle sobs that deepened as they dampened his shoulder.

He put his arm around shaking shoulders and gruffly said, "It's over now, sweetheart."

"It was awful."

"You exaggerate."

"I saw everything. Everything."

That was good. A witness. Well, a living one, which would make them so much easier to question.

"Am I safe?"

Varti sincerely doubted it. "Perfectly safe."

The pink ringlets tilted, and the man—yes, certainly a man—wrestled off his wig and bunched it up in his lap. Large eyes fringed in white lashes searched Varti's face. The pupils were horizontal bars, and there was a shining twist of horn high on his forehead. Folk, then. He had the aesthetic of a Brighte Childe. Where was Phil? He'd know what to do.

"You're a kind soul."

"I'm good with girls."

The man kissed his cheek, just a quick peck, but it was enough to make Varti's face flame.

"Stay with me," the fellow begged.

"Forever."

He laughed weakly. Then came a fresh wash of tears.

Varti pressed the man's head into his shoulder and stroked short, pale hair. Very unprofessional. Stupid curse.

They stayed like that for a long time, until Phil came striding their way. "You're all right?"

"Never better. I waylaid our killer."

"I got your message. Gathered a cohort together and came as quickly as I could."

The witness unclenched and whispered, "Philtrum?"

"Malcom!" Phil's expression faltered into dread. "Oh, no. Oh, Mal. Is it Salsify? Sweet Ireeni, I need to sit down."

He lowered himself to the bench on Malcom's other side and bent forward, face in his hands. Varti was afraid that he was crying, too, but when Phil lifted his face enough to meet Varti's gaze, he'd pulled himself together.

"This is Malcom Freylee, a friend. As you may have already surmised, he's a performer. The victim ...." Phil's voice caught, but he soldiered on. "I'm sorry. I've only ever known him as Salsify."

"Alphonse Halcyon," supplied Malcom. "Philtrum, is this Weller? You're his Varti?"

"You must be mistaken."

Phil waved a hand between them. "Sorry, Mal. Yes. Meet Varti Weller, my fabled quartermate."

"Zounds. Alphonse and I were half-sure Philtrum made you up to keep us from inviting ourselves over." Malcom made a soft keening noise that ended in a sob.

Quickly standing, Phil removed his cloak and swung it around Malcom's shoulders. "We'll have you looked over, but can you answer a few questions. I need to ask."

"I know," he said in a small voice. "I'll try."

Malcom turned toward Phil, freeing up Varti to peer around. Where had Sylvester gone? Slipped away into the shadows, his promised anonymity intact. More badges were arriving, and copper tape was being unrolled, cordoning off the section, even though the curfew meant there would be no gawkers or reporters until sunrise.

Dr. Kang and one of his interns turned up with a two-badge escort, reminding Varti that he might be helping pick through another crime scene.

He didn't want to.

"Varti?" Phil said softly, in that tone that meant he'd been trying to get his attention for a while. "Do me a favor? Mal doesn't want a doctor, and he doesn't want to answer any more questions tonight. But he also doesn't want to be alone. Bring him around to Ramage's for me? Stay with him. I'll set up a meeting at the Bastion for tomorrow. Be his bodyguard until then."

"Why me?" Varti griped. "I have no interest in him or his testimony."

"Let's call it fate." Phil sounded awful, even though he was trying to smile. "Malcom's stage name. I only just realized you wouldn't have any way of knowing. It's Comfrey."

Varti's first thought was to wonder why it sounded so familiar. It was almost as obscure as Salsify. A woodsy, folksome name. And then it hit him.

Back at the beginning.

On that first oddsome day.

*Fifth of Forest, gathering wolfberry, comfrey, and thornapple.*

# 54

## *Protective Custody*

Determined to have a more normal day, Varti left Ramage's roost before sunup, intent on getting in his morning run. He needed to clear his head, to think. But Aril—or possibly Burr—was waiting for him at the foot of the ladder.

Ramage's cooks had taken charge of Malcom the night before, much as Ramage had insisted on looking after Varti. Had something happened? He trailed after them to an open doorway. Beyond was a soft-lit bedroom, for a night lamp glowed on a bedside table. Sound asleep on an extravagant four-poster bed was Phil, still dressed in his uniform. He hadn't even taken off his boots.

Curled against his side was … well, it *had* to be Malcom. Varti wouldn't have recognized him without all the ruffles and paint. His face was almost boyish in its roundness, and now that his hair wasn't flattened from wearing a wig, it stood out around his head in wispy tufts. And that shining horn hadn't been part of a costume.

"Must be a troll," he muttered.

With a smile and a headshake, Burr—or it really might have been Aril—pushed him through the door. Malcom stirred and his eyes blinked open. They were an uncommon shade of blue, and they regarded Varti sleepily. But then they widened into wakefulness and immediately began to water.

Guessing he was a harbinger of bad memories, Varti backed up a step. Except Malcom reached out and whispered, "Don't go."

Varti balked.

Phil woke enough to groan, "Blighted bane. Too early."

"Sorry to bother you. It was nothing important," Varti retorted.

Phil's eyes popped open, and Varti could see the moment he remembered where he was ... and why. Sorrow. Regret. Resolve. He gave Malcom a parting squeeze, swung his feet to the floor, and asked, "Am I late?"

"Yes."

He patted at his vest, sighed, and said, "My deck's in my cloak. Be right back." His voice came from further away. "Will my good and generous mother permit breakfast in bed this morning?"

Aril—or Burr—slipped off in the direction of the kitchen, leaving Varti to navigate a conversation that could only be awkward. But when Malcom reached for him, he shuffled to the edge of the bed. And uttered a slur.

"It's all right. I know. Philtrum explained. Last night. So ... I know that you don't mean it. Or that you meant to say something much kinder. Sit?"

"No." Varti didn't sit, but he didn't leave.

Malcom pulled and bunched blankets in his lap. "Thank you. If you hadn't been there, I don't know wh-!" He faltered, then

345

shook his head. "Just ... thank you."

"It was nothing."

They fell into a tense silence, which Phil interrupted. Lowering himself slowly onto his side of the bed, he quietly shuffled his guidance deck. "A double reading, I think." And he offered half the deck to Varti, the other half to Malcom.

Malcom's hands trembled. "I'm afraid to look."

"You can close your eyes if you want," Phil offered. But then he breathed, "Ohhh. You're cardmates."

"What?" Malcom dared to look at the upturned cards on his palms. "What does that mean?"

"I don't think Varti would see it as betrayal if I tell you that he's turned up these same cards in recent readings. This could mean that you're kindred souls. Or it's very likely confirmation that you're sharing a path. I'm sorry it's been a perilous one, Mal."

Varti wondered at the odds.

It didn't feel like a coincidence.

Phil's readings were too honest.

"Fifth of Forest, gathering wolfberry, comfrey, and thornapple," said Phil, his fingertip brushing small purple flowers. "It's considered good fortune to turn a namesake card. And this is Salt of Ages. Touch salt, Mal. You're in the right place, with salt magic as protection."

Malcom sniffled and nodded.

"And now you." Phil checked the upturned cards on Varti's palms. "Eighth of Skies, attended by bright hopes and promises."

A central figure with radiant wings, high in the blue, offered open palms to eight different elemental sprites.

"Straight on, this card predicts one of two things. Either you'll cross paths in significant ways with eight new people, or you'll soon behold a Brighte Childe's smile. Inverted as it is, the meaning shifts into a warning. Be wary of the next eight people you meet, because they will break their promises and disappoint your hopes. Or you'll soon behold a Brighte Childe's tears."

"Am I his Brighte Childe?" asked Malcom.

"You and Salsify are both Brighte ones. And it's impossible to ignore that he was the eighth victim. I'm quite sure that Varti is disappointed that he couldn't prevent his death." Voice thick with apology, Phil added, "It's wracksome no matter who, but to lose a friend ...?"

Varti curled his fingers around the cards on his other palm, preferring to focus on the upturned one instead of Malcom's renewed tears.

Clearing his throat, Phil said, "I can't ever remember someone calling so urgently for the same card."

Varti had drawn The Howl. For the third time.

Six times were a charm, so this was half lucky.

To Malcom, Phil said, "Varti recently acquired a big gray hound. Doggerel has gone missing, but I think this means they're meant to find each other again."

Varti was still getting his morning jog, but not in the usual way. In a turn of events that was as surreal as it was nostalgic, Phil loped easily at his side as they ran through the Burrows.

"We should run together more often," Phil remarked.

Varti knew that for a lie. Or a wishful bit of empty optimism.

"We *could*." Phil sounded defensive. "If I made an effort."

There was no way, and they both knew it.

"It's a nice idea, anyhow."

Varti wished he could reassure Phil. Almost without thinking, he framed the things he wanted to say in four-word bursts.

*Save me next Newday.*

*Let's run the wall.*

*I'll buy us sandwiches.*

*We'll go see Nani.*

*Take her out driving.*

They neared the previous night's murder scene, where copper tape and copper-caped badges dissuaded the curious. Hexadille Porter was already there, snapping pictures while another woman—presumably her partner—spoke in urgent undertones to the ghostly form of the victim.

Alphonse Halcyon had been Folk. Varti hadn't realized until Phil's reading, when he'd called him a Brighte Childe. Then again, he hadn't been asked to collect the pieces this time, so he'd had no hint. But here was a ghostly representation of the card he'd turned up, because even with indistinct edges, it was possible to see wings shivering behind Salsify's slender shoulders.

The fairy noticed Phil, and with a blur of wings flew at him … and right through him.

"Hush, there, Salsify. I'm here. I see you." A tear slipped down Phil's cheek. "I'm sorry."

Varti bit his lip, but the curse was in a foul mood. "We're here to run you off. Comfrey is mine now."

Even knowing that Phil's exasperated glance was intended

for the curse, Varti felt deeply, doubly bad. So unprofessional. So cruel. This. This is why they confined him to basements.

Phil patiently said, "You can tell, can't you? That he's folk-spelled."

Suddenly, Varti was face to face with the ghost.

"Yes, he's the one. My quartermate," said Phil. "Varti arrived first and took care of Comfrey."

Salsify grew more distinct, and his hand came up to graze against the side of Varti's face. Not a proper touch. Varti couldn't feel fingers or palm. But his skin cooled. Only to warm again with embarrassment when the ghost smiled and mouthed a few words. Varti didn't deserve so much kindness from someone he'd failed.

"Ugly," he growled. A nice, straightforward opposite. Because everyone knew that fairies were lovely.

This one stayed close, as if trying to warm himself against Varti while Phil conferred with Hexadille and Rowena. Varti couldn't speak, couldn't offer a reassuring touch. But he could see this ghost, and that might be a comfort. Maybe it was, because they searched each other's faces for several long knicks.

For some reason, Varti didn't feel embarrassed. Only calm.

Salsify's wings began a slow, rhythmic beat. That was good.

The ghost edged closer, head dipping as if to whisper something.

Varti strained to hear, but there was no sound. However, a chill seeped through his clothes, and Salsify seemed to be trying to capture Varti's exhalations.

"He's cold," said Phil, who came up behind Varti. And to Salsify, "Does it help at all, getting close to us?"

The ghost reached for Phil, and Varti involuntarily stepped

back, bumping into his quartermate. Phil placed a steadying hand on his shoulder and bowed his head, making it easier for Salsify to reach.

Ghostly fingers brushed freckles.

Phil earnestly said, "Come with us? Varti and I can take you to where Comfrey is. You won't be alone while we sort out what to do."

Salsify's attention returned to Varti, gaze searching. As if asking permission.

"Over my dead body." Which was as indelicate as it was erroneous. Varti couldn't imagine leaving this soul adrift in the Burrows. Better to have him haunting a friendlier, more familiar place.

Was this why Holmes was letting Benedick's ghost make itself at home in his front hall?

Which brought Varti to another, more troubling question. Was it possible that Holmes's former assistant was also a true ghost?

A scant knell after Varti started his tocking, Phil sent word that a meeting had been called in Sarah Yamada's office. He tossed the message at Kel, saying, "He's taken leave of his senses."

She scanned the summons and brightened. "I'll be ready."

Because Badge Kel Mirza was officially listed as a member of Phil's investigative team.

They exited the lift in the heart of the irregulars headquarters, and Varti hung back, letting Kel do all the talking.

He was also trying to decide if he should be marking the next eight people he met. Or six now, since Hexadille and Rowena might count. Unless, of course, meeting Salsify satisfied the guidance deck's portent.

"Weller. Mirza." Dharm, Yamada's assistant-cum-bodyguard, greeted them solemnly. "This way, please."

Varti had never been particularly sensitive to magical security measures, but his hair stood on end as they passed through a series of wards that sent his nerves jangling.

Kel was either oblivious to or unbothered by their intangible buffeting.

Dharm opened a door and urged them through ahead of him into a large office. Other badges had already arrived, some seated at the conference table, others making changes to a large city map. Varti noticed with traces of envy that this one *did* include the surrounding countryside. He moved that direction, curious if any settlements besides Concordia, Tarnish, and Plover were part of the Hedge's patrol.

But then someone barred the way.

Malcom Freylee grabbed one of his hands and tried for a smile. It wobbled off course, and Varti feared the man was going to burst into tears. But then Phil was there, a hand on each of their shoulders.

"We have been waiting for you to begin. I didn't want Mal to have to relive last night more than once, but this once is necessary." Phil was using his official, on-the-job tone, but his eyes betrayed him. This was personal, and it was wracking him.

"Hello, Varti," said Malcom. "Philtrum said you found Salsify for me. It ... it's less hard, knowing he isn't truly gone. *Thank you.*"

Kel had kept close. "Brighte Childe?" she ventured curiously.

"Oh. Yes. Probably." Malcom offered his hand, palm down, fingers arched. Almost like he expected Kel to kiss it.

She did slip her hand under his, but only to give it a few bobs. "Weller did all right, then?"

Malcom nodded seriously. "I owe him and Philtrum so much. *Everything.*" And turning slightly, he asked, "Isn't that right, Salsify?"

Kel went very still as a ghost wafted to Malcom's side. "Knells bells," she breathed.

Varti was somewhat more interested in details that hadn't come to light until now. Because he'd only ever seen Malcom in full skirts, then tucked in bed. What had sounded like heeled boots on the cobbles turned out to be cloven hooves. Pale, shaggy fur covered Malcom's hindquarters, which were jointed like a faun's. But he couldn't *be* a faun. A long, whiplike tail with a tufted end swished nearly to the floor, and there was his horn to consider. A short, spiraling twist that was more like an iridescent seashell than the sorts of antlers Varti was used to seeing.

All at once, in the innermost place where all of Varti's words were caged, he decided to think of this man as Comfrey. Because that was the name that connected them.

The door opened, and Dr. Kang arrived with apologies for delaying everyone. Then Dharm struck a bell on the corner of Yamada's desk, calling the meeting to order.

Once everyone was seated, Sarah Yamada shuffled a couple of papers before addressing their witness. "I will firstmost thank you for cooperating with Kemp and for agreeing to answer any questions his team will bring to this table. All here are sworn to your protection by the laws of the royal city of Newcomb and by our duty to uphold them."

She paused.

Comfrey offered a small, "Thank you."

Waving that aside, Yamada said, "I will need some … clarification. Malcom Freylee, your ident number in the city registry belongs to one Comfrey Lee, a human female, which cannot possibly be accurate. I don't understand how so great an oversight came to be, but I'll need you to declare yourself. Also, your appearance doesn't align with any of the selcouth races currently on record. With all due respect, what are you?"

# 55
## *One of a Kind*

VESPER 13, FOUR NINETY-EIGHT
FARADAY
9 KNELLS, 47 KNICKS
ON THE FIRST FACE OF THE CLOCK

Comfrey folded his hands on the table and answered in a quiet, steady voice. "I'm proof that children can still be stolen. My adoptive parents found me in their daughter's cradle. While I'm grateful that they didn't immediately pitch me into Lake Tethys or abandon me at the base of a scape tree, they never got over their wariness of me. Or the loss of their little girl.

"As soon as they found placement for me in an early academy with facilities for boarding, they abandoned their house, hopped a train, and never looked back. And since paperwork wasn't a priority, I'm still living in Comfrey Lee's place."

Yamada frowned. "You're a stole-away?"

"That's not how I introduce myself, but yes. I'm what the ancient stories refer to as a changeling."

Dr. Kang chimed in. "And your variety? I've never seen anyone with your features!"

"That's the consensus. Unless another changeling arrives to help me build a family, I'm one-of-a-kind. My academy instructors let me decide for myself, and I chose to embrace a fable and give it form." Comfrey's smile was a weary thing. "By all means, let the record show. I'm a unicorn."

Varti took careful notes throughout the meeting. Yamada only called him out once, wanting to know why he'd resorted to anonymous testimony in order to convey his discovery. A witness would have been so much more helpful.

Phil pointed out that Varti couldn't have revealed his source even if he wanted to, so the anonymity would have to stand. Which was almost entirely true. Because at the toss of a quadricentennial cog, four words could have cleared matters up in no time.

*Sylvester Thornapple assisted me.*

*I don't understand why.*

*He definitely knows things.*

*Trusting him? So unwise.*

*But he came through.*

*Wolfberry, Comfrey, and Thornapple.*

*We share a path.*

*I know it's true.*

The meeting ended with Yamada peevishly asking, "You made contact with Holmes? Why isn't he here?"

"I did send a message," Phil said. "Shall I place a call?"

While he went to do so, Comfrey reached for Varti's hand again. He didn't say anything, didn't even look Varti's way. Holding on was apparently enough.

Or not.

Because Comfrey sniffled. Which pulled Salsify near enough that the temperature around Varti dropped significantly.

So Varti tried. At the very least, he could distract them. "I hate all Folk on principle. You're an obscenity. No wonder you were abandoned."

Rusting slagheaps.

Not helpful.

Confrey turned to him, eyes wide. "No holds barred."

"I am fairer than Faire. I am truer than Oracles. I'll bet you're a terrible actor."

His eyes narrowed. "I wasn't much of an academic, but the arts? The stage is my rightful realm. I make an impression on people. I know how to stroke egos … and echoes … and endlings. We're not sure if it's part of my legacy or if it's a knack, but it's *very* effective."

Cold settled across Varti's shoulders.

Comfrey lifted their joined hands. "You aren't impervious. Philtrum should have introduced us sooner."

Something writhed within, and Varti's heart pounded. Was Comfrey speaking to his curse? No, not simply speaking. Challenging.

"Hussy," he snapped.

"And you as virgin as new-fallen snow." Comfrey leaned closer, lowering his voice even further. "Let me rest my head in your lap and gaze adoringly. Because in tales that's how my kind were captured."

Varti was almost cross-eyed, Comfrey was so close. "Yes, please. No. Not happening." Which wasn't at all convincing. He got the sense that his curse was more anxious than he was. Because Varti could tell that Comfrey didn't mean it. He sternly said, "You're making me uncomfortable."

The man gave his hand a small squeeze. "And you make me feel safe."

That's when Phil returned. He shot a look Varti's way, probably checking that Comfrey and Salsify were still in his keeping. But no, there was a hand sign. Kel was at Varti's elbow an instant later.

"Pardon me, gentlemen." Her smile was grim. "Weller's being summoned. I'll hang back with you."

Comfrey quailed.

Kel helpfully announced, "He calls me a blighty wench."

"Poxy, too," Varti complained. "She'll be the next to abandon you."

Which was the strangemost recommendation Varti had ever given. And the most effective. He was able to reach Phil's side in time to hear his hushed report to Yamada.

"Mr. Holmes has refused your invitation. If we want a meeting with him, it'll have to happen at his Bridge District office. He's summoning us."

Yamada traded a look with Dharm, then muttered, "Vexsome derelict. Fine. We'll go."

Phil grimaced and said, "His man said there was one other condition."

Her tone was barely civil. "Yes ...?"

"He's summoning *us*," Phil repeated, pointing between him and Varti. "Only me and Weller."

Yamada's jaw clenched, and she spoke through her teeth. "Fine. Take care of it. Report back."

Varti was already on the move, Phil close on his heels, when

Yamada's frustration boiled over.

"Make a note, Dharm. The man's still an utter ass!"

Enzo attended a morning lecture and a practicum without seeing Arty. "I think he's busy with Owen."

Skrik patted his cheek.

Purdle said, "Is a ghost more interesting than us? I don't see how. I'm really very mysterious. Not that anyone ever notices."

Tuppence peered up at the row house and asked, "Are you late?"

"There wasn't any sort of schedule," Enzo said vaguely. When Mr. Hudson had turned him out the night before—so he wouldn't miss any classes—it had felt a lot like being dismissed. Without any sort of invitation to return.

So he was presuming, showing up like this. But where else would he go? The Hound was here, and he was every Basker's reason for being. Even now, generations later, Enzo's whole upbringing had centered around learning his duty and taking it up anew.

"This place?" demanded Tuppence. "The Hound is here?"

"Quietly, please." Enzo nodded apologetically to a couple who edged by on the far side of the walkway. "But yes, he's here."

"Can you tell?" She backtracked to his side and lowered her voice. "I cannot. I thought I would be able to tell."

"No, not really. If Mr. Holmes hadn't declared himself, I wouldn't have been able to guess." Which meant that if Plenilune Marsk hadn't directed Enzo to the Hound, he might have given up, moved on to another city, and missed him entirely.

"I do not like it," said Tuppence.

"Why not? I found him. That was the whole goal. And Mr. Hudson suggested I stay on as a kind of assistant or something."

"I do not like that a man of the House of Basker cannot recognize a fell beast, even when they are standing right in front of him." Her many scarves fluttered as she shook her head. "Danger can be potent or stealthy or patient or swift. But not all of those things at once."

"Usually." Enzo opened the gate for her. "But that rule of thumb only applies to Realmish entities. The Hound is an existence that predates the Sundering. He's been here much longer than the fae, though in the aftermath of everything, there were those who proposed that he may have slipped into our world from another Realm."

"Is the Hound potent and stealthy and patient and swift?"

"Yeah, sure. All of those things and more." Enzo smiled. "He's amazing."

"What about weaknesses?"

"What do you mean?"

Tuppence flatly said, "The killings. Have you forgotten the killings?"

"Oh! But those weren't the Hound. Mr. Holmes has been sequestered here, under careful watch. The most recent death vindicates him. He's innocent of all."

She slowly reached up and gently flicked his forehead. "Dolt."

"What? Why?"

Skrik said, "Innocent of one does not prove he is innocent of all."

"But …! Oh. Well, I suppose you *could* argue that point. But the pattern is the same. It follows that the killer is the same. And it's not the Hound."

Tuppence shook her head at him.

Skrik patted his cheek.

Enzo looked to Purdle, hoping for some clue to what he was missing. But the sprite was gazing intently at the black door with its equally ominous wreath, almost as if he could see through it. He cheerfully announced, "My friend is here. Mr. Weller."

And then the door opened, even though none of them had tried knocking.

Mr. Hudson smiled benignly. "Good of you to drop by. Enzo, I believe you can contribute to the discussion underway. However, if it wouldn't be too much trouble …?" He inclined his head in Tuppence's direction. "You are clearly a formidable ally. Would you be willing to guard our door? It would put everyone at ease, knowing you're here."

Tuppence hesitated.

Skrik said, "It's a good plan."

Purdle said, "Strength within and strength without."

With a firm nod, Tuppence drew two glittering blades.

"Oh, dear! Perhaps something more discreet. This district only expects to see weaponry on the parade grounds. Have you ever been? Morning exercises always draw a crowd." Mr. Hudson gestured toward the weapons, his smile still genial.

And by some miracle, Tuppence bowed to his request, for her blades disappeared back wherever they came from. Enzo's last glimpse as the door closed behind him was of his guardian standing quietly on the bottom step, keeping watch.

Enzo looked more closely at Mr. Hudson.

The man beamed and beckoned him further. "Into the sitting room with the rest. Your usual chair. I'll bring tea."

It was almost a relief to obey. Not because of any sort of compulsion. Enzo would have noticed that. But because it was so much simpler, not being in charge. Also, because there was a chair at Mr. Holmes's fireside that Enzo could consider *his*.

He edged through the door, half-hoping for some sign of welcome from the Hound, but Holmes bent at the waist, intent on something Mr. Weller was doing at a square table that hadn't been in the room before.

Kemp was there, too, and his smile was real. "Enzo! Glad you and yours could make it. Varti's sorted something important, and he's updating our case file. See for yourself."

He stepped close enough to gather that Mr. Weller was laboring over a map. He'd traced several routes with different colored pens—orange, green, red, yellow. Choosing another pen, he confidently marked another path in royal blue. Each line began in a different part of the city. Some curved along, following the trolley line, but it became increasingly clear that they intersected in one place in particular. Purple, brown, and finally a sky blue line tracing a route from the Theater District to that same point, only it didn't pass through. That's where it ended.

Enzo ventured, "What's on Loyalty Road?"

Holmes glanced up. "*Under* Loyalty Road," he crisply corrected. "The most recent victim died in the Burrows."

"Okay ... yeah. Under. So he's mapping in three dimensions. You know, I was in that area just the other day. Or nearby. When was it?" He checked his watch and thought back. "Wednesday?"

"They call it Williday here," reminded Purdle.

"Eight lines. Eight lives," said Skrik.

Enzo was embarrassed to have put the killings out of his mind. His quest was accomplished. He'd found the Hound, and he was satisfied that *his* fell beast wasn't behind the recent string of murders. But Kemp and Weller were with the local police, and they were still looking for the culprit. Enzo studied the map with more care.

He didn't know the city.

Couldn't fathom their customs.

Never would've found the Hound without help.

But maybe he could still contribute. Because he was a lifelong expert in ... well, in a lot of things. But he knew everything that could be known about the creature they were trying to corner. So Enzo touched the rainbow-hued intersection Weller had created and said, "Loosed beasts like small, enclosed spaces. Anything will do. A box. A bottle. And in a weakened state, it will retreat from the usual protections—blest charms, runic rings, fairy lights, and the like."

Wide eyes locked onto him.

Mr. Weller moved first, lunging partway over the table to grab him by the front of his sweater. His expression wasn't hard to read. He was angry. Furious. But then his expression cleared into something more earnest and honest, and his question almost wasn't one, it rang with so much certainty.

"Are there more hounds?"

"Oh, that's very good," said Purdle. "You didn't waste your words today!"

Holmes stared at him, thunderstruck.

Skrik patted his cheek and whispered, "Dolt."

Enzo held up his hands, unsure what to say next. He'd promised not to betray Holmes's secret, but they were definitely facing another fell beast. How much could he say?

"You're thick as your knit and six times as woolly," groused

Weller, which was enormously unfair.

"Tell him," urged Purdle. "It was a *good* question."

"Yes, there are several fell beasts. In some ancient cultures, they were worshiped as gods, but others feared them as demons of war, chaos, and despair. Those were the unfettered ones. Loosed beasts. They're really much happier when they find a ... umm ... a suitable host." Enzo very carefully didn't look at Holmes. These were facts. Straight out of a book. Not at all secret, provided you had the right books.

Kemp quietly asked, "You know what's going on?"

"Well ... yeah. The whole reason I came to Newcomb was because I was searching for something similar. Your killer ... it's probably another fell beast. Different from mine. I couldn't guess which one."

"Why didn't you come forward with this information?" Kemp asked.

Enzo didn't have a good answer for that. "Because I'm a dolt?"

Holmes snapped, "How many beasts are there?"

"A dozen. At least, that's the traditional number."

"Do you know where they are?"

"No."

"Are they all canine?"

"No. But they're all considered dangerous predators."

Holmes began to pace. "What forms do they take?"

"I didn't really look into other cultures and their worship. My family specialized. The Hound was our ... well, our everything." Quailing before the man's fierce gaze, Enzo cautiously listed, "Dragon. Snake. Firebird. Tiger ...?"

"An animal spirit." Kemp traded a long look with Weller before adding, "But not a dog."

"Definitely not!" Enzo said staunchly. "Well, I really don't think it could be him."

"I've heard of forest deities taking the form of a boar." Kemp's smile was humorless. "A vengeful pig?"

Enzo slowly nodded. "Yeah, I remember something about a boar. It's an option. But why vengeful?"

Phil waved a hand at the map. "Weller found a connection. All of the victims shared a fondness for the same mother's cooking. Varti's confirmed it to my satisfaction. We were speculating that the killer chooses their victims from among the people who visit The Swirly Pine."

"Swirly's?" Enzo grabbed the edge of the table. "Okay, wow. I really have been there. Arty brought me. He said that everyone in the city loves it."

Kemp said, "You're both lucky not to have been targeted. Remember what Owen said about sync ratings?"

"Enzo is under our protection," Purdle said haughtily.

Which was true. Enzo carried enough charms to fend off most threats. Then again, he'd removed most of them the other day, so he wouldn't drive off the ghosts Kemp had been tracking. Thanks to that, he was down to … well, not much. He patted his hips, checking for pocket charms. But he was confused by the pig thing. "Why a boar? It could just as easily be an ape or something."

"Oh, I don't have any idea what kind of animal we're dealing with," said Kemp. "Ignore my attempt at a joke."

Enzo was ready to add the local sense of humor to the list of things that made him feel like an outsider.

Weller said, "Swirly Pine is literal."

"I don't get it."

Purdle said, "He's lying."

Enzo searched the officer's face. He was all lean lines, heavy brows, and large nose. The lies weren't his fault. Enzo understood that. But Weller had gotten to the Hound first, and that small fact rankled. This was his family's legacy. His duty and responsibility. His mission in life.

"You're an ignoramus. Get one of your pets to explain it."

"They're not pets!" Enzo raised a hand, changed his tone. "No, you know that. I see. It's turned around."

Purdle was making a reeling motion with his hands.

Skrik made the snuffling sound that was the closest he came to laughter.

Enzo's own words seemed to hang in the air. *It's turned around.* "Ohhh. Oh, gracious sakes. It's not really The Swirly Pine, is it?"

Kemp offered an encouraging, "There you go. Simple enough once you learn the trick of it."

He guessed he was the last to know, not that it actually mattered. The Swirly Pine had nothing to do with trees. The shop's true name was masked by a simple bit of wordplay. Finally in on the joke, he muttered, "The Pearly Swine."

# 56
## *The Royal View*

VESPER 13, FOUR NINETY-EIGHT
FARADAY
4 KNELLS, 22 KNICKS
ON THE SECOND FACE OF THE CLOCK

When it came to circle-craft, Enzo had experimented with many materials for their construction. Salt and sands, chalk and charcoal—these were traditional. But he'd fiddled with everything from flower petals to peppercorns with varying degrees of success. Child's play.

This was similar. But more … illicit.

He'd wondered why Jamie's big duffle had clanked so much. And if Nunc's furtive glances meant they were out of bounds. He hadn't spoken up, even when Arty suggested that Tuppence keep a lookout in the alley below. Now, with paint fumes thick in the air, Enzo couldn't think of a polite way to ask if he was party to a crime.

Finally, he raised his hand. "What are you doing?"

Arty straightened then waved at the rooftop. "Isn't it obvious?"

The guys were putting the finishing touches on an elaborate painting on the flat roof of a six-story building that offered a very nice view of the Bridge District. They were high enough up

366

that nobody at street level had taken notice.

Enzo asked, "This is vandalism, isn't it?"

"It's art!"

"But ... do you have permission to paint here?"

Arty's gaze held amusement. "Nobody said we couldn't."

"That's not the same as getting a permit. Or ... however things like that work here." Enzo wondered if he sounded old. "Who owns this building?"

"This old dear belongs to the royal family." Arty gave the roof a couple of thumps with the heel of his boot. "It's fine. We're using it for its intended purpose. Your Mr. Kemp called us up, didn't he?"

"I don't follow."

Arty waved to include Jamie and Nunc in his statement. "We've been waiting our whole lives for this."

Enzo wasn't sure how to politely counter that. None of them were even sixteen yet. Except maybe Jamie. But his air of maturity was more about the confidence with which he carried himself. Sky blue and pale yellow and spring green paint flecked the dark skin of his arms. He rattled a can of white spray paint, eyeing his handiwork before adding highlights.

"We're good, Enzo. This rooftop's been used like this for so long, the layers of paint have added a span to the height of the building."

"There *are* layers," volunteered Purdle, who'd been exploring a small, spindly-legged water tower and the dilapidated shed that occupied the far corner of the roof.

The building was old, its edges ringed by a low stone wall that was pitted by years and crusted with lichen. They'd stolen up the side using a fire escape a couple of hours ago. Since then, the flat gray surface had bloomed with a dozen colors.

"See that line?" Arty directed his attention to a thick set of cables overhead. They ran down toward the lawn below, disappearing inside a sort of pavilion on the edge of the green.

"What's the fancy building?"

"That's the Oratorium. For royal declarations, speeches, stuff like that." Arty's finger traced the line back up to where it vanished from view at the top of the city walls. "There's a cable car the royal family use to descend, and it passes right over this spot. Plus, there's a viewing platform up there, with a set of binoculars in a fixed position. Know where they're trained?" He thumped his boot again. "Right here. And do you know what? Nobody's ever been allowed to build a structure that would obscure the royal view."

"Of this spot."

"Too right."

Enzo glanced between the wild swirls and starburst that Arty and his crew had created. There were overlapping blobs that might have been letters, but they were so misshapen. He ventured, "Is the royal family interested in street art?"

"It's for messages." He stood straighter. "This is ours."

So the graffiti was *some* kind of message. Or a signal. "What does it mean?"

"It means we've been called up. We're on the job!" Arty gazed up at the palace. "I'm sure the queens will be glad to know it, after all this time."

Enzo cut a look at the ornate glass-and-steel palace that overlooked the Bridge District. His lessons hadn't included anything about politics or royalty yet. "There's more than one queen?"

Arty favored him with a pitying look. "They symbolize the ongoing peace. One from here, one from there."

"And your queens are keeping a watch on this roof, waiting for you to send them a message." Enzo had to ask, "Why?"

"It's always been this way, hasn't it?"

"Has it?"

"Since the beginning." Arty's pride was obvious. "The city borrowed our name—basically stole it—but we're the rightward heirs and all that. Hand-picked and sworn in. Trained on the sly. Called up when there's a need."

"You're part of a secret organization?"

"That's what I've been telling you. Consider yourself inducted. So you'll need to keep it mum, just like the rest of us." Arty revealed, "We're the *real* Irregulars, with orders handed down from a place old as Olde, *older* even. Baker Street."

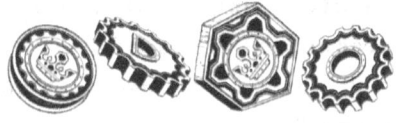

Graffiti complete, Arty enacted the next part of his plan. Shouldering their gear, he led the way down into the Burrows, just ahead of the deep knells of the curfew bell. "I asked Patina and Seelie to get there early, reserve our favorite table."

Normally, Enzo would have been delighted to spend the night someplace as lively as The Swirly Pine. But as they aimed for a booth in the back corner, he was uncomfortably aware that anyone here—including his new friends—might be the fell beast's next target.

He hung back, asking Skrik, "Are there any protections on this building?"

"Nothing."

"Can we do anything about that?"

The shadow imp took a moment to answer. "I could hide the door."

Purdle tutted. "That might leave someone out in the dark. This is a *shelter*. People are safer inside than out."

Tuppence said, "I could guard the front door, but there are three floors, all windowed."

Enzo hadn't even noticed that there were upper stories. "Am I due a boon? It's been a while …?"

Purdle tapped his chin. "I bestowed a rather large one on my good friend Weller, but … if it was a *small* wish, I could grant it."

Tuppence asked, "Why are we bothering with defensive tactics? This is a hunt. We should be going after the beast."

"Enzo!" called Arty, waving from the booth.

"We should hear him out. *Then* decide."

Skrik muttered, "He is more dangerous than he looks, but he is no match for a fell beast. It could kill him."

"Worse, it could claim him," said Tuppence.

"We won't allow it," soothed Purdle. "Isn't that why we're here?"

Enzo whispered, "An hour. Is that a small enough wish? After that, I'll figure something out."

Purdle straightened his tiny crown. "They call it a *knell* here."

"One knell, then."

The sprite's sweet smile was all the answer he needed.

The Swirly Pine had become an unassailable haven for the next hour. Long enough for him to hear out Arty, who'd brought them all here, straight into danger.

Conversation dropped away when a fresh platter of the house special arrived, piping from the fryer. But after Arty had consumed three, he returned to the problem at hand. "How do we trap a fell beast?"

"A complex pattern of circle-craft and command. And a suitable mooring."

"Easy?"

Enzo blinked. "Honestly? Not really, no."

"But can you do it?" challenged Arty.

"Well, sure. I think."

"So that's sorted."

Enzo frowned. "No, it really isn't. I'd need someplace to create the circle."

"Can you use one of the big ones on campus? The ready-mades for class demonstrations."

"Possibly ...?" But he was already shaking his head. "We'd have to lure the beast from here to there."

"Bait?" suggested Arty. "We're pretty fast on wheels."

"Not fast enough."

Nunc asked, "How big a circle are we talking?"

Enzo idly sketched runes on the tabletop with his finger, mind racing. "Big. About ... twice the size of the ... the *art* you worked up earlier."

"*There's* an idea," said Arty.

"Been a while since we did any installations in a high traffic area," said Nunc.

"Good thing there's a curfew on," said Arty. "Toughest part of street art is keeping the pedestrians from mucking through the works."

Jamie offered a low, "Too true, mate. Too true."

Patina leaned forward. "Here in the Burrows? I like it."

"Close to its lair," whispered Seelie, her feathers puffing.

Arty picked apart one of the turnovers, offering half to Skrik. "It can work. We've got the room, and we've got the knells. And if we put in a call to Kemp, he'll show up before we land in too much trouble. Enzo, you craft the circle. Seelie can help. Me and Jamie and Patina will posh up the edges, give it some style."

Nunc asked, "How much paint's left?"

Jamie prodded his duffle and looked doubtful. "Spray's no good. Runes require precision."

"Options?" Arty asked, eyeing the jars of sauce on the table. "We could get salt from the kitchen ...?"

Their hour was nearly up. "Skrik, I need some things. Actually, it's a lot of things."

His oldest friend touched his cheek and gruffly said, "Rely on me more."

# 57
## *Fallible*

VESPER 13, FOUR NINETY-EIGHT
FARADAY
4 KNELLS, 42 KNICKS
ON THE SECOND FACE OF THE CLOCK

Having made his report—such as it was—to Holmes, Varti had assumed he'd be going back to his basement office a failure. He was keenly aware that he hadn't met the man's challenge. Oh, Doggerel had been vindicated, but not because Varti had found the killer. Thomas and Durst had been more effective, since they could provide the necessary alibi.

So the job opening had closed.

And Varti's unspelling was off the table.

Because someone else was going to stop the killings.

Now he was enduring another report, Phil's to Yamada.

Duty had never been more of a struggle, but Varti would support Enzo Basker, whose value to this investigation kept multiplying. His special knowledge was going to be more important than Varti's map savvy. Enzo knew a fell beast's habits, its needs, and presumably its weaknesses. And he was capable of magic.

Unlike Varti, who was feeling increasingly superfluous. But when he tried to steal out, Phil grabbed his arm and wouldn't let go. Holding him there while he framed plans based on Enzo Basker's family's secrets.

Varti stood at attention, but he wasn't really listening anymore. This went beyond frustrating, straight to depressing. But why?

He'd made his current post in Files & Evidence his own, led his team for more than a decade, devoted himself to working within his limitations. His department was an essential part of the Bastion's innerworkings, and he was proud of what he'd accomplished.

But it wasn't enough. Not when he knew what he'd lost.

And it wasn't simply that he'd failed. He'd lost to Enzo.

No, not only that. He'd lost *someone*.

And Varti wanted him back.

"I'll meet you at Ramage's," said Phil. "I have to arrange some things, but I'll be there quick as I can."

Varti's lip curled. "Off to canoodle with the hussies at Covey."

Phil mildly chided, "Don't talk about Ramage's sisters that way."

"They are entirely respectable. And sphinx down is golden."

His best friend's gaze dropped guiltily. "I have no idea how you always know."

Varti often wondered if Phil hated that he *did* pick up on personal details as quickly as he did work-related ones. It wasn't as if he could stop seeing, sorting, and surmising. Living with Varti meant that Phil had very little in the way of privacy.

But Phil softly said, "You're the best of us, Varti. That's

never changed."

This time, Varti's gaze dropped. Which must have been too honest for his curse's liking because he next trod on Phil's foot.

They parted ways, Phil limping toward the trolley station while Varti chose a brisk pace toward the city center. At this knell, the sun had already disappeared from Newcomb's portion of sky. Lamps burned throughout the bridge district, and the few pedestrians on the walkways looked to be in a hurry. It was almost curfew.

Before he reached the innermost of the six bridges for which the district was named, Varti stepped around a flower cart, skirted a newspaper stand, and ducked into an alcove lined with pneumatic postboxes. And waited to see who was following him.

A scant knick later, Durst rounded the corner, his undulation in disarray until they spotted him. The gorgon's hands swung loose at his sides, but there was a long weapon case strapped to his back. His expression didn't change, but a concert of hissing felt like scolding.

"I will walk with you," said Durst.

Varti stayed put.

"Mr. Hudson thought it best, and Mr. Holmes made it an order."

"Don't make excuses. No need to be shy about it. Driss wanted me."

Durst's lips twitched.

As they continued on together, Varti dared to hope that Durst knew the rules for that folksome game of tiles that Ramage kept around. Although cards or a few rounds of trilby would be a fine way to pass the time until Phil could break away and join them. Which might take them into the night watches.

Would Comfrey like to play?

Or was that rude to suggest games, given recent losses?

Though Salsify was still with them.

"So you can speak unwitting truths, provided you think they are lies."

Varti slowed to a standstill and stared up at Durst. "I realize it's never come up before, but I never lie."

"You told the truth."

"I'm always honest." Varti couldn't remember what he'd said that had Durst so amused.

"You are fallible. And so are your lies." He strolled on, forcing Varti to follow.

The Speckled Hen came into view, as did the harpy pacing out front, encouraging passersby to find shelter before the bells rang their warnings.

Varti tried again, "I never make mistakes."

"You can be mistaken." Pointing up, Durst added, "Driss *did* want you."

Varti wished he could protest the shocking double standard that emerged as the evening progressed. Because Durst cheated at cards.

In the spare room where Comfrey had been staying, he and Varti and Durst crowded around a table no bigger than a platter. Close quarters, with barely enough room to drop bobbin bets between the glasses Comfrey topped off between hands.

The problem was ... Durst's snakes were stealing peeks.

"I have three-of-a-kind," Varti warned.

"No. You do not." The gorgon dropped four more bobs on the growing pile.

"He has a pair of threes," said Comfrey, who kept lapsing into giggles for no apparent reason.

Except that he was correct about the pair. Varti turned to find Salsify peering over his shoulder. *All* of them were cheating. He muttered, "Ill repute in abundance. I'll be bringing my claims to court."

Nobody believed him.

Except possibly Driss.

Varti felt bad.

Durst displayed a winning hand and blandly remarked, "Would you cheat if you could? Or does your contrary spelling keep you from dishonest dealing?"

Comfrey considered him curiously. "Have you ever tried to lie?"

Varti hadn't ever tried to lie in order to get the curse to contradict him. Usually, he tried to skew his lies in revealing ways.

Comfrey dealt, Durst opened the bidding with a knob, and Varti said, "Finally. A decent hand."

Nobody believed him.

Not even Driss.

Because the little cheater checked.

When Phil turned up, Varti's purse was flat, proof of a stubborn integrity.

"I've made certain that our quarters at The Green Man are perfectly safe. For all of us. You, too, Salsify." Phil's smile was weary. "Let's go home."

"But ... curfew ...?" protested Comfrey.

"Nobody will question a quick walk under badge escort." And to Varti, "It took so long because I've been clear to the Academy of Mages and back. To pick up Owen. He's probably snooping."

Varti was horrified. What had possessed Phil to bring a journalist into their quarters?

Phil added, "You're welcome to join us, Durst."

The gorgon silently stood, clearly ready to go.

Because Phil was extending hospitality to assassins as well.

Nobody else had returned to The Green Man yet, but Phil had Mr. Whilom's key, and they were soon creaking their way upstairs. Lamps were already lit, and Varti immediately noticed one of the changes Phil had overseen, because a narrow cot had been added to their living area, tucked beside the radiator. Far more concerning was the miniature copper man perched on the edge of their table, legs swinging, arms folded as he studied Varti's case wall.

As they crowded in, the golem found his feet and gesticulated excitedly. Though as soon as Salsify drifted over, he froze.

Phil said, "Owen, meet Alphonse Halcyon. A friend. Another victim. The eighth."

More gyrations, then the golem stomped over to a tiny input deck and began typing. Phil went to see what he was saying. Flustered, Varti dove into routine. He hung cloaks that were badly in need of steaming. He adjusted the radiator settings and watered his plant. He cleaned and wound his watch, then hesitated over polishing boot buttons. Durst's boots were lined up next to his, and they were so big, Varti's could have nested inside them.

He glanced Durst's way, to where the gorgon stood outside the circle of lamplight. He'd propped a shoulder against the wall beside a window and gazed out into the night. With a vague hope that assassins didn't boobytrap their footwear, Varti lined Durst's boots up beside his and Phil's and set to work.

"No, I don't have connections to all of the victims. Although Jacob Oswald, the seventh victim, was working for our team at the time he died."

Varti moved closer, wanting to see what the golem was asking.

ARE YOU BEING TARGETED?

"I don't think so, no. Although Oswald died in the alley outside this building."

Owen spun to face Phil. He threw his tiny hands wide. More keystrokes.

HERE? IT FOLLOWED YOU HERE?

OH, WHAT DO I CARE?

I'M IMPERVIOUS TO DEATH

BUT YOU? SIGNIFICANTLY LESS SO

HOW CAN YOU BE SO SURE YOU'RE SAFE?

"A potent combination of hedge magic and salt magic. According to Purdle, it will keep the killer out. We're safe. *And* off the record."

I WILL ABIDE BY OUR AGREEMENT

LUCKY FOR YOU. THIS ROOM'S A TROVE

WHO MAINTAINS THIS GLORIOUS MAP?

"The map is Weller's. You remember my quartermate ...? Badge Varti Weller, head of Files & Evidence.

Owen waved a finger between Varti and his map, then typed.

I WANT IT

"Where shall I have it delivered?"

The little golem clasped his hands over his heart and affected a swoon.

Phil gently pointed out, "He's lying. And I know you know he's lying. In the weeks after the incident, you tried repeatedly to corner him for an interview."

WAS THAT HIM?

SLIPPED MY MIND

Owen was definitely lying, and he wasn't trying to hide it. Varti's distrust spiked. He'd seen too many people do this, saying one thing—the acceptable, legally-defensible thing— while meaning a poorly-obscured and culpable truth.

Or in the case of journalists, embellishing dull truths with insinuations that stayed just shy of slander. And waylaying ravaged badge candidates in the hopes of spinning their recent trauma into an exposé.

NO OFFENSE, WELLER

JUST DOING MY JOB

"Don't be silly. I have nothing but fond memories of you." A small hand waved his lie aside.

DON'T BE GRUDGESOME

WATER UNDER THE NINE BRIDGES

I'M PART OF THE TEAM NOW

Part of the team? Did he mean Phil's investigation team? But of course that's what he meant. He was here, wasn't he? Phil had brought him in, just like he'd brought in Varti.

He wrestled with a writhing sense of injustice, tried to step away from his feelings and think clearly. Was Owen a possible asset?

He had connections. No, he had *former* connections.

He was unkillable. They could send him into dangerous places.

He was incorporeal. Spying was definitely in his wheelhouse.

But no matter his potential, Varti couldn't ignore one simple truth. A journalist didn't belong in the middle of an investigation. Phil had to see that Owen wouldn't keep quiet about any juicy details he overheard. Death wasn't going to stop him from blabbing, not when he had access to an input deck.

Varti finally rasped, "I'm glad you're here."

Phil's expression grew increasingly worried. Like he'd only now realized that Varti might not have liked O. N. Acres any more in death than he had in life. Phil was usually more careful about the people he brought home.

Whatever Varti's face was doing, it sent Owen into a quick series of keystrokes.

KICK MY CLAPPER

HE STILL HATES ME

"Nothing could be further from the truth," Varti said smoothly.

Into the sudden lull, snakes hissed. And Durst was reaching behind his back, possibly for a weapon.

"Pardon us." Phil's tone, while polite, carried a note of command. "Varti and I need a moment. We'll just … step into the hall. Won't be more than a knick."

# 58

## *Locking Time*

### VESPER 13, FOUR NINETY-EIGHT
### FARADAY
### 11 KNELLS, 37 KNICKS
### ON THE SECOND FACE OF THE CLOCK

Dark, empty, and cold—the creaking hall with its ancient wainscoting, faded runner, and night-black skylight wasn't the most convivial place for a conversation. But Varti and Phil faced each other in their stocking feet outside the door to their quarters. Varti couldn't begin to imagine how this conversation would go. Except … badly.

"This is my fault."

"No."

Phil sighed. "It *is*, and I'm trying to apologize. I know we went through a rough patch with Owen, but that was years ago. He and I have been friends for a while now. He's smart and resourceful and–"

"A good kisser?" Varti bit his lip so hard it hurt.

"I was going to say *funny*." Phil touched his elbow. A familiar gesture. He wasn't blaming Varti for anything he might say. "He's not really even a friend, not like you and me. More of a longstanding acquaintance. We'd run into each other here and there. He's as gossipy as a roomful of aunties, and he's always on the lookout for a good story. If I needed some information, I'd give him a tip in trade. Harmless stuff. Nothing important." Phil's tone turned pleading. "He's not a bad guy. I let bygones be, but I should have realized that you'd still have a key to grind. Maybe a whole ring of keys."

So. Owen had been cultivating a source inside the irregulars. All of his chance run-ins with Phil had been calculated.

"You're a security leak," he said flatly. Which wasn't fair. Holmes had also named the reporter as one of his sources.

"Owen's the one who gets around. He cozies up to people who can be useful to him. Like he said, it's all part of the job. If it's any comfort, Yamada has known about our *friendship* since the beginning. I've basically been assigned to Mr. Acres. I'm his insider, so he leaves the rest of the irregulars alone."

Tit for tat.

By the book.

Under orders.

So why was Varti still furious?

Phil quietly said, "Try."

"It's simple."

"Yeah, I know."

"Nobody listens to me."

Phil nodded thoughtfully.

"Nothing's changed." But so much had changed, and so fast. "I just want to be alone."

"I wouldn't do that." Phil frowned. "But you *know* that. And I don't think this is about Mal and Salsify."

"Yes." In frustration, Varti nodded, turned up his palm, and tapped his toe. "Promised," he ground out. Rusting crenellations, that actually hurt.

Phil leaned closer. "What was all that?"

"A lie."

"Someone promised you something?"

"You did, you faithless whore," he muttered. "Forever cuckolded in my own quarters."

"Durst?"

"*Finally*, you see it."

"Enzo?"

Varti's conscience pricked, and he whispered, "He makes me happy."

"What? Did Holmes's assistant do something? He's been helpful. Or … wait. Do you mean the promise you share with Purdle?"

"Yes. I'm so glad we're of one mind in everything."

Phil beckoned for more. "I'll get there. Eventually." And then he really did get there. "Holmes, then?"

"No."

"You tracked him down, brought him on board. Yamada's pleased about that, by the way." Phil hugged himself. It really was cold in the hall. "What could he have promised you? Something you want. Something related to the case? Something …?"

"It's more of a threat, really."

"Would Mr. Hudson know?"

"Nobody from Hibernacle House knows we made a bargain."

Phil muttered, "Ashes, I'm slow." And opening the door, he jerked in surprise. "Oh! Durst. Just the man I needed. Join us, please?"

The gorgon had to have been standing on the other side of the door. He stepped into the hallway, pulling the door shut behind him.

"We're having a crisis of communication. The spelling he's under never cooperates with me, and I want to know what's been promised. Did Holmes offer Varti something?"

Durst bent so that his faceted goggles were level with Varti's eyes. "Do you want this man to know?"

"Phil's an idiot. Let's tell Owen instead."

Snakes nosed Varti's hair, and one pressed against his cheek, cool and silken.

He gently cupped his hand over that one, grumbling, "Vespertide, and you without your bonnet." Which was almost true, which probably meant the curse was still wary of Durst. So he gave a simple opposite. "No."

Durst's regard shifted. "If Mr. Holmes is satisfied with the outcome of this case, he will find the means for *Varti*'s unspelling." He gave teasing emphasis to Varti's given name.

He grumbled, "Success is my sole responsibility."

Phil frowned. "Mr. Holmes can't possibly expect you to apprehend that monster alone. We work as a team. And Enzo is the one who ... oh. Oh, ashes. I see."

Varti knew he did. He was good at people.

"You want to get to the thing first."

"No."

"But we don't know how to stop it or contain it. That's Enzo's area of expertise. We need him to confront the killer because nobody else has any idea how to confront a fell beast."

Wrong.

Wrong!

There *was* someone else who must know. Someone who may have already been trying to do just that.

Varti fumbled for his watch. Eleven knells, forty-nine knicks.

Nearly midnight.

Phil checked his own watch. "Are you planning to call for Purdle?"

He was, but not here.

Shoving past Durst, Varti went inside and stepped into his boots. He was soon fully equipped and cloaked and on his way back out. Phil interrupted him, though. "A reading. Please?"

His best friend placed the cards on Varti's upraised palm and murmured, "What can you do alone?"

Hisses filled the air over their heads, and Phil blinked up at Durst. "Oh. Of course. You won't be alone." Cutting the deck, he turned up the first card. And then slowly, slowly, he revealed the second.

Varti stared at the cards, waiting for the reading. When the delay dragged on, he glanced up.

Phil was visibly shaken, but all he did was reclaim his cards and address Durst. "I'll put out a call. My team will be armed and ready within the knell. Varti won't be able to manage it, so you'll have to call for us. Give your location. We'll back you up."

"How?" asked Durst.

Turning to his own gear, Phil snagged his whistle and the copper slot key that gave him access to any of the Bastion's report stations throughout the city. He gave clipped instructions, but he didn't say a word about Varti's reading. Judging by the stubborn look on his face, he didn't want to explain why. So Varti turned his back and left with Durst ... but without guidance.

Varti wasn't in a roundabout mood. He ran straight down the center of Livery Road, his lamp and club banging against his thigh. Durst hadn't been joking when he said that Varti couldn't outrun him. The gorgon easily outstripped him, then carefully measured his strides until they were running even. They definitely made an oddsome sight, but with the curfew in force, nobody was around to take note.

In the distance, Old Ebonnel began the midnight toll.

They passed The Speckled Hen, its windows still alight even though it was locking time. Varti caught a flash of blue feathers and wondered if Ramage was harboring people who'd needed to get indoors. Maybe he should drop by on his way home. Make sure Ramage wasn't ruffled or careworn.

By the time they crossed Century Plaza into the Bridge District, the carillon's final knells shivered into silence and the scents changed. Wet leaves on the pavers. Cold lavender in the door garden. Varti struggled with the gate catch, his hands were shaking so much.

Durst reached around him and calmly eased the works. In doing so, he put Varti in range of Driss and company, and flickering tongues brushed his skin. But that didn't worry him half so much as the oncoming confrontation. Truly, he wasn't the same person he'd been a twelve-day ago. And for that, he was fiercely glad.

Varti rapped smartly on the black door.

He was prepared to stand pounding for as long as it took to rouse someone from the rooms on the second or third floor, but in a handful of heartbeats, Thomas opened up.

With a knowing smile, the man said, "Come, Mr. Constabulary. Let's get you in out of the drear, hmm?"

Durst said, "He needs a word with Mr. Holmes."

"I was just telling him that we were due. The kettle's on. He's waiting in the sitting room."

Varti searched Thomas's face and wondered how much of his geniality was an act. The man returned his gaze with an expectant air, as if awaiting instructions. At the risk of offending him, Varti spoke, but it was only to grumble, "This will go well."

"Not necessarily." Thomas drew him inside with a hand around his back. "This should be interesting."

In the sitting room, which was only lit by the fireplace, they found Holmes in a morose slump, lost in the shadows of a deep wingback chair, staring into the flames. He swung a hexagonal pocket watch on its chain, with a rhythmic *whirr* and muffled *slap* each time it hit his palm. He spoke first.

"Locking time, Weller? Dashed rude if not for the fact that I can't afford to sleep." And with a perfunctory wave at the other chairs, he ordered, "Distract me."

He went right back to staring, but this time, Varti noticed something in the shadows above the mantle. Eight sheets of paper had been tacked in a long row under the map Varti had marked up earlier. Could Holmes see them in such moody light? Was he considering the case?

Varti wasn't flattered by the man's demand, and he tried not to be insulted, either. He had his own reasons for being here. If they alleviated Holmes's boredom, it would be an incidental upshot.

He brought out his quadricentennial coin and cast about, in need of water, and moved toward a vase of flowers. But then Thomas walked in.

"Oh, dear me, no! There's no need to upset the asters." The man carried an elaborate soup tureen by its handles. Setting it carefully on the table, he murmured, "Here we are, Mr. Weller. Will it do?"

Varti couldn't recall ever summoning Purdle in Thomas's presence. How the man had known what was needed was … well, it was unaccountable. But most welcome. Varti dropped his coin into the tureen and held his breath.

Flits later, the water stirred, and Purdle burst into the room astride Cubit. He looked startled and sniffed at his arm before peering down into the tureen. "Lavender water? That's very hospitable of you, Weller! However, I mustn't stay long. Enzo might need me at any moment, but Tuppence is there, so it should be all right."

Holmes's voice emerged from the shadows of his chair. "What is young Mr. Baskerville doing that might require oversight?"

"Basker," Purdle said primly. "His surname changed to Basker long ago, just like your Saturday turned to Chromday."

"I have not forgotten the old calendar, even if the founders— in all their pomposity—refashioned it in their own likeness." And with weary patience, "Where is Mr. Basker?"

"Hunting."

A dangerous drawl. "What is his quarry?"

"The other beast, of course. Arty wants to see if he can harness it, and Enzo had to admit that if it works, it would be a good way to keep it from killing again."

Holmes asked, "Do *you* think it will work?"

"I believe in Enzo. And he believes in Arty. Friends are fearsome things, don't you think? They have a strangely strong influence. Almost like a contract, but less strict and less certain."

Varti couldn't understand why Holmes was still just sitting there.

Didn't he realize that they were needed? That it was time to join the hunt?

But all Holmes offered was a bland, "They're going to get themselves killed."

This was vexsome on several levels, not the least of which was the fact that Varti needed to succeed first. And for that, he needed something from Holmes. Staring hard at Purdle he waited to see if he could speak. Because this was not the time to accidentally waste words.

"Yes, yes. Your day is new, and my boon is bright and ready." With a gracious flutter of fingers, Purdle said, "Tell the truth."

So Varti stalked forward and planted his hands on the arms of Holmes's chair. Face-to-face, Varti didn't ask for what he wanted. He demanded it.

"Give me my dog."

# 59

## Team

Purdle reacted first. "You're invoking the Hound? That's supposed to be Enzo's right."

Holmes drawled, "You expect me to give that monster free rein?"

"No." Varti wasn't going to back down. This was too important.

"Why?"

Stupid question. Pointless question. Holmes knew he couldn't answer. "No reason."

"I'm not Toby."

Which made no sense to Varti.

Holmes's gaze slid sideways, and he rubbed at his temple. "You've set it off."

"Bad dog. Wretched thing. Stay," he growled.

The man roughly pushed him aside, escaping his chair. But he didn't go far. Pacing before the fireplace, he snapped, "No. I refuse."

Thomas pointed out, "You've acknowledged that Doggerel isn't the killer."

"That thing is a creature of ... of instincts and impulses, lacking reason, Defying logic."

Durst spoke up. "Instincts can serve well enough, especially when it comes to tracking down and killing one's quarry."

"Would you rather Varti proceed without help?" asked Thomas. "He means to, and I cannot see that going well."

Holmes staggered, catching himself on the mantle. He raked a hand through his hair, which was looking increasingly disheveled. And increasingly gray.

Varti whistled softly and patted his leg.

The expression that overtook the man's face was the strangest mix of incredulity and ... resignation. Holmes stalked out.

Varti followed him into the front hall, where the man was already halfway up the staircase.

Pointing to the floor, Holmes commanded, "Stay."

Stranded at the foot of the stairs, Varti's ears strained, following each thudding step, up to the third story, followed by the slamming of a door.

Thomas slipped to his side, peering up. "Oh, dear. It *will* be all right, though."

"I know."

"I'll just ..." he murmured, starting up the stairs after his employer. His steps were much lighter, but there was nothing to muffle their sound. Not with all the clocks silenced.

Durst strolled out of the sitting room and offered him the quadricentennial cog. "The little one returned to Enzo."

Several of his snakes lifted, their gazes fixed upward as a light rap sounded, followed by the distant murmur of Thomas's voice. Varti couldn't hear his words, but the sudden shift in his tone was unmistakable. Then came a scuffle and clattering of claws as an enormous gray dog came hurtling down the stairs, tail flagging.

Varti was mentally reeling through routes and patrols and the position of access panels. His options were severely limited because Durst looked like trouble and Varti couldn't manage without him. But then he realized something important. They were in the Bridge District, not far from military quarters. And he could go right now and get the one person who would never forgive him if he left her out.

He knew the address in Kel's file. Knew it was in a cluster of ancient bungalows along the edge of the parade grounds. Knew she went through dawn exercises there every single morning.

So he set off at a jog, intent on adding to his team.

He rapped sharply.

Grumbling and steps.

The door swung wide to reveal an armed woman with short blue hair and a resentful scowl. She looked him up and down, took in the ungainly dog at his side and the gorgon at his back ... and smirked. "Kel, you blighty wench! Your boss is here!"

Varti was really kind of pleased.

Kel stumbled out of a door that had to lead to her bedroom. She was in a state of disarray and disbelief, but then she smiled—wide and wild—and disappeared into her room again. Her voice carried just fine when she hollered, "Only need a knick!" Followed by an exultant, "Knelling, belling *yeah*!"

# 60

## *Circle-Craft*

VESPER 14, FOUR NINETY-EIGHT
CHROMDAY
1 KNELL, 6 KNICKS
ON THE FIRST FACE OF THE CLOCK

**E**nzo wasn't willing to craft what amounted to a huge family secret onto a public road, especially not with the permanence of paint. So he politely refused Jamie's offered supplies in favor of simpler tools. String. Chalk. Silver. Sand. It was enough to make a beginning.

"Can one of you find something I can insert here?" He'd found a brass fitting in amidst the pavers, which would be a big help. Using his hands to describe his need, he added, "To make a circle."

Nunc peered up and down the empty street. "Anyone see a mercy making the rounds?"

Enzo assumed he was being sarcastic.

Arty rattled through the tools in his belt, muttering, "I mean … it doesn't need to be a staff. Just slim enough … and steady."

"Here!" Seelie bustled forward, yanking something from her belt. Pushing the end into the hole, she said, "I'll want that back. It's my best one."

Enzo inspected the brush, which might have been meant

for paint or ink, then dropped a knotted loop of string over it. "Okay, this works. Thanks."

She pushed into his personal space. "I'm a mage, too. I can handle basic stuff. Are there parts you can share out?"

His first impulse was to say no. He was so used to working alone ... or with Skrik's or Purdle's support. But he didn't want to insult Seelie, so he considered her offer. "This would go faster if the frames were already in place. Once the outer ring is down, can you give me seven concentric circles within it? About this far apart."

He showed her the distance between his hands.

She compared it to her own handspan. "Simple as a snap, easy as whistling."

Enzo unspooled string. Arty and the rest of his crew backed up, making room for him as he chose a distance. For an incorporeal beast, the snare needed to be large.

Nunc muttered, "That is *not* going to go unnoticed."

"Especially once I'm done with it." Jamie was rubbing his hands together. "Nice scope. Room to *express*, y'know?"

Enzo carefully set his line and dragged the thick chalk across dark stone. Smooth as butter, the white glittered with crushed crystal. Skrik had found the good stuff. Finishing the first ring, he relinquished the simple tools to Seelie and turned to Arty.

"Do whatever you want on the outside, but don't step inside." Spying the cans of paint, he thought to add, "No overspray."

"Not a drop," Jamie promised. "I have a knack for it."

The teens huddled together, deep in discussion, and Enzo moved on to next steps. Handing a pouch of coins to Purdle, he said, "I want to hide what I'm doing until the circle's complete."

"Using the knobs for anchors?" Purdle hefted a thick,

hexagonal coin. "That's what they call these silver ones. Knobs."

"That'd be great. Thanks." And recalling another detail, Enzo whispered, "Skrik? I want lavender. Dried works in a pinch, but the fresher the better. Ask Mr. Hudson if you can take cuttings?"

With a nod, the imp melted into a crack.

Enzo tried to gather his wits for the task ahead, but he was distracted by Arty's crew. They'd reached some kind of consensus, and they were farther along than he was, with Arty, Patina, and Nunc making sweeping strokes with chalk outside of his circle.

Blue chalk forming curling storm clouds.

Yellow chalk adding banners and stars and flickers of lightning.

Green chalk circles, still too rough to tell what they'd become.

The teens paced the edge, pointing and gesturing and arguing. But while they worked, their eyes were bright, intent. And they were smiling. Happy with their plans. Heedless of the potential danger.

"I know what to do." Tuppence squared off in front of him, her gaze full of challenge. "Put me in the center."

"What? Umm ... I don't know about that. It would be risky for you."

"I have done it before. I have succeeded before." Tuppence's chin tilted proudly. "I know this."

Enzo thought fast and gave in. "Once the circle is ready, I'll place you myself."

"In this, you show good sense."

It really was the only thing he could do. Without access to better resources, Tuppence was their best option for an anchor, for she was heavy with the weight of years and blood. He offered his hand, steadying her over the boundary Purdle had already established. He softly urged, "Protect Seelie for me?"

Tuppence drew herself up and vowed, "The Darke Childe who befriended us will be safe."

Patina gave a whistle, a bright, rising sound, and Arty straightened. Enzo followed their gazes. Two officers in green cloaks were hurrying their way. Neither of them was Mr. Weller.

"I've got this." Arty waved for the others to keep going, but first he turned to Enzo, his fist coming up. "Hand out. Take these."

Enzo reached out, and Arty dropped six metal disks onto his palm. Each was studded by a magenta crystal. "Are these ...?"

"Crumbs, yeah. I want eyes on this. Tap the crystal. Tell them where to stand so they're out of the way." And then he was jogging forward to greet the local police, arms wide as he invoked the name of Philtrum Kemp.

One of the officers left, possibly to confirm.

Then Skrik was on his shoulder, and the scent of lavender filled the air. The imp said, "You do your part. Arty will do his."

He was right. He was good at that. So Enzo chose his starting point, let Seelie pass by, and knelt to begin the first ring of runes. He'd always wanted to try this. Had always assumed he'd need to in order to recapture the Hound. Seven circles to seek him and call him and lure him and trap him and hold him, to bind him and—if absolutely necessary—to end him.

The echoing darkness of the tunnel faded from notice as Enzo's fingers took on a faint glow. With slashes of bright chalk, he brought symbols into alignment, and the air hummed with the power of them. Seelie made soft clucking and cooing sounds, and he lifted his head.

A dozen more officers had joined the first two, and Nunc had them lining up along the edges of the circle, lamps on full, brightening the whole area. Jamie must have been painting for a while now, but Enzo hadn't noticed. His protections had fended off the chemical smell.

Arty was saying, "Sure, he's young, but he's a specialist. Regius Professor Coquelicot herself will vouch for him. His numbers? Staggering. It's why Highmost Perior Kemp called us up."

"You're all mages?" asked a mustachioed fellow skeptically.

"Ever seen one work?" countered Arty.

"Not really," he admitted.

Another member of the patrol chimed in, "Me, neither."

"Well, this will knock you widdershins. You'll be bragging to your mothers come morning," Arty promised. "Thanks for the extra light, by the way. You're a clutchward crew."

Which was met by hearty assurances that they were only doing what they could.

Enzo was impressed. Young as they were, these original Irregulars were very good at teamwork. And it was nice to be part of something. Well, part of something other than a ponderous legacy that had come unmoored five centuries back.

Purdle came over then, all his silver spent. "He's coming. From there."

"Who is?" asked Enzo, squinting uncertainly into the lamp-sparked dark. Had Mr. Kemp finally made it?

The sprite replied matter-of-factly. "The Hound."

# 61

## *Artistic License*

Vesper 14, Four Ninety-Eight
Chromday
1 Knell, 31 Knicks
on the first face of the clock

**V**arti increased his pace as soon as the clustering lights and green cloaks of the foot patrol came in view. Were they too late? But ... no. The badges were assembled in orderly ranks, with no air of alarm or uneasiness. He slowed to a walk, looking for some clue to why so many regulars had been diverted here.

Kel said, "I'll find out," and lengthened her stride.

Varti glanced Durst's way only to find the gorgon missing. So he wound his fingers into Doggerel's wiry ruff and worked his way through the crowd, hoping for a glimpse of red hair.

Phil didn't seem to be present.

Enzo was, though.

The young man knelt in the center of a bafflingly intricate series of circles, a stub of chalk poised in his fingers. However, his attention was locked on Doggerel, eyes wide behind his spectacles. Varti's fingers tightened, which caused the dog to peer up at him, his gaze searching. Was the Hound letting Holmes see? Would that man decide that despite Varti's plans and demands, Enzo was contributing more to the case's resolution?

"They're acting under Kemp's direct orders." Kel rejoined him. "Or so they say. Did you know he called in the mages?"

"Yes. All according to plan."

"Nobody I talked to is in charge. None of them know who is, but they're supporting this lot." Kel frowned. "I should call this in. Yeah?"

"You're useless."

"He's calm." She indicated Doggerel, who chose that moment to yawn. "He'd be riled if we were in for it. So I'll call this in, get Kemp in the loop, then help you sort this out."

She jogged toward the nearest report station, her own slot key already in hand. Varti wondered when it'd been issued. He outranked her, and he didn't have one.

While she called for the irregulars, he strolled along the edge of the flamboyant frame that four teens were adding to Enzo's nested circles. Varti eyed their handiwork critically. Based on the style, these four were the source of graffiti all through the city. How on earth had Enzo gotten mixed up with them?

As he worked his way around, his focus shifted. He noted their position, in the center of the road, directly in front of The Swirly Pine. People were crowding in the shop's windows, watching from a safe distance, trying to see.

Doggerel sneezed. The air was thick with the smell of fresh paint.

What were these badges thinking, allowing something so permanent to deface a main road. Varti eyed the artwork unhappily. At first.

The imagery was an interesting mix of stylized storm clouds and royal dogs, who were the traditional guardians of the city.

In the midst of swirling lines and toothy grins, he came across a painted cenotaph stone. The artist had added a name—GEMMA.

Moving along, Varti found more of these markers at intervals. Each bearing a single name—ASTER, TESS, POLLY, WILLA. Then came JACOB and OWEN. He stopped in front of ALPHONSE. A memorial for Salsify. These kids were creating a tribute to the victims. One that assumed this man, the eighth victim, had been the last.

They were putting a lot of faith in Enzo.

One of the teens stepped up to Varti, hand extended. "I'm Arty. Owen's been staying at my place, but Kemp said you needed to meet him."

So this was the teenaged cogger who specialized in ghosts.

Varti ignored his hand and said, "He makes fun of you behind your back."

"You know what? He raves about you behind yours. No hard feelings. Must be rough." Arty next proffered his hand to Doggerel. "You brought a tracker? Not sure he'll be much help. From what Enzo said, the thing we're trapping doesn't have any substance."

So this was a trap.

Kel returned, lifting her chin Arty's way before announcing, "Kemp's on his way. Where's the big guy?"

"Turned himself in," said Varti.

"Are we taking this lot in, too?" she inquired, scanning the graffiti. "Be a shame. This clangs."

"We're sanctioned," countered Arty. "Queens' business."

"Bold claim." Kel caught Varti's eye. "If you trace all the he-saids and she-saids back to their source, this young man's the one who's been giving orders."

The kid feigned surprise. "Are you accusing me of something, ma'am?"

"Bet you don't often have the badges lighting your way while you decorate alleys."

"This *is* a first," said Arty.

"First of many," offered Varti.

Kel said, "Be a shame to scuttle it. Brightens up the place."

"Back to it, then," said Arty. It was hard to say if he was excusing himself … or dismissing them.

"Dharm gave me a message for the patrol," said Kel. "I need to work through the ranks, checking sync scores. I'll circle back to you after. Yeah?"

Varti muttered, "I don't care."

"I can take care of myself," she assured.

He watched a while longer, taking note of the young mages assisting Enzo. Adding descriptions would have to do for his file. Maybe Phil would be able to fill in their names.

Spiraling outward, Varti left the best-lit area and made for a lamppost further along. He was searching the shadows for some sign of Durst … or any other lurking danger. A low growl made him stop. Doggerel was staring into the dark space between two buildings.

Varti jumped when the dog's jaws closed over his wrist and tugged.

It got him moving. Resting a hand on Doggerel's back, Varti let himself be led. It should be Durst, and reconnecting with him was probably wise.

But it wasn't him.

"Fancy meeting you here," said Sylvester Thornapple.

# 62

## *Vantage*

P ushing off the wall where he'd been leaning, Sylvester ambled Varti's way. "Back together, I see. And in fine fettle! But I wonder if you appreciate your position. You're in a heft of danger."

"From you."

"Me? No. In fact, I'm in an even more pressome place." Sylvester slowly raised his hands. "Your snaky escort has me in his sights."

Varti smiled. "You'll get what you deserve."

Sylvester looked to Doggerel. "We're friends after a fashion ...? My treat at the Banderole & Bugle. A meaty bone upon the hearth. Just the thing in Vespertide."

Doggerel pricked an ear, as if considering the offer.

"*Two* bones. I know your gentleman friend won't mind a second evening out. What do you say?"

This apparently met with approval, because Doggerel walked to Sylvester, reared up on his hind legs, and planted his paws on Sylvester's shoulders. The man grunted under the weight, and the Hound turned his head to peer up into the darkness above.

Varti followed his line of sight and caught the briefest glint of faceted crystal.

Sylvester said, "He's found a safe vantage. Shall we join him there?"

Should he?

Turning back toward the circle, he wrestled with his sense of duty and a growing sense of uselessness. He'd wanted to charge in, to hunt down the fell beast with Doggerel, and to ... what? Enzo was clearly the one with the know-how to put a stop to the killing streak. And Arty was better equipped to lead a cohort than he was. But did that mean he should retreat into the proverbial rafters?

Sylvester said, "Come away, Weller. There's nothing you can do."

"There must be."

"So you *do* realize it. Then let's both be wise. Your gorgon found the rungs set into the wall, but I know where the stairs are, and they'll be easier for those on four feet."

Varti was completely torn. As a badge, he belonged with the foot patrol and Kel, keeping Enzo and those kids safe. But they were building a trap for a fell beast. Didn't that mean that Doggerel was at risk? That thought stirred his feet to follow.

A door marked with the logo for the public works.

Four tight turns up a set of utilitarian stairs.

Another access door leading onto a shallow balcony.

Then came more stairs, these disappearing into the shadows above.

Sylvester crowded against the rail on one side and waved an arm, inviting Varti to precede him. Doggerel bolted up the stairs, and Varti followed with more caution. They were nearly to the tunnel ceiling, and the closer they came, the more sounds reached him. Drips and hisses and clicks coming from pipes, gauges, knobs, and wheels. The catwalk provided access for maintenance—steamworks and gasworks, plumbing and pneumatics.

They took a turn, seemingly out into open air. There were still pipes overhead, but the way felt precarious, even though the metal grating was firm underfoot. Narrow walkways fanned out in a hex pattern. Ahead and to the right, he could see Durst silhouetted against the light bleeding up from below. He'd found a platform overlooking the center of activity, and he'd brought out a long rifle with a powerful sight and curving chambers. A sniper's weapon.

By the time Varti reached him, Doggerel was seated at his feet, peering through the rails.

Sylvester shamelessly used Varti as a shield. "Thank you for staying your hand." He went through his rigamarole of an introduction, but Durst showed no sign of hearing or caring.

Varti said, "Mr. Thornapple lies constantly, and he cheats at cards."

"Is that so?" Durst swung his weapon around, pointing it just above Varti's shoulder.

"Now, now, gents. Let's all be friends. Deal me in, and you'll find I play fairly. But what's this?" Sylvester's tone changed. "Ah. This isn't a typical rifle."

Varti could acquit himself well enough on the firing range, but he wasn't cogsome about varieties of weaponry. All he could really tell, even at this range, was that Durst's weapon was some variety of air gun.

"Can you see it, Weller?" Sylvester's voice held just a hint of awe. "It's subtle. Shy, perhaps? Or as sly as I?"

Durst lowered the weapon, tucking its length against his side. He grimly asked, "Who is he?"

"My nemesis."

Sylvester smilingly offered, "Friends after a fashion. Sometime collaborators."

Varti announced, "I trust him completely."

"I share your reservations. But my hand is stayed." Durst jerked his thumb in Doggerel's direction. "For now."

"Your sly gun won't have any effect on the monster." Sylvester nodded significantly toward the street below. "Now *that*? That will work."

Their view of Enzo's circle was perfect. The mage had finished six concentric circles, having filled them with Realmish symbols. Pale chalk had taken on an eerie glitter, proof that there was magic at work. What was interesting was that the surrounding painting was similarly lively. Maybe it was a trick of the light, but Varti kept catching movement out of the corner of his eye.

Storm clouds roiling past borders.

Lightning flickering from within.

Guardian dogs shaking their manes.

Then a fresh cohort arrived, cloaked in copper, with Phil at the front. He jogged alongside a dark-clad figure armed with double swords. Black hair streamed behind him in a long tail, and it took several flits for Varti to recognize him. Dharm normally kept his hair in a tidy knot. It was strange, seeing him fitted out for battle instead of a board meeting.

Varti leaned forward, wanting to let Phil know where he was, yet unable to shout.

All at once, his cloak shifted, and there was the faint jingle of a chain.

He glanced down, disbelieving. Was Sylvester actually trying to steal his pocket watch?

But no. The watch wasn't the man's goal. One of Varti's handcuffs snapped shut over his wrist, and the other closed around Sylvester's. Varti tried to pull away, but the chain wrapped around the railing.

"Let's stay safe together." Sylvester cleared his throat. "Your dog has no collar or I would have included him. Do you have something that would serve, Durst? It would be for the best."

The gorgon calmly unshouldered his weapon case, unclipped the strap, and beckoned to Doggerel. He cocked his head, then growled softly.

Sylvester said, "If you want to be bound to that mage instead of this rail, I can only assume you have your reasons."

Varti said, "Enzo doesn't want you." And working his way around to a different sort of lie, he added, "I'll rejoice to finally be shed of you, wretched thing."

Doggerel snorted, but he also submitted. And not a moment too soon.

# 63

## *Eyes in the Dark*

VESPER 14, FOUR NINETY-EIGHT
CHROMDAY
2 KNELLS, 49 KNICKS
ON THE FIRST FACE OF THE CLOCK

V arti's attention snapped downward as a whistle piped below. Phil was calling out instructions. The assembled badges shuffled backward, leaving their lamps behind, so that the ring of light remained. In the very center of his circle-craft, Enzo knelt to place something. There was an air of finality to the action.

Much closer to hand, Doggerel began to growl. Varti bent to test the leather strap, worried Durst had fastened his makeshift collar too tightly.

Sylvester swore under his breath and tugged Varti upright before pointing with his free hand.

Durst murmured, "Do *not* move. Keep quiet."

Varti couldn't see anything in the darkness on the opposite side of the tunnel, but Durst leveled his gun along the same line Sylvester had indicated. On the rooftops, then. Somewhere amidst the shadowy peaks and pilings.

And then ... eyes.

Phil's report about Owen's death had mentioned eyes. For

some reason, Varti had pictured a lurid red. He couldn't imagine why, now that a pair of mercury-flame eyes stole along the roof of a three-story building with security bars on its windows.

It was definitely peering over the edge, but Varti couldn't figure out the shape of the thing, assuming it had one. Loosed beasts liked small, enclosed spaces. That's what Enzo had said. But this one was on the prowl, and those on the ground didn't have an inkling.

He should raise the alarm.

That was the right thing to do.

But something shivered through the still air, a vibration without sound. Varti's ears popped, and then Enzo's softly gleaming circle—now empty of people—lit with sudden brilliance.

"The barrier is down," announced Durst. "Are we sure that little one is just a sprite?"

Varti glanced at Sylvester, who'd met Purdle and might have an answer. The man had turned his back to the circle, and his gaze collided with Varti's, eyes wide with silent pleas. At the same time, Doggerel tried to lunge over the catwalk railing, only to have Durst's strap jerk him back.

"Troublesome." Then Durst grabbed for the Hound's scruff, muttering, "With all due respect, sir. *Stay.*"

Sylvester whispered, "Don't let me go."

It wasn't difficult to piece together the problem. Varti said, "You wanted me safe."

"Are ulterior motives a lie?"

Varti doubted it. He could only be grateful for Sylvester's intervention, since he'd brought Doggerel into a perilous situation. And Holmes with him.

Sylvester groaned and tugged his cap low over his eyes.

Varti seized his arm. "I'm detaining you for questioning."

"I beg you to try," the man whispered.

Doggerel whined and tried to wriggle free.

Durst hissed through his teeth, then ordered, "Do not panic."

Right before serpentine coils—huge and heavy—looped around them all.

Enzo withdrew an ancient coin from the inside pocket Skrik kept reinforced with shadow runes. The heavy bronze disk had been worried by many hands over the centuries, rendering the original images indistinct. Tuppence had been obtained by the Baskervilles at some juncture, jealously guarded by each generation, then handed down at the very last. A deathbed variety of bequest.

She would come to Enzo one day, but Tuppence was still ruled by his grandfather's wishes. That didn't make it any easier to risk her here. But she was resolved, and Enzo knew she was right. If they were going to do this now, it had to be this way.

"I added protections for you," he murmured, setting her upon a page torn from his journal. The circle he'd drawn wasn't much larger than she was, but he'd taken pains over every rune. "You'll be safe."

Tuppence didn't answer.

Couldn't in this form.

Enzo rearranged stalks of lavender, hiding her at the center of his trap. Straightening, he stepped carefully over his handiwork, joining Seelie outside the circle's boundary, where Mr. Kemp waited.

"My friends," said Enzo, indicating Arty and the rest. "They can't be here."

"Hey!" Patina protested. "We're part of this! We planned it!"

Arty set his hand on her shoulder and simply asked, "Why not?"

"Your sync scores. This fell beast is desperate, and you make an appealing alternative to my plans for it. Go inside. Let me handle the rest."

Kemp signaled to a woman in a green cloak.

She escorted the teens away, toward The Swirly Pine.

Skrik muttered, "That one. And that one. And that one."

"What about them?" asked Kemp, scanning the assembled badges.

Enzo said, "They either have Realmish heritage or their linking numbers are elevated."

"I don't think it will matter," piped up Purdle. "Those with patrons have protections. And once my barrier drops, your circle will be the only thing the beast can see."

Kemp said, "I'll pull my cohort back to a safer distance. We'll support you as best we can, but ... I'm not sure there's anything we *can* do. I'm open to suggestion."

Purdle said, "Turn out your pockets."

With a bemused smile, he did. A silver charm, a ring with two small keys, a flat tin of mints, and a few coins.

"The smallest one, please. The bobbin."

Kemp offered the copper coin with an expectant air.

"Make a wish," ordered Purdle. "A good one. But it should be as small as it is important."

A slow smile added a merry light to the man's eyes. "Will it do?"

"You're really very good at this!" exclaimed the sprite. "Give the coin to Cubit. It's time."

Purdle always knew.

So as soon as Cubit took the coin into his mouth, Enzo turned to face his handiwork, lifted his hands, and began an incantation so old, the language was lost to time. But the family records included a transliteration, so he knew the meaning of the syllables that he spoke. That they were weighted by an ancient longing. That they were captivating in the truest sense, and that their secret was a legacy hammered into him. That he was doing something historic.

"It's here. It's watching," warned Skrik.

"I *told* you it was time." Purdle gave a casual wave, and his barrier dropped.

For a breathless second, nothing happened, and Enzo struggled to grab air. But then every chalk-stroke sent up a vertical beam, crisp columns that held for several heartbeats before flying apart, scattering in every direction. Seeking.

A keening howl raised every hair on Enzo's arms.

The Hound.

Dread curling in his gut, Enzo thought to ask, "That friend of yours, the officer. Weller."

Purdle smiled. "I like his surname. Don't you? It's just right. Very fated feeling."

"He had a dog with him."

"Yes."

"Do you suppose …?"

Skrik said, "Yes."

"The Hound?" Enzo whispered.

"Yes," confirmed Purdle. "Are you surprised? I told you they are often together. That's how we met ... remember?"

"But that's going to be a *problem*." Enzo's circle could stop a fell beast. *One* fell beast. "Are there two of them?"

Purdle pointed up and away to the right. "Doggerel is that way. That's my friend Weller's name for him."

"The one you want to trap is there." Skrik pointed up and away to the left. "Also, Arty is far less obedient than you were at that age."

"Is he not in the shelter?"

"Not," acknowledged Skrik.

"Very not," agreed Purdle.

Varti realized what must have happened. Durst. They were becoming increasingly wrapped in snake coils.

The gorgon sharply ordered, "Do *not* look. My eyes are uncovered."

He forced his gaze forward.

"This was the only way to hold them both and keep my hands free." Durst sighed and said, "I need a blindfold. Until it is in place, eyes forward. All of you."

There was some jostling, and Varti realized that Sylvester was struggling against the constricting coils.

"He's bound to be ticklish. If you want to get free, try that." Varti wondered how clearly the man was thinking.

Then a furred hand pressed over Varti's eyes, and Doggerel's gruff voice was in his ear. "Do not let go of your friend. And ... *he* wants me to take your necktie."

Why had the Hound taken this shape?

And … *he.* Could Holmes be helping him?

There was a tug to loosen the bowtie that Varti always wore for work. After some fumbling, it slithered free, and Durst said, "Thank you, sir."

The gorgon was indeed addressing Holmes, his employer, within the Hound.

Doggerel said, "He wants to know how well you can see while blindfolded."

"Well enough for most things thanks to my undulation. But there will be no sniping." And then, "It is safe now."

The clawed hand lifted, and Varti blinked up at Doggerel, whose features remained entirely canine. So the Hound remained ascendant, but he was clearly conferring with his alter ego. Doggerel's other hand was clamped over Sylvester's face. "This one risked himself to protect us. Wily. Worrisome."

"You are too kind," Sylvester muttered. "Falling gods, how can you even think?"

"*I* am not alone."

Varti rested a hand lightly on one of the thick loops of muscle that knotted the three of them together. Smooth as silk. Gleaming faintly. He wondered if the scales were the same green as Durst's undulation. And if there was a pattern. Daring to look into the gorgon's face, he was startled by the alteration. Not only were the goggles gone, Durst no longer wore clothes.

His skin was bared to his hips, where scales took over. Something gleamed dully on his upper arm—metallic, ornamental.

Above the green silk of Varti's necktie, Durst's undulation was looking wilder than ever. Were the snakes larger? Definitely longer. Driss and a couple of his companions had no trouble reaching Varti to bump noses before returning their attention to the action below.

"Do as you threatened. Detain him," ordered Doggerel, who shimmied out of the way, shoving him and Sylvester closer together. Then to Durst, "Get rid of this collar."

"Is that wise, sir?"

"Varti did not bring me here to cringe in the rafters."

"What can you do?" asked an incredulous Sylvester.

With a dark chuckle, the Hound answered, "Hunt."

"Arty!" Enzo exclaimed, concern outstripping a brief flicker of annoyance. Genius or not, he was out of his depth. "Go back inside."

"Nah. I saw my crew safe, and I'm back to help."

"You're vulnerable here."

"No more than you are, old man."

"This isn't about your age!" Enzo protested. "You're exactly what the beast is seeking."

"As if *you* aren't primed and ready for occupancy."

Enzo *was* shy on protections at the moment, but he trusted his familiars. "I have Skrik and Purdle. Their contracts are a formidable deterrent."

"Yeah, well, I'm not without means." Arty unclipped something from his belt. "You've got your legacy, and I've got mine."

Another howl clawed its way up Enzo's spine. Officers shouted warnings, and a few whistles blew. Some were pointing to the roof of a nearby building. Eyes like a flare of magnesium peered briefly over the edge, burning afterimages into Enzo's retinas. All else was a shadowy billow, boiling around those eyes, formless and angry.

"It's there," said Enzo. "The fell beast."

"Sure about that?" countered Arty, whose gaze briefly flicked to something in the opposite direction. He went right back to fiddling with the dials on what looked like an oversized pocket watch. "Should you be letting me distract you?"

Oh, Enzo was distracted all right. Because a monstrous dog dropped from seemingly nowhere, crashing against an upper-story ironwork balcony, then leaping to the gabled roof next door, where he briefly disappeared into shadows. But a few seconds later, he came careening out of an alley, running upright at first, then picking up speed on all fours as he veered around the officers, totally ignoring Enzo and his circle.

Kemp ran over, exclaiming, "Rust and ashes, that was *Doggerel*, wasn't it?"

"The Hound," Enzo whispered.

The Baskerville family's legacy launched himself at the building where the other fell beast had been, clambering hand-over-hand up the stonework.

The lady officer who'd been in charge of getting Arty's crew to safety jogged up. "This one got away. Sorry, sir."

"So I see. Just wait a flit, Kel. Arty, what do you have there?"

The teen snapped the casing shut and smiled up at the redhead. "Help."

"Can you be more specific? Otherwise, I'll be escorting you inside myself."

"That would be a mistake."

"So you say." Kemp quietly ordered, "Tell me what you're planning. I'll hear you out."

Arty toggled a switch on the device's side and smugly countered, "How about I *show* you?"

# 64

## *Chasing Immortality*

E nzo wasn't prepared. At all. Whatever Arty unleashed, it wasn't something described in any of the books in the Basker library. Nor in any of the sections he'd read in *Imponderabilia*. Copper threads corkscrewed upward, multiplying as they went. Oh, Enzo knew the fizzing hiss of it, the bitter tang of it, the building pressure that danced along the periphery of all his senses.

Magic.

Old magic.

Skrik growled as a ring appeared next to Arty—a couple of yards across and fit with gears and cogs and clockfaces. It flickered and drifted out of focus, proof that it wasn't physically there. The intricacy of the design was unusual. Magic held to strict patterns, but these felt like personal touches. Modifications?

Enzo whispered, "What is it? Can you tell?"

Skrik said, "A way."

That's what the imp called cracks. They were *his* way. Just like water could become a path for Purdle. Enzo asked, "So it's like a door?"

"No." Skrik growled softly. "Death is a way."

The thing began to turn, and as it rotated every which way, picking up speed, it became a sphere of copper light. The air changed, and the orb suddenly shattered outward, then collapsed back inward, coalescing into the figure of an older gentleman with a cane. He peered around, taking in everything and everyone, before acknowledging Arty with a nod.

"Been a while," Arty offered. "We've got citizens in need of protection. And for the record, the Hound isn't the problem. I need him safe, too."

The man reminded Enzo of the ghosts—translucent and silent—only he retained that coppery luster. He carried himself differently than the victims. Dignified. Confident. And he wore a formal suit with a short cape that wasn't much different than the uniforms of the police.

Despite his apparent age, he stepped briskly, cane swinging as he made a circuit of the street art framing Enzo's trap. He didn't act like a typical dweller. He was too ... self-assured. Too powerful.

Enzo asked, "Is he a ... what did you call them here. A keepsake?"

Arty laughed. "Nah, he's something else entirely."

Skrik muttered, "Realm-took."

The woman Kemp had addressed as Kel exclaimed, "Knells bells! Do you not recognize him?"

"I'm sorry?" Enzo had no idea who this guy might be.

Kemp said, "Sorry. I'm also at a loss."

"Foreigners and woodfolk," she grumbled. "That's one of the Founders!"

Trapped on the catwalk, Varti found his relegation to the fringes of action increasingly vexsome. Was he doing enough? If all he did was protect one citizen of Newcomb—if Sylvester was safe—was it enough? Was he incapable of more?

After Doggerel's precipitous departure, Sylvester had sunk to a seat among Durst's coils, hat pulled low, shoulders hunched. Still linked to him by their cuffs, Varti leaned anxiously past the rail, trying to track his dog's progress. Bypassing Enzo's magic circle, Doggerel threw himself at the buildings on the opposite side of the road. The monster responsible for the killings retreated from view. Scared off? Fleeing.

Meanwhile, something was happening beside the circle.

Coppery light unfurled around the young cogger Varti had met earlier. He was a mage, so his use of magic wasn't a complete surprise. But it was showy, and the way Enzo, Phil, and Kel surrounded him was telling. Were they trying to stop him ... or support him? And then another figure appeared. Luminous and indistinct at this distance. Was there another ghost involved? Or did Arty have a familiar?

Phil shouted orders, and the assembled badges broke formation. Soon, he and Kel had them standing in ranks off to one side, *away* from the building that Doggerel had scaled.

And the ghostly figure—a man by his gait—completed a brisk stroll around Enzo's work, then raised both arms. His cane glittered as if capped by a starburst, and from every direction, glowing particles swarmed, then reformed into sheer hexagonal panels. They appeared first between him and the badges, locking together in a shimmering wall. At the swing of his arm, more panels spanned outward, rippling in Varti's direction until he was peering through ... what? A magical barrier?

Yes, it had to be. Now that there were panels just below the catwalk, Varti could see that they sparkled with Realmish writing. The network was reminiscent of the dome that had been part of Newcomb's original construction. Their shifting glitter and sheen made it difficult to see what was happening below, but there was a welcome upshot.

Sylvester heaved a shuddering sigh and tentatively straightened.

"Did the barrier clear your head?" asked Durst.

"That ... does seem to be the case." Sylvester touched Varti's shoulder in silent gratitude. "What happened?"

"A god has descended," said Varti. As if *that* could happen.

Squinting through copper tracery, Sylvester muttered, "What has that boy done?"

"Keep looking away," commanded Durst, whose coils simply vanished. Several flits later, his big hand appeared in Varti's line of sight, his necktie draped over his palm. "I am finished. You are safe."

"In more ways than one," countered Sylvester. "This wall has significantly dampened the effects of young Mr. Basker's mischief."

Durst peered through his weapon's sight. "I do not recognize the entity they have summoned."

"Entity?" echoed Sylvester. "I'll grant it fits better than a god descending, but he's not some random entity. And not a gent I

421

would cross. Best to remain beneath the notice of his sort."

"You have no idea what's going on," Varti accused.

"Of course I do. Let him take a gander, Durst. There's a dear." Sylvester beckoned to the gorgon, who turned over his weapon.

Varti struggled with the weight of it, then tried to find a line of sight.

Durst mildly said, "Show him."

Which was oddsome. Especially when Varti's view suddenly snapped into clarity. On a famous face. Or infamous, if the stories were to be believed.

"All of the Founders dabbled in immortality, one way or another. Memoirs and portraits and statues and scholarships. But legacies weren't *his* style. Handing things down meant giving them up." Sylvester said, "That's him, isn't it, Varti? Or an uncanny likeness, at the very least."

"How nice." Varti couldn't really tell if the figure was a ghost or a god, but he was definitely using magic. A wilesome twist, if the mathematician turned mastermind had somehow turned mage. Something that would worry Varti less if he could confirm that the man was still gone. Because James Moriarty was supposed to be long dead.

"One of Newcomb's founders," Sylvester explained to Durst. "A rumored traitor to the crowns. Not my first choice for a guardian deity."

Durst took back his gun, using its scope to study the situation. "These barriers are protecting the enforcers and the civilians. But your guardian deity left an opening."

Varti had noticed that as well. Hard not to. A long passage led from the circle into the darkness beyond. Or more properly, it invited whatever lurked in shadows to walk into Enzo's trap.

Several facts added up.

The badges behind the barrier were safe. The same must be true for those sheltering inside The Swirly Pine and other businesses along the road. Sylvester had been spared, and Doggerel had found a way to resist the trap. But for all its elaborate styling, Enzo's trap *wasn't* working.

Varti feared that was Doggerel's fault. By giving chase, had he driven off their killer? Was there something Varti could do about that? Mind racing, he searched his pocket for the key to his cuffs. "I'm staying here."

Sylvester asked the same question he'd put to Doggerel. "What can you do?"

He wasn't being dismissive. He was waiting for an answer.

Varti didn't have one. But he wasn't going to let that stop him.

Across the way, a sudden clamor rose—snarling and growling and squealing. Something tumbled off a roof, fell to the pavement, still rolling. Two beasts broke free of each other, Doggerel and the bright-eyed shadow creature. The loosed fell beast Enzo had described.

A muffled *shhh-whump* made Varti jump.

Durst had fired his weapon.

Below came a cry, shrill with anger, and Varti's heart lurched. But Doggerel wasn't hit.

He'd taken bipedal form again, and he crouched a short distance from the other. The shadow roiled and split, then melted to one side before gathering together again. On the ground where it had been, the pavement was pitted, but it was hard for Varti to see exactly what had happened.

"You hurt it. *Through* the barrier," said Sylvester in consternation. "What are you using for bullets?"

Eyes still fixed on his prey, Durst pulled a slim projectile from a carrier at his belt and offered it on the palm of his hand. Crystal within a twisting cage of metal, all etched by runes.

"I'm staying here," Varti repeated, and his key clicked in its lock.

Sylvester grabbed his arm. "Hold on. Look there."

Moriarty wasn't just using magic. He was … shifting?

No, not changing forms. It was only his cloak. The fabric gained fullness and length, flowing away from his shoulders until it became a river. Copper-lit water churned away from his position, whipping toward the fell beasts, parting them. Doggerel paced along the opposite bank—back up, head low, barking furiously.

Varti shook free of Sylvester and gave feet to his third claim, finally making it a lie. "I'm staying here!"

# 65

## *Coins*

"**W**hy is there a river?" exclaimed Enzo. He knew about the awe-inspiring capabilities of keepsakes, who took on lives of their own, but this ...? This kind of effortless influence over reality was definitely ascribed to gods.

"It's the James, of course," said Arty, sounding proud. "Newcomb wouldn't exist if it weren't for the James."

As far as Enzo could tell, the man he'd summoned up was human. The lady officer had recognized him as a historical figure. One of the architects or engineers of the city who'd made peace with the Folk. So definitely just a human. But Skrik had referred to him as *realm-took*.

That was a new term, but it didn't take much imagination to guess what that meant. Especially after reading Marsk's meandering journal entries that hinted at the very same thing.

"Does that guy have the patronage of a water elemental? Or ... *did* he ...?" Enzo posed aloud.

Purdle didn't look convinced. "That *might* explain it. Or

part of it."

"Are you serious?" laughed Arty. "I mean ... he might've been *their* patron."

"He certainly has access to a lot of power." Enzo was feeling even more wary of this guy than he had been of Marsk.

"Within limits," said Arty.

Kemp ventured, "If you had access to someone so amazing, why wait until now to call for his help?"

"Limits," Arty repeated. "There's rules he's gotta follow."

Enzo checked his circle. The runes were still intact, but with his wavering attention, their reach had dwindled. He quietly asked, "Will it still work?"

Skrik said, "Yes. *If* you focus."

That was going to be harder than it sounded. Distractions kept coming. Officer Weller burst through one of the barrier walls, running at full tilt toward the Hound. He didn't even slow for the phantom flow of the James. Just plowed right through.

Purdle asked, "Should I go?"

"You want to, don't you?" Enzo could tell.

"I've been thinking. He's been *folk-spelled*. That has consequences."

Enzo pivoted, addressing Arty. "That man ... Weller. He doesn't realize that he's vulnerable." And glancing at Kemp, he asked, "How long ago did the folk-spelling happen?"

"Graduation. He was cursed during our graduation. It's been more than a decade ...?" He tapped his fingers, as if trying to do the math.

Kel spoke up. "Fourteen years. Why's he vulnerable?"

"The spelling—or curse, if you prefer—integrates with a soul, makes a home for itself inside. It's quite entrenched by

426

now. It's *synchronized* with him."

Kemp's expression darkened. "The thing's changed his sync score."

Kel was already running.

With a hushed oath, Kemp ran after her.

Arty calmly turned to Moriarty and said, "The Hound *and* Weller, please. They're a priority. Kemp and Mirza, too. Don't let that thing touch them."

Enzo thought the summon seemed ... amused. But he graciously inclined his head and casually redirected the flow of his river. It occurred to Enzo for the first time that the flow hadn't harmed the loosed beast, only separated it from the Hound. Because Arty had asked him to protect the Hound ...?

Tuppence's complaint came to mind. Why waste time on defensive strategies? This was a hunt. Enzo ventured, "Your Founder hasn't attacked."

"Doubt he could. Not directly." Arty's gaze followed Kemp and Kel. "They're a couple of knobs. And they think *I'm* being reckless."

Skrik gently tugged Enzo's hair and ordered, "Focus. For Purdle's sake, at least."

Because Purdle had gone after his friend Weller. A tiny hero astride his trusty newt, slowly trundling into the fray.

Varti had become a creature of routine. Oh, there was variation in his days, but always within a familiar framework. He logged in evidence. He updated case files. He clipped a lot—a rusting slagheap lot—of newspaper articles. *Danger* for him had dwindled down to the threat of paste sticking in the fine hairs on his fingers … or the nearest vending machine running out of Aubade's.

But he was sure as certain that he'd been in the wrong place on the catwalk.

And even surer what place was the right one.

Doggerel. He needed to get to Doggerel.

So Varti ran down clanging stairs and pounded across pavers, and he didn't break stride when he hit Arty's barrier. Passing through was a relief, but on the other side, a weird tension hung in the air. Ominous. Oppressive.

Doggerel. He needed to get to Doggerel.

But … then what? There needed to be a next step. Varti swiftly considered all the moving pieces in this confrontation.

Enzo's circle. The crux of a plan crafted by someone who understood fell beasts.

Arty's … patron? A merciful barricade, which might spare many. But also a mysterious river that had raised Doggerel's hackles.

Newcomb's serial killer. Far more shrewd or resilient than Enzo had anticipated. If it latched onto anyone here, they would die.

Doggerel's potential. Surely someone else had worked out that the best weapon against a fell beast was another fell beast.

Holmes's influence. His cooperation would give the Hound an edge. The compass in the clockworks, pointing true.

The only part Varti hadn't accounted for was his own. It wasn't as if he could tell anyone what he thought. So why was he here? Getting to his dog needed to lead to more.

Doggerel spotted him then and left off barking at the twisting river, standing to his full height, ears pricked. The illusory water swirled closer, threatening to swamp Varti, and the Hound let loose a quakesome howl that rattled every pipe and tile in the tunnel.

Putting on an extra burst of speed, Varti closed the remaining distance, only to be grabbed up. With an underlying growl, Doggerel said, "*He* thinks you are reckless, but I know you are brave."

"His good opinion means nothing to me."

"You have mine." The Hound jumped back, putting more distance between them and the river. Slopping Varti's ear with a hasty lick before putting him down, Doggerel complained, "It knows. It wants to run."

Varti nodded. "Let it go, and good riddance."

"It would not go far. It would keep trying." Doggerel sounded amused when he added, "He and I ... *agree*. Give this beast to the Baskerville brat."

"A brillsome pet."

"Our kind are not easily contained. We are never truly tamed."

"So insulting." Really, Doggerel's claims might as well have been compliments. Or at the very least ... acknowledgement.

Doggerel had taken a position between the beast and its escape route, but that in itself wasn't enough to get the thing moving in the rightward direction. Varti could only think of two options. Be chased. Or be lured.

Rust it all, was he only good for bait?

All of a sudden, Kel came running their way. The river swung around in a curve that chased her, but she also managed to outrun its strange flow. She gave Doggerel a once-over, then turned her back on him, keeping her gaze fixed on the shadowy monster crouched on the opposite bank. "New information, sir. You're compromised. Vulnerable to that thing."

Phil came into view then, his gaze fixed on Varti.

"Oh, realms," Kel breathed, starting forward. Because burning white eyes had fixed on Phil.

Doggerel was quicker, making an incredible leap that placed him between Phil and the monster. An instant later, a hair-raising sizzle rent the air, and a paver under it shattered with a spray of crystal shards.

Durst. Varti shouldn't have discounted the gorgon, whose ammunition could hurt the creature, at least temporarily.

The thing screamed.

Doggerel barked warnings.

Varti made a rude gesture in Durst's general direction.

Phil doubled over, breath coming in short bursts. "Did Kel tell you? Curse messed with your sync scores. Changed your rank. Boosted your appeal."

That couldn't be right. He was next to useless when it came to anything magical. But ... Phil was telling the truth.

With a crooked smile, Phil added, "On the bright side, you probably qualify for the irregulars now."

Varti snapped, "Lovely. I had no other plans."

Phil's expression wavered, and he turned away. Squaring his shoulders, he said, "One thing at a time. We've this lot to sort. Oh. Oh, ashes." Raising his voice, he called, "Do you need ... help ...?"

Purdle waved regally from Cubit's saddle as they crept through midair at the newt's plodding pace. "Are you offering to escort me? Like a color guard? I've always thought that must be grand."

Varti and Kel jogged forward to flank the sprite.

At the same time, another of Durst's bullets rammed into the ground. The fell beast screamed again. This time, Doggerel's bark was more like laughter.

The phantom river lapped closer, and Varti sidestepped warily.

"Stop avoiding the water," Purdle chided. "It doesn't mean any harm. Can't you tell?"

Kel craned her neck, peering back toward Enzo and Arty. "He did say the old duffer can't hurt anyone." She rounded on Varti. "The James. It's *his* river. Moriarty's trying to protect your poxy arse, so stop avoiding it and *use* it."

"That's what I said!" Purdle pointed at Kel. "You're a good listener. I *like* you. Come here."

She blinked.

"Hold out your hand," he instructed. "Cubit has something for you."

The newt promptly spat a bob onto her palm.

"That's ... very generous ...?"

"I know! I've been on a magnanimous streak. Which is why I need to set a condition. No more blessings or boons left for a while. So save it up. The longer you wait, the bigger the hope. Just ..." He mimed a toss. "Into water. *Still* water. Not a river, please. I don't do rivers."

"Got it." Kel kissed the bob and slipped it into her vest pocket.

Phil crowded close and grabbed Varti's shoulder. "The Drowned Man. One of the cards you turned up. It was The Drowned Man. I thought ... Sweet Ireeni, I was so afraid that it meant .... But I was *wrong*. We need to be in the water."

Varti added Phil, Kel, Purdle, and the phantom river to his

pile of moving pieces, and he shook his head. Rather than bait, it would need to be bait and switch.

Seizing Phil by the necktie, he growled, "You stay here. And try to stop me. Otherwise, Holmes's new assistant will be a blighty wench, and he'll love her more than I ever could."

Phil frowned and shot a look at Kel.

She shrugged. "All I really got was that you're with him. The rest is straight out of the *Hex*."

"You take the *Hexagon*?" Phil asked lightly.

"Only if they're spilling royal tea."

Varti tried to think of a better way to lie. Couldn't his curse tell this was a matter of life and death?

But then Phil said, "You're in the running for the position he's considering. Weller thinks you'll be the one to end this, and he's envious. Though ... I have to wonder ...." With a faint smile, he asked, "Are you more worried you'll lose him to her, or her to him?"

Because of course Phil would turn a perfectly viable plan into a hacksome love triangle. Varti let go the necktie and grabbed Phil's hand none too gently. "Your name's the only one inscribed on my heart."

Phil gave a small squeeze. "I'll get there. Keep trying."

"Tibbs wants cogs. Hexadille fancies bobs. You're crowns and laurels over knobs and only knobs."

Kel, who'd been watching Doggerel pace the river's edge, cut Varti a flatsome look. "Coins?"

"It's a thing we made up ages ago, but he's got them all widdershins. Tibbs likes bobs, I did suspect Hexadille was into cogs, and I've always and ever been a dodger. More to the point ... that thing has also shown a preference. It wanted a woman.

The first five victims were ladies."

She got down in Varti's face. "You've seen my file."

"No."

"You *know* my sync score."

"I wouldn't have noticed."

"And you think it's enough to be pullsome?" She was right to be skeptical.

"You confuse me, too. Always flirting."

"Oh, realms no," she laughed. It was a friendly sort of rebuff. The kind that didn't sting.

"He means me." Phil rubbed Varti's knuckles with his thumb, then let go. "Kel, do you have a trinket I can do a bit of hex-craft on? It's simple magic, just a party trick, really. But Weller thinks if we flirt with that thing, it'll give chase."

"How'd you get *that* from what he actually said?"

"Let's call it a knack."

Kel displayed her watchchain. "Take your pick."

Varti kept a wary eye on the cornered beast while Phil lapsed into the gently lilting tone that he usually reserved for card readings. And apparently party tricks.

When he finished, Kel asked, "What's it done?"

"I usually tell people they've captured a piece of my heart."

The trinket had taken on a warm glow. There was a softness to the swirl of colors that was pleasant. Attractive.

"And that works?" she asked incredulously.

Phil laughed and didn't admit how well. "The magic is harmless and won't last for long, but by holding it close, it might be mistaken as the overflow of *your* soul."

She checked that her watchchain was secure, bounced on the balls of her feet, eyed the river, then declared, "Good to go."

"Keep it a secret from Doggerel," said Varti, bending to pick up a handful of crystal shards from one of Durst's spent bullets.

"Right," said Phil, hurrying to the Hound's side. They'd need to work together.

When Varti straightened, Kel was right in front of him. She grimly said, "Fourteen years, sir. You had better not ditch me for the irregulars. Not when things have finally started clanging."

"Kiss my clapper," he invited.

"I like you, Weller, but not that much." And then she really did confuse him. By kissing his nose.

She walked to her starting point, a spring in her step.

Purdle drifted to Varti's side. "Some contracts are sealed with a kiss."

Varti hadn't promised her anything. Not really.

"Do you think that's why she kissed the bob?"

"Flagrant disrespect."

"I liked it. Did you like it?"

Varti didn't think his opinion on the matter was going to be a factor.

"Fourteen years of waiting," Purdle mused aloud. "To hold onto a wish for so long ... that's strong magic."

If he could have, he would have disagreed.

That wasn't strong magic.

That was a strong woman.

Enzo muttered, "I don't understand why it's staying away." All seven of the circles flowed with magic, but only the first two actions had been accomplished—seeking and calling. "The lure *should* be irresistible. But … the Hound ignored it, too."

Skrik said, "There's more than your magic in force."

"Variables," offered Arty. "Grandad might be levering back your pull."

"Okay, sure. It could be the barrier." Enzo considered the graceful arch of rune-etched panes. "I don't think we're at odds, but there are consequences to coordination. Can we …? Sir, could you tighten your boundaries?"

"Instead of walling off the whole street, close us in with the beast?" Arty demonstrated with his hands, creating a much smaller dome. "That might even amplify the effect of your circle-craft."

They both looked hopefully at the old guy.

He spared them a faint smile. And shook his head.

"No?" Arty scowled. "I mean … I get it. He can't endanger us. Against the rules."

"So he'll diminish the effectiveness of my mage-craft, then discount its efficacy?" Enzo was annoyed enough to argue. "You aren't abiding by rules if you can twist them. Let's be honest, sir. Newcomb won't be safe until I trap the beast. Don't become the only thing standing in my way."

The figure stalked closer, annoyance plain on his face.

Skrik hissed a warning and doubled in size. Enzo had to widen his stance to steady the additional weight.

"There's such a thing as being over-protective, and that can be counter-productive," reasoned Arty. "It's not like you've never taken any risks, you dodgy old gaffer."

Moriarty slowly inclined his head.

"Do it. Plenty of failsafes in place, and Enzo's a wiz." Arty repeated, "Do it."

The gentleman gave the whole scene an assessing look, then capitulated with a silent rap of his cane upon the pavers at their feet. His barrier flexed and contracted. It was still a wall, and it would still keep the people beyond it safe. But its upper edges knit as they lowered, and the far edges changed from canyon to enclosure.

Now, Enzo could see a confrontation, newly lit by the fragments of else light cast by the Founder's river. The loosed beast was there, a tangle of darkness trapped between the barrier and the river. Maybe it noticed that it was trapped, because it wailed a complaint. The answering snarl from the Hound left Enzo a little breathless.

Arty asked, "Better, yeah?"

"I hope so. The trap won't spring unless the fell beast crosses the boundary, fully entering the circle."

"That's not gonna be a problem," Arty said, pointing. "Our badges are finally making the most of the James."

Kemp and Weller were coming back. Not straightway. They were weaving too much to be making headway. They circled and skipped and waved at the pursuing snarl of darkness. Weller appeared to be pelting it with stones.

Newcomb's serial killer would leap for them, but each time, the river curved upward, arching over the men's heads, knocking the beast aside. And as it collected itself for another bid, the Hound would be there, forcing it to back down, to find another path forward.

Weller sprinted out of the river, shouted something, and disappeared again into the cloaking flow.

Kemp was revealed then, jogging along with ... yes, that was

Cubit tucked into the crook of his arm. The beast lunged, and the river bucked. The Hound jumped for the beast, jaws snapping, and it shrilled in wordless frustration.

"Realm take me," Arty laughed. "Did you hear him?"

Enzo strained his ears, trying to make out words. And then Weller's voice came clearly.

"I saw her first! Get your own!"

Then Kemp cheerfully shouted, "Run, Mirza! We'll cover your retreat!"

And the river gave a lazy swirl, revealing the position of the third officer. She wasn't running. Facing the fell beast, she was taking slow, purposeful backsteps.

Weller was pleading with the monster now. "I'll swear off unicorns. You can take his bed. Or mine, but only if you mind the coverlet."

Kemp's copper cloak looked well against the ribbon of river that rose to deflect the fell beast's next bound. Knocked sideways, it wailed when a projectile sliced through it, slamming into the pavement with a crash and clatter.

Moriarty turned, peering up toward the tunnel roof, and offered a polite salute.

"What was that?" asked Enzo.

"Sniper on the catwalk. I've had eyes on him for a while. He's *absolute*. A gorgon, if you can believe it."

"Umm ... okay. That'll be Durst. He works for Mr. Holmes."

"Wonder what would happen if those two got a proper look at each other, y'know?"

Skrik said, "The gaze of a gorgon means death, even to a god."

The James swirled in tight curves that piled up, obscuring the location of the circle. Maybe the Founder couldn't do harm—not directly—but he clearly wasn't opposed to laying the groundwork for it.

"Don't let it get to her," sang out Kemp. "That would be disastrous!"

"You're a better actor than the unicorn, but the woodfolk accent grates against my ears."

"I didn't know you loved my accent."

"It's your cooking I can't get enough of," countered Weller.

"I *can* cook, you know."

"You'd make a wonderful mother!"

Enzo frowned. "I think they've lost the thread."

"Doubt it'll matter. The critter's more interested in Badge Mirza anyhow." Arty tentatively asked, "Can your Hound not swim?"

"I have no idea."

"He's really skittish about the water."

The big gray dog kept dancing away from the Founder's river, like he didn't want it touching him. In fact, the Hound snarled at *it* nearly as often as the other fell beast. But Enzo couldn't imagine why.

Weller was close enough now for Enzo to tell that Purdle had hitched a ride atop his friend's head. He knelt in the man's black hair, yanking at curls as if they were reins.

"Closer, cloooser," coaxed Arty in an undertone. "That's the way. Any flit now."

Phil ducked under the river.

Weller emerged farther along.

"It's like a game of hop-toad," said Arty. "But with deadlier stakes."

Enzo noticed that the river wasn't the only thing on the move. The Founder's barrier had been closing in behind, making it impossible for the loosed beast to backtrack. And then Skrik announced, "We have company."

On the opposite edge of the circle, with her feet set over the cenotaph bearing her name, stood the ghost of Willa Cyrine, her weapons drawn as she faced her killer's approach.

"She ... umm. Why's she here?" asked Enzo. "Did you know that would happen?"

"Nah, but it's gog-worthy. Wonder if she'd be open to future collaboration. Like Owen."

Kemp started waving his free arm. "Go, Kel! It's all you!"

The woman turned and sprinted their way, skidding to a stop just short of Willa. For several long moments, the two women just stared at each other. But then Kel wheeled, planted her feet in the same stance Willa's ghost had taken, and they faced the oncoming blot together.

"That's done it, I think," said Arty. "Point of no return. Say ... how close is too close? For us, I mean?"

"Oh ... umm. Good question."

Arty started backing up.

Enzo followed his lead. Only to realize that they'd left the woman—Kel—in a bad place.

She flung her arms wide and cried, "Come on, you vile pollutant! Want to test our mettle? Show me how much you want me!"

Why was she still standing at the front? Did she not remember that the whole goal was to get the beast into the circle. "Skrik can you ...?"

But Moriarty got there first.

He stepped lightly around the circle, offered a flourished greeting, and took her hand. Literally. Enzo hadn't realized that despite the man's ghostly appearance, he had substance.

Bowing over her hand like a courtier, he smiled up into her face.

Calm as you please.

Despite the oncoming monster.

Enzo knew Kel said something, but it wasn't loud enough to carry.

With seconds to spare, the gentleman lifted his arm, creating a billow of the cloth that was also a river, twirled her as if they were in a dance, and … she disappeared into the folds.

That … that could be bad. Enzo took a step forward, but Arty seized his arm and yanked him to a stop. And then all of his and Seelie's careful preparations flared in welcome as the perilous snarl of vicious intent collided with his runes.

The beast's cries might have knocked him and Arty flat if not for the stalwart presence of Moriarty, who'd set himself between them and the whirlwind struggle that wracked magical boundaries.

Rune-lights formed delicate chains that twisted upward and pulled down, inexorably containing the shadow beast.

Trapping.

Holding.

The shadow diminished, but then there was a worrisome increase. Was the creature breaking free? "No," Enzo whispered.

"No," Skrik confirmed. He'd resumed his usual size, and his small hand patted Enzo's cold cheek. "Leave the rest to Tuppence."

The shapes inside the circle flickered in and out of focus. Fur. A claw. A paw. Scales. And then the flapping of too many scarves, followed by an outpouring of brilliant white light that stank of heat and vanished with a sigh of lavender-scented finality.

When Enzo had blinked the stars from his eyes, the burrow road was empty. Everything was gone, even the Founder and his barriers. The sudden silence had a stunned quality.

Next came the sound of running feet, and Seelie was at his side, her eyes alive with wonder. Jamie punched his shoulder, and Nunc shook his head in a show of amazement. Patina's voice ... yes, there she was, talking fast to Kel, who hadn't been realm-took after all. Only removed from danger. And Arty ...? He'd gone to Willa. Probably already in negotiations about inhabiting some of his clockwork.

Purdle was back on Cubit, leading the way for Kemp and Weller. They had their arms around each other, staggering slightly. A big gray hound walked at Weller's side, tail swaying, leaning into him with enough weight that it was pretty likely that Kemp was the only thing keeping Weller upright.

"Quickly," urged Skrik. "Before anyone else tries to pick them up."

Enzo dragged his attention back to his circle. "I need to wash it away," he mumbled. "Brooms and buckets and water ...?"

"I can bring things." The imp melted into the nearest crack.

Stepping across chalk lines gone dull and gray in the aftermath, Enzo brushed aside a few stray sprigs of lavender. Tuppence's bronze coin was there upon his paper protections, which had darkened like toast and singed along the edges. Beside her rested a large, silver medallion. He tested it with a fingertip—only warm, not hot—then weighed it in the palm of his hand. Straightening, he confirmed that all of the silver coins Purdle had placed were gone.

Bringing light to his fingertips, he explored the new coin, which was twelve-sided. Runes from his circle etched the outer edge, the ones to bind. He ran his thumb over the raised image on its shining surface. A bouquet of lavender, captured in exquisite detail.

Slowly turning it, the light revealed a long-eared, long-legged hare caught in a twisting leap.

"It's over Tuppence. Are you all right?"

And she was there before him, all flapping scarves and scowling.

"Did you think I would fail?" She hugged herself and looked away.

"No. Never that, Tuppence." And gently, carefully, he asked, "Did that ... bring back bad memories?"

She remained moodily silent.

"I thought I saw ... umm ... there at the end. You were ...." Enzo dared to ask, "Are you a fell beast as well?"

Tuppence stiffly said, "That is not a thing you need to know, young master. Not at this time."

"Will there come a time?"

"Not if the young master is so reckless as to leave Tuppence behind."

He carefully placed the bronze coin in his pocket, then offered her the silver one. "What do you think we should do about this one?"

"Rest is good for rage. She needs rest."

"May I trust her to you?"

Tuppence looked startled, then flustered. She rearranged her scarves, then snatched the silver medallion from his hand. "I must be looking after you properly, for you to have grown so wise."

And so the bound beast found safekeeping in a pocket, and the royal city of Newcomb was made safe.

# 66

## Kemp and Weller, Weller and Kemp

VESPER 22, FOUR NINETY-EIGHT
NEWDAY
8 KNELLS, 9 KNICKS
ON THE FIRST FACE OF THE CLOCK

**V**arti dropped a bag from Currant Bun next to the waiting hamper from The Speckled Hen, then made as much noise as possible pushing through Phil's beaded curtain. If his quartermate didn't budge up soon, they were going to be late. Propping a hip on the mattress, Varti hummed a lullaby.

Phil cracked an eye and smiled. "Go on with you," he mumbled.

"I've been dreading today."

"I'm excited, too. We owe dear Nani a grand outing." Phil further rumpled his already-rampant hair. "This past week has been endlessly grindsome. Was there ever a harder-earned Newday?"

A lot had happened.

The Queen lifted the curfew in an official ceremony that had required every badge to muster to the parade grounds in full regalia.

Another true ghost had been located. Jacob Oswald had—

rather predictably, according to his colleagues—taken up residence at an exclusive supper club. And refused to leave it.

A carillon service had been arranged for the murder victims, and Phil's team had been front and center. So they'd been right back into dress uniforms in order to accept bouquets. From Princess Ethelmae. Kel had been widdershins all week over the honor of it.

Headlines that had begun in triumph were already moving on. Newcombers were eager to put the whole matter behind them.

"Stay abed, you fecksome squanderer," said Varti.

"I will if you'll bring my deck."

By the time he fetched it, Phil was sitting upright, propped against his headboard. He patted the place at his side, and Varti handed off a bottle of Aubade's before joining him—huddled close against the chill of the Drears, sharing the morning.

It was just the two of them again.

Because even Doggerel was gone, returned to the office at 221 Old London Road. *Eventually* returned. Because Varti had stubbornly kept his dog until Williday. Those four days had been good, and if Holmes was angry, he could rust off.

Comfrey had remained their quartermate while packing up the rooms he'd shared with Salsify. After today, he'd be moving in with another theater district friend. But before that, Phil and Varti were escorting him and Salsify to Keepsake Chapel, where they'd decided to explore a more Realmish alternative to what Enzo's young friend Arty could provide.

It had taken a week of dropped clues and bizarre insults and four-word clarifications to get Phil to realize that they could spin two gears with one cog.

Nani would get her drive into the countryside, though by carriage, not steam cycle.

Comfrey would have hands to hold for what might turn out to be a last goodbye.

And everything would go back to normal.

Kemp and Weller, Weller and Kemp.

"You've drawn nothing but tame cards all week," Phil remarked.

"The deck's gone sour and stingy. I want ...." But Varti stumbled over what he'd been about to say. Because it was true?

Phil considered him closely. "You're missing the excitement, aren't you?"

"It's not that." But it was.

"You miss Doggerel."

"No," he lied softly.

And it wasn't only him. Sylvester Thornapple hadn't put in another appearance, and Durst had his own work, assuming he hadn't already moved on. Varti had no excuse to find out if the things he'd dreaded had come to pass. Holmes could have closed up shop, taken on Enzo Basker, and returned to Hibernacle House.

The map on the wall in the other room was bare of pins.

He had no new leads to follow on the BENEDICK case file.

Even his role as a member of Phil's team had run its course.

"It's not over," he mumbled.

"I know, right? Wait. You don't know. Oh, ashes." Phil actually looked rather tragic. "Don't hate me. It's been a thicket. My whole week. I should have said something sooner. I'll be seeing Enzo tomorrow afternoon. Loose ends stuff."

"Save it. I want my reading first."

Phil capped his coffee and began to shuffle. "I'm sorry, Varti. Even if I *was* thicketed, I should have spoken up. He has an idea for finding Willa's familiar, and he asked me to accompany their search party. I imagine your friend Purdle will be there. Come along?"

"Can't."

"Good. We're meeting at nine knells. In the Bridge District." Varti's heart leapt.

"Enzo seems to think that Mr. Hudson will be helpful." Varti's heart clattered.

"Now lend me your hands," Phil said with a smile that was a little too teasing.

But the weight of cards created a calm between them, and Varti watched closely while Phil took a shallow cut and turned a small stack onto Varti's other palm.

"Last of Forest, also known as Brink of Wilds, gathering stone and moss and whispers."

The card showed a chapel built on the edge of a wood, with stone markers ornamenting a small, grassy park. Whoever created the card must have been inspired by Keepsake Chapel, with its ancient and overgrown cemetery.

Phil traced a curving path with his fingertip. "Brink of Wilds is a boundary card that suggests a choice. To stay on the safe path, crossing into the tamer suit that comes next in the deck. Or you might stray from your current path and into the waiting wilderness. Embracing change.

"Stone suggests the solidity of your belief. You'll choose when you're sure. Because of the chapel on the card, belief implies some level of devotion, though not necessarily one that's religious in nature. Moss usually refers to years.

446

Something old as Olde. Maybe even ancient. And whispers? Some interpret these as guidance, but it can also mean ghosts or memories or a recurring omen."

He cut the cards again, turning up a second card.

"Oh! *This* is rare. A neighboring card. Eleventh of Forest, gathering axes, ancients, and avians."

So after a full week of bland, tame readings, Varti had called to both Eleven and Twelve of Forest. He'd been hoping for The Howl, but twice wild, and on a day when they were forest-bound? It felt … promising.

This card showed a many-antlered figure seated upon a bramble throne, an axe leaning against his knee. Birds hid in amidst his branching tines, and one perched upon the axe haft, beak open in song. It was a blue bird with sweeping tail feathers.

"Helve," said Phil. "He's a forest deity, and the woodlands hereabouts are dotted with tiny chapels dedicated to him. Eleventh of Forest straight-on as it is here, grants permission. You may clear out any thickets and build with the forest's blessing.

"In conjunction with Brink of Wilds, I think it's fair to say you need to choose *where* to build." Phil sought his gaze before adding, "But this is astonishing for another reason. The contract token that we think will lead us to Willa's familiar …? Enzo believes that they'll turn out to be a forest creature. Because she also carried a trinket belonging to Helve."

Varti said, "I had completely forgotten that."

"Neighbor cards and neighbor days with forest-bound paths."

Phil lapsed into a silence. Varti elbowed him lest he fall back asleep. And then he fanned out the cards, searching for one in particular. He held it up.

"The Drowned Man," said Phil, gaze full of questions.

"One card per reading. It's how you always do things."

"Oh, I see. And you're right. I've been remiss. Your reading from before, I withheld it. Here, I'll show you." And he searched for the card. "It was another last card, a boundary card. Last of Vesper, which signals the end of a season, is more commonly called Else-Bound. Your second card was Else-Bound, and combined with The Drowned Man, I thought it meant you were going to leave me. That I was about to lose you."

"I'm not going anywhere."

Phil gathered and straightened his cards before quietly answering, "I wouldn't try to stop you."

Varti knew better. Phil probably did, too.

Which meant they were both liars.

# 67

## Contract Token

Vesper 23, Four Ninety-Eight
Rowday
4 Knells, 3 Knicks
on the second face of the clock

E nzo was very nearly late, mostly because Purdle had *wanted* to be late.

"It's fashionable," he insisted.

"But is it *friendly*?" Enzo countered.

"Is it not? Depending on the situation, I can see why it might be vexsome. Isn't *that* a lovely word? Don't I sound like a local? But now that you've brought it up, I do wonder about the lateness. Newcombers *do* keep a great many clocks around. Practically everywhere! Is it possible that punctuality is *more* fashionable? What do you think, Cubit?"

Hurrying inward from Farrukh station, Enzo passed three bridges before spotting the lavender-thick dooryard of 221 Old London Road. A small group of people had gathered there. Mr. Hudson looked quite dashing in a long velvet coat of forest green. He stood with Durst, whose undulation was tucked under a drab turban. Enzo had only expected Kemp, but the flutter of a green cloak betrayed Weller, who hung back.

"Enzo!" Kemp called, all smiles. "And good morning to you,

Skrik, Purdle, Cubit. We've been getting acquainted. Have you met Roke?"

"No. Thank you for handling the arrangements." Offering his hand, Enzo said, "Hello, sir. Thank you for joining us."

"Roke Suthering," offered a Folk whose indigo cloak was so long, it brushed the cobbles. They'd needed to wait for the sun to drop below the city walls in order to accommodate his particular needs. He was one of the varieties of Darke Childe that couldn't abide direct sunlight.

In the false twilight unique to the city, he'd thrown back his cowl, revealing pale skin with a grayish cast, pointed ears, and monolid eyes that were completely black. His smile was too tight to reveal his fangs, but Enzo knew they were there. These Folk might not subsist on blood, but they'd quickly earned the nickname *vampire*. A total misnomer. By rights, they identified as nocturnes.

With great dignity, Roke added, "Thank you for your efforts on my granddaughter's behalf."

"You mean Willa!" exclaimed Purdle. "Yes, I can see it. She has your eyes."

Expression gentling, Roke said, "She does."

Kemp said, "We're all here. Enzo, how would you like to proceed?"

"Did you bring it?"

Roke's hand emerged from under his cloak. When he unfurled fingers tipped by black claws, Willa's ring rested on his palm. When the personal effects of the victims had been returned, the suspected contract token had gone to him. He was cooperating with the search on the condition that he could take part.

"Okay, good. Umm ... we'll take a walk. And I'd like Mr. Hudson to lead the way."

"What direction?" inquired the man.

"Whatever seems best ...?" Enzo didn't deserve any credit. This wasn't his plan at all. Mr. Holmes had suggested it, Mr. Hudson had agreed to it, and Mr. Kemp had tracked down the ring. But Enzo had wanted very much to do this. Knowing there was a bereft familiar out there, possibly injured or in distress? He had to try.

Mr. Hudson tucked his arm through Enzo's and smiled. "This may go more smoothly with our dear Mr. Weller at the fore. Can you find us a path with less fanfare, Mr. Constabulary?"

Weller presented himself, his gaze sullen.

"Let's aim for someplace with trees," said Mr. Hudson. "Fullnis Park?"

Weller rolled his eyes but set off, almost immediately turning down a side street. Durst hurried to walk alongside the man, and Kemp brought up the rear, chatting amiably with Roke.

"What do you make of Willa's newfound devotion to Helve?"

Her grandfather said, "Her choice comes as a surprise. We talk often, but ... I *do* think she was keeping some things to herself lately. I thought perhaps palace business. Or a new love. But a newfound familiar would be at least as distracting."

"What sort of familiar do you think she would attract?"

Roke ventured, "Something Brighte. A sun sprite or a flower fairy?"

"From everything I learned, those would definitely be appropriate. I'm really very curious what we'll discover."

Meanwhile, Weller had turned onto a curving lane overhung with trees.

The man abruptly complained, "I hoped to never see you again."

Which inspired a low chuckle from Durst. "Are we on the other side of your regard, my undulation and me?"

"My nature is not so changeable. Keep your friends out of sight."

Rather than taking offense, the gorgon tugged at the folds of his turban, and a few snakes wriggled free, bobbing their heads excitedly in Weller's direction.

He grumbled, "It's your own fault if they become frostbit." And more softly, "Go away, Driss. I've tired of you."

Durst said, "They do not believe you."

Mr. Hudson patted Enzo's arm and asked, "Should I be worried about our tagalongs?"

He checked on Kemp and Roke, who were lost in conversation. "No ...?"

With a small shake of his head, Mr. Hudson pointed up.

It took most of a minute for Enzo to spot them. Arty wheeled across a skybridge, headed in the same direction they were. Then Seelie darted across the roof of a building. And Patina ducked down an alley as they passed by. The real Irregulars were snooping.

Skrik softly said, "They are protective of you."

"Our friend Arty looks after his own," agreed Purdle. "I'm the same way. Don't you think?"

They left the avenue, took a covered path, waited at a crosswalk, and entered a beautiful park filled with towering Werifesteria trees. This was definitely the sort of place where a forest deity would feel at home. Enzo asked, "Is there any place here that's dedicated to Helve?"

"Yes," said Weller.

"No," said Durst, interpreting.

Mr. Hudson said, "I don't think that will matter. There's a hint of portent in the air, don't you think?"

"Is there?" Enzo asked, peering around. There were people everywhere—coming and going or resting on benches. The splash of several nearby fountains didn't quite cover the calls of gathering birds. He wondered how many roosted here at night. Whole flocks, by the sound of it.

A familiar mechanical hum passed by to one side, and Enzo turned in time to see Arty and his whole crew zoom by on their monocycles, bound toward the skate park. Arty offered a fleeting smirk and a casual wave.

Then someone asked, "Mr. Weller?"

"Not here," the man quickly lied, hiding behind Durst.

Far from offended, a broad fellow in religious robes made a gesture with his hand. A blessing? He said, "Good eventide to you all."

"Serendipity strikes!" softly exclaimed Mr. Hudson, who soon had the priest-like person by the hand. "How are you and Badge Weller acquainted?"

"He's my confessor," blurted Weller.

"Friend of a friend. My name is Ammil, and I was sent. To you, I think."

"That *is* a first. How delightful." Mr. Hudson coyly asked, "Who sent you, I wonder?"

"As this is Rowday, my guide is Ireeni, for the augurs foresaw a long walk and an eight-fold encounter."

Kemp exclaimed, "Eighth of Skies!"

"Set alongside The Peregrinator." Ammil turned the jingling chains that looped his neck, and finding one in particular, he pressed it between his thumbs and murmured a blessing over

453

Kemp, whose whole countenance radiated delight.

Then Mr. Hudson put their problem to the priest, spinning out everything that had led them here.

Enzo was intrigued by the number of coincidences Mr. Hudson had apparently triggered. And to a greater degree, he was intrigued by Ammil himself. Gargoyles were a variety of Folk that were famed for their sturdy build and impressive strength. Ammil's gray skin was several shades darker than Roke's, and his lower jaw jutted, so that two small tusks rested lightly against his upper lip.

Kemp said, "Roke and I, Hudson and Enzo, Purdle and Skrik, Weller and Durst. That's eight!"

"You've forgotten Cubit!" protested Purdle.

"*And* Driss," added Varti, pointing at the peeking snakes.

Ammil mildly said, "Gorgons are numbered by their tails. And I daresay Cubit *must* be numbered since Mr. Weller is already an acquaintance. Eight new encounters in all, and now that I have heard your story, you should return with me."

"To the cathedral?" asked Mr. Hudson.

"To the cloisters." Ammil said, "The one you seek is there."

Varti wished he could ask Durst so many things. About Sylvester Thornapple. About Sherlock Holmes. About evenings out and games of chess or trilby or cobble-take or cards.

He contented himself with whistling softly to Driss and lifting a hand so the peekaboo snakes could nose his fingertips or press into the warmth of his palm.

Eventually, Durst said, "He keeps sending me for eggy buns."

Varti muttered, "Doggerel hates them."

"He blames you."

"I had nothing to do with his addiction."

"Grumbles about you all the time." Durst seemed to enjoy playing tattletale. "Seems to me that if you are always on someone's mind, that is a fair beginning."

Varti insisted, "I've been completely forgotten."

"You left an impression." Gazing up at the Composite Cathedral, he blandly added, "You have a tactical advantage."

"Holmes adores me."

"He has acknowledged you."

Varti could tell the words were true, but it was still hard to believe them. Doggerel was the one he thought of fondly. Holmes was more like ... sulky baggage lashed to the boot.

They didn't enter the cathedral proper, instead navigating the cloisters. Rather than returning to the courtyard he'd visited with Sylvester, Ammil led them another way. It was different, but with similar trappings. Winking candles and snapping torchlight and a pantheon of shrines. Then they turned into a small garden with a low-sprawling tree surrounded by standing stones. There was a creature there, stacking more of the smooth rocks, setting them with patient *click*s and *clack*s. It startled and froze where it crouched.

"You are safe, little one," said Ammil. "These gentlemen are here to ease your fears."

The small person slowly straightened from their task. Compared to Varti, they would have been a bit over knee-high. Slender limbs looked like bark lashed together by twining vines, but the face that turned their way wasn't wooden. Their face was heart-shaped, with the delicate features associated with sprites, pixies, and other Smalle Folke. Cupped ears reminded him of a bat's, but they appeared to be shaped from leaves. And both the top of their head and their lower parts rustled with a covering of ragged leaves. Brown on brown on brown, with eyes that glowed a sickly green.

They ran to Ammil, trying to hide in the folds of his vestments.

Then came words. So many words. Something Varti could no longer offer. They took turns introducing, explaining, apologizing, soothing. And slowly, so slowly, the little one believed their words and came out of hiding and gasped when Roke knelt to proffer the ring. Only then did they stray from the safety Ammil represented, to reach for and retake the contract token, whimpering as they cradled the thing to their thin chest.

Varti couldn't hear what Roke said, but the air stirred, and dry leaves rustled.

Edging closer to the nocturne, the fae creature pushed the ring onto Roke's finger, and with a groan Roke gathered the little one into a gentle embrace. Willa's familiar pressed their cheek to his, tipped their face toward the dusky sky, and blinked hard, as if to hold back tears.

Roke's tears flowed freely as he murmured promises and endearments.

"That's done it," Thomas said in low tones. At some point, he'd slipped to Varti's side. He watched the mourners with a wistful smile on his face. "A contract sealed in tears may be bittersweet, but all the stronger for it."

Varti fielded the portentous aside without comment. Or … he would have *preferred* silence. But words slipped out nonetheless.

"My contract will be with Doggerel."

"What an interesting idea. I wonder if that's even possible. Young Mr. Basker is sure to know." And then Thomas said, "You'll come by, won't you? Tomorrow."

And just like that, Varti knew he was standing on the Brink of Wilds.

# 68

## *A Proper Rival*

VESPER 24, FOUR NINETY-EIGHT
VONNEDAY
6 KNELLS, 12 KNICKS
ON THE FIRST FACE OF THE CLOCK

Varti sincerely doubted that Thomas had meant for him to show up on their front step before sunrise, but his morning run had taken him straight to the Bridge District. Out of uniform and empty-handed, he knocked.

Thomas opened the door, saying, "Bless you for being an early riser."

And handed him a leash.

And closed the door on him and Doggerel, who gazed up at him expectantly. So they ran along the James and through the parade grounds, then zigzagged back and forth, across all six bridges.

The carillon was just tolling seven knells when Thomas flagged him down, three newspapers tucked under his arm. He held the gate for Doggerel, who took his own leash between his teeth and saw himself through the open front door.

"That'll do wonders for his mood. Same time tomorrow?"

Varti mutely shook his head.

"This is all very … experimental. Both of them are quite

stubborn, but I have high hopes." Thomas lifted a finger and took a conspiratorial tone. "He'll be around this afternoon. To *your* offices. It's nice to see him making an effort."

"I'll have Henna put out the kibble."

With a light laugh, Thomas said, "Pining is for plays and lovers parted, not for those meant for partnership."

Not an assistant. A partner.

But whose?

It was two knells on the second face of the clock, and Kel had just gone off to thrust their morning's summary reports under the noses of the lead investigators on each affected team. The elevator *ding*ed on the floor above, pulling Varti's attention from a lackluster report he was annotating with green ink.

There was no denying a sense of impending doom.

As of this past Chromday, Files & Evidence had a new intern. These assignments were a recurring necessity that always ended up being six kinds of awkward. *Every* division took on their fair share of last-year academy students or fresh graduates, helping them sort out their aptitudes before the periors and purnals handed down final assignments.

Usually, Henna looked after their interns, and Kel made up excuses why they shouldn't bother Varti. But for some reason, the new guy—a skittish academy student called Wim—kept seeking Varti out.

Henna insisted he was a good kid.

Kel thought he was trying too hard.

The only thing Varti could say with any certainty—if he'd been able to say anything at all—was that Wim was a klutz.

Three … two … one …. The elevator *ding*ed at Varti's office level, and there came the clip-clop of hooves. Wim was fairly dancing in place, which was noisier than you might think in enclosed spaces. Like basements.

Varti quickly slid his potted plant closer to the center of his desk, lest it fall prey to wheeling hindquarters or the nervous flick of a tail. The young centaur clattered into view, eyes wide as he wrung his hands.

"*Really* sorry, sir!" Wim's voice had a tendency to crack when he was nervous. Which was perpetually. "I know Ms. Henna said not to bother you, and I *tried* to tell them that you weren't able to speak to anyone, but … they want to speak to you anyhow! And it's just me upstairs, so there's nobody else to ask." Lowering his voice to a loud whisper, he asked, "What do you think I should *do*?"

How could the boy both insist that Varti couldn't speak yet persist in asking him to do so?

Footsteps sounded on the spiral staircase, and the boy covered his mouth with one hand and pointed up with the other.

Varti understood being nervous and eager to please, but this was ridiculous.

*Nobody* could be frightened of Phil. Especially not a chestnut colt from the same hometown. For pity's sake, their families were probably friends.

"Steady on, Wim. We're hardly a threat." Phil added a sheepish, "Really, Weller. I did try to explain."

The other half of that *we* stalked into view. Sherlock Holmes looked … annoyed. And in a particularly predatory way. No wonder Wim was spooked.

Phil tried again. "While not an irregular, Weller is a valuable member of my team. We meet here in his office from time to time, so you'll get used to seeing me around. Go on back upstairs and cover the front desk. We need a private word."

"Yessir!" squeaked Wim, noisily making his escape.

The elevator *ding*ed away, and Phil rubbed his face. "Was I that awkward when I was seventeen?"

"You were entirely suave. A brillsome exemplar."

"At least I outgrew it ...?"

"Your charms have dimmed considerably with the passing years."

Phil smiled and shook his head, then indicated Holmes. "I'm here at this good gentleman's behest. Would you be so good as to bring me these files?"

The slips he turned over were requests for two very familiar case files.

Varti shot a look at Holmes, who twirled a finger, demanding he hurry it up.

SET UPON BY DOGS. The file and its speculations were pointless now, since the case was officially closed. But the notes would show all the work Varti had put in. Everything he'd recorded in obscurity.

How long had it been since Phil had heard Varti's own words?

BENEDICK, even more of a surprise. Varti hadn't realized Holmes had noticed that he'd even started the file. Then again, he wasn't the sort of man anyone should underestimate. Because it was plain as porridge that he was going over Varti's head to gain access to Benedick Carraway's evidence locker.

Good.

Doggerel would be pleased.

Varti guided Phil to a reading desk, and his best friend accepted the folders with a brisk nod. All business, either because of the curse or because Holmes was watching.

Only after Phil had begun to read did Varti attempt to confront the man.

"I've missed you." Well, that was blunt enough.

"You used to say that to Durst."

"Until he bested me at cobble-take. Now, we're bitter enemies."

Holmes looked away, rubbing his thumb across his fingertips. "I cannot decide if you are applying for a position as my assistant … or my nemesis."

"Nobody likes rivalry." Which was a strange lie. Varti assumed it meant Holmes had been telling the truth when he said he hadn't had a proper rival in years.

"It can … keep things interesting."

"You missed me, too."

The man shook his head. And meant it.

Good. Varti hated lies.

"Our arrangement," Holmes began. "I'll honor it. Look into Benedick's murder, and I'll find the method for your unspelling."

The terms had changed.

But Varti found he didn't mind. Not when another investigation meant prolonging their association.

"And … as it happens, there's a new case. One I cannot refuse." Holmes stiffly added, "I am accustomed to working with an assistant. Someone who can keep up."

"You're making up reasons to keep me around."

"No. I'm not." Withdrawing a long, lustrous envelope from

462

his breast pocket, Holmes offered it with the quirk of a brow. The seal—the royal seal—had been broken. "A summons from the palace." He coolly added, "You're good with dogs. That should prove useful."

# THE END

*Thank you to everyone who takes the time
to read, rate, review, and recommend my stories,
wherever they may be found.*

FORTHRIGHT

# *Acknowledgments*

Fiddling a new world into existence? Definitely my kind of fun. Finessing every last detail in a book that's thick with them? Somewhat more daunting. Which is why I must wholeheartedly thank the brillsome cohort who helped me roust a lot—a rusting slagheap lot—of pesky mistakes from the *Folk-Spelled* manuscript. In no particular order, since these aren't even all numbers:

**Two**—Lady Reagan, who caught every contraction used by cast members who shouldn't … err … should not.

**Y**—Laura Hobbs, who was quickest to put two and two together. Clever girl.

**Theta**—caitelatte, who put up with my purnals and periors, then crosschecked my hexes, knells, and homophones.

**Eight-one**—Wendy "Lady Ismene" Davis, who makes allusions to my stories almost as much as I do. Bless your calendar sense.

**Green**—Eldest, who deserves a round of applause for coming up with the Pig in Heels. You're a rare wit, and I have reason to be glad of it.

**J**—Travis Baldree, who sussed out stragglers whilst bringing the cast to vibrant life with his narration. Grab the audio book, folks. It's worth every knob & bob.

**Ampersand**—Mart Lett, cover illustrator and creative force behind a growing stack of character sheets, cast portraits, and guidance deck cards. *Thank you* falls short. Find more of their art at www.mart-lett.com.

**never more than**
FORTHRIGHT

a teller of tales with a fondness for unlikely friendships, wary alliances, unforeseen consequences, hard-won trust, diverse cultures, found family, local legends, and all manner of folksome things. Author of the **Immortal Holmes** series, paranormal mysteries with a steampunk aesthetic set in an alternate history & also the romantically-inclined **Amaranthine Saga**, along with its cortege of short stories & serials.

**ForthWrites.com**
patreon.com/forthrightly

## ALSO BY FORTHRIGHT

### Amaranthine Saga

*Tsumiko and the Enslaved Fox*
*Kimiko and the Accidental Proposal*
*Tamiko and the Two Janitors*
*Mikoto and the Reaver Village*
*Fumiko and the Finicky Nestmate*
*Pimiko and the Uncharted Island*
*Rhomiko and the Confirmed Bachelor*

### Songs of the Amaranthine

*Marked by Stars*
*Followed by Thunder*
*Dragged through Hedgerows*
*Governed by Whimsy*
*Hemmed in Silver*
*Captured on Film*
*Bathed in Moonlight*
*Flattered by Flowers*
*Scribbled in Margins*
*Pressed into Service*

### Amaranthine Interludes

*Lord Mettlebright's Man*
*Suuzu and the Nine Nippets of Legend*
*Coop and the Elderbough Trackers*
*Alder Woodacre and the Acorns of Affection*

### Patreon Exclusives

*Bard & Barbarian*
*Kimiko and the Cycle of Moons*

# *Navigating Newcomb*

### Four Seasons

Milvine (spring) – 90 days
Fullnis (summer) – 90 days
Vesper (autumn) – 90 days
Bittern (winter) – 90 days

**Calibration Days** is the annual festival that concludes the old year. During the unnumbered days between years, Newcomb's many mathematicians and astronomers recalibrate timepieces & restart the calendar.

### Days of the Week

Newday (Sunday)
Rowday (Monday)
Vonneday (Tuesday)
Williday (Wednesday)
Trouday (Thursday)
Faraday (Friday)
Chromday (Saturday)

### Units of Time

Flit (second)
Knick (minute)
Knell (hour)
First Face (a.m.)
Second Face (p.m.)
Tocking (shift)

### Night Watches

6-9 knells – Wicking Time
9-12 knells – Winding Time
12-3 knells – Locking Time
3-6 knells – Echoing Time

**Bobbin** [small copper coin] Familiarly known as a "bob," this counts as small change. A bob is grooved along its rim like a pulley or … y'know … a bobbin.
CU = \$.33

**Cog** [small pierced silver coin] This is the most common coin in circulation. A cog is the usual price for items in a vending machine. Its edges have teeth. They are effectively gears, and they mesh neatly with dodgers.
AG = \$2; 6 CU = 1 AG

**Knob** [thick hexagonal silver coins] A knob is marked by a crown on the face and a laurel wreath on the reverse, which led to the commonly used idiom fo confusion: *"I can't make crowns or laurels of it."*
AAG = \$6; 3 AG = 1 AAG

**Dodger** [large silver coin inset with a gold hexagon] While a doger is a coin, it's not what you'd call pocket change. One is roughly equivalent to a day's wage for many people in Newcomb.
AU = \$48; 8 AAG = 1 AU

**Ingot** [large, heavy elongated hexagon of gold] Ingots are often referred to as "flash." You wouldn't drop an ingot at your local bob & knob or bun cart, but you might see them stacked on the betting tables in high-class, high-stakes gambling houses.
ING = \$288; 6 AU = 1 ING

**The Royal City of Newcomb.** This *barely* qualifies as a map, but I wanted to give you the placement of each district, the river, the spoke roads, trolley stops, and palace, as well as some of the secondary roads that lead in and out of the city. Arrows point to a handful of places that are important to Varti, Enzo, and the rest.

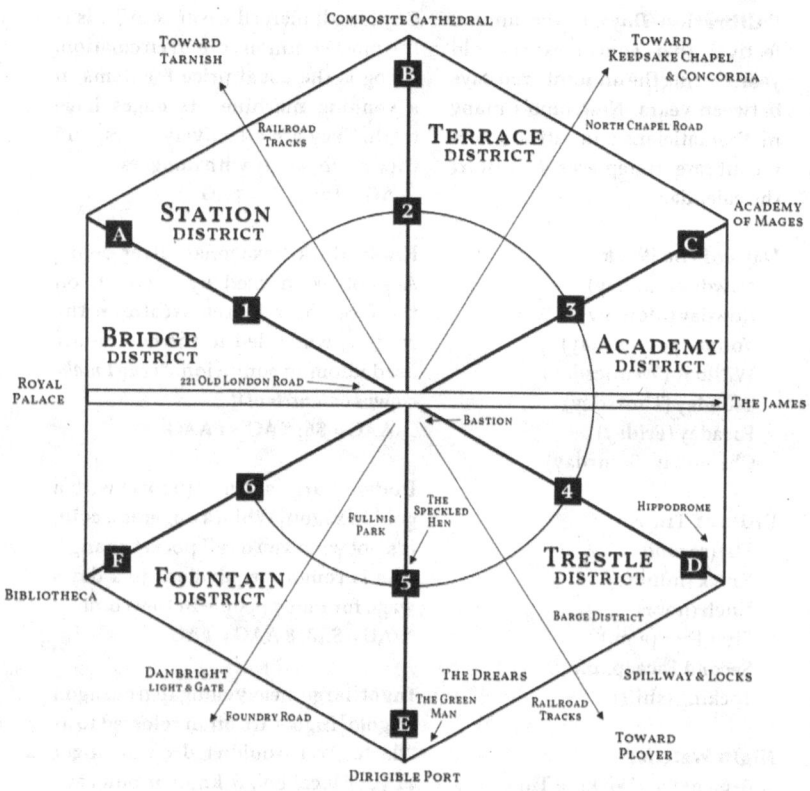

**Trolley Stops**
1. Farrukh Station
2. Newsome Station
3. Chromwell Station
4. Vonneffe Station
5. Rowan Station
6. Trouvaille Station

**Spoke Roads**
A. Industry Road
B. Piety Road
C. Loyalty Road
D. Cannery Road
E. Livery Road
F. History Road

## *patreon.com/forthrightly*

Find your way to forthright's Patreon account, where you'll discover
exclusive stories, sketch peeks, behind-the-scenes details, first looks
at official art, and the chance to hop onto my art card mailing list.

# THE SERIES CONTINUES
YOU HEARD IT HERE FIRST

ELSE-MOORED

AN IMMORTAL HOLMES NOVEL

**Kimiko AND THE CYCLE OF MOONS**

For all those who really wished they could see the *entire* courtship of Kimiko MIyabe and Eloquence Starmark, I have good news! The **serialization is updating now.** All the drama at Kikusawa Shrine (and New Saga High): two roommates, three sisters, twelve kisses, and the long-awaited stirring of a sleeping landmark. Friendship. Courtship.

Become a patron at https://www.patreon.com/forthrightly

# Bard & Barbarian

BY FORTHRIGHT

*Imber was only a boy when he met the divine beast
who would one day share his adventures.*

A serialized fantasy that's currently a Patreon exclusive. Access to the ongoing adventure is available at all tiers of support. Now with bi-weekly audio installments, narrated by Travis Baldree. Become a patron in order to read along.

https://www.patreon.com/forthrightly

# cozy fantasy from an author you already trust

SPOILER: FORTHRIGHT HAS OTHER PENNAMES

# GALLERIES OF STONE by C. J. MILBRANDT

*Magic mountains. Master sculptors. Living statues.*

The trilogy is complete. Available in print & digital.
Audio editions narrated by Travis Baldree.

Book 1: *Meadowsweet*
Book 2: *Harrow*
Book 3: *Rakefang*